HIGH TIME FOR LOVE

"What do you call that thing you're wearing?" he asked, fingering the flimsy material. It was smooth and silky, and he longed to run his hands over the softly rounded curves beneath.

Samantha sipped her wine and her eyes locked with his. "This is a caftan," she said. She could feel the heat rising between herself and Jeff. A part of her—the safe, sensible Samantha she knew so well—wanted to run away, to put distance between herself and this man. But the new Sam, the Samantha she was just getting to know, was tired of running. She shivered and took another sip of wine, then leaned closer to Jeff. He took the empty glass from her and placed it on the table. Then he gently drew her into the circle of his arms.

"There's nothing to stop us from loving each other, Sam," he said.

"Are you sure?" She was in his arms now, and she felt as though she were wrapped around his heart, but still she was afraid.

"I'm sure," he whispered, his lips brushing her hair, his breath warm against her face.

She lifted her face then, her eyes begging for his kiss. This was her night, her time.

It had been so long, and she had been so lonely. . . .

IT'S NEVER TOO LATE FOR LOVE AND ROMANCE

JUST IN TIME (4188, $4.50/$5.50)
by Peggy Roberts
Constantly taking care of everyone around her has earned Remy Dupre the affectionate nickname "Ma." Then, with Remy's husband gone and oil discovered on her Louisiana farm, her sons and their wives decide it's time to take care of her. But Remy knows how to take care of herself. She starts by checking into a beauty spa, buying some classy new clothes and shoes, discovering an antique vase, and moving on to a fine plantation. Next, not one, but two men attempt to sweep her off her well-shod feet. The right man offers her the opportunity to love again.

LOVE AT LAST (4158, $4.50/$5.50)
by Garda Parker
Fifty, slim, and attractive, Gail Bricker still hadn't found the love of her life. Friends convince her to take an Adventure Tour during the summer vacation she enjoys as an English teacher. At a Cheyenne Indian school in need of teachers, Gail finds her calling. In rancher Slater Kincaid, she finds her match. Gail discovers that it's never too late to fall in love . . . for the very first time.

LOVE LESSONS (3959, $4.50/$5.50)
by Marian Oaks
After almost forty years of marriage, Carolyn Ames certainly hadn't been looking for a divorce. But the ink is barely dry, and here she is already living an exhilarating life as a single woman. First, she lands an exciting and challenging job. Now Jason, the handsome architect, offers her a fairy-tale romance. Carolyn doesn't care that her ultra-conservative neighbors gossip about her and Jason, but she is afraid to give up her independent life-style. She struggles with the balance while she learns to love again.

A KISS TO REMEMBER (4129, $4.50/$5.50)
by Helen Playfair
For the past ten years Lucia Morgan hasn't had time for love or romance. Since her husband's death, she has been raising her two sons, working at a dead-end office job, and designing boutique clothes to make ends meet. Then one night, Mitch Colton comes looking for his daughter, out late with one of her sons. The look in Mitch's eye brings back a host of long-forgotten feelings. When the kids come home and spoil the enchantment, Lucia wonders if she will get the chance to love again.

COME HOME TO LOVE (3930, $4.50/$5.50)
by Jane Bierce
Julia Delaine says good-bye to her skirt-chasing husband Phillip and hello to a whole new life. Julia capably rises to the challenges of her reawakened sexuality, the young man who comes courting, and her new position as the head of her local television station. Her new independence teaches Julia that maybe her time-tested values were right all along and maybe Phillip does belong in her life, with her new terms.

Available wherever paperbacks are sold, or order direct from the Publisher. Send cover price plus 50¢ per copy for mailing and handling to Penguin USA, P.O. Box 999, c/o Dept. 17109, Bergenfield, NJ 07621. Residents of New York and Tennessee must include sales tax. DO NOT SEND CASH.

FULL BLOOM
STACEY DENNIS

**ZEBRA BOOKS
KENSINGTON PUBLISHING CORP.**

ZEBRA BOOKS are published by

Kensington Publishing Corp.
850 Third Avenue
New York, NY 10022

Copyright © 1994 by Stacey Dennis

All rights reserved. No part of this book may be reproduced in any form or by any means without the prior written consent of the Publisher, excepting brief quotes used in reviews.

If you purchased this book without a cover, you should be aware that this book is stolen property. It was reported as "unsold and destroyed" to the Publisher and neither the Author nor the Publisher has received any payment for this "stripped book."

Zebra, the Z logo, and To Love Again Reg. U.S. Pat. & TM Off.

First Printing: December, 1994

Printed in the United States of America

To my beloved CANINE *friends, past and present.*

For Frosty, Taffy and Nit-not, and the two furry tyrants who currently rule the roost, Saki and Tigger. Truly "woman's best friends"!

One

Jeff heard the barking, and then he saw the woman. Even from a distance there was something hauntingly familiar about her.

The early-morning stillness faded away, and Jeff lowered his coffee mug to the table. He opened the door of his newly rented cottage and stepped outside. He'd just finished congratulating himself on finding the perfect place to relax and write his book, and now this. Was it a dream or a nightmare?

He walked to the side of the road, waited while a dusty pickup rattled by, and then strode across the road to the woman and her dogs. They were large, white, and hairy. Handsome enough, he supposed, if you were into dogs. But he wasn't. Never had been.

The woman had her back to him, and she was bent over, talking softly to one of the dogs. Jeff waited.

Then she straightened and smiled at him.

"Hello, Commander. It's good to see you again."

Jeff stared. He felt his jaw collapse and his eyes widen. Memories fought their way to the surface of his mind. That voice, the smile, the coppery curls . . . was it possible?

"Sam? Samantha?"

Sam nodded, her smile widening. "It's me, Jeff. It's been a long time, hasn't it?"

A long time? It had been more than thirty years since Jeff and his father had summered in Cape May, since Jeff had met Samantha on the beach, when she was fourteen and he was eighteen.

Memories washed over him. The Wildwood boardwalk, hot dogs smothered in mustard and sauerkraut, the tangy scent of salt air.

"The lease was signed Sam Wells," he said, shaking his head. "You're my landlady?"

Sam laughed. "Afraid so. Think you can get used to a landlady named Sam, Commander? Of course, I don't look much like a lady now with these faded jeans and . . ."

Jeff was shaking his head. He felt like a heel, like a creep of the first order, but there was no sense prolonging this reunion. There was no way he could write a book living right across the street from a kennel. But he stared at Sam, trying to find the right words. She was beautiful, a cute young girl turned into a lovely, mature woman. She was also heavily, unmistakably pregnant.

What he remembered most was her smile and the sound of her laughter. It had always reminded him of crystal bells. Crystal bells. Ah well, he'd been only eighteen then, and everything had been intense. Through the years he'd learned that romance was just a word, and even committing to marriage didn't guarantee a happy-ever-after.

A couple of sharp barks brought him back to the matter at hand. Dogs. Several of them. And their shrill barks made his head spin. He stared, then squared his shoulders and faced the woman he'd never expected to see again. The warm spring sunshine played across his back and the smell of fresh, growing things tickled his nostrils. Jeff disregarded those pleasant feelings, folded his arms across his chest, and frowned.

Some kind of sled dogs, he thought. But what did he know? The closest he'd ever come to having pets were two goldfish he'd won at a fair. The dogs were nice-enough-looking animals, he supposed, but certainly not what he wanted for neighbors.

Samantha gave the animal a final pat, straightened, and turned to face him. Lord, but he liked the shape of her lips, he thought crazily, realizing that his months of celibacy were catching up to him.

Sam smiled at the look on Jeff's face. She knew he was struggling with memories just as she was. Her smile broadened. "The beach in Wildwood? A girl named Sam? It was a great summer, wasn't it?"

There was something in her eyes, something in the way she cocked her head to one side. That voice, Jeff thought. He felt dizzy, and his normal cool aplomb deserted him as he stared in fascination, unable to tear his gaze from the woman's blatantly protruding belly. Dogs, a beautiful pregnant woman, and a voice from the past. Suddenly the memories assaulted him full-scale. The feeling of being flung back into the past intensified. Suddenly he smelled the salt air, heard the waves crashing on the beach, tasted the hot dogs and the creamy chocolate fudge the boardwalk was famous for. And he remembered the girl. Sweet and shy, certainly not as well rounded and confident as the woman before him, but familiar enough to make him ache with the memories.

Fourteen . . . she'd been only fourteen to his eighteen, but there'd been an instant rapport. Was it because they'd both known what it was like to lose a parent?

Jeff's mother had died when he was two years old and Sam's mother had walked out on her when she was twelve. Sam had been rescued by her aunt, a blue-eyed, cheerful woman named Daisy.

"It really is you." It felt like a dream, like something that would happen after a wild night and a few too many bourbons.

Then she smiled again, and the sun, so recently hidden behind a cloud, suddenly beamed down on Jeff's shoulders.

"Well, I'll be damned!"

"It's me, all right." Sam's hand was lying on the big dog's collar.

Jeff glanced at the animal, saw the way it leaned protectively against Sam's jeans-clad leg while regarding him with a level, intelligent caution. Or at least that's the way it seemed to Jeff, but how could he be sure? He knew next to nothing about animals, dogs in particular, but despite himself he felt a grudging respect.

"Lord, Sam! I can't believe this. After all these years . . . who would have thought? Well, how have you been? What have you been doing with yourself?" He stopped, took a deep breath, and laughed. "Hell, I can see the answer to that, can't I?"

Jeff shifted uneasily. He felt like a real ass,

but he had to be honest. "Look, Sam, I'm afraid there's been a big mistake. When I rented the house I was looking for a peaceful retreat, a quiet place where I can work undisturbed. I'm planning to write a book now that I'm retired. I sure didn't bargain for barking dogs and . . ." Jeff's dismay grew as he watched a veil slide down over Sam's incredible green eyes. A man could drown in those eyes. He'd felt that way at eighteen, and the memories were sweeping over him relentlessly. With an effort Jeff pulled his thoughts back to the matter at hand. What he'd shared with this woman years ago had been nothing more than puppy love. And that was then; this was now. Sam was obviously married and about to have a child, and he was looking for peace and solitude. He wanted a chance to get his bearings while he decided what to do with the rest of his life. He sure didn't need old memories filling him with confusion.

His eyes swung automatically to Sam's swollen belly. Come to think of it, wasn't it kind of late in life for Sam to be incubating?

"Don't you like kids and dogs, Commander?" Sam asked seriously, her head tilted to one side. The laughter had disappeared from her eyes, and her face had a tight, tense look.

"Look, it's not like that," Jeff said, and now he did feel like a real jerk. "Sure I like kids and animals, but this just won't work. Please refund my deposit so I can look for another place to live." He didn't like feeling like the bad guy, but it was just the way things were. He wasn't into kids and animals. He never had been. His life had been dedicated to his military career.

"Can't," Sam stated flatly. "Today is Sunday and all the banks are closed. I deposited your rent check late Friday afternoon." And she had. Jeff's check had arrived just in time to allow her to pay her past-due utility bills, and she was counting on future rent checks to carry things until the kennel started paying its own way. If not for Doug's meager insurance policy, she wouldn't have been able to hang on this long, but she was near the end, and if Jeff walked away . . .

"Then write me a check," Jeff said, restlessly shifting position as an unusual fragrance wafted around him. "I'm sure I can trust you." It wasn't a flowery scent. It was clean and fresh, strong and earthy, like the woman standing in front of him. Jeff decided he was definitely losing it. How could a man have erotic thoughts about a woman who looked like she was ready to deliver a baby at any time? He tried to concentrate on how he could get his money refunded instead of how it would feel to kiss Sam again. Lord, why was the memory of lying on a blanket at the beach with a sweet young girl at his side and feeling the hot sun on his skin suddenly so vivid? He could almost feel those first wondrous stirrings of manly passion again. He swallowed, determinedly bringing his thoughts back to the present as Sam laughed. He was forty-nine, almost fifty years old. He'd been married and divorced, so why was he feeling like a lovestruck kid all of a sudden?

"I don't think you should be too trusting," Sam warned. She shifted her body and absently rubbed her back. "I deposited your check on Friday and wrote checks to pay my bills Saturday morning. There isn't any money left in my account. I'm afraid if I wrote you a check, it would bounce as high as the kennel roof." She hated feeling so round and frumpy, and this pregnancy was so different from when she'd carried Tim. Then she'd been young and fearless, confident that everything would come up roses. Now she knew different. And she was starting to wonder if she really was too old to have this baby.

Jeff was momentarily speechless. His money was gone and he was looking at a damsel in distress on top of everything else. Just what he needed!

"Are things that bad?" he asked, raking his fingers through thick, dark brown hair. Instantly he was sorry he'd asked. He didn't want to get involved with this woman, yet he felt an urgent need to understand her situation. Where was her husband? A woman in her condition shouldn't have to worry about bouncing checks. He and Sam had been friends once, if only for a brief time, so it was only natural that he'd be curious. But curiosity killed the cat, Jeff, he reminded himself; none of this is any of your business, and if you're smart you'll make tracks out of here just as fast as possible.

Then Sam shrugged, and her hand left the small of her back to curve protectively over the mound of her belly. "Whoops; junior's acting up," she said, her eyes round with a strange combination of wonder and regret. "Gosh, it's a weird sensation when the little guy starts doing acrobatics."

"I'll bet," Jeff agreed. He was intrigued despite himself. Creating a new life was a miracle; Sam would get no argument from him about that. He'd seen enough of the other side to know.

Impulsively, he stepped closer. It was crazy,

and he felt like a fool, but he couldn't resist. His hand inched out toward Sam's rounded belly. He hesitated, but the temptation was too great. "May I . . . ?" During his brief marriage he'd thought about being a father, but after the divorce he'd shoved all those thoughts away, and he'd told himself over and over that it was best that there'd been no children to be ripped apart by a broken family.

Now Sam laughed, and Jeff's lips curved in response. The sun was suddenly brighter, and Sam's laughter sounded like crystal bells tinkling in a summer breeze, just the way Jeff remembered it. "Sure," she said. "Here, give me your hand."

Her touch was a shock to Jeff's nervous system. He couldn't remember when he'd last felt so alive and alert. He suddenly realized that a part of him had never forgotten Samantha, or that crazy, wonderful, totally innocent summer.

Carefully, Sam guided Jeff's hand to her belly. It was a strong hand, she thought. Warm and strong. She was tempted to close her eyes and pretend, but no, there was no point in that. Doug was dead, she was a widow, and she would be raising this child alone. Still, there was no harm in letting herself enjoy the fantasy for just a minute.

Jeff was so caught up in the moment, he

missed the fleeting look of sadness that darkened Sam's eyes. He'd had some pretty awesome moments in his life, but feeling Sam's baby moving inside her was something he couldn't even begin to describe. For the first time in years he felt a stab of regret at not having children. He coughed. "That's really something. The little devil can really kick! Your husband will be sorry he missed this," he said. There was a lump the size of a Florida grapefruit in his throat. He withdrew his hand reluctantly, faintly embarrassed by the shared intimacy. "But then, I suppose this happens all the time, doesn't it?"

"Quite a bit lately," Sam admitted. She hesitated, then lifted her chin. "My husband died two weeks after I learned I was pregnant."

Jeff's breath caught in his throat and his hand instinctively moved to capture Sam's fingers. He pressed gently, wishing he had the guts to take her in his arms. "I'm sorry."

"Thanks," Sam said, her voice stiff with dignity. "Naturally, I wish things could have been different, but the baby and I will be okay. We're not alone. There's my aunt Daisy and my son Tim. Tim is twenty, and he still lives at home."

"You have a twenty-year-old son?" For some reason Jeff had a hard time imagining Sam mothering a grown son. Then he grinned as another memory surfaced. "Remember all the bratty kids we were always trying to escape that summer? God, they followed us everywhere. I tried just about everything to get rid of them, didn't I? But you always wanted to play with them." He sobered. Sam didn't want to hear his adolescent remembrances. "Well, I'm sure you're glad to have your son with you now. You shouldn't be alone at a time like this. How is your aunt?"

Sam smiled, but a look of weariness passed over her features. She absently rubbed the mound of her belly and sighed. "Aunt Daisy is as fine as a seventy-eight-year-old lady with arthritis and various other problems can be. I meant what I said before about your rent check, Jeff. I can't give it back to you, at least not right now. Couldn't you give the place a try? Maybe it won't be as bad as you think. The dogs aren't that noisy. Muffy yaps a little, but the Samoyeds are usually very well-behaved. And they have good, even dispositions, if that's what you're worried about." If only Jeff would stay and give the place a chance! They needed his rent money so badly.

"I can believe that," Jeff said, his gaze swinging to the big white dog standing guard at Sam's side. He looked at the dog quizzically. "Is the dog pregnant, too?"

"She is," Sam said. She looked down at the dog proudly. "This, Commander Brooks, is Polar Princess, one of my best bitches. Isn't she gorgeous? She's due to whelp in a few weeks. I already have a waiting list for her pups. When the pups are sold I'll be able to give you your money back, but in the meantime . . ." She shrugged helplessly.

Before Jeff could form a reply a small bundle of black-and-white fluff came flying across the scraggly lawn, yapping for all it was worth. The creature flung itself at Jeff's legs, then ran in eager, excited circles around Sam and Jeff, yipping all the while.

Maybe the big dogs were well-behaved, Jeff thought, his dark brows raised questioningly, but this. . . . "Muffy?" he asked.

"Yep. Cute, isn't she? Muffy loves everyone. Watch out, though; if you pet her, she's likely to piddle. She gets overstimulated."

"Right," Jeff said, attempting a smile. He had no intention of ever petting the animated dust mop, but he had a feeling Sam wouldn't appreciate that sentiment. It wasn't as if he disliked animals; it was just that in his well-ordered, disciplined life there had never been room for anything as frivolous as a pet, and if there had been, he certainly wouldn't have chosen anything like this fuzz ball.

But Muffy seemed determined to change the status quo. She ignored Jeff's lack of response and proceeded as though he'd given her a green light. With her large, shiny, shoe-button eyes peeking out from under a black-and-white fringe, and her shaggy plume of a tail wagging ecstatically, she was pretty hard to resist. Against his better judgment, Jeff bent down and patted her head. As Sam had warned, the thrill was obviously too much for her. Muffy promptly squatted and piddled all over Jeff's perfectly polished brown shoes, all the while looking up at him adoringly with her Betty Boop eyes.

"Oh, dear! I'm sorry! I . . ." At first Sam looked thoroughly chagrined, but then, as she absorbed the shocked expression on Jeff's strong-featured face, she had to laugh. And once she started she had a hard time stopping. Jeff's expression was priceless—a combination of shock and dismay, of righteous indignation warring with amusement—as his dark eyes met her laughing ones. Sam shrugged. What did it matter, anyway? The man didn't like her big belly or her dogs, and he'd likely be out of here the second she refunded his rent check. She'd been crazy to think it could work, that a dignified, retired naval commander would want to live across the street from the Snow Storm Kennels. But they weren't into the tourist season yet, and Sam had thought a year-round tenant would be better in the long run.

Sam's backache intensified, and she massaged it automatically. Maybe some men liked dogs and slightly disheveled, extremely pregnant women. Maybe the old Jeff she'd once known would have, but not this man. He was different. Older, quieter, more reserved. Maybe being in the military had done that to him. Let's see, he was probably about forty-nine; old enough to be set in his ways, as Aunt Daisy was fond of saying. But it didn't matter. If he left, Sam knew she would have to start hunting for another tenant immediately. That was the reality. The fantasy didn't matter.

Just because she and Jeff had once shared a few innocent kisses on the beach . . . just because they'd discovered the wonder of first love together didn't mean that more than thirty years later they could pick up where they'd left off. And she wouldn't want to, anyway. She'd had a husband, and things hadn't worked out. She wasn't looking for anymore hurt or rejection. All she wanted to do was raise her dogs and her baby.

"Look, I really am sorry," she said when she

was finally able to speak. "I didn't mean to laugh, but you have to admit I warned you. If you'll wait right here, I'll get something to clean your shoes. Bad girl, Muffy," she scolded, but without much conviction.

Discipline, Jeff thought grimly. That's all the salt-and-pepper mop needed. A couple of stern reprimands and the creature would think twice before piddling on anyone's shoes again. He shook his head, torn between a spurt of anger and a crazy feeling of amusement. In the end the amusement won. Was all this really happening or was he dreaming—or, more accurately, was he in the middle of a nightmare?

"Please," Sam repeated, "let me clean your shoes and at least offer you a cup of coffee. I feel terrible about all this."

Briefly, Jeff closed his eyes and counted to ten. A pregnant woman and a piddling, yapping pup. Could things possibly get any worse? It was certainly not the peaceful, relaxing atmosphere he'd looked forward to. Still, a cup of coffee did sound good. A stiff shot of whiskey would have been better, but he'd settle for coffee. And he was curious to hear what Sam had done with her life besides getting pregnant. "Coffee sounds great, but forget about cleaning the shoes. Just give me a damp rag." Now he did grin. "I may be a male chauvinist, but I'm not about to have a pregnant woman bending over to clean my shoes!"

Sam returned his smile. "You've got a deal, Commander. I don't bend too easily these days." She felt something stir inside her, something she thought had died with her husband. Jeff Brooks was a good-looking man, all right. He was tall, over six feet. Just right. Sam had always figured that if a man was tall enough to look up to, he was just right; and Jeff was certainly a man to look up to.

Sam led the way to the house. She figured Jeff was a man who knew exactly what he wanted and how to go about getting it. He'd been a handsome boy, and now he was a devastatingly attractive man. A hint of silver at his temples lent dignity to his masculine good looks. Mature. She liked that, and the way his dark eyes gleamed when he smiled, the way his lips had curved as he felt her baby move inside her. Sam smiled. Strong, yet tender; a potent combination. And she liked the way he smiled, too. And the way he was built, not as slender as she remembered, but certainly not fat. Just broader and older. Not too muscular, just strong and solid.

Jeff walked behind Sam, watching the slightly awkward sway of her hips with fascination. How could a woman so heavily pregnant still retain a certain grace? And the dog, Polar Princess . . . her time was near, too, yet she also had a graceful, almost regal look about her, despite her increased girth. They made a pretty picture, the expectant mother and her pregnant dog. Jeff thought that if he weren't so hung up on the idea of writing his book, he might enjoy hanging around just to see how things turned out . . . Sam's baby and the pups. But writing the book was a goal he'd set for himself, and a debt he felt he owed his father and all the other elderly people who spent their final years feeling lonely and unneeded. If his book helped people to understand the special needs of the elderly, it would be worthwhile.

"Mom! Hey, Mom!"

A tall, long-haired young man came careening out the door of the modest, brick-front house. "She's doing it again, Mom! Aunt Daisy's acting up again. Now she won't take her medicine. And she won't let me change the channel on the television, and she insists on keeping that ragged old scarf on her head. What are you going to do about her?"

Sam winced. "Calm down, Tim. I'll take care of Daisy. Can't you try and have a little patience?" She turned to Jeff. "This is my son, Tim. Tim, this is Commander Brooks, the man who rented the house across the street. He used to come to Cape May for the summer when I was young."

"Hey," Tim acknowledged, his brown eyes sweeping Jeff curiously. "So you're the new tenant. What do you think so far?"

Jeff extended his hand and smiled. "I'm the tenant for the moment," he answered, "But I'm not sure . . ." His words trailed off as he watched Sam visibly sag. The light went out of her green eyes, and Jeff could almost see new lines of worry burrowing into her forehead. "We'll see," he finished quickly.

"We're going to have a cup of coffee, Tim," Sam said. "Where is Aunt Daisy?"

Tim shrugged. "Parked in front of the television, as usual," he said. "At least she was a few minutes ago. I still say the way she acts lately is weird."

"She's old, Tim, and she's not in the best of health. Her arthritis bothers her, and I think she's just trying to get a little attention. I've been so busy with the kennel lately, I haven't spent enough time with her."

There was something in Sam's voice, an odd mixture of anger and resentment and guilt. Jeff watched silently as Tim shrugged again, looking slightly ashamed. He felt a tug of sympathy for both Tim and Sam. He knew all too well how hard it was to deal with aging relatives, and for someone in Sam's predicament, it had to be nearly impossible.

"Is there anything I can do to help?" he asked. He instinctively reached out to steady Sam as she mounted the front steps. For some unexplainable reason he wanted to lighten this woman's burdens. He longed to bring that slightly mischievous smile he remembered back to her lovely face, and he wanted to hear her silvery laugh again.

Sam shook her head. "Thanks, but Aunt Daisy doesn't think much of strangers these days. I guess you could say she's a little eccentric. She behaves pretty well for me, though I'm sure I'll be able to get her to take her medication."

But it was not destined to be one of Aunt Daisy's better days. She seemed determined to make a liar out of Sam. She wasn't about to be cooperative in any way, shape, or form.

"Who's this?" she asked, her faded blue eyes narrowed suspiciously as she glared at Jeff.

Jeff smiled at the elderly woman who was frowning so angrily. He couldn't help remembering his dad and the summer the two of them had spent in Cape May. It was one of his fondest memories. And then he and his dad had packed up and gone home to Ohio before the feelings bubbling inside Jeff and Sam could ripen into anything serious. Jeff pushed the memories away. They'd both been too young, anyway.

"This is Jeffrey Brooks, the new tenant for the house, Aunt Daisy. Remember? I told you he was coming." Sam gently touched her aunt's shoulder.

"Humph! Nobody tells me anything anymore! I might as well be a tree standing in the middle of the yard for all the notice I get. And I don't like strangers. You know that, Sammy girl. What do you do for a living, young man?" she demanded. "Not into anything unlawful or underhanded, are you? What did you say your name was? Jeremy?"

Aunt Daisy leaned closer to peer into Jeff's face.

From the corner of his eye, Jeff caught the flush that colored Sam's cheeks.

"Aunt Daisy, please . . ."

"It's all right, Sam," Jeff said quickly. "Your aunt is right. She's just being cautious, and rightly so. You're two women alone here and . . ."

"They're not unprotected," Tim said sharply,

coming up behind Jeff. "I'm here to look after them."

"Sure. I didn't mean . . ."

"You didn't answer me, young man. Are you up to no good?"

"No, ma'am, and my name is Jeff." Jeff spoke seriously, but he couldn't quite hide his smile. With her shapeless print housedress and floppy pink slippers and her mop of unruly gray-brown hair partly covered by a bright red-and-green-printed scarf, Aunt Daisy reminded him of a cartoon character he'd once enjoyed. Too bad he wasn't planning to write a book of humorous fiction. Pregnant landladies, dogs of assorted sizes and shapes, senile aunts and irate sons . . . then he looked at Sam and his smile faded.

Obviously, she wasn't finding the scene amusing. There were lines of strain around her mouth and she looked very tired.

"I'll wait for you in the other room," he said quietly.

Two

Later, after Sam had finally managed to cajole her aunt into taking her medicine and lying down for a nap, she poured two steaming mugs of coffee and lowered her bulk into a chair across from Jeff. What a terrible impression they had all made on him! She wouldn't blame him if he ran shrieking into the streets.

"I'm sorry about all this," she said. "You must think you've stumbled into a nut house. Believe me, Aunt Daisy is really a sweet person. She's not always so unreasonable. Sometimes our lifestyle is almost normal."

Sam stirred cream into her coffee and flushed, remembering the way Aunt Daisy had stubbornly clamped her lips shut on the spoon when Sam tried to give her her medicine.

"Hey, it's okay," Jeff said quickly, wanting to ease Sam's discomfort. "I've seen old people act a lot worse." He fell silent, remembering.

Watching Sam cajole and coax her aunt had been like watching the rerun of an old movie.

How many times had he played the same scene with his father? How many times had he raked his fingers through his hair in frustration as he tried to reason with a man who was so lonely and unhappy he could no longer think coherently? Suddenly he realized Sam was watching him, and she looked concerned.

"My dad," he explained. "His last few years weren't as good as they should have been. Being in the military, I couldn't keep him with me. He was lonely and unhappy, and I finally had to put him in a nursing home. It was just about the hardest thing I've ever done." He nodded in the direction of the other room. "It's not the best solution, but it may be an option you'll eventually have to consider."

It wasn't any of his business, of course, but in the space of the last few minutes he'd decided that Sam was overwhelmed and overburdened. She was pregnant, trying to run a kennel and care for a cantankerous old woman, not to mention looking out for her son. It made him tired just thinking about it.

Sam shook her head adamantly. "I'll never put Aunt Daisy in a nursing home. She took care of me when my mother walked out. I'm sure it wasn't easy for her, but she never once made me feel I was a burden to her. The least

I can do is return her unselfish kindness. And anyway, it's not like she's seriously ill. I sometimes think she acts up out of boredom. I'm always running from one chore to another, and Tim . . . well, he marches to his own drumbeat. Aunt Daisy probably feels neglected."

Sam sipped her coffee and shifted position. These days there was really no comfortable way to sit, but everything would be all right once the baby was born. It was what she'd been telling herself for months, as if the baby's birth would wave a magic wand that would solve all her problems and make all of them, even Aunt Daisy, happy and contented.

Jeff took note of Sam's restless movement and felt sympathetic. He wished he had the nerve to offer her a back rub. He didn't know much about pregnant women, but he'd read something once about pregnancy and backaches. He shook himself mentally; it was crazy. Disregarding the brief relationship he and Sam had had as teenagers, he'd known her less than an hour, and yet he felt inordinately protective. He could just imagine what she would think if he suddenly started rubbing her back.

"Have you always lived in New Jersey?" he

asked, desperate to change the subject and get his mind back where it belonged.

"I left for a while, after I married Doug," Sam explained. "Aunt Daisy was younger then, and she insisted that I get on with it and live my own life. So Doug and I traveled around for a few years."

"His job kept him on the road?" Jeff asked.

Sam laughed, but it was not a joyful laugh. "You could say that, I suppose," she answered. "Actually, we lived and worked at a circus for a while."

"A circus? As in lion tamers, clowns, and elephants?" Jeff asked, looking stunned.

"The very same. Doug thought he wanted to be a trapeze artist. He wasn't too happy when I wouldn't agree to go on the high wire with him. I stayed on the ground and sold tickets."

Jeff shook his head, unable to think of an appropriate response.

"Then we went out to California for a while. Doug worked as a lifeguard. He liked that, but I never felt comfortable in California. I didn' feel as though I fit in. Then I got pregnan with Tim, and Aunt Daisy had a mild stroke I told Doug I was coming back, with or with out him. He was between jobs then, so h came, too. When Tim was born he made up for everything."

Sam hesitated, then decided that she might as well be honest and up front. "I guess you could say that Doug and I weren't exactly compatible. I suppose I should have ended the marriage, but I felt as though I'd be depriving Tim of a father." The last few words flew out of Sam's mouth in a rush. What on earth was she doing, spilling all this to Jeff? He'd merely asked if she had lived in the same place all her life. He hadn't requested a life history.

"So you came home," Jeff said.

"Yes, and I've never been sorry. I love it here," Sam said. "Cape May is such a quaint little town, and there's something tranquil yet exciting about the ocean. Of course, as far as Aunt Daisy is concerned, nothing is like it used to be. According to her, the old days were definitely better. She doesn't even like the Victorian Mall they put in a few years ago. She said it's too commercial." Sam paused to catch her breath, then smiled. "Now what about you? What have you been doing all these years?"

Jeff frowned. "I got married, but it only lasted a couple of years. Marcie said I was too rigid, that living with me was like being in boot camp, and she didn't like being dragged from one naval base to the next. She said she wanted to settle in one spot and put down roots."

"I'm sorry," Sam said quietly.

"Yeah. So am I," Jeff said. "Or at least I was at the time. Later I realized it was probably for the best. And at least we didn't have any kids to be torn between us."

"Children do make a difference," Sam said. "Anyway, isn't it crazy how you ended up back here after all this time?"

Jeff grinned. "I guess I was homesick for the Wildwood boardwalk. And I thought I'd like to try my hand at one of the casinos in Atlantic City. I guess you don't get to do that very often, do you?"

Sam's green eyes widened. "Are you kidding? I've never even seen the inside of one of them. When Doug was alive he liked that kind of thing, but it scares me. I guess I never felt like I had money I could afford to throw away."

Jeff nodded. He resisted the urge to fold Sam in his arms. It didn't sound like her life had been very easy. He felt bad when he saw her eyes darken with memories. Judging from the tightness around her mouth, and the way her shoulders sagged, they still bothered her.

Glancing down, he saw that his coffee cup was empty. "I guess I better go," he said, noting that Sam kept her eyes lowered. "I'll start looking around tomorrow and see if I can find a more suitable place. You can pay back my rent money when the princess, here, delivers her royal babies. It really was great to see you again, Samantha, and I'm sorry our business arrangement isn't going to work out."

Sam eased her bulk out of the chair and winced. "Thanks," she said, "and I am sorry for the inconvenience. I guess I just wanted to rent the house so bad, I didn't think things through. This isn't the most tranquil atmosphere for a writer, is it?"

She was trying hard to conceal her disappointment. Oddly enough, it wasn't simply the loss of a paying tenant that bothered her. There was something about Jeff that moved her, and it wasn't just old memories stirring. Pregnant women were entitled to a few little idiosyncrasies, weren't they?

Was it the stunned, shy look that had touched his eyes when he'd felt her baby move inside her? Or was it the gentle, understanding way he'd treated Aunt Daisy? Something told Sam that here was a good man, a man who could be trusted, even if he wasn't particularly fond of her dogs. And that could change. Maybe.

Sam grinned ruefully and gave Jeff her hand. Her thoughts were drifting in the wrong direction again, but it was understandable. Her pregnancy had been difficult. Doug's death, the early weeks of violent morning sickness, waiting for the results of the amniocentesis, Aunt Daisy's crazy antics, and Tim and his aimless drifting. It had all taken a heavy toll, and now, faced with a few kind words, a compassionate touch, and the sweet ache of memories, she was going off the deep end.

Fourteen. She'd been just weeks away from her fifteenth birthday when Jeff and his father came that last summer. She was still awkward, shy and unsure of how to act around the opposite sex. Jeff had given her her first taste of womanly confidence that long-ago summer. He'd held her hand and told her she was pretty, and he'd stolen a few chaste kisses under the boardwalk. It had all been so innocent, and they hadn't made any promises. They'd been too young and unsure of themselves for that, but Sam had never forgotten that summer, or the young man who had made it so special.

Jeff saw the softening in Sam's face, read the memories in her eyes . . . the same memories that tugged at him. He gripped her slender hand briefly. It was feminine, yet strong and capable. He stepped back, afraid to lengthen the contact. Feelings were stirring inside him that he hadn't felt in a very long time.

"Goodbye," he said, then hurried outside. He was almost desperate to get away before . . . what? Before he offered to help Sam deal with her aging, unhappy relative? Before he told her not to worry about paying back his deposit? Or was he afraid he'd want to reach out and feel the wonder of Sam's child moving inside her again?

A door slammed, and Jeff turned to see Tim plop down on the lawn with several fluffy white puppies. Despite his resolve to remain uninvolved, he walked over.

"Hello again," he said. "What have we here?"

Tim didn't bother to get up. Instead he picked up one of the pups and held it out to Jeff.

"This little guy is the pick of the litter. He should sell for four or five hundred dollars, but knowing Mom she'll probably get three hundred. Multiply that times six, deduct all the vet's bills, the lost hours of sleep, various vitamin supplements and puppy meal, not to mention the cost of heating the kennels in the winter and air conditioning them in the summer . . ."

Jeff's eyes narrowed as his brain did a few quick calculations. "Not too lucrative, hmm? How come you only get three hundred for the pups if they're worth five?"

Tim shrugged. "Mom's tender heart. She can't bear to think of any of her babies going to a less-than-perfect home. Let me tell you, she screens prospective buyers like she was an adoption counselor. She ends up selling puppies cheap to people she thinks will really appreciate and take care of them."

"You don't approve?"

Again Tim shrugged. He lowered one wet-nosed pup to the ground and picked up one of the others. "It's not for me to say. Mom's the boss. This is her kennel."

Jeff grinned. The pups were cute. He had a sudden, crazy urge to pick one of them up, but he curbed his desire by jamming his hands into his pockets. "How do you tell one from the other? And how come their noses are all spotted?"

"You get to know their personalities after awhile. See how much bigger these pups are? These three are males, and those are females.

Usually the males are bigger. As for the noses, they're solid pink when the pups are born, then they get spotted like this. By the time these babies go to their new homes their noses will be solid black. See the black rim around the eyes? That's what the AKC calls black points. All Samoyeds have them."

"Well, I've learned something new today," Jeff said, nodding. "Thanks for the information, Tim."

"Any time," Tim said nonchalantly. "Are you going to hang around awhile, or are you making tracks out of here?"

Jeff started to speak, then stopped. A half hour earlier he'd have said he was on the way out, but now he just wasn't sure.

"I don't know," he answered honestly. "The house is just right, but . . ."

"Yeah, I know. Barking dogs, batty old ladies, and a pregnant woman. Crazy, huh? Mom's okay, though. She's a pretty neat lady, and she's got a good heart. I just wish she wouldn't nag me so much, you know? She's always after me to get a job. She doesn't like any of my friends. Sometimes I just feel like taking off, you know? But then I figure that she needs me, even if she won't admit it. I don't think Aunt Daisy's going to be much help when it comes time for Mom to go to the hospital and have the baby, do you?"

Jeff slowly shook his head, already regretting his decision to stop and chat with Tim. Why did he feel so responsible for a woman he didn't even know? And it wasn't his problem how Sam got to the hospital, was it?

Three

"You don't have to do this, Tim," Sam said, wearily reaching up to flip a strand of auburn hair off her forehead. She finished mixing the disinfectant in a bucket. "I can manage. You ought to be out looking for a job. Do you realize your twenty-first birthday is coming up soon? You can't hang out here for the rest of your life, you know."

"Why not?" Tim grinned disarmingly, anxious to ward off yet another confrontation with his mother. He didn't mind working in the kennels, at least until he could find a way to do what he really wanted to do. In fact, he had some ideas to make the kennel a paying proposition, if he could just get his mother to listen. . . .

"Come on, you know what I mean," Sam said. When Tim looked at her like that he could melt the heart of a lion, which was exactly the problem. She could never stay mad at him, and she simply didn't know how to be firm with him. "One of these days you'll meet a special girl and you'll start thinking of marriage and a family. You can't support a family playing with puppies and brushing dogs."

"I guess not," Tim said slowly, "but wouldn't it be great if everyone could make a decent living doing something they enjoy? Like you, Mom. Is there anyplace else you'd rather be than right here, surrounded by your dogs?"

Sam was silent for a minute, thinking. Darn that Tim! He got her every time! In all honesty she couldn't imagine a life without her dogs and the kennel. She'd loved dogs from the time she could walk and pick out pictures of puppies from magazines. But she was pretty sure Tim didn't have the same dedication. Oh, he liked the dogs, and he was good with them, but for Tim the kennel was just an excuse to get out of looking for a real job.

"You know how I feel about all this, Tim," Sam said, waving her arms as if she wanted to encompass it all. "But you also know that we're barely scraping by. If it weren't for your father's insurance money and Aunt Daisy's rental property . . ."

"Then why don't you pack it in and get an office job, or maybe you could go back to school and be a nurse or a teacher."

Tim's expression was blandly innocent, but

Sam knew that he'd turned the tables on her once again.

"Touché," she said, laughing. "You know I'd mortgage my soul before I'd part with my dogs. The thing is, I know I can eventually make this venture pay off. Oh, I don't expect to be rolling in hundred-dollar bills, but I really believe I can turn a decent profit. It's just going to take a little time."

Tim continued wiping the kennel floor with disinfectant, but he couldn't keep the excitement from his voice. "That's right," he said eagerly, "and I've got some ideas that may help. I was thinking . . ."

"Help! Help! The house is on fire! Help!"

The panicky cry came from the house, and terror gripped Sam as she awkwardly struggled to her feet.

Tim was already off and running toward the house and Aunt Daisy's frantic cries.

Please God, no, Sam prayed silently. Please let Aunt Daisy be all right, and don't let our house burn down. Please!

By the time Sam reached the house Tim was scolding Aunt Daisy. He looked much older than twenty as he angrily shook his finger in Daisy's face. Sam sniffed the air, relief washing over her in giant waves as she realized it was just another false alarm. Aunt Daisy had been pulling these little tricks frequently in the past few weeks, and Sam couldn't figure out why. Was it simply boredom? Resentment because Sam and Tim didn't spend more time with her? Or was her elderly relative really losing touch with reality?

Sam's eyes focused on Tim, and her hands curved protectively around the mound of her belly. She fought to catch her breath, and waited for the earth to stop spinning. "Is everything okay?"

Tim nodded grimly. "This time, but I swear, Mom, something's got to be done, and soon. She's getting worse every day. One of these times it will be for real."

Sam faced her aunt. "Aunt Daisy, isn't this going a little too far? I'm really not in the best shape to be running, you know."

The funny little gleam faded from Aunt Daisy's eyes and was quickly replaced with regret and guilt. "I'm sorry, Samantha. You know I'd never do anything to hurt you or the little one, but I didn't know where you or Tim were, and Muffy's run off someplace. I called and called and no one answered so . . ."

Sam's irritation abruptly drained away. So that was it: Aunt Daisy was bored and lonely.

She'd always been an active woman and she enjoyed people. Being left on her own most of the day while Sam and Tim worked in the kennels just wasn't working out, but what was the alternative? Was it really time to start thinking of a nursing home, or some sort of retirement situation where Aunt Daisy could have the companionship of people her own age? Or would that be a cop-out?

"Come on, dear," she said gently, putting an arm around her aunt's stooped shoulders. "Let's have a cup of tea and talk, all right?"

Tim shrugged helplessly and turned away. His mother had endless patience; he didn't know how she did it. He loved his great-aunt, too, but sometimes . . . and what would happen after the baby was born? With all the work to be done in the kennels, plus a new baby to care for, his mom simply wouldn't have time to pamper Aunt Daisy.

Tim went back to the kennels while Sam sat with the old woman. As he scrubbed, he wondered how he could get his mother to listen to the ideas he had for the kennel. He'd been doing a lot of reading, when he wasn't out with his friends, and he was pretty sure he'd figured out a way to make the kennels pay their way and then some. But it would take some money and, as his mom had pointed out, they were barely scraping by. It was crazy: They needed to make more money, but they needed money up front so they could make more money.

For lunch that afternoon Sam and Tim ate grilled cheese sandwiches. Tim had apple pie for dessert, while Sam settled for a plain apple. Aunt Daisy had eaten earlier and had gone upstairs for a nap, and now Sam had a rare moment of peace. She patted her rounded tummy and smiled, visualizing a happy, healthy baby boy or girl. Soon now, she'd hold her child in her arms and everything would be all right. The baby would help her deal with the pain and guilt she felt over Doug's death.

She hadn't expected a child at this time of her life, and at first she had been stunned and frightened. Would the baby be healthy? Was she too old to give a child the love and care it would need? Briefly, she'd considered an abortion, but she knew she couldn't do it. This was her child, flesh of her flesh, and it would be every bit as precious as Tim was. And she would find a way to raise it alone. Her lips twisted bitterly as she remembered Tim's early years. For all intents and purposes, she'd raised Tim alone, too, because Doug had shown little interest in his son. He'd always been too busy with his various get-rich-quick schemes.

Tim shoved a forkful of pie into his mouth, chewed a moment, then asked, "Well, what do you really think of our new tenant, Mom?"

Sam's smile faded, and the apple she was eating stopped just short of her lips. "He seems nice enough," she answered casually. "Of course, I remembered him as a somewhat shy, awkward eighteen-year-old. He's a lot different now. But I guess it doesn't really matter what we think of him. He won't be staying long. I guess you noticed that he wasn't too thrilled to discover that his new home was right across the street from a kennel. He'll probably be moving out soon."

"Most people wouldn't be happy living across the street from a kennel," Tim acknowledged, pushing his empty plate away, "unless they happened to be dog people like us. You know, Mom, I've been doing a lot of thinking, and I've got some ideas."

Sam heaved herself up out of the chair. "We don't have any extra money right now, Tim." Her son always had ideas, and his ideas always required money. Sam knew Tim meant well, but . . .

Muffy streaked through the kitchen just then, in hot pursuit of the tiny stray kitten

Tim had rescued recently from a tree in the yard.

"Speaking of ideas, taking in that kitten was not one of your best," Sam said, quickly reaching out to collar Muffy as the Shih Tzu made yet another pass at the frightened, hissing feline. "Easy, Muff," Sam said. She turned to Tim. "Maybe you'd better see what you can do about finding a home for that critter. I don't think we need any more confusion around this place, do you?"

Tim shook his head and grimaced. "I'll see what I can do."

When he finished straightening the kitchen for his mother Tim put the kitten in a cardboard box and tried to think of someone who might be interested in a nice, healthy kitten. Suddenly he had a brainstorm. Why not? Wasn't his mom always telling him to be more forceful?

Fifteen minutes later Tim was comfortably ensconced in Jeff's carton-filled living room, the cardboard container at his feet.

"Settling in, huh?" He grinned at Jeff, then rolled his eyes heavenward as he mentally tallied the boxes and cartons stacked around the room. "You must be as big a pack rat as Mom. Need some help?"

"Thanks, but I'll manage," Jeff replied. "I

decided it wouldn't be fair of me not to at least give this place a try. Uh, what's in that box you're holding?" He had a strange feeling he didn't really want to know, but his curiosity was getting the better of him. "It's not . . . alive, is it?" Tim hadn't brought him a puppy, had he? A furry, fuzzy, noisy, piddling . . .

"It's sort of a housewarming present," Tim answered slyly, feeling really proud of himself. A person couldn't very well refuse a present, could he?

"Why do I get the feeling I'm being conned?" Jeff asked, his tone sharpening. "What's going on, Tim?"

"Okay, okay, I'll come clean." Tim sobered. "I found this little guy in a tree the other day. He's hardly old enough to be away from his mama. I just couldn't abandon him, could I? But Mom says he has to go. Muffy keeps chasing him all around the house and . . ."

"So you're trying to pawn him off on me? You actually thought I'd want a kitten?"

"Hey, he's really healthy, and who knows, he may turn out to be a champion mouser."

"Mouser?" Jeff was absolutely certain he was going into shock. He'd survived war games in basic training with recruits who were dizzier than Tim, but this was the ultimate! Pregnant women and senile old ladies, barking dogs, and now this innocent-looking young man talking about mousers!

"Sure," Tim said, nodding vigorously. "Look, I don't know where you're from, Jeff, but New Jersey isn't just famous for its tomatoes, you know. We also grow very large, ferocious field mice. Every self-respecting home needs a reliable mouser."

Jeff started to laugh then, and for a couple of seconds he wasn't sure he'd be able to stop. The whole situation was so ridiculous. Here he was in the middle of unpacking, longing for nothing more than peace and quiet, and some crazy kid was sitting in the middle of his living room trying to give him a kitten. For all Jeff knew, the darn thing might be a female, and with all the pregnant females he'd seen so far, could this cat be far behind?

"I'm not afraid of mice, Tim, no matter how large or ferocious they are. Sorry, but your sales pitch isn't going to work. I'm not interested in acquiring a pet. I just want to think and relax and write my book. As soon as I get my computer set up I'll start working."

"Computer? What kind is it? Do you have a printer and a modem? How large is your hard drive?"

"Hey, slow down," Jeff said, laughing. "What

FULL BLOOM 51

is this, the Timothy inquisition? You sure are nosy!"

Tim grinned sheepishly. "Sorry. It's just that computers fascinate me."

"Yeah? What kind do you have?"

"Hey, I didn't say I had one," Tim answered, his face clouding. "I just said I like them. Look, I'd better get going. Are you sure you don't want this cat? If I don't find a home for him, Mom will make me take him to the SPCA, and you know what will happen then."

Jeff seriously doubted Sam would make Tim take the kitten to the animal shelter. He knew he should hold firm, but then he made a fatal mistake; he looked into the cardboard box.

It really was a small kitten. Tim was probably right: It didn't look old enough to be away from its mother. Bright green eyes stared up at Jeff imploringly, making him think of a prisoner pleading for a stay of execution.

"I don't suppose it's litter trained?" he snapped.

"Absolutely," Tim assured Jeff quickly. "He's a real smart little guy. He won't be any trouble. It's not like you have to walk him or anything."

"Oh, hell," Jeff muttered. What did a little more craziness matter? He was convinced he was smack-dab in the middle of a nuthouse anyway, so why not join in? "Okay," he said grudgingly. "I'll give it a try, but if things don't work out, you're getting him right back, understand? And it better be a him!"

"Great! You won't be sorry, Jeff. Here, I bought you a bag of stuff for his litter pan just to get you started."

"Thanks, I guess. Look, Tim, I really do have to get back to work now, otherwise I'll still be unpacking next week."

"Sure. I'll get out of here and let you get on with it. See you later, Jeff."

Tim could hardly wait to tell his mom that Jeff had decided to stay, at least for a while.

Jeff closed the door on Tim's retreating figure and started to laugh. Kittens and kids! What next? Then he stopped laughing and his brow puckered in a frown. Kid? How old was Tim anyway? He vaguely remembered Sam saying he was twenty, but he talked and acted more like a young teenager. Something didn't quite add up. He made a mental note to ask Sam the next time he saw her.

Halfway across the room, Jeff stopped. What was he doing? He knew the smart thing to do was hunt for another place right away, someplace quiet and serene. Instead he was unpacking and settling in, almost as if he intended to stick around permanently. And now he was responsible for the welfare of a tiny, totally helpless kitten. Why was he letting himself get involved this way? How would he ever get his book written if he allowed himself to get wrapped up in his pregnant landlady's family problems? He didn't have the answers. Oh, they were there somewhere, buried under tons of rationalizations. There was definitely a reason why he was staying, but he wasn't ready to face it yet.

Bright and early the next morning Jeff drove his Blazer over to Wildwood. He'd read in the local paper that they were opening a brand-new senior citizens' center, and he wanted to find out more about it.

He found the place easily and nodded approvingly as he saw that the building was large and in an easily accessible area of town. Inside he noted a sparkling-clean, cheerful interior. The first person he met was a short, rotund little man named Frank Fenwick.

"I've got a couple of reasons for being here," Jeff explained. "First of all, I'm writing a book about senior citizens, and secondly, my landlady's aunt is feeling kind of lonely. I was wondering if something like this might not be good for her."

Frank smiled, his lips seeming to spread

from one ear to the other. He clapped Jeff on the back. "Let me show you around, young fellow," he said.

"Frank? Oh, Frank, can you come over here for a minute?"

Jeff watched curiously as a tiny, birdlike woman held out a platter of cookies to Frank and insisted he try one.

"These are for the dance tonight," she said. "What do you think?"

"The best I've ever tasted, Elsie," Frank said, biting off a chunk and closing his eyes in ecstasy. "Elsie is our master chef," he said, with a wink at the blushing little woman. "Don't know what we'd do without her."

"You're having a dance tonight?" Jeff asked. "Is that a regular thing or is it a special occasion?"

"Regular thing," Frank said, ushering Jeff into a spotless kitchen with a huge oven and stainless-steel sinks. "Here's where we prepare the food for our dos," he explained. "Yep, we have a dance every Wednesday evening. From seven until eleven. We have real good times. Mostly the women outnumber the men, but we make do, and everyone seems to enjoy themselves. Friday mornings the ladies have an exercise class. Some of the gals say the exercises help their arthritis and such. Mondays are for the men. Us old fellows like to work out, too, you know." Frank chuckled. "Keeps the flab at bay, you know."

"I'll bet," Jeff said. He was impressed. Several women, most of them looking to be about the same age as Daisy, were bustling around in the kitchen, wearing ruffled aprons and laughing and chatting as they prepared the evening's refreshments. A couple of white-haired gentlemen were hanging balloons and crepe-paper decorations from the ceiling with the help of a man who looked to be about Jeff's own age.

"That's Mark Fisher," Frank explained. "He volunteers a few hours every week to help us out. Say, how would you like to give us a hand, young fellow? We can always use a strong back and a healthy heart."

"I'd be glad to help out," Jeff said, "and I'd like to bring my friend over to meet all of you."

"Well, that would be fine, young fellow," Frank said. "That would be just fine."

Driving home that afternoon, Jeff was thoughtful. The center seemed to be just what Daisy needed, a chance to get out and mingle with her peers. To do something besides vegetate in front of the boob tube. And who knows, maybe the exercise class would help her arthritis.

He wished his father could have enjoyed the benefits of such a center. He was sure it would have made a big difference in the quality of the older man's last years. But he couldn't change that now, and he had a feeling his dad would approve of what he was trying to do for Daisy.

Four

Thursday morning dawned bright and clear, unusually warm for early May. It was barely 7:30 when Jeff took his coffee and wandered out into the front yard. Almost a week had passed since he'd moved in, and he had finally finished unpacking. His computer was set up, but for some reason he couldn't get it running. Ruefully, Jeff admitted that his primary talents didn't lie in the field of electronics. He knew how to run the word-processing software the salesman had sold him, and he'd taught himself how to format blank disks and run the letter-quality printer he'd purchased with the computer, but that was the extent of his knowledge. If the computer failed to cooperate, he was lost.

Shrugging, Jeff promised himself that he'd get out the phone book and find a competent computer person to help him out. He was still looking forward to starting his book but, oddly, the project had lost some of its original appeal. It just didn't seem as urgent as it once had. Was the peaceful country setting getting to him, or was he simply unwinding after years of a rigorous, demanding military career? Maybe a little of both, Jeff thought, looking around at the trees that were just beginning to leaf out. No wonder they called New Jersey the garden state! He remembered the taste of the world-famous Jersey tomatoes, and he had to admit they were delicious. Tim had told him that Sam planted a dozen tomato plants each spring, and that she'd be ready to put the seedlings in the ground any day. He wondered if he'd be around to taste them when they ripened.

Leisurely sipping his coffee, Jeff admitted that it was nice not to have to adhere to a rigid schedule, nice to be able to linger over coffee in the morning, nice not to give orders or take them. He still wondered if he was making a mistake by hanging around here. He was prepared to make a commitment to Daisy now, and he wasn't sure that was a good thing. Sure, it made him feel noble to think of helping the elderly woman, but he was leery of getting too involved in Samantha's family affairs. Pregnant women seemed so vulnerable. Every time he saw Sam waddling around the yard with her dogs he had the crazy urge to run over and offer to help, to feed the dogs or clean the kennels, anything to lighten her load. It scared the hell out of him. After his brief, ill-fated marriage Jeff had decided to keep his relationships with women casual. He wasn't interested in taking vows or making promises. He was fine on his own.

Jeff eyed his somewhat unkempt yard, deciding that it would be a good idea to borrow a rake from Tim and start cleaning up. He glanced across the road. All was quiet at Sam's place; no barking dogs or petulant aunts. Evidently, everyone was still sleeping.

Wandering around the yard, Jeff smiled, forced to admit that, so far, the kennel hadn't proved to be as much of a distraction as he'd feared. He was actually beginning to look forward to the periods when Sam or Tim turned the big dogs into their runs for exercise.

There was no denying the dogs were beautiful animals, and even if he hadn't been taking frequent peeks out of his windows, it would have been obvious that Sam took perfect care of her dogs. But how on earth was she going to manage when her baby was born? And how was she going to handle her aunt's cantankerous behavior?

Shaking his head, Jeff drained his coffee cup and silently chastised himself for doing it again. He couldn't seem to stop thinking of Sam and her problems. He couldn't help worrying about her. And Aunt Daisy fascinated him. She was totally unlike his own father and yet exactly the same in some ways. He had a strong hunch that there was nothing wrong with her that a little socialization and physical activity wouldn't cure. What the heck! Why not try and help the woman and do some research for his book at the same time? What could it hurt?

It was about 9:30 when Jeff heard the knock. He opened his front door and confronted Tim's grinning face.

"Hey, how's the kitten?" Tim asked. "I thought I should check, you know? Mom warned me not to bother you, but I figured you wouldn't mind just this once."

Once again Jeff was struck by the thought that Tim's behavior did not match his chronological age. But the young man's open friendliness was impossible to resent, and besides, Jeff was more than ready to desert his uncooperative computer for a while.

"Come in and see for yourself," he invited. "Cat already thinks he owns the place."

"Cat? Is that what you named him?"

"Can you think of something better?" Jeff asked. "I never had a pet before, you know."

"No kidding? Boy, you must have had a deprived childhood."

"No, I don't think so," Jeff replied thoughtfully. "It was just that my dad worked long hours, and I was in school all day. We never seemed to have time."

"Well, Cat looks contented enough. Tell the truth; aren't you glad you said yes?"

Jeff couldn't help smiling. "I suppose so. He *is* good company. How are things going at your place? Your mother feeling okay?"

"Mom? Oh, sure. She's as healthy as a horse. Always has been. Aunt Daisy's acting up, though. Twice in the past couple of days she's gotten out of the house without me or Mom seeing her. She was already down by the road when I spotted her and, boy, did she put up a fight when I tried to take her home. I tell you, one of these days there's going to be big trouble!"

"That's too bad," Jeff said thoughtfully. Apparently, there was no time to waste if he was going to help Aunt Daisy find contentment. "There's a new senior citizens' center in Wildwood. Do you think Daisy would be interested? It looks like a pretty decent place. They have weekly dances and exercise classes and all sorts of activities for the elderly. I'm planning to volunteer a few hours a week to help them out."

"Hey, that sounds great. The only thing is, Mom doesn't really have the time to be running Aunt Daisy back and forth these days, you know?" Tim grinned. "Not to mention the fact that she's having a hard time getting behind the steering wheel."

"I'll be glad to take Daisy," Jeff said. "It will be good research for my book."

"That reminds me," Tim said. "Did you get your computer all hooked up?"

"Not exactly," Jeff said. He raked his fingers through his hair and frowned. "It's hooked up but not running," he admitted, throwing the troublesome equipment a disgusted look. "I guess my only recourse is to call a computer technician to take a look and help me figure it out."

"Could I have a look?" Tim asked. "I took computer courses in school and I got all *As.*"

Jeff couldn't miss the eagerness and excitement in Tim's eyes. He wasn't crazy about some green kid fooling around with his expensive equipment, but he didn't have the heart to refuse.

"Okay, but be careful, will you? I've got a king's ransom tied up in this stuff."

"Don't worry, I'll treat it as if it were my

own," Tim promised, tossing his jacket on a chair. He sat down in front of the nonfunctioning computer. "I'll bet I can work out your problem in nothing flat."

Fascinated by Tim's self-confidence, Jeff sat down and made himself comfortable. The computer wasn't working anyway, so what harm was there in letting the kid fool around a little?

"Okay, that should do it," Tim announced a couple of hours later. "Want to give it a try?"

"You mean you actually got it to work?" Jeff roused himself, realizing that he'd dozed off while Tim was puttering. He couldn't remember the last time he'd slept during daylight hours, but for the last few days he'd felt different, more relaxed. He grinned and decided lightning wasn't going to strike him down just because he'd napped while the sun was up. "You really fixed it?"

Tim grinned proudly. "There really wasn't all that much to fix. You just didn't have everything set up right. Boy, this is some system! You could do just about anything with this baby!"

Jeff peered over Tim's shoulder curiously. Sure enough, the blinking yellow curser was doing its thing. He shook his head in amazement.

"Hey, thanks, Tim. This is great. How much do I owe you? You have no idea what a relief it is to have this thing working. Now I can get started on my book."

Tim grinned proudly. "No charge, Jeff. I'm just glad I could help. Well, I better get going. Mom and I have to take the newest batch of pups to the vet to be checked out. That's going to be a real fun trip! We have to take Aunt Daisy with us. She'll be bored and . . ."

"No, you don't have to take her," Jeff said firmly. "How about letting me baby-sit Aunt Daisy while you and your mom go to the vet? Believe me, I've had plenty of experience with elderly people. Aunt Daisy and I will get along just fine, and it will give me a chance to talk to her about the senior center."

Jeff realized that he was actually looking forward to spending some time with the feisty Aunt Daisy, and he was pretty sure it wasn't just because of his proposed book.

Sam's jaw dropped a half hour later when Tim showed up with Jeff in tow. Now what had her son done? she wondered. She'd warned him about pestering Jeff.

"Hi," Jeff said. "How are things going?"

"Just fine," Sam managed. He was a handsome man, all right. Even a woman in Sam's delicate condition could see that. But what was he doing in the kennels, and why was Tim grinning like a fool? Suddenly Sam wished she'd taken the time to comb her hair properly, and that she was wearing something soft and feminine instead of the bleached-out jeans and loose shirt she had grabbed that morning. Then she shrugged. Jeff hadn't come to see her. He was probably just killing time.

Even in old clothes she was striking, Jeff thought, and that watermelon mound of a belly couldn't detract from her appeal, but that wasn't why he'd come over. He reminded himself he was just trying to return a favor.

"Is everything okay at the house?" Sam asked Jeff. She remembered the leaky faucet in the bathroom sink and flushed guiltily. She should have had it fixed.

"Great news, Mom," Tim broke in before Jeff could reply. "Jeff has volunteered to sit with Aunt Daisy while you and I take the pups to the vet."

Sam reached out to her son for support and slowly hoisted herself to her feet. She felt more awkward with every passing day. Sometimes when she sat on the sofa and couldn't get up she felt like a beached whale.

The pups tumbled around her feet now, like fat cotton balls, dark eyes glistening with lively curiosity, their pink-and-black-spotted noses wriggling as they sniffed and snuffled each other.

Jeff watched the show with a smile. If he were a dog person, he'd be sorely tempted. Thank goodness he wasn't.

"That's impossible, Tim. We can't impose on Jeff like that," Sam said. She turned to Jeff. "Thank you for offering, but . . ."

"I won't take no for an answer," Jeff said stubbornly, determined to win this round. "I insist," he continued, thick, dark brows drawn into a line of determination. He'd noted the dark circles under her eyes. "You and Tim will have your hands full with these little guys, and for the moment I don't have anything else to do. Besides, thanks to Tim my computer is functioning perfectly, and as soon as I get my notes organized, I'll be able to start working on my book. So you see, I owe you one. If I'd had to call a computer technician it would have cost me a bundle. Tim saved the day."

"Really?" Sam looked stunned.

Jeff's gaze swung to Tim just in time to see the young man frown unhappily.

"Really," Jeff said. "This is one bright guy you have here." He clapped a hand on Tim's shoulder. An idea was spinning in his head, but he knew he'd need to think it through before he acted on it. "Where's Aunt Daisy?

It's time we got acquainted. There's something I want to discuss with her."

Sam opened her mouth to protest, then shrugged. Who was she to look a minor miracle in the eye? It would be nice not to have to worry about Aunt Daisy for a couple of hours. Of course, she was reasonably certain this would be the first, last, and only time Jeff willingly volunteered to "aunt-sit." A few hours with Daisy would probably cure him for life.

After getting Jeff and Aunt Daisy settled and taking a quick shower, Sam climbed in the back of the station wagon with the puppies while Tim drove.

"I wish you wouldn't try to drag Jeff into our personal lives, Tim," Sam said unhappily as they drove toward the vet's. "He made it perfectly clear that he wants peace and quiet so he can concentrate on writing his book. I promised to refund his rent check when I get paid for the pups. After that I don't know when we'll get another tenant. The way things are going, one afternoon with us would send a normal person screaming into the streets."

"I don't think Jeff's going anywhere," Tim said, grinning. "In fact, it looks as if he's settling in real good!"

Sam chewed her bottom lip. Was it possible

that Jeff had had a change of heart? "I still don't think you should run over there all the time pestering him, Tim."

"He likes me," Tim answered. "And I like him. He's an okay guy. And he didn't think I was pestering today when I fixed his computer."

Sam fell silent. High praise from Tim. Never having known what it was like to have a real dad, her son had enjoyed precious little male influence in his life. It would be wonderful if . . . there, she was doing it again, just what she'd warned Tim not to do. Cut it out, Sam, she chided. It's never going to happen. A man like Jeff isn't going to let himself get sucked into your problems, and besides, he doesn't even like dogs!

A half hour later Sam watched intently as the veterinarian checked each pup and pronounced it healthy. She was sure all the puppies were fine, but it was important to have professional confirmation.

"Okay, Sam," Dr. Gregory said a few minutes later. "This group looks good to me. They can go to their new homes any time now."

"Good. Now I can catch up on my bills."

"You're doing a beautiful job with these

dogs, Sam. Every one of them is a credit to the breed. Are they all sold?"

Sam grinned proudly, picked up one of the pups, and cuddled it against her cheek. "Every one. Why? Do you want one?"

Dr. Gregory smiled. "I wouldn't mind. Maybe we can work something out when Princess whelps. That's pretty soon, isn't it?"

"A few weeks," Sam answered, "but I already have twelve people waiting, and since an average litter is six or seven it looks like you'll have to get in line."

Dr. Gregory shrugged. "The story of my life. Anyway, it's good to see you doing so well with the kennel. I know it's been your dream for a long time. Speaking of impending births, when is your little one due?"

"Soon," Sam answered. "Hopefully before Princess delivers. I'm getting anxious."

Dr. Gregory's kindly face sobered. "It was sure too bad about Doug. A real freak accident."

"Yes. Well, Tim and I better get these little fur balls home. Thanks again, Dr. Gregory. I appreciate your extending me credit this way. I'll send you a check just as soon as I collect for these little beauties." For some reason, thinking or talking about her late husband didn't hurt as much as it had a couple of months earlier when the mention of Doug's name would have sent Sam into a fit of tears.

"Dr. Gregory's a nice guy," Tim remarked as he helped Sam load the puppies into their crates. "What would we have done if he hadn't given you credit?"

"I don't know," Sam said, shaking her head. "I honestly don't know."

Five

Jeff quietly studied Aunt Daisy as the elderly woman sat in front of the blaring television. He was quite sure she wasn't the least bit interested in what was being said, and he was equally sure she was scrutinizing him just as he was her. The first time he'd seen her he'd detected a sharp intelligence in her faded blue eyes. But there were lines of discontent around her eyes and her mouth, and he suspected that more than anything else, Aunt Daisy was bored and lonely, just as his father had been. He also had to wonder about her medication. From personal experience he'd learned what damage overmedication could do. Maybe when he got a little more comfortable with Sam he could ask her.

Suddenly Aunt Daisy turned on him. "Who are you anyway?" she demanded, glaring angrily. "I don't know you. I don't even like you!"

"How can you know you don't like me if

you don't know me?" Jeff asked reasonably. "Maybe we can be friends. I'd like to be your friend."

"Why?" Aunt Daisy asked suspiciously. "No one wants to be bothered with a cranky old woman. Where's Sam, and what's happened to Timothy? Did you find him a job yet? Sam's worried about him, you know."

"I know," Jeff said agreeably, "but don't worry. Tim will be all right. He's a bright fellow." He paused and took a deep breath. "I'm Jeff, Aunt Daisy. I rented the house across the road, and I'm writing a book. You may be able to help me."

"Is that so?" With surprising agility, Aunt Daisy turned, picked up the remote control box, and turned off the television. "I think I'd rather talk to you than listen to that rubbish. Tell me, are you married? Do you like babies? Sam's having a baby, you know, and she has no husband. Poor Doug! It's a shame. He was too young to die, but maybe things will work out for the best in the end. They weren't getting along very well, you know. They had a big fight the night of the accident. If you want to know what I think, I believe Samantha blames herself. She won't admit it, but I can tell."

Jeff was having a hard time absorbing everything at once. Not sure how to reply, he kept silent and let Aunt Daisy talk.

"Yes, you're right. Tim is a good boy," Aunt Daisy said, nodding. A memory lightened her gaze and a smile curved her lips, giving Jeff a brief glimpse of what she must have been like as a young woman. "He was always a good boy, but Sam worries too much for her own good. Thinks she has to take care of everything herself. I'd be glad to help around the house, you know, but she won't let me. She treats me like a helpless cripple. I've got arthritis, and Samantha keeps pushing pills at me. That fool doctor she takes me to . . . he thinks the answer to everything is in a little pink pill. But Tim will be all right. He's a good boy." Aunt Daisy's eyes narrowed suspiciously and she tapped Jeff's arm. "What's the matter with you? Cat got your tongue? How am I supposed to get to know you if you don't open your mouth, Jake?"

"Jeff. My name is Jeff. You're right about Tim, Aunt Daisy," Jeff replied. Then he couldn't resist. "What about Samantha? Is she a good girl?"

Aunt Daisy laughed out loud. "Samantha? 'Course Sam's a good girl. A bit of a tomboy, and she does dote on those smelly dogs of hers, but she's good, all right. There's none better. Do you like Sam, Jack?" Aunt Daisy chuckled. Of course he did. Why wouldn't he?

Jeff was startled. He was still marveling at Aunt Daisy's outspoken ways. He saw her studying him intently, and he caught the gleam of mischief in her eyes. He grinned, suddenly realizing that Aunt Daisy was even sharper than he'd originally thought.

"Well, what's the trouble, young man? *Does* the cat have your tongue?" Aunt Daisy chuckled at her own little joke and looked very pleased with herself. "You do like Sam, don't you, Jim?"

"Oh, I like Sam, all right," he admitted. "I like her just fine, Aunt Daisy. But I'd really like to get to know you better. Did you know that there's a new senior citizens' center in Wildwood? They have weekly dances and exercise classes for ladies like yourself. The man who runs things, Frank Fenwick, said they'd love to have you join them. What do you think?"

"They have dances?" Aunt Daisy asked, her eyes sparkling. "My, I haven't danced in a long, long time, but I used to be something on the dance floor. Goodness . . . you say they have exercise classes for old ladies like me?

Why, I don't believe I have anything suitable to wear to a dance."

Jeff smiled. "We'll get you a new dress," he said, "and Frank said some of the ladies claim exercising helps their arthritis."

"You don't say? My, I wonder if Sammy would have time to drive me."

"That's not a problem, Aunt Daisy," Jeff said. "I'm going to be donating some time at the center and I'd be glad to take you over."

"You would? Well, my goodness, you are a nice young man, aren't you, Jake?"

"Absolutely," Jeff said.

"Well, that's fine, Jim," Aunt Daisy said. "I knew you were okay the minute I laid eyes on you." Then she leaned back, closed her eyes, and began to drift off. Her breathing deepened and she began to snore softly.

By the time Sam and Tim returned from their trip to the vet Aunt Daisy was stretched out on the sofa, sleeping soundly. Jeff sat in an easy chair, reading a magazine and looking quite content.

Sam eyed the peaceful scene with something close to disbelief. "She didn't give you any trouble?" Absently, she kneaded the small of her back. She ached almost constantly these days, and she was convinced she looked just like one of those helium balloons she sometimes saw in the windows of the florist shops. "I was worried."

Jeff could see that her back was bothering her. "No need to worry," he said. "Aunt Daisy and I got along just fine. She seemed really interested in the senior citizens' center. How did everything go with you? Pups all okay?"

The faint look of weariness fell away then as Sam warmed to her favorite subject. She smiled proudly. "A-OK. Dr. Gregory even wants a pup for himself. He said they're a credit to the breed." How could a man look so relaxed and yet so alive . . . so incredibly male? Sam wondered. And why would a pregnant, balloon-bellied woman even care?

Sam lowered herself into a chair, deciding that her advanced pregnancy was affecting her brain. A woman about to deliver a child wasn't supposed to be thinking such things, was she? It was her hormones, Sam decided; they were all out of whack. As soon as the baby came she'd be fine. She'd revert to her normal, sensible self. But in the meantime she had to keep a tight hold on her emotions. She wasn't interested in making a fool of herself with Jeff.

And she was much too old for silly, meaningless flirtations.

Jeff noted the confusion that passed over Sam's face, saw the gentle way her hands smoothed over the bulge beneath her peach-colored smock. She looked younger than he knew her to be, despite the lines of strain and weariness around her sea-green eyes. He couldn't help wondering how she would look after the baby was born. Although he'd vowed not to, he was getting more and more involved with this family. After just one afternoon with Daisy he was determined to brighten the older woman's life. He genuinely liked Tim, and Sam . . . well, he had the darndest urge to take care of her, to ease her backache and lighten the load she was carrying.

"That's great," he said, dragging his thoughts back to the present. "Say, Tim, what do you say we help Aunt Daisy to her room? She'll be more comfortable there."

"Sure. Hey, Mom, why don't we invite Jeff to stay for dinner? We've got plenty of leftover lasagna, haven't we?"

Sam could have throttled her son cheerfully. What on earth was he doing, inviting Jeff to stay for dinner, and leftovers at that? Now he'd put Jeff on the spot and . . .

"Unless you don't like lasagna. Do you?" Tim looked blandly innocent, but Jeff had a funny suspicion that the young man was trying his hand at matchmaking.

"I love lasagna, especially leftover. It always tastes better the second time around."

"Great. Then it's settled; you'll stay. As soon as we get Aunt Daisy settled I'll set the table. It's been a long time since we've had company." Tim was grinning like a three-year-old turned loose in the middle of a toy store.

Sam took a deep breath, counted to twenty, and rubbed her aching back a little harder. This time Tim really had gone too far. Over and over she'd cautioned him about pestering Jeff, and what did he do? First he pawned a kitten off on him, and now he'd gone and invited the man for supper, putting him in a position where he literally couldn't refuse.

Slowly, Sam made her way to the kitchen, opened the refrigerator, and pulled out a foil-wrapped pan of leftover lasagna. At least Tim was right on that score. There was plenty, and if she did say so herself, she made great lasagna. She slid the pan into the oven to reheat, then sneaked a quick look in the mirror. No doubt about it, she decided, she looked like a beach ball with legs. No man in his right mind would be interested in a woman who looked the way she did. Sighing, Sam decided that, for the moment at least, romance could not be one of her top priorities. And, all things considered, life really wasn't that bad. She was healthy, and as soon as the baby was born, she'd have more energy and be better able to cope. Perhaps Aunt Daisy would be more content, and maybe, just maybe, becoming a big brother would inspire Tim to get out and make his way in the world. Things would work out. They had to.

"May I help?"

Jeff's deep voice startled Sam. The paring knife she'd been holding clattered to the floor, and she felt herself flush.

"Sorry. I didn't mean to sneak up on you." Jeff bent and picked up the knife, turning on the faucet and deftly rinsing it off. Instead of handing it back to Sam, however, he gently nudged her out of the way and began chopping green pepper. "Why don't you sit down and relax for a few minutes? Let me and Tim take over. This kind of thing is hardly new to me. I've done my share of KP."

He smiled, and Sam's heart did a somersault. Yes, indeed, Commander Jeffrey Brooks was one good-looking male animal, and he had more than enough sex appeal to make a pregnant woman's heart beat faster. She had a crazy urge to giggle.

Sam smiled back, picturing Jeff peeling potatoes and washing dishes. Oddly enough, she thought he looked right at home in her kitchen, wielding her paring knife.

She hoped the change of position would ease her persistent backache. "Thanks," she said. "I'd be a fool to turn down that offer."

Jeff hummed a little as he expertly quartered a juicy tomato. It was good to see Sam smile, good to see her relax a little, and it made him feel good to think he could help make it happen. It was just because she was pregnant and a widow, he told himself. Any man worth his salt would feel protective toward a woman in this situation. And, of course, there was the fact that he and Sam had once been friends, maybe even a little more than friends. If they hadn't been so young, who knows how things might have turned out?

Sam levered herself into the one comfortable chair in the room, Aunt Daisy's old rocker. It had a worn but still comfortable floral cushion. She was positive the baby had dropped. Her obstetrician had told her to expect labor to begin at any time, and for the past couple of days she'd felt different. Now she realized what it was. It was virtually impossible to sit comfortably, yet when she stood on her feet for any length of time her back ached constantly. Hurry up, little one, she said silently. It's about time for you to make your entrance into the world.

"Hard to get comfortable?" Jeff asked, shooting a sympathetic glance in Sam's direction.

Sam nodded and grimaced as she shifted positions. "Fortunately, I don't have much longer." She patted her belly tenderly. "This little alien is due any time now."

Once again the ill-fated paring knife clattered to the floor. Sam couldn't hold back a grin at the comical look of fear and disbelief on Jeff's handsome face.

"Any . . . time?"

"Don't worry," Sam said. "I'm sure I'll have plenty of time to get to the hospital. From what I remember, babies usually take their own sweet time. Of course, I'm a lot older now than I was when Tim was born, so this birth may be a little different."

"Oh, sure. I wasn't worried. It's just that . . . well, I guess I didn't realize that the baby was due so soon."

"Didn't you ever want a family, Jeff?" Sam asked curiously. It was hard to imagine such an attractive man being alone, and she had the feeling that, if he'd just loosen up a little, Jeff would make a wonderful father. A good husband, too, she thought, letting her mind wander just a little. And he'd probably be a magnificent lover.

Sam's illicit thoughts were interrupted when she saw Jeff's eyes darken. He turned back to the cutting board and began chopping with a vengeance.

"Like I told you before, I tried marriage once," he said flatly, unable to keep the bitterness out of his voice. "Marcie said that living with me was like being in military school. She thought I was too rigid. She just walked out one day, without even giving me a chance to change. We didn't really have time to have kids."

"I'm sorry," Sam said softly. "I didn't mean to dredge up painful memories."

"It's all right. It was a long time ago. Sometimes it seems like a dream . . . like it never really happened." He smiled. "I was thinking that in a way the time you and I spent together as kids seems more real than my brief marriage. Crazy, isn't it?"

"Not really," Sam answered. She shifted her weight and grimaced as a tiny spasm shot through her belly. "I've never totally forgotten that time. It was special; at least it was for me." She smiled. "You know what they say about never forgetting your first love."

"It was special for me, too," Jeff said softly. "When I saw you that first day . . . well, I almost couldn't believe my eyes."

Sam laughed. "I imagine I look a wee bit different than I did in the old days, but it was a great summer, wasn't it? I cried when you went home."

"Me, too," Jeff said. A lot of men probably wouldn't have wanted to admit that to a woman, but Jeff felt comfortable with Sam, unless he let himself dwell on how close she was to giving birth.

"Okay, how are we doing in here?"

Tim strode into the kitchen and Sam sighed with relief. Talk about perfect timing. The conversation had definitely started to veer in a dangerous direction.

"Everything is under control," Jeff said, appearing as glad to see Tim as Sam was. "Table all set?"

"Yep. Want me to whip up some garlic bread, Mom?"

Sam nodded, enjoying the rare treat. It was nice to let someone else take over for a change.

When everything was ready Tim insisted on escorting his mother to the dining room.

Sam's eyes widened, and she gasped as she saw the carefully arranged table. Tim had used their best tablecloth and napkins and Aunt Daisy's prized Blue Willow china. In the center of the table was a copper bowl filled with fresh-picked yellow and red tulips.

"Why, Tim, this is wonderful! We'll have to invite . . ." Sam stopped in midsentence, appalled by what she'd been about to say. Now she was doing it—insinuating Jeff into their lives when she knew very well that the man had neither the intention nor the desire to get involved. She gave herself a mental shake. It had to be her delicate physical and emotional condition that was making her think and say all the wrong things. She hoped the baby would hurry up so that things would get back to normal.

She didn't want to look at Jeff, but she couldn't help herself. Their eyes met and a tingle raced up Sam's spine. Jeff looked so at home in her dining room . . . so right. There was tender concern on his face as he regarded her, and before she could move he was at her side, helping her sit down. His hand on her arm was gentle, his flesh warm and comforting. Sam felt a sudden rush of tears. This was what she had been craving, what she'd been deprived of throughout her pregnancy; a man's tender, caring concern. She knew that lots of women went through pregnancies alone these days, and she wouldn't have had that kind of concern even if Doug had lived, because he'd been incensed by the idea of her midlife pregnancy. He'd demanded that she have an abortion, and that was what they'd argued about the night he had his accident. Sam squeezed her eyes shut to stop the tears. She could still feel Doug's selfish rage, the heat of his anger at her for daring to go against his wishes. She could still hear his lament that she was a stupid broad.

"That's the bad part of being a bachelor," Jeff said, sitting down across from Sam a moment later. "When I cook for myself I don't fuss with nice linens or fresh flowers. It's pretty much paper plates and Handiwipes. This is a pleasant change of pace. Thank you for including me."

They had just finished eating when the telephone rang. Tim shot out of his chair as if he'd sat on a hot pan. "I'll get it," he called over his shoulder as he careened into the kitchen. "I know it's for me."

"Kids," Jeff said, shaking his head good naturedly. "Then again, Tim doesn't really fall into that category, does he? How old did you say he was, anyway?"

"Tim is twenty, soon to be twenty-one," Sam

replied, "but I know what you're thinking. He acts like sixteen, doesn't he?"

"He does seem young."

Sam sighed. "That's my fault, I guess. Aunt Daisy and I both babied him. When Tim was born he was very frail. It was scary, and then he got rheumatic fever. He was sick for a long time. I guess we coddled him a little too much, and now I don't know how to rectify the situation."

Jeff nodded. Now that he'd gotten to know the family better it wasn't hard to picture Sam mothering her son, even if the young man was now a full head taller than her. He'd watched her with the pups and with her elderly aunt. She was a natural at nurturing. "It must have been a hard time for you, too. How did you get so good at mothering? You were what, about twelve when your mother left, weren't you?"

"Yep, twelve," Sam said, reluctantly remembering that unhappy time. "I was just reaching the age where a girl really needs her mother." She paused, a soft smile curving her lips. "Fortunately, Aunt Daisy was ready and willing to step in and fill the void. I can't imagine what would have become of me if I hadn't had her."

Twelve years old and trying to be brave about losing her mother.

FULL BLOOM 87

Tim came bouncing back into the dining room. "Hate to leave this lovely little party, but some of my friends are heading over to Wildwood to the boardwalk. Can I borrow the car, Mom?"

Jeff saw the sharp annoyance that colored Sam's face.

"What about me? What if I need the car?"

Tim grinned. "Come on, Mom, where would you go? You can barely get behind the wheel as it is . . . whoa! That's right; how will you get to the hospital if you go into labor and I'm not here?"

"Hey, I'm here," Jeff said quickly, "and fortunately I'm better at driving cars than I am at fixing computers. Why don't you go ahead and have some fun, Tim? I'll look after your mother."

"But . . ." Sam couldn't help being warmed by Jeff's words, but it wasn't right to impose on him this way, and she knew she should resent Jeff for upstaging her authority.

But Tim was already gone, and Jeff reached across the table to pat Sam's hand reassuringly. He wanted to wipe the cloud of worry off her face. The peach color of her smock lent a pretty glow to her skin and complemented her reddish-brown hair and green eyes.

"Let him go, Sam. It'll give you and I a chance to get better acquainted."

Sam was silent. Was this the same man who had looked so aghast when he saw Polar Princess and learned he'd rented a house across the street from a dog-breeding kennel? The same man who had insisted he needed peace and quiet so he could write his book? The same man who had almost gone into cardiac arrest when Muffy piddled on his shoes?

"Was I out of line?" Jeff asked when the silence stretched between them. "I'm so used to issuing orders, I sometimes forget myself."

"No, it's all right, but I guess I'm just not used to anyone else taking responsibility around here." Sam heaved herself to her feet. Her back immediately began to throb and she winced.

"Are you okay? You're not . . . having labor pains, are you?"

"Not yet," Sam said, "but I have a feeling they're not far off. I hope I can have the baby and get back home before Princess whelps. This is her first litter, and I want to be here to comfort her."

Jeff shook his head. About to go into labor herself and worrying about her dog!

He followed her into the living room. It

wasn't dirty, just messy and disorganized. It took all his willpower not to start picking up magazines and straightening sofa cushions, but this wasn't his house, and none of what was going on was his responsibility. And if he got too pushy, Sam might well slam the door in his face. She might be pregnant and somewhat vulnerable at the moment, but she was no weakling, that was for sure. He had to keep reminding himself of that.

"Sit down and put your feet up," he suggested to Sam, taking her arm and guiding her toward the old but comfortable-looking sofa.

She smiled gratefully as Jeff helped her lower her bulk. "Mm," she murmured. "That does feel better." It was nice being with Jeff this way, but she couldn't help wondering if he was just hanging around out of some misguided sense of responsibility. He'd told Tim he could go out, and now he probably felt he had to baby-sit Tim's mother. The thought made Sam wince. She was responsible for herself and always had been. She didn't want anyone thinking he had to take care of her.

Jeff put his coffee cup on the table and sat down beside Sam. "Let me massage your back," he said. "I can see that you're hurting."

Sam's eyes widened in surprise. "You'd really do that?"

"In a heartbeat," Jeff said. "Now try to relax."

It was awkward sitting behind Sam and trying to rub her back, but Jeff gave it a good try. As his strong hands moved down Sam's shoulders to her nonexistent waist, his mind screamed a warning: Go home, Jeff. Get out of here and forget you ever looked into those gorgeous sea-green eyes. Forget the way it feels to touch her, the way you want to coddle and protect her. He remembered the way it had felt to put his hand on her belly and feel the child move inside her. Awesome was the only word to describe it.

But Jeff ignored the signals. He rubbed Sam's back until she groaned with pleasure and relief; then he gently lowered her back against the sofa cushions.

"Coffee time," he said huskily, moving to a chair across from her.

A few minutes later he slowly sipped the hot liquid, carefully averting his eyes. He hadn't expected to feel so . . . so protective, so tender toward Sam. But didn't most men feel that way about pregnant women? As though they needed to be handled gently and sweetly?

"That was nice of you," Sam said softly. "Thanks."

Jeff cleared his throat. "No problem. I was just thinking that I owe you an apology."

"Why?" Sam asked. "What for?"

"It's about the dogs," Jeff said. "They really aren't as bad as I thought they would be . . . with noise, I mean. And I have to admit that they're beautiful animals. How did you get started with the kennel?"

Sam wriggled into a more comfortable position and began to talk, her eyes shining. She was rarely at a loss for words, but she was especially fluent when speaking of her beloved Samoyeds. Actually, she loved all dogs, and someday, if things went well, she wanted to try raising Old English Sheepdogs, too.

"I didn't even know what a Samoyed was until I met Hank Richards," she explained. "I was visiting a friend outside Philadelphia, and she had to take her cat for a shot. Hank was there with a litter of Samoyed puppies. He told me all about the breed and I fell in love. I bought one of his pups, and that was the beginning. Eventually, I hope to be able to make a comfortable living from my kennels," Sam explained. "Did I mention that Polar Princess is working on her championship?

When that happens her pups will be even more valuable than they are now."

"Unless you give them away to make sure they get good, loving homes," Jeff said, unable to resist teasing her a little.

Sam grinned. "Tim told you."

"Yep. In a way, I think I can understand it. You really love them, don't you?" Jeff emptied his coffee cup and leaned back, feeling wonderfully relaxed and content.

"Yes. Do you think I'm foolish for caring so much? Because I do love them, all of them. They're more than just a way to make a dollar."

Talking about her dogs kept Sam from dwelling on the insistent ache in the small of her back, and the strange tightening sensation that was creeping around her belly.

"I can see that," Jeff said. "No, of course you're not foolish for loving the dogs, but I do wonder how thin you can spread yourself, Sam. I don't know a lot about babies, but I've heard rumors that they require a lot of time and attention, and I guess baby dogs aren't all that different. And with your aunt to look after . . . hey, that reminds me. I visited the senior citizens' center in Wildwood the other day. It would do her good to get out a little, spend some time with her peers."

Jeff waited, hoping Sam wouldn't be offended by his wanting to help her aunt. Thinking back, he remembered that Sam had been extremely responsible even at fourteen. There'd been times when she couldn't join the other kids because she had to hurry home from the beach and start dinner for herself and her aunt or do some other household chore.

Sam's chin was set stubbornly and her eyes flashed emerald fire. "If she wants to go, I'll take her," she said.

"Sure, I know you would. But you don't have to. I'll be happy to chauffeur her around. Don't be ashamed to admit that you might need a helping hand now and then, Sam. With Daisy, or in some other way. Why, I'll bet Daisy would be delighted to help in small ways. It would alleviate her boredom and give her a sense of being needed. Even if you just let her do a few simple chores around the house, it would ease your burden a little. I think Daisy is just lonely, Sam. And I think she feels useless. We had quite a talk this afternoon."

"But she has arthritis," Sam protested, "and it seems like her mind is wandering lately."

"Because it's not being used," Jeff said.

"She sits in front of the television vegetating. It's a wonder her brain doesn't totally atrophy. And you need to be careful about overmedicating her. That can happen easily with elderly people. Doctors prescribe one medication for arthritis, another for blood pressure, a third for depression, and sometimes they don't check to see how everything interacts. Anyway, think about it, and see if you can't think of something she could do to help you around the house. You might be surprised at the change in her."

"I wish," Sam said. "Sometimes things do seem to close in on me. Aunt Daisy . . . Tim . . ."

"Sounds like it's been rough," Jeff said. He hesitated, then took the plunge. "How did your husband die, Sam?"

Jeff waited for the shutter to drop over her eyes, for the sadness to drag down the corners of her mouth. He didn't want to reopen old wounds, but he sensed that she needed to talk about it.

"It was an accident; at least that's what the police said. Doug and I, we had an argument about . . . money." Sam wasn't deliberately lying, but she couldn't tell Jeff how ugly Doug had been when he discovered she was pregnant. "He wanted me to sell the dogs and the kennel. He didn't like living with Aunt Daisy. But he'd always had trouble keeping a job, so I thought that living here in Aunt Daisy's house would solve several problems. Instead, it made Doug even more restless. Anyway, we fought and he stormed out of the house. He was speeding and ran into a concrete abutment. They said he . . . died instantly."

Tears streamed down Sam's face now, and her hands trembled as she angrily tried to brush them away. "I just keep thinking that I shouldn't have argued with him. That if I hadn't . . ."

"Don't fall into that trap, Sam," Jeff said quickly. "You can't go through life blaming yourself for a tragic accident. You're not responsible."

But her late husband was, Jeff thought angrily, visualizing the scene and the man Sam had described. An immature, ne'er-do-well husband, storming out of the house in a rage, leaving behind a pregnant, tearful wife. His jaw tightened.

Sam saw the change come over Jeff's face, saw the way his muscles tensed. "I'm sorry. I didn't mean to dump on you," she said. It would be different if they were both younger. Young people were usually more tolerant, more easygoing. As it was, she and Jeff were probably both set in their ways, with established patterns of life. "You don't have to stay and baby-sit me. I'm sure you'd like to go home and work on your book. Or is it too late? Do you work best in the morning or the evening?"

"I'd really like to stay for a while, if you don't mind," Jeff said. "I think this baby is getting ready to make its appearance, and I wouldn't want to miss the big event."

Sam summoned all her willpower. With what was probably her last ounce of physical strength, she straightened her slim shoulders and managed a weak, thoroughly unconvincing smile.

"Really, it's not necessary," she insisted. "You don't have to look after me. I'm fine, and it's not like I'm alone, you know. I have . . ."

Jeff interrupted with a smile. "I know. You have Aunt Daisy and Tim, but Tim's not here at the moment, and although Aunt Daisy is a real sweetheart, I'd have to wonder at her driving ability late at night, especially since there's a thin cover of fog out there. And no car."

Sam bit her lip; then her eyes met Jeff's steady, encouraging gaze. She shrugged and grinned. "Okay; you win. Stick around, Commander Brooks. This may well turn out to be one of the most interesting nights of your life!"

Six

"Whoa! Here it comes again!" Sam reminded herself to relax and remember all the things she'd learned in her Lamaze class. She turned pleading eyes on Jeff. "Have they .. found Ellie yet?"

Ellie was Sam's best and oldest friend. She was also her labor coach and had promised to be on hand when the big day arrived. Well, the time had come, except that it was night instead of day, and getting later and darker with every passing moment, or at least that's the way it seemed to Sam. And Ellie wasn't home.

Sam took a deep, cleansing breath and held it as her contraction built and reached a peak; then she let it out slowly, forcing herself to relax as the pain slowly ebbed away.

"So far, so good," she said, sneaking a glance at Jeff's pale, worried face. Good grief, even like this he was handsome, she thought crazily. And he was so sweet, so concerned.

Maybe she was dreaming. Then, as another contraction stabbed her belly, she knew she wasn't. This was real, all right!

"Of course I haven't gotten to the hard part yet," she added a couple of minutes later, when she could speak again. "That comes when I reach the transition stage of labor, and by then I'll be safely installed in the hospital with Ellie and Dr. Bergstrom at my side." She managed a brave smile. "It's been a while since I've done this, but I guess it's like riding a bike. You never forget." But having a baby at forty-six was different from having a baby at twenty-five, Sam decided. She'd been fearless then. Now she felt helpless and vulnerable. And there were more things that could go wrong. She was nowhere near as blissfully confident as she'd been when Tim was born.

"I don't know about that," Jeff muttered. "I'll feel better when you're settled in the hospital." He was terrified. He knew he was sweating profusely, and it wasn't even hot. "Ellie's husband said she should be home at any time. I'm sure she'll call soon."

Driving Sam to the hospital was one thing, but filling in for an absent labor coach was definitely above and beyond the call of duty. He wasn't qualified; he'd had no experience with pregnant women. And he wasn't anxious to start now, not with Sam. Yet, what choice did he have? If Ellie didn't show up in time, someone had to help Sam.

Jeff wiped perspiration from his forehead. The night was cool, but he felt like he was on fire. He'd been in sticky spots before, even life-and-death situations, where he'd been totally responsible for the welfare and lives of many men, but this was by far the scariest, most mind-boggling event of all. Just the thought of participating in the delivery of Sam's child practically paralyzed him.

"Are you okay?" he asked worriedly. "Can I get you something? A pillow? Maybe we should just go to the hospital. You can wait for your friend there, can't you?"

Free of pain for the moment and feeling remarkably content, Sam giggled. Which was very odd, since she'd never, ever been a giggler. But Jeff was adorable. Forty-nine years old, but right now he reminded her of a scared little boy. Were all men like this when confronted with the miracle of birth? She wondered if he had any idea how cute he looked. She had a sudden pang as she wished the baby she was about to deliver belonged to Jeff.

"I'm fine," she said. "And it's too early to rush to the hospital. Dr. Bergstrom said I have plenty of time. My pregnancy has been perfectly normal. Actually, I'd really like to wait until Tim comes home...."

"Oh, no!" Figuring that Sam knew more about this giving birth business than he did, Jeff had given in to all her whims so far. Instead of racing to the hospital at the first warning twinge, he'd followed Sam's instructions and had helped her get as comfortable as possible. He'd timed the contractions and listened while she called her doctor. He'd refrained from waking Aunt Daisy and he'd massaged Sam's back, but when it came to waiting for Tim to come home he was drawing the line.

"Look, you'll be better off at the hospital," he said, his chin jutting stubbornly as he strode toward Sam's bedroom to pick up the suitcase she had packed and ready. "I'm going to wake Aunt Daisy, and then we're heading for the hospital. I'll call Ellie's husband and tell him to have Ellie come to the maternity ward and meet us there."

Sam opened her mouth to protest, but one look at Jeff's stern, no-nonsense profile changed her mind. This man meant business. Now she was getting a glimpse of the former naval commander, the man who issued orders and expected—no, demanded—that they be obeyed without question. "Okay," she said without argument. "Whatever you say." Aside from the fact that she simply wasn't up to debating with Jeff, it felt kind of nice to have someone else in charge, to have someone looking after her for a change. She started to smile, but made a grimace as another contraction grabbed her.

Jeff shook Aunt Daisy gently. "Wake up, Aunt Daisy. It's time to take Sam to the hospital."

Daisy woke instantly, almost as if she'd been waiting. "What is it? Is the baby coming?"

"Yes. Sam's fine, Aunt Daisy, but it's time to take her to the hospital."

"Well, of course it is! She can't have her child here, can she? Where's Tim? Is he driving? I don't like riding with that young man. He careens around corners and runs right through red lights. He's going to kill himself one of these days. I keep telling Sam, but no one listens to me anymore. Are you listening, young man? What kind of driver are you? Not a speeder, are you, Jack? I don't hold with speeding."

"No way, Aunt Daisy, but you've got to hurry and get dressed so we can drive Sam to the hospital."

"If you expect me to get dressed, you'd better get out of my bedroom, young man! I was raised with proper modesty, not like the young people today, running around half naked! Go on now, get out of here so I can get some clothes on. Goodness, I wish I'd put those curlers in my hair last night. Well, no time for that. We can't keep Sam and that baby waiting, can we?"

Jeff backed out of the small bedroom. "Okay, she's coming," he informed a panting, red-faced Sam a few minutes later. "What's happening now?"

Sam held up her hand and shook her head, indicating that Jeff would have to wait for an explanation. At the moment, she was otherwise occupied.

Jeff watched her for a minute; then, sensing that she was in perfect control, he dialed Ellie's home once more.

"Sorry," Ellie's husband said. "She's still not home. Look, how far along is Sam, anyway? How many centimeters is she dilated?"

"Centimeters? Dilated?" It sounded like a foreign language to Jeff, and why was Ellie's husband asking him all this stuff anyway? "How the hell should I know?" Jeff yelled. "I'm not a doctor! Look, we'll be heading for the hospital in a few minutes. Can you have Ellie meet us there?"

"Sure thing. Hey, try to relax, old man. After all, it's not even your kid."

They waited until Sam was between contractions; then Aunt Daisy took one arm and Jeff the other. Sam's pains were coming faster now, and increasing in intensity. She looked slightly pale. There were no more protests about leaving for the hospital too soon.

"I'll sit in the back with Samantha," Aunt Daisy said. "I may not have firsthand knowledge of this birthing business, but I'm real good at hand-holding."

Jeff had to chuckle. "I'll just bet you are," he said. He quickly slid behind the wheel and buckled his seat belt. "Well, it looks like you're getting your wish, Sam. You'll have your baby and be back home in time for Princess to whelp."

"Umm," Sam murmured. "Shut up and drive, Jeff. I think my little . . . acrobat is in a hurry."

"Silly dogs," Aunt Daisy said. "One of these days those dogs will be taking over the whole house! Don't know why you couldn't have picked a nice, ladylike hobby like embroidery, Sammy girl." But she held Sam's hand tightly, and with her free hand she massaged the hard mound of Sam's belly. "My, you do have a tummy. It'll be all right, Sammy girl," she crooned gently. "You did this before, remember? Tim was a cute baby, wasn't he? I wonder if this little one will look the same? Maybe it will have your red hair, Sam."

"Auburn, Aunt Daisy. My hair is auburn," Sam managed between contractions. "Lucille Ball had red hair."

"My, I used to enjoy her shows," Aunt Daisy said. "We don't get good shows like that anymore. Of course, some of the talk shows are interesting. That Phil Donahue is good. Did you know that if a man decides to change himself into a woman, they have to cut off his . . ."

"Aunt Daisy, please!" Sam moaned.

Glancing in the rearview mirror, Jeff saw Aunt Daisy shrug. "All right, dear, now you just calm down. It's not good for you to get excited. Before you know it, that sweet little baby will be here. My, won't that be grand?"

Although he was still unfamiliar with the area, Jeff made pretty good time. Twelve minutes and thirty seconds after he pulled out of Sam's driveway he was helping her into the emergency room at the hospital at Cape May Court House.

"Oh, dear, this brings back memories, doesn't it, Samantha? We spent a lot of time here with Timothy, didn't we?" Aunt Daisy looked a little uneasy, and Jeff gave her arm a reassuring pat.

Sam made a funny, grunting noise, but she shook her head stubbornly when a nurse tried to get her to sit in a wheelchair. "Can't sit," she insisted. "I . . . have to walk. Oh, where is Ellie?"

"It doesn't look as if that dizzy blonde is going to make it," Aunt Daisy said waspishly. "Knew she couldn't be counted on in a pinch!" She turned to Jeff. "Looks like you'll have to fill in, young man. I always did think that Ellie was a scatterbrain. Can't be trusted in an emergency." She eyed Jeff speculatively, then shrugged. "I guess you're it, Jack," she said. "There's no one else. Sammy won't want an old lady like me in the delivery room with her."

A nurse interrupted. "Look, I need some information before I send this woman up to the maternity floor. Who is in charge here? Who's responsible?" The woman wore a faintly disapproving look as she turned to Jeff. "Are you the father?"

"No. I'm just a friend."

"Humph! That's what they all say when it comes right down to it. Well, which one of you will take responsibility for the lady's bill?"

"Me," Sam said. "I'm responsible for myself."

"She certainly is," Aunt Daisy said, beaming proudly. She patted Sam's hand, then leveled a stern, no-nonsense look at the nurse. "Now you just take my niece upstairs where she belongs, missy, and then I'll give you all the information you need. She's about to have a baby, you see, and she's not interested in hanging around here to chitchat."

"Well! And just who are you, madame?"

"Just call me Daisy, honey, and lighten up, will you? We're here for a birthing, not a funeral!"

Fifteen minutes later, Jeff sat on a hard wooden bench across the hall from where Aunt Daisy sat, chatting away with the nurse in charge of admissions. He definitely felt shell-shocked. His military experiences were starting to seem tame in comparison to what he was going through now. Somehow he'd allowed himself to be steamrollered into agreeing to stand in as Sam's labor coach. Sam had been spirited away to the maternity floor, and he'd been given a crash course in the Lamaze method of natural childbirth. In a few minutes someone would take him to scrub, they'd give him a white smock thing to put on, and he'd be taken to join Sam in the labor room. He almost wished he was the fainting type; if he passed out cold on the floor they'd have to find someone else.

Aunt Daisy plopped down beside Jeff and patted his hand. "Well, thank goodness that's taken care of. I thought that silly nurse would never stop asking foolish questions. Imagine, she actually had the nerve to ask if Sam was married! As if my niece would even consider having a child out of wedlock! Of course, nowadays a lot of women do, don't they? Especially with all this nonsense about ticking time clocks! A lot of foolishness, if you ask me. By the way, what is your name again? It's not Fred, is it? I knew a gentleman named Fred once." She cocked her head and glared at Jeff. "Come to think of it, Fred wasn't much of a gentleman. He got me out in his car one night and tried to put his hand up my . . ."

"Jeff. My name is Jeff," Jeff said distractedly. "I hope Tim finds the note I left for him. Sam will be okay, won't she? It's dangerous to have a child at her age, isn't it?"

"Now, don't you worry," Aunt Daisy said, patting Jeff's hand. "Sam will be fine, Jim. She's had all the necessary tests and the little one is fine. They can do that now, you know. Look right inside a woman's belly and see if the baby is normal. Why, they can even tell the sex, but Sam said she didn't want to know. It's really sweet of you to be so concerned, Jake." She leaned over and peered into Jeff's face. "Are you in love with Samantha? My, wouldn't that be grand! Samantha would have a husband and the baby would have a daddy. Have you ever been a father, Jack?" Daisy smiled, nodded, and began to hum softly.

"Jeff. No. I'm not a father."

Aunt Daisy shook her head and stopped humming. "Don't worry. It will happen when the time is right."

"I'm not looking for a wife. I'm writing a book and . . ."

"Every man should have a wife. It's not natural to be alone. They did some kind of study and found that married men live longer than single men. I had a husband once, you know. Harold. I wish I had someone of my own now. Folks aren't meant to be all alone." Her face took on a wistful look. "I did date some, but things just never worked out."

"No, I suppose folks shouldn't be alone," Jeff mumbled. But Aunt Daisy was alone, and so was he. Sam would have her baby now, and someday she'd probably remarry. Tim would eventually find a nice girl and settle down.

Jeff couldn't help wondering what the future held for him. Would he ever have the courage to remarry? Did he even want to?

He'd been alone for years now, and he'd depended on his naval buddies for occasional companionship. Some of the married men had invited him to their homes, and here and there he'd had a taste of marital bliss. Some of the experiences had left him feeling lonely and bereft; others had only reinforced his conviction that he was better off staying single. Not all marriages were made in heaven, he'd discovered.

Jeff thought back to his brief youthful marriage. It had never been a really happy union, and there was no reason to think things would be different if he tried again.

A young nurse's aide interrupted his meandering thoughts. "Follow me," she said. "We'll get you suited up so your wife can get this show on the road."

"She's not my . . ." Jeff stopped. What difference did it make what this young woman thought? All that mattered was Sam and her baby.

"Are you sure I'll be able to do this?" Jeff asked nervously as the girl helped him into a sterile hospital gown. "I want to help, but . . ."

The nurse smiled. "You'll be fine. Your wife needs you now, and that's the only thing that matters."

Jeff followed the young woman down the

hall. This whole thing was crazy, unreal. It was like he'd tripped and fallen into a deep pit and couldn't dig his way out. He knew he had to see this thing through no matter how hard his heart pounded in his chest. As the nurse said, Sam needed him, and there wasn't anyone else. Jeff's throat tightened. Sam was used to having everyone else lean on her; now, for a few hours at least, it was her turn to lean. He pasted a bright, cheerful smile on his face as he entered the labor room.

"Hey, how's it going?"

Sam lay in a high white bed. Her green eyes looked huge in her pale face. She tried to smile, but it was plain to see that she was scared and hurting. "I wasn't sure you would come," she said slowly. "Ellie said she'd be here, but she isn't, and it's not fair to expect you to get involved this way."

"Hey, it's okay. I won't let you down, Sam, and who knows, Ellie may walk in the door at any minute. If she does, you can throw me out." Jeff brushed a few strands of damp auburn hair off Sam's forehead. "Are you sure you're okay?" he asked.

His insides were all knotted up. He knew Sam wanted Ellie, but at the moment it seemed that neither of them had a choice. Jeff stifled a groan. How the hell had he gotten into this mess in the first place? It was almost as scary as being in a trench in a steamy jungle with enemy fire all around.

Suddenly, Sam's eyes widened and she groaned. Jeff watched, stunned. He could actually see the great mound of her belly tighten under the crisp white sheets.

"Breathe, honey," he commanded instinctively, frantically trying to remember everything the nurse had told him. "No, don't pant. Not yet. Just take a deep breath. That's right. Okay, again. Easy . . . breathe. Good. You're doing great." There was actually a baby there inside Sam's belly, a real, live baby. It was an awesome thought.

He was rubbing her belly now, his big hands moving in gentle, soothing circles on her taut skin. Thank God for the nurse's instructions, and the television show he'd seen recently, where a woman had gone into labor in a disabled elevator.

The nurse entered the room then and smiled. "Well, look at this! Aren't we doing fine?" She stood by as another strong contraction gripped Sam. When it subsided she moved to the foot of the bed.

"Let's just see how things are coming along," she said.

Sam kept her eyes closed as the nurse examined her. Her breathing evened out and the lines on her forehead smoothed. At least she wasn't doing this alone. It had been different with Tim. She'd been young then, full of hope and optimism. Now . . . well, she was just glad Jeff had agreed to pinch-hit for Ellie. But she felt bad that he'd been forced into this situation. "Thanks, Jeff," she murmured. "That was a big help. When did you learn to be such a great labor coach?"

Jeff grinned, picked up the damp cloth lying on the bedside table, and gently patted Sam's forehead. "About five minutes ago," he replied. "A real crash course. Want some ice chips?"

"Yes, please. Oh, that's good. Thank you." For a moment, Sam was silent, savoring the delicious coolness on her dry lips. Then she looked up at Jeff solemnly. "I'm sorry you had to get roped into this. I'll bet you wish you were a million miles away." Being a labor coach had to be a harrowing experience for a bachelor like Jeff.

He grinned and placed another ice chip on Sam's tongue. A funny little ripple went through him. It was such an intimate gesture, and he was beside Sam for one of the most important events of her life. "You know, a few minutes ago that might have been true," he said, "but now . . . I don't know. I think I must be getting into the spirit of this thing. I'm kind of excited, and there's nowhere else I'd rather be."

"Really? You're not disgusted? I was afraid . . ."

"Nothing to be disgusted about," the nurse chipped in, giving Jeff a stern look as she straightened Sam's sheets. "Giving birth is a normal, natural process. Bringing a new life into the world is a beautiful experience, and it was meant to be shared."

"But . . ." Sam looked as if she wanted to explain the complicated situation, but Jeff gently placed a quieting finger across her lips. Smiling, he shook his head. Let the nurse think what she wanted. In a curious way, he sort of liked the idea that they all thought he was the father of Sam's child.

"Birth often brings people together," the nurse said, shooting Jeff a meaningful look as she swished out of the room in a crackle of stiff white uniform.

When she left Sam and Jeff looked at each other and started to laugh. "You realize that she thinks you're the . . . guilty party, don't you?" Sam asked, gasping. "She thinks you're . . . the father of my baby."

"I know," Jeff said softly, reaching out to

smooth Sam's forehead, "and this may sound crazy, but right now I almost wish I was."

Sam's green eyes widened with surprise; then another contraction gripped her and there was no time for idle talk.

"Please," she said, as the contraction ebbed, "is it time to go to the delivery room? How much longer?" She was so tired, and the contractions seemed so much stronger than what she remembered from Tim. But she was much older now, she reminded herself. It was bound to be harder.

The doctor arrived a few minutes later, a tall man swathed in white. He examined Sam briefly, patted her hand, and smiled.

"Well, Samantha, this is it. Your baby is just about ready to be born. We're moving you to the delivery room, and soon you'll be a mommy again. How does that sound?" He glanced at Jeff. "You coming along?"

"I . . ." Jeff wasn't sure what he should do. Did Sam want him to go all the way with her, or would she want him to bow out now that the doctor was here? It wasn't his baby, after all, and birth was such a personal thing. Maybe he'd just be in the way.

"Please," Samantha whispered tiredly. "Please stay with me, Jeff." She thought she couldn't bear it if he left. Just knowing he was beside her was giving her strength.

Nothing could have stopped him then, not the whole National Guard! Sam wanted him with her. He was important to her.

He grinned, feeling like a kid who'd just discovered a shiny red bike under the Christmas tree. "Try and get away from me, lady," he answered huskily. "This is one event I don't plan to miss!"

Everything happened in double time then. A gurney was wheeled into the room and Sam was expertly transferred onto it; then the nurse and the doctor practically raced down the hall to the delivery room.

Jeff trotted behind, both scared and exhilarated. This was it then, the home stretch. In a few minutes Sam would be a mother again and he . . . a sudden feeling of desolation swept over him. His excitement waned as he reminded himself that he was just a bystander . . . a stand-in. If Ellie was here he'd be relegated to the waiting room with Aunt Daisy. He had no stake in this birth. None at all.

"Let's go, coach," the doctor said, breaking into Jeff's thoughts. "Get behind her and lift her up a little. That's right, just like that. It will make it easier for her to push, and it eases the back pain."

FULL BLOOM

Jeff positioned himself behind Sam and lifted her so that she was leaning against him. They were both damp with perspiration, but Sam's soft warmth felt wonderful. Once again he felt the excitement build. What did it matter why he was here? He was, and he intended to make the most of it. Maybe he was just a stand-in, but he was here for Sam when she needed him, and that counted for something, didn't it? And this might be his one and only chance to participate in the miracle of birth.

Sam strained and grunted, and Jeff could feel her muscles tense against him. She was probably working harder than she ever had in her life. He felt a surge of pride and bent down to kiss the top of her head. She was some woman!

"I . . . I'm glad you're here, Jeff," Sam managed, between pants. "I'm not sure I . . . could have done this alone. How will I ever repay you?"

"Invite me over for lasagna some night," Jeff quipped. Then he looked up and saw the mirror suspended over the table. He felt the color drain out of his face.

"Oh, my God, I can see it, Sam! Your baby! It's coming!"

Sam tried to laugh, but it ended on a sob

of pain. "Now do you . . . believe I'm really . . . having a baby?"

The next few minutes blurred as Jeff concentrated on helping Sam work through the last intense contractions. She was really tired now and she was having a hard time concentrating on his commands.

"Come on, honey, just one more," Jeff heard himself coaxing, amazed at how calm and competent he sounded. He wiped beads of perspiration from his forehead. This was definitely a night he wouldn't soon forget!

"Okay, here we go," Dr. Bergstrom said. "One more good, strong push and you'll be home free, Samantha. I'll be putting your little baby in your arms in just a few minutes."

Jeff lightly squeezed Sam's shoulders, filled with an excitement beyond anything he'd ever known before. The tension in the room was almost palpable. Everyone was watching and waiting to welcome Sam's baby into the world.

"Once more, honey," he said, echoing the doctor's instructions. "Just once more!"

"Ahhh!" Sam pushed with all her might. Her face turned crimson, and Jeff felt her strain against him.

He wished he could lend her his strength, wished he could take her pain on himself. But he couldn't do either one. All he could do was be there.

Then, suddenly, it was over. He heard the doctor's triumphant cry. "A girl, Sam! You have a fine little daughter."

Sam felt the tension drift away, felt the pain flow from her weary body as her child was delivered. She lay, limp and exhausted and happier than she'd ever been in her entire life. A girl. She had a daughter! A feeling of euphoria slid over her and she went limp.

Jeff gently lowered Sam to the pillows, finally able to relax his own muscles. He couldn't tear his eyes away from the tiny, wriggling body Dr. Bergstrom had laid across Sam's stomach. He'd never seen a newborn before. He'd never realized that a child could be so small and vulnerable. With a sense of wonder he realized that the little girl was totally helpless. Without loving parents to care for her she wouldn't survive. A rush of warmth filled Jeff's body. He reached out and stroked the baby's satiny cheek. Immediately, the tiny mouth turned toward his finger.

"Isn't she beautiful?" Sam asked. "Isn't she the sweetest thing?"

"She's wonderful," Jeff said without hesitation. "And so are you. You are one brave, gutsy lady, Samantha Wells."

Sam was so tired. She longed to close her eyes and drift off. She knew she looked her worst, but somehow it didn't matter. Jeff was at her side. He'd been there when she needed him, and the way he looked at her daughter made tears well up in her eyes. Impulsively, she reached out to clasp his hand.

"Thank you," she said simply. "Thank you." How could she ever tell him what it had meant to have him here by her side? How could he ever understand how frightened she'd been? She knew the statistics about older women giving birth. She'd read up on all the things that could go wrong, the birth defects that even amniocentesis couldn't foretell. And now it was over, and she and her daughter were both okay. She'd heard the doctor say that the baby looked perfect, and had scored a nine on the Apgar.

For Jeff it seemed natural to return the pressure of Sam's hand in his, natural to lean down and kiss her cheek and allow himself to feel all the wild, crazy emotions churning inside him. For just a moment he rested his cheek against hers. He couldn't speak. All he could do was feel, and what he felt couldn't be expressed in words.

A half hour later, Jeff found Aunt Daisy in the waiting room, giving the nurses a hard

FULL BLOOM

time. When she spotted Jeff she leaped off her chair like a woman half her age, arthritis and all.

"Well? What is it? A boy or a girl? Is Samantha all right? Did that fool doctor get here in time? How's Sam? Can I see her?"

"Calm down, Aunt Daisy," Jeff said, grinning like an idiot. Why on earth did he feel like passing out cigars? But even the weary, overworked nurses were smiling now, so maybe all this craziness was normal. "Sam is fine and so is the baby. It's a girl."

"Oh my! A little girl . . . just what we wanted. Oh, my!" Aunt Daisy was grinning just as foolishly as Jeff, and suddenly they were hugging each other and dancing around the room like tipsy teenagers.

By the time they got home the sun was coming up. Jeff went into the house with Aunt Daisy to give Tim the news.

"I'm sure glad Mom's okay," Tim said when they told him. His face was filled with relief. "I was worried about her. When I got home and saw your note I didn't know whether to come to the hospital or just stay put. I was kind of scared. Mom is pretty special, you know?"

Jeff clapped a hand on Tim's shoulder. "Yeah," he said, "I know. Look, how about if

I make coffee and some breakfast for us? We should have some kind of celebration, don't you think?"

"A celebration! Oh, good!" Aunt Daisy was beaming, Tim was grinning foolishly, and Jeff felt something warm and wonderful inside. It was like being part of a real family.

Aunt Daisy set the table, Tim made the toast and poured juice, and Jeff scrambled eggs, and then they all ate as if they hadn't seen food in a month. And, in the hospital a few miles away, Sam slept, dreaming of her infant daughter and a tall, strong, dark-haired man.

Seven

Sam held her baby daughter to her breast. Until now she had never believed in miracles, but Amber Dawn had changed all that. The birth itself was a miracle, after all the years she had waited. She had wanted another baby after Tim, even though Doug was a less than satisfactory parent. She knew she had enough love for both of them. But it had never happened, and after several years, as her marriage slowly and steadily deteriorated, she had decided it was probably for the best. Then, when she'd least expected it, when she'd thought it was too late, she had discovered she was pregnant, and at first her feelings had been ambivalent: It was too late. She was too old. It wouldn't be fair to the child. Now every time she looked at the baby's tiny features she was awestruck. Amber was so beautiful, so perfect, so completely hers. She wondered if she would have felt as fiercely protective if Doug had been at her side. Then, although the thought saddened her, she had to admit that she and Doug probably would not have stayed together in any case. Her marriage had been in serious trouble long before she got pregnant. She and Doug had been moving in different directions for years, with Sam struggling to build a safe, secure home, while Doug drifted aimlessly from one mediocre job to another . . . from one empty dream to the next. Sam briefly closed her eyes, remembering again how Doug had reacted to the news of her pregnancy.

"You've got to be kidding!" he'd yelled. "A kid? Why? Why do you want to tie yourself down that way, babe? We've been all through that family stuff, and anyway, I've been thinking that it's time we thought about blowing this town and heading south. I hear there are plenty of good jobs down in Florida, and all that sun and surf. . . ."

Sam remembered arguing that she couldn't leave Aunt Daisy and Tim, and she'd reminded Doug that her aunt's old house was the only real security they had. In the end she had flatly refused to even consider moving to Florida. And it hadn't been just giving up her beloved tomato plants or the change of seasons she loved so much; she simply hadn't trusted Doug. And now she thought how pathetic he'd been, a middle-aged man trying to act like a carefree youngster.

Amber stirred, and Sam was brought back to the present. Rightly so, she decided, nuzzling her chin against the baby's fuzzy little head. This was her future now, this beautiful little girl. If he had given her nothing else, at least Doug had left her this wonderful legacy. And the past was better left alone.

"Samantha?"

She looked up to see Aunt Daisy smiling from the doorway. That was another miracle, Sam decided. Ever since she'd brought Amber home from the hospital her aunt had seemed happier, more alert. And she was actually helpful.

"Yes, Aunt Daisy?"

"I just wanted to tell you that I'm going out for a while, dear; that is, unless you need me here. Do you?"

"Why, no, I suppose not, but where are you going? Is Tim taking you somewhere?"

For the first time Sam noticed that her aunt was dressed in her best cotton dress. Her gray hair was neatly arranged in a bun and she was even wearing a touch of lipstick.

"No, not Tim," Aunt Daisy explained. "It's that nice man who rents our little house. What is his name again? Jack? Or is it Jake? Oh, dear, I am terrible with names."

"It's Jeff," Sam corrected automatically. "But why is Jeff taking you out?"

Aunt Daisy nodded happily. "We're going to the new senior citizens' center in town. You know, the one they opened in Wildwood a few months ago? I've been wanting to go, but you and Tim were always so busy. . . . Anyway, Jim thinks I should join. He said it would be good for me to spend some time with folks my own age. After all, you're busy and so is Tim, and sometimes I do get a little lonely."

"I know," Sam said, lifting the baby and putting her over her shoulder. She patted Amber's back, waiting for the obligatory burp. It came, and she carefully laid the baby in her cradle. She should have been the one taking Aunt Daisy to the center, but there was never enough time for all the things that needed to be done around the house and the kennel.

Aunt Daisy came and looked down at the sleepy infant. "My, she's a darling little girl, Samantha. But even little girls need a daddy, you know. You're going to have to do something about that one of these days. Maybe you could consider Jake. He's a nice man."

"Jeff, Aunt Daisy. His name is Jeff."

"Of course. Isn't that what I just said?"

When she heard the knock on the door Sam was sorely tempted to run and hide. Aunt Daisy meant well, but God only knew what she was likely to say. When she got an idea in her head . . .

But it was too late to hide. Sam watched helplessly as her aunt ceremoniously ushered Jeff into the living room to view the sleeping infant.

"Isn't she lovely?" she cooed. "I was just telling Samantha that this little girl is going to need a daddy. People think only boys need their fathers, but that's not so. Poor Timothy, now he got the short end of the stick in the daddy department, didn't he, Sammy? I'm sure Timothy would be a much happier young man if he'd had a father who had taken an interest in him . . . a man to model himself after. He'll be all right, of course; it's just that it would have been better if he'd had a daddy. So we must make sure that Amber has a nice man to look after her."

Jeff stood over the cradle, looking down at the baby. Every time he saw Sam's child he was filled with a strange, totally foreign emotion. It was nothing he could put a name to, but just looking at the tiny little girl made him feel good. Jeff was so wrapped up in his feelings that at first he was unaware of both Sam's discomfort and Daisy's rambling discourse. Then Sam's anger penetrated his thoughts.

"Aunt Daisy, stop it right now! You're embarrassing me and Jeff. If you're going out, maybe you should get ready and go!"

Jeff's eyes widened. It was so unlike Sam. She was always so patient with Daisy.

"Sam, is there anything wrong? Did I say or do something?"

"Oh, no, it's not you." Sam shook her head. "I just don't want Aunt Daisy to start bombarding you with . . . look, I've got to get out to the kennels. Tim is going to keep an eye on Amber for me while I sit with Princess. We think she's just about ready to deliver."

"Oh, good, more babies!" Aunt Daisy smiled and clapped her hands. "Even if those doggie babies don't smell as sweet as this little one, they're still cute."

Sam felt her anger slip away. How could she stay mad at her sweet, irrepressible, well-meaning aunt?

"Shall we go, Jim?" Aunt Daisy asked. "I don't want to miss the orientation."

"I'll have her back by bedtime," Jeff promised, watching the cloud lift from Sam's face as she tenderly tucked a lightweight blanket over the sleeping baby. "If you need any help with the dogs later, I'd be glad to volunteer."

Sam couldn't meet his eyes. What must he think of her, of Aunt Daisy . . . of all of them? "Thanks," she managed, "but that won't be necessary. Shouldn't you be working on your book?"

God, she was beautiful, Jeff thought, and now that the bulk of her pregnancy was gone he could see the grace of her newly slim figure. She wore her maturity well. She was even more attractive than he remembered her as a girl. He had a sudden wild urge to haul her into his arms and kiss her senseless. He grinned to himself, wondering what Aunt Daisy would make of that little development. She'd probably cheer, he thought. Then he saw the fire in Sam's sea-green eyes, and the determination in the lines of her body. She was annoyed with her aunt and hell bent on showing Jeff just how strong and independent she was.

He grinned, and this time it showed.

Sam frowned, wondering what Jeff found so funny. Lord, but he was a handsome man! She felt her blood warm as she imagined what it would be like to lie in those strong arms, to nestle close to the broad, solid chest. She had hoped the baby's birth would rid her of these crazy, impossible thoughts, but instead they had gotten worse. Free of the draggy feeling that had accompanied the last stages of her pregnancy, her body was waking up, and she was feeling things she didn't want to feel. Oh, well, maybe her hormones were still slightly out of whack. Maybe she couldn't be held responsible for the wild, irrational thoughts she was having. And what was it Ellie had said about middle-aged women turning into sex maniacs?

Aunt Daisy just watched and smiled.

A few hours later, Sam handed Tim a sheet of paper with written instructions on Amber's care. "Okay, Tim," she said. "Here's all you have to do. Just keep an eye on Amber and call me when she wakes up. Too bad she's not sleeping through the night yet. I have a feeling tonight's the night for Princess, and since it's her first litter it may be a long night."

"Don't worry about us, Mom," Tim said cheerfully. "Amber and I will get along just fine. And in a pinch I can always call Aunt Daisy. She's really perked up lately, hasn't she? Did you see how she was gussied up?"

"It's good for her to get out," Sam said shortly. "I don't know why I didn't think of taking her to the center myself."

"You've had a lot on your mind lately, Mom, and you're not superwoman, you know, even if you try and act like it sometimes."

Sam's frown deepened. What was this, pick-on-Sam day?

"I better get going," she said. "I don't want Princess to get anxious."

Daisy chattered away as Jeff drove toward town. Jeff listened and nodded at the appropriate times, mentally gauging the change in the elderly woman since he'd first met her. She was much livelier, much more alert and cheerful. He knew Sam had cut back on her medication, and that Daisy was thrilled with her great-niece. But it was more than that. When he'd first broached the idea of her joining the senior citizens' center Aunt Daisy had hesitated. Looking almost shy, she'd confided that it had been years since she'd socialized with folks her own age. She had admitted that she'd forgotten how to dance.

"All the more reason you need to join," Jeff had insisted. "You're not the only person your age who's lonely, you know."

"I keep telling Samantha what a nice man you are, Jake," Aunt Daisy said, breaking into Jeff's thoughts. " 'Course, I'm sure I don't need to tell her. Sam's no dummy, you know. Personally, I think she's a little gun-shy after what happened with Doug. But she'll loosen up now that the baby's here. She's a cutie pie, isn't she, Jeremy? I'm so glad you were with Samantha when the baby came. I knew that dizzy blonde, Ellie, couldn't be depended on."

Jeff smiled, remembering. "It was quite an experience, but I'm sure Sam would rather have had her friend at her side."

Aunt Daisy chuckled. "Maybe, and maybe not. Like I said, Samantha's no dummy. Why would she want Ellie when she could have you?"

The senior center was as Jeff had first seen it, bright and clean and cheerfully decorated. Daisy tried to hang back, but Jeff wouldn't allow it.

"Come on, Daisy," he said firmly, taking her arm and propelling her through the door. "The first few steps are the hardest. After that it gets easy."

"Humph! Always knew you were pushy, Jack!"

Jeff laughed; Aunt Daisy was a stitch. And it made him feel good to think he could have a hand in helping her lead a happy, wonderful life.

"Look," he said, "there's a lady with a nice smile. Let's go say hello."

He took Daisy's hand, like a parent leading a child on the first day of school. "Hey, what's this? You're shaking. Are you scared, Aunt Daisy?"

"Scared? Me? Don't be silly, Jim! Do I look like a flibbertigibbet to you?"

"Not a bit, Aunt Daisy," Jeff said quickly. "I think you're wonderful." And he really did.

Jeff helped Frank Fenwick and some of the other seniors decorate for the dance that evening, while a sweet-faced little woman took Daisy off for orientation. It was something they did for all new members, Frank explained, as he hammered nails into place so the others could hang crepe-paper hearts and flowers.

"It's funny," he told Jeff, "but most of the new members seem a little reluctant at first . . . sort of like they're not real sure they should be here."

Jeff nodded. He'd sensed that in Daisy, as if she wanted to join in but wasn't sure she should.

"Is Daisy a relative of yours?" Frank asked. He put his hammer down and gratefully accepted a diet cola. A white-haired lady wearing a ruffled apron handed one to Jeff.

"Thanks, Ada," Frank said, giving the woman a friendly wink.

Jeff took a long swallow. He couldn't have said why, but he was having a great time.

These seniors were so lively and eager. They were all enjoying themselves so much. "Daisy is the aunt of a friend," Jeff said. "From what I hear she's been pretty morose lately. My friend thinks it was mainly boredom, and I agree. She was spending all her time sitting in front of the television, and taking too much medication. Personally, I think she's a lot sharper than anyone realizes. How did you get involved in all this, Frank?"

Frank grinned. "Self-defense, I suppose. I was suffering some of that boredom you mentioned. I knew I had to get moving to do something to keep the brain cells from turning to mush. You've had some experience with an elderly person's loneliness, haven't you, young fellow?"

Jeff started to shake his head, then he nodded instead. "My dad. I was in the military and couldn't spend a lot of time with him. Toward the end he deteriorated badly. I can't help blaming myself."

Frank clapped a hand on Jeff's shoulder. "Don't start heading down that route, Jeff. We all do the best we can. Sometimes it's enough, sometimes it isn't. Now take my situation: My wife, Marge, came down with Alzheimer's about six years ago. I didn't know how to deal with it, or where to go for help. Our kids are all scattered, and they have families and lives of their own. There wasn't much they could do. I bumbled along as best I could, trying to watch Marge and keep her safe, and then one day I knew I just couldn't do it anymore."

"So you put her in a nursing home?" Jeff asked.

"Had to," Frank said, "but it just about killed both of us. We'd been together for forty-three years, through good and bad. I felt like I was deserting her."

"But if you couldn't keep her safe . . ."

"That's what I had to realize. Keeping Marge at home wasn't what was best for her."

Frank tipped up his can of cola and took a long swallow. "She's gone now; passed away a couple of years ago. I guess some folks wouldn't understand my saying this, but it was a blessing for both of us. I miss her . . . always will," Frank said quietly, "but I know she's resting in peace now. She's safe."

Jeff nodded and clapped a hand on Frank's shoulder. "I understand," he said.

Frank stood up and picked up his hammer. He nodded. "Somehow I thought you would," he said.

After orientation the seniors were all served a hot lunch. Jeff sat between Frank and Daisy, amazed at the quality of the food.

"This chili is great," he said. "Who made it?"

Two women at the far end of the table laughed and admitted they were the chefs.

"Chili is my specialty. My children used to love it."

"Wait till they taste my chicken and dumplings," Daisy whispered to Jeff. "Bet you didn't even know I could cook, Jeremy."

"Thought your name was Jeff," Frank said, dipping a piece of corn bread in his chili.

"It is," Jeff said, turning away from Daisy. He lowered his voice. "But she can't seem to remember it."

"Oh." Frank went on eating, as though that was a perfectly normal occurrence.

Before Jeff and Daisy left Frank asked them if they could think of some ways to raise money for the center. "We depend mostly on donations, and folks try to be as generous as possible, but times are hard for everyone these days, so I thought if we could all put our heads together and figure some way to raise some extra money, it would be a big help. We sure don't want to shut this place down."

"No way," Jeff said adamantly. "Let me think about it for a few days."

Jeff drove Daisy home for a nap that afternoon and promised to take her back for the dance at seven.

"Mom's still in the kennels with Princess," Tim told Jeff, after Daisy had gone off to lie down. "The way things look, she'll probably be there all night."

"Think she'd mind if I peeked in?"

Tim shook his head. "You better not, Jeff. The dogs don't know you that well, and a whelping female can get pretty nervous."

"Oh. Okay. Well, I'll just go on home, then. Is Amber okay?"

"See for yourself," Tim said. "I have to admit she's a cute kid."

Jeff looked down at the sleeping baby. She was on her tummy, and her round little behind was poked up in the air. She made soft, wheezing little sounds.

Jeff backed up and cleared his throat. "Well, I better get out of here before I wake her. See you later, Tim."

Jeff sat in front of his computer later that evening, but the screen remained blank, as blank as his mind. He'd expected his outing with Aunt Daisy to give him some ideas for his book and it had, but everything he'd seen and heard had fled from his mind the minute he sat down at his desk. At this rate he'd never get the book written.

Actually, he'd enjoyed the little jaunt with Aunt Daisy more than he'd expected to. He'd originally looked at it as a way to get some research done on his book, but it turned out to be more than that. Frank had reminded Jeff that there was a real need for centers like the one he'd recently opened in Wildwood, and now Jeff was trying to think of ways the center could raise money. He'd been good at organizing in the service. Perhaps it would stand him in good stead now.

Before he left the center after the dance Jeff had committed several hours a week to the senior center. Everything Frank had said had hit a nerve.

Finally, Jeff switched off his computer and stood up. He'd agreed to help out at the center, and he was looking forward to it, but that wasn't helping him write his book. For the moment he had a severe case of writer's block.

He peered out the window in the direction of Sam's place. Sure enough, all the lights were on in the kennel. Sam was probably out there right now, helping Princess deliver her puppies. But what about Amber? Wasn't Tim supposed to be watching the baby while Sam took care of the dog?

Jeff began to pace, and as he paced he worried. Was Tim competent to look after a newborn? There was no doubt he was a decent kid, but taking care of an infant was an enormous responsibility. What if something came up he couldn't handle? What if he fed the baby too much, or not enough? Did Tim even know how to change a diaper?

Jeff stopped pacing and stared out the window toward the kennel. He wished he could go and help Sam, but she'd made it abundantly clear that she didn't appreciate his interference. But, damn it, she hadn't said he couldn't visit her family, had she? And after spending an entire evening helping her deliver Amber he was at least entitled to visitation rights, wasn't he? In his heart Jeff knew that Sam wouldn't leave Amber Dawn with Tim if she didn't have perfect confidence in his baby-sitting abilities, but there was no harm in an extra pair of helping hands, was there?

Sam sighed wearily and smoothed her hands over Princess's belly. The big dog's eyes were wide with anxiety; something was happening, and she didn't understand what it was.

"Easy, pretty girl," Sam murmured soothingly. "Soon you'll have your babies lying next to you and you'll forget the hurt."

Suddenly, Princess stiffened, hunched her

back, and strained with all her might. Silently, Sam urged her on, feeling each surge with her dog. Then she saw it, the bulging sack protruding from Princess's vulva. The bitch strained again and again, and finally the pup was free. Princess immediately began chewing at the sack to free her baby. Sam smiled. Everything seemed to be progressing normally, so she wouldn't interfere. Her job now was to calm and reassure the new mother, and hope that the dog's natural instincts would take over. If there weren't any problems she would refrain from handling the pups until the delivery was completed.

Again and again the scene was repeated until there were seven tiny, wriggling pups in the whelping box. By then Polar Princess was quivering with exhaustion. Sam watched carefully, making sure the bitch expelled all the afterbirth; then she gently rubbed each puppy with a clean terry towel. All but the last pup had already nursed, so now Sam laid the newest arrival against Princess's swollen teats. As soon as the little guy began to suck she was satisfied.

When the new mother had been allowed to relieve herself and had been given some warm milk Sam helped her settle in the whelping box to feed her babies. Seven pups; Sam had hoped for six, so the last one was a bonus.

Wearily, Sam raised herself to a standing position and rubbed her back. She'd been bent over for what seemed like days and she was almost as exhausted as Princess looked. She'd gone back to the house a couple of times to feed Amber, and Tim had assured her he was doing fine as a baby-sitter. But now . . . good Lord, it must be later than she'd realized. Why hadn't Tim called her?

She raced back to the house as fast as her feet would carry her. If anything had happened to her baby . . .

Sam stopped short at the living-room doorway. She took in the scene in front of her in shocked disbelief. Tim was nowhere in sight, nor was there any sign of Aunt Daisy, but Amber, her precious little baby, was sleeping quite peacefully, nestled against the broad chest of Commander Jeffrey Brooks. And Jeff was humming an odd, tuneless melody, a contented smile on his face.

"What in the world? What are you doing here?" Sam demanded. "Where's Tim? If he's gone off somewhere, I'll . . ."

Jeff held his finger to his lips, cautioning her not to disturb the sleeping baby. It was the first time he'd ever held such a tiny infant, and it was an incredible experience. There was simply no way to describe the emotions swirling around inside him as he cradled little Amber against his heart.

Sam took a deep breath and checked the questions trembling on her lips. She was going to wring Tim's neck! She . . . her anger began to fade as her fears were replaced with wonder. Was this really Jeff holding her little girl so tenderly? Jeff Brooks, the stiff, stern commander? The man who didn't like noise or piddling dogs? Was that actually a smile of contentment on his face, or was her imagination playing tricks on her?

"Jeff, what's going on?" she whispered. "I don't understand. I left Tim in charge. If he went out and . . ."

"Relax," Jeff said softly. "Tim is in his room, asleep. The kid was falling asleep here on the sofa, so I sent him to bed. Do you have any idea how late it is?"

For the first time all evening Sam looked at her watch. "Four-thirty?" she shrieked. "In the morning? Oh, Lord!"

Jeff nodded, shifting ever so slightly as Amber settled into a more comfortable position.

"Daisy is also sleeping," Jeff informed her. "I think all the dancing she did wore her out."

"Dancing? Aunt Daisy was dancing? Oh, that's right . . . at the center. But who with? What about her arthritis?"

"I guess she temporarily forgot all about it," Jeff replied, grinning. "You should have seen her, Sam. She was great. She looked like a different woman. She met a lot of people her own age and had a wonderful time. I think the center is going to be good for her. I'm taking her back again next week."

Sam rolled her eyes heavenward. Aunt Daisy dancing up a storm and Jeff holding her baby and looking as though he was actually enjoying it. What next?

"Anyway," Jeff continued, "you made it very plain this afternoon that you didn't want my help in the kennels, so I decided to stop by and visit with Tim and the kid here. Just to make sure everything was okay. There's nothing wrong with that, is there?"

Sam shook her head and slowly sank down on the sofa next to Jeff and the baby. Amber looked fine. In fact, she looked pretty darned cozy, as though she wouldn't mind staying nestled in those strong, masculine arms indefinitely.

You've got good taste, daughter, Sam thought, willing herself not to stare at the back of Jeff's hands. Suddenly, she wished she could trade places with her baby girl. What would it be like to snuggle against Jeff's chest, to feel his heart beating against her? To let the scent of his aftershave tickle her nostrils?

Sam shook her head and blinked. "No, of course not. I appreciate your concern, but I still don't understand why Tim is in bed and you're here. It was Tim's responsibility to look after Amber, and he was supposed to call me when Amber woke up for her last feeding."

"We decided not to disturb you," Jeff said, sounding quite proud of himself. "I heated one of the supplementary bottles you keep in the refrigerator. Amber loved it."

There was only one way to keep her thoughts from straying in the wrong direction, and that was to focus on her anger. And she sure had every reason to be annoyed. Tim's irresponsibility, Jeff's high-handed takeover. Who did he think he was anyway, deciding what her baby should eat?

But Jeff looked so wonderful holding Amber like that, and the baby seemed positively euphoric. It was awfully hard to stay angry, and it suddenly became impossible when Jeff carefully deposited the baby on the sofa beside them and stood up, holding out his arms to her.

She was so tired, so drained . . . so alone, and Jeff's arms looked so inviting . . .

"You're dead on your feet," Jeff said. "Otherwise I would be sorely tempted to kiss you until you begged for mercy. Let it go, Sam.

Accept the fact that someone helped you out for a change. That's not so terrible, is it?"

"No, but . . ."

"No buts tonight," Jeff said firmly, stroking her hair and trying his darndest not to let her unique, earthy scent get to him. This was not the time for romance; Sam was nearly comatose. What she needed now was a few hours of sleep. Reluctantly, he pointed her toward the stairs. "I'll carry Amber for you," he said. "You'd better get some sleep. Before you know it this little gal will be ready for breakfast."

"Thank you," Sam said softly, wearily trudging up the stairs after Jeff. She was tired; too tired to think straight. "I do appreciate what you did," she said softly.

And that was Jeff's undoing. He laid Amber in her crib and took Sam in his arms. He bent his head, touched his lips to hers, and felt the skyrockets burst all around him. Lord, it felt good to hold a woman again, but this wasn't just any woman. No one but Sam could have made his heartbeat so erratic. Sweet, fiercely independent, feisty Sam, and her crazy but wonderful family.

Sam leaned into him. She was tired, all right, but she wasn't dead. She could still feel, and what she felt was incredible. Jeff's arms were warm and strong, and she felt small and safe and cared for. And more alive than she'd been in a very long time. She'd always thought that by this time of her life sex would be relatively unimportant, that it would be more of a routine function than something so exciting she would have trouble catching her breath. And Jeff! His enthusiasm was that of a man half his age! How was it possible?

Before she could voice any of the crazy feelings buzzing around inside her, Jeff was gently putting her away from him.

"Go to bed," he said, almost gruffly. "I'll see you tomorrow."

As he walked across the yard with the predawn stillness all around him, Jeff brushed the lint from Amber's baby blanket off his pants. He grimaced. If only he could brush away the sweet infant smell as well, the feel of a soft, warm little body cuddled trustingly against him . . . the warm, earthy scent of the baby's mother.

He was getting in too deep and he couldn't help feeling nervous and a little scared. Who needed all this, anyway? A crying baby who peed on your lap and upchucked on your shoulder, an eccentric old lady, and a young man without a shred of responsibility who acted half his age? And last, but not least, a rotten-tempered, ungrateful, beautiful, green-eyed, auburn-haired lady who had the remarkable ability to raise his blood pressure and his temperature with a mere glance. Yeah, who needed it? Did he really want to start something with Sam at this stage of his life? Hell, he'd been single for years and he'd made out just fine. He had a few friends, the freedom to come and go as he pleased . . . no ties, no responsibilities, no family. No one to really care if he lived or died. No one to share a sunset with. No one.

Eight

"And if you ever do anything so irresponsible again, I'll never . . ." Sam stopped, thoroughly confused. Despite her lack of sleep she'd woken with a clear head and a smile in her heart. She could still feel Jeff's kiss, still see the way he'd looked holding her baby daughter. How could she be mad at Tim when things had turned out so wonderfully?

"Oh, never mind," she said. "I guess there was no real harm done." She carefully measured coffee into the pot and kept her eyes hidden. If Tim got an inkling of what she was really thinking . . .

Tim shook his head in bewilderment. What was wrong with his mom, anyway? It wasn't like her to back down this way. A sudden thought struck him and he grinned mischievously. "Ah, I get it. Did you and the good commander have a little tête-à-tête when you got home last night? Is that why you're so chipper this morning?"

"Don't be ridiculous," Sam said quickly. If Tim got the idea there was something going on between her and Jeff, she'd never have any peace.

"Stop looking at me like that and get out to the kennels, will you? I want you to check the new arrivals."

"Okay, but I still think . . ."

Sam whirled from the sink and placed her hands on her hips. "Want to live until tomorrow, Tim? Then you'd better get out of here today. Right now. Get!"

Sam tidied the kitchen, her thoughts continually straying to Jeff. She felt a little scared when she thought of him, of the implications of getting involved with him. She was feeling things she didn't want to feel, thinking things she shouldn't be thinking, like how wonderful it would be for Amber to have a man like Jeff on whom to practice her feminine wiles. How nice it would be to have a strong, decisive man to lean on once in awhile. Wishful thinking, Sam, she chided herself. She was mentally insinuating Jeff into her family, willing him to take the place of the husband she'd lost, the father her daughter would never know. It was all wrong and, more importantly, it was futile. Jeff would have to be certifiably insane to get involved with a woman who was responsible not only for herself and a tiny infant, but also for a cantankerous old lady and an immature young man. Add to that the fact that she had a virtual mountain of unpaid bills, a house that constantly needed repairs . . . the list went on and on, and finally Sam decided enough was enough.

She was suffering from a mild case of post-natal depression. It was affecting her judgment, making it impossible for her to look at life rationally. It wasn't serious and it would pass. In a few weeks, when Amber started sleeping through the night and she herself got some uninterrupted sleep, she'd be as good as new, and maybe even better, because now she had a daughter as well as a son. She had a new child to love and care for, and with Princess's babies she was well on her way to a successful breeding kennel.

But was it enough? Could her family and her kennel fill all the empty places in her heart, or was that something only a special man could do? And what if she couldn't have that man? What if it was all an impossible dream?

Tim stared at the new mama and her wriggling, snuffling babies thoughtfully. A good crop, he decided, sizing up the three largest males as potential champions. Even so soon after birth it was possible to see that some of the pups were superior. He sighed, wishing that his mother would at least listen to some of his ideas for the kennel. They were good ideas, he was sure of it, but so far he'd been unable to get her even to listen to what he had in mind. Of course, they would need a computer, and he knew they didn't have that kind of money right now. Asking her to buy a computer would be like asking for the sun and the sky. Maybe, Tim thought slyly, he should try and enlist Jeff's help. Despite the prickly way she sometimes acted around their tenant, Tim was sure his mom really liked the guy. Maybe even more than liked. He grinned. Unless he missed the target all around, Jeff wasn't totally immune to his mom's charms either. And he couldn't think of anything nicer than having his mom hook up with a decent guy like Jeff. Frowning, Tim took Princess out to get a little exercise. His dad had been a jerk; sad but true. The guy had cared about no one but himself. When Tim was younger he'd wondered why his mom had put up with it, but now that he was older he knew she'd been trying to keep the family together because of the way she'd been dumped as a kid. But maybe staying with his dad had been the wrong thing for her to do. Then Tim shrugged and grinned. As Aunt Daisy was fond of saying, things usually turned out for the best. If his mom had left his dad, they wouldn't have Amber now, and Tim had to admit that she was a pretty cute kid, even if she was awfully noisy and demanding. Someday he'd like to have a little girl like that, and maybe a son as well. He wondered if Jeff had ever wanted kids.

Sam checked Princess and her fuzzy brood several times that day, with little Amber riding contentedly in a carrier strapped to her back. The baby seemed to enjoy accompanying her mother on her rounds, and Sam loved the feel of her soft, sweet-smelling body against her. "Don't worry, sweetie," she murmured, reaching behind her to pat the baby's well-padded behind. "You'll never have to worry about your mama leaving you."

Jeff had been standing silently in the afternoon shadows. He knew it was wrong to eavesdrop, and maybe he was too damned nosy for his own good, but something deep inside wouldn't allow him to back off and leave Sam to her own devices. There was something sweetly vulnerable about this aggravating, maddening redhead.

"Hi there," he said, stepping out of the shadows before Sam could turn and catch him spying on her. "Just thought I'd walk over and see the new arrivals. Do you mind?"

At close range Jeff thought Sam looked different somehow. She should have had circles under her eyes, should have looked tired and draggy, but instead she looked fresh and radiant and very pleased with life.

"Hi," she answered, sounding almost shy. "Aren't they great? They all seem healthy and vigorous, and Princess hasn't rejected any of them so . . ."

"Rejected? Why would she do that?" Jeff peered into the whelping box curiously. As far as he was concerned, the tiny, wriggling creatures were far from beautiful, but he knew that would change. In a few weeks they would become fat and fluffy. They would be adorable; irresistible to people like Sam, who loved dogs. But what was this about the mother rejecting?

Amber began to whimper. Sam unstrapped the baby carrier so she could take her daughter in her arms. The minute little Amber saw her mama's face she stopped fussing.

"Sometimes if there's something wrong with a puppy, the mother will reject it and refuse to feed it. It sounds cruel, I know, but it's nature's way. You know, survival of the fittest?

Of course, if that was to happen, I'd try to bottle-feed the rejected pup. Sometimes that works, but most of the time a rejected pup will die."

Jeff looked solemn. "It does seem cruel. Are you saying that if something was wrong with one of Princess's pups she would be able to detect it even if you couldn't?"

Sam nodded. "That's right. A bitch normally checks each of her babies as it's born. She licks them all over to stimulate bodily functions, and she also smells the puppies' breath. That tells her something."

"That's incredible," Jeff said. "I guess you can tell I don't know much about dogs."

Sam grinned. "I got that impression, but you know what they say—it's never too late to learn." She felt herself flush. "If you wanted to, I mean."

Jeff's brows rose a fraction of an inch and a devilish grin played around his lips. Last night Sam had been exhausted, but right now she looked well-rested. He stepped a little closer.

"How about it, Sam? Does that go for you, too? Is it too late for you to learn how to play? How to loosen up and enjoy life?"

She tried to laugh and failed miserably. It

came out sounding suspiciously like a sob, and it was all the ammunition Jeff needed.

"Come here," he said. He drew her into his arms, baby and all. "Ah, Sam, this has been building up for a long time. You feel it, too, don't you?"

She nodded wordlessly, her body singing a wild melody as Jeff held her to him. Then she raised her face for his kiss and the whole world tilted. The touch of his mouth was firm and strong, not yet demanding, but rather sweetly cajoling. Laughter bubbled up inside her as Amber wriggled between them.

"She's a great kid," Jeff said, breaking away to look down at the squirming infant, "but right now I wish she was someplace else. How about it, Sam? How about chucking all your responsibilities for just one evening and going out to play? Dinner and dancing: How does that sound? When was the last time you went dancing? I promise to curb my inclination to give orders and take charge if you'll just relax and concentrate on having fun."

For just a moment Sam followed the dream. She could close her eyes and feel herself dancing with Jeff, floating around the dance floor in a filmy, frothy dress, with her hair pinned high on her head and . . . then reality returned with a thump as she felt the familiar dampness on her chest. Amber needed to be changed. Anyway, she wasn't really the type for frilly dresses. Her tastes ran more to jeans and boots and country music. Probably just one more indication of how ill-suited she and Jeff were.

"Sounds sinful, Commander, but I'm afraid I have to decline," Sam replied. "I really wouldn't feel comfortable going out and leaving Amber with Tim for an entire evening. Not yet, anyway. I can't overlook what happened last night. I love Tim, but he's not always as dependable as he should be."

Jeff groaned; one step forward and three back. That seemed to be how things went with him and Sam. He opened his mouth to speak, to try to change her mind and convince her that she needed and deserved some pleasure in her life. But then he looked at her and saw the bleak regret in her eyes, the way she unconsciously bit her lower lip before turning away. She wanted to play; she just didn't know how. Jeff's jaw tightened stubbornly as he decided it would be his personal mission to teach Sam how to relax and enjoy herself. Somehow, some way, he'd figure out how to do it.

"Okay," he said easily. "Maybe some other time. Have a good day, Sam."

He walked away whistling, and Sam watched

him until he went into his house and closed the door. Then Amber got tired of being ignored and started to protest. Sam put the baby up to her shoulder and started walking back to the house. It was for the best, she told herself. She and Jeff were too different, too far apart. He was neat and she was messy. She loved animals and he could take them or leave them. He was free and unencumbered, while she was drowning in family responsibilities. The list went on and on, and it was better not to start something that couldn't be finished. The thought should have comforted Sam, given her a righteous feeling. She was doing the right thing, the sensible thing. So why didn't she feel good about it?

Neither Sam nor Jeff had noticed the shadow near the doorway, nor did either of them hear the sound of an elderly woman clucking her tongue in dismay. And they didn't hear the pleased chuckle either, when Aunt Daisy decided it was high time she stepped in and had her say.

"So, how's the new tenant working out?" Ellie asked as she and Sam shared coffee and fresh-baked banana bread the next morning.

Ellie grinned. "I already know he was a great labor coach."

Sam rolled her eyes. "Where were you when I needed you, pal? The poor guy was steamrollered into doing something he wasn't prepared for. It's a wonder he didn't run shrieking into the streets."

"Mm, but he didn't, and I see he's still here, despite your noisy, smelly, hairy dogs." Ellie's grin widened. She sniffed the banana bread appreciatively. "That must tell us something."

"I think he just feels sorry for all of us. He's got this thing about Aunt Daisy. He feels like he neglected his own dad, so he's been taking her to the senior citizens' center. And he's letting Tim use his computer. And then here I am, a pregnant widow, all alone . . ." Sam bit off a piece of bread and chewed thoughtfully.

"Only you're not pregnant anymore," Ellie reminded Sam, her bleached brows arched. "And speaking of, uh . . . you're going to be careful from now on, aren't you? I mean, Amber is a sweetheart, but you don't need any more babies, Sam. You really are a little old for this sort of thing. Next time you might not be as lucky."

"Babies? Hey, wait a minute, I'm not even . . ."

"Maybe not yet, but it will happen, and

maybe when you least expect it. That's why I think you should be prepared."

"Ellie, you are outrageous! What makes you think I'm planning to jump into bed with Jeff, or any man, for that matter?"

Ellie was a picture of innocence as she held up five fingers and began ticking them off. "Well, first of all, you're a great-looking female." She folded down her thumb. "Secondly, you've just had a baby, and we all know what childbirth does to a woman's hormones. Puts them in high gear, or at least that's what happened to me after each of my kids. I couldn't wait to get the green light and jump Tom's bones." With a wink, Ellie folded down her index finger. "Now, third . . . well, I've seen Jeff, and a woman would have to be blind and certifiably insane not to want to . . ."

"Ellie, stop!" Sam cried, putting her hands up to her flaming face. "God! You make it sound like I'm in heat, like one of my dogs!"

"Is there really that much difference between us and them?" Ellie asked innocently. "Come on, Sam, you're too young to put it in cold storage, so why not? God knows you're entitled after what you put up with from Doug."

"I've got responsibilities, Ellie," Sam insisted. "Tim, Aunt Daisy, and now the baby. I . . . I'm not free to indulge myself that way."

"Why not? What do your family responsibilities have to do with your sex life, Sam? You're a full-grown, consenting adult. You should be able to do both."

"I'm not sure I know how," Sam said quietly. She flushed. "Doug was the only man I ever slept with, Ellie. I'm not very experienced."

"Good God! I'll say!" Ellie said. She shook her head. "Wow! Sam, you've really got to do this. You owe it to yourself, and I'll just bet that Jeff is great in the . . ."

"Did I hear my name being bandied about?" Jeff asked. He was standing just outside the screen door, looking in.

"Oh! I . . . didn't hear you come up. Have you . . ."

"Just got here," Jeff said. "I'm looking for Daisy. Frank called and said they're having a meeting today to find ways to raise money for the center. I thought she might like to go."

"Come on in and I'll go find her. The last time I looked she was putting curlers in her hair." Sam knew she was red to the roots of her hair. She could only pray that Jeff hadn't overheard Ellie's outrageous remarks.

"I've got to be going," Ellie said, squeezing past Jeff at the door. "Nice seeing you, Jeff, and don't be a stranger. Tom really enjoyed that chess game."

"So did I," Jeff said. "Tell him one of these days we'll have a rematch."

Nine

Sam went about her household chores mechanically, one moment chastising herself for not accepting Jeff's invitation, the next assuring herself that she had done the right thing. The last thing she needed was a sticky romantic situation to put a strain on the fragile friendship blossoming between herself and Jeff. There really wasn't any room in her life for romance at the moment, no matter what Ellie thought. And as for sex . . . well, how in the world would she ever manage that? And what man would want to stand around waiting for a convenient time?

But Ellie meant well. She had been Sam's best friend for a long time. She'd seen her through a lot of rough times. She'd been at Sam's side through the ordeal of Doug's funeral, and she'd been supportive throughout Sam's pregnancy, even though she'd confided that she would have dealt with a midlife pregnancy differently. Ellie was a dear and valued friend who just wanted her pal to be happy, but in this instance Sam was convinced Ellie was on the wrong track.

"You've got enough to worry about, Sam, old girl," she reminded herself firmly. "Amber, the kennel, Aunt Daisy . . ." But why was it that lately she had to keep reminding herself of her responsibilities? Why was she feeling so unsettled, so dissatisfied? Why did she sometimes feel as if she wanted to escape from it all?

Tim poked his head around the door frame. "I'm going across the street to help Jeff, Mom." He frowned as he studied his mother. "Since when did you start talking to yourself?"

"I'm not," Sam snapped, annoyed that Tim had snuck up on her this way. "And what can you possibly help Jeff with?"

Tim's eyes narrowed angrily and his jaw tightened. "Obviously, Jeff doesn't see me quite the way you do. If you really want to know, he asked me to help him program his computer."

"Oh, Tim! I just meant that Jeff's equipment must be very expensive. Do you really think . . ."

Tim's face hardened. "Thanks for the vote of confidence, Mom." His voice was bitter and his eyes looked bleak. "That's just what I need. Why is it that you don't think I can do anything right?"

"I do! I mean . . . it's just . . ." Sam's voice trailed off helplessly. The damage was done. And maybe Tim was right. Maybe deep down inside she did think of him as a child, but he was *her* child. As a little boy he'd needed her concern and protection. She groaned as a lightbulb seemed to explode in her skull. Good grief! Tim was almost twenty-one years old, a grown man! Why did she have so little confidence in him? No wonder he sometimes looked at her with such resentment. "Tim, wait! I didn't mean . . ." But he was already gone.

"Stupid fool!" Sam raged. "Stupid, stupid, stupid!"

"Hey, hey, is that any way to talk about the mother of my favorite kid?"

Jeff had come in unnoticed, but for some reason Sam wasn't surprised or startled by his sudden appearance. He seemed to have a knack for showing up just when she needed him the most. He crept into her life at odd moments the way he'd crept into her heart and . . . oh no! She was doing it again. This had to stop.

"Why were you berating yourself that way,

Sam? You're a lot of things, but stupid isn't one of them." He was standing right in front of her now, and he tipped her chin up so he could look in her eyes. "What's wrong, honey?" The *honey* had slipped out, but he wasn't sorry. It was how he felt, and he was too damned old to be coy and play games.

"Oh, Jeff! I've made a royal hash of things," Sam said. "I hurt Tim's feelings, and I'm beginning to wonder if it's my fault he's the way he is. Maybe I damaged his self-esteem or something. And if I've messed up like this with him, what kind of mother will I be to Amber?" She needed reassurance, needed strong arms around her . . . needed Jeff to tell her everything would be all right.

"You'll be a very good mother, I'm sure," Jeff answered. His voice was gentle, his hand under her chin warm and safe. Carefully, as though she were made of glass, he drew her into his arms and nudged her head onto his shoulder. He stroked her hair and inhaled the scent of her. And she sensed him smiling. "You're much too hard on yourself, Sam," he continued. "You've been carrying a heavy load for a long time. Of course you've made a few mistakes along the way. You're only human." Jeff grinned as Sam lifted her head to look at him. "Even I make mistakes once in awhile."

Sam started to smile, but her expression grew sober as Jeff slowly lowered his mouth to hers. The instant their lips made contact her blood turned to liquid fire. She swayed against Jeff dizzily. It was 10:30 A.M. Daisy was in the den watching a talk show on television; Amber was upstairs, napping; Tim was across the street. For the moment, at least, they were alone, but it was only an illusion. Then Jeff broke the kiss and looked at her with . . . what was it? Lust? Longing? Loneliness? Maybe a combination of all three, she thought crazily. But which one of those emotions was responsible for making her wriggle even closer to Jeff's hard, masculine body? Was it lust or loneliness that made her want to chuck everything and hop in the sack with him?

A loud shout of laughter and the sound of a baby's fretful wails brought them both back to earth. Jeff grinned ruefully, rolled his eyes heavenward, and dropped his arms. "I think the fates are against us, Sam. Want me to get the baby while you check on Daisy?"

Sam started to protest, then abruptly changed her mind. What was so wrong about accepting a helping hand? "Thanks," she said. "That would be great."

She watched Jeff go sprinting up the stairs to the nursery and took a moment to wonder at his comfortable familiarity with her home, his ease in dealing with all the members of her little family. When had it happened? How? Jeff was a bachelor; the only family responsibilities he'd ever had were to his aging father, and he still talked about needing peace and quiet to write his book. On the other hand, he seemed to be spending more and more time in her house, where peace and quiet were unknown commodities. Sam's eyes widened as she realized that Jeff had become a very important part of her life. She tried to imagine being without him. Who would hold her when she was tired or discouraged? Who would offer tidbits of wisdom on dealing with Aunt Daisy's quirks? Who would stand beside her to admire Amber's beauty?

Suddenly there was another wild shout of laughter from the den, and Sam shook her head and hurried to check on her aunt. Duty called, and there was simply no time to worry about her personal feelings for the enigmatic naval commander who had dropped back into her life without warning. Maybe there never would be.

Sam caught a glimpse of the television screen and silently groaned. At the moment her most pressing wish was that Dr. Ruth would go off and visit the tribes in Africa—anything other than extolling her sexual expertise to Aunt Daisy!

"My goodness, Samantha, what is the matter with you?" Aunt Daisy swung her gaze away from the television reluctantly and peered at Sam over the rims of her bifocals. "Why, you're all flushed. Are you running a temperature? Not coming down with some nasty bug, are you, dear? My goodness, what would we do if you got sick? Why, this whole place would fall apart!"

Sam shook her head. Sometimes talking to Aunt Daisy was like being on a roller coaster and not being able to get off.

"I'm fine, Aunt Daisy," she said. Actually, she wasn't fine at all. Maybe she did have a fever. Maybe that's why she felt so warm and tingly, so achingly, meltingly . . . With an effort, Sam checked her wayward, wanton thoughts and forced a smile. She raked her hands through her hair and pushed the offending strands out of her eyes.

"I just wanted to see if you needed anything.

Are you hungry? I can fix you an early lunch, if you like."

Daisy shook her head vehemently. "Good heavens, Samantha! Go on about your business and leave me be! It's much too early for lunch, and anyway, Dr. Ruth is coming on next. You know how I hate to miss her show. She's quite the expert on sex, you know. I want to hear what she has to say today. Maybe you should watch, too."

"No thanks," Sam answered, "and I really don't think you should be watching a sex show, Aunt Daisy."

Pulling her gaze away from the television, Aunt Daisy glared at Sam. "Well, why on earth not? I'm over twenty-one! Loosen up, Sammy girl! There's nothing that old woman can say that will shock me. After all, I'm human, you know. I had a full and satisfying relationship with your uncle before he passed away, God rest his soul. What do you think . . . ?"

"Aunt Daisy, please!"

Daisy's eyes gleamed wickedly. She cocked her head to one side like a little bird and regarded Sam with a knowing look. "I bet I know what's ailing you, Sammy girl. You've got the hots for that handsome hunk, Jack, haven't you? Well, I can't say I blame you. If I were twenty years younger, I'd give you a run for your money." She chuckled. "Not that it would do me a bit of good. I've seen the way that man looks at you, Samantha. He's got it bad!"

Just then Jeff appeared, a rosy, wide-eyed Amber nestled in his arms. " 'Morning, Aunt Daisy," he said cheerfully. "How are you today?"

Sam noted the teasing smile that hovered on Jeff's lips. She felt her cheeks warm. How much of Daisy's silly tirade had he heard?

"Well, good morning, Jim. It's nice to see you, dear. Are you having lunch with us today? I'll be ready to eat as soon as Dr. Ruth's show is over." Daisy tugged the hem of her print dress over her arthritic knees and smiled. "My, don't you look wonderful holding that baby! Doesn't he look natural, Samantha? Why, anyone who didn't know better would think you're father and daughter. And wouldn't that be grand? Babies need fathers as well as mothers, you know. Take Tim; he'd be better off if he'd had a good man to mold himself after."

"Aunt Daisy!" Sam raised her voice warningly, but before she could say anything else Amber was deposited in her arms.

"Here you go," Jeff said pleasantly. "I think this pretty little lady is ready to eat. I changed her diaper, so she's all set in that department." He smiled at Sam. "Why don't I keep Aunt Daisy company while you feed Amber, and then we can all have lunch together?"

If Amber hadn't been cuddled in her arms, Sam would have thrown them up in surrender. "Why not?" she muttered. Aunt Daisy was trouble enough on her own, but with Jeff egging her on . . . what chance did she have against those two?

In the blessed quiet of her bedroom Sam rocked and nursed Amber, slowly regaining her composure. She looked down at her tiny daughter, overwhelmed by the feelings of love that swept over her. Amber sucked vigorously, but her eyes were squeezed shut, as though she, like her mama, wanted to shut out the rest of the world and just enjoy the tranquillity of the moment.

"That's what we'll do, sweetie," Sam said, smoothing the baby's wispy auburn hair gently. "This time is just for us. No one else matters."

But it wasn't true, of course. They all mattered. Tim, Aunt Daisy, and now Jeff, as well. Sam almost wished it wasn't so; then she felt ashamed of herself. She couldn't even imagine what her life would be like without her family. What's more, she didn't want to. Sure, they annoyed and exasperated her at times, just as she probably bugged them. In the end it didn't matter. They were family, and families stuck together for better or worse.

But Jeff wasn't really a part of her family, unless . . . Sam shook her head. She was doing it again, dreaming dreams that couldn't possibly come true. Sure, Jeff was physically attracted to her; they both knew that. And she was attracted to him. And let's face it, they were both horny. They wanted to jump in the sack together, but what about after? Would it go beyond that? And if it didn't, could she handle that?

Sam was buttoning her blouse when she heard a sound behind her.

"Sam? Aunt Daisy wanted me to ask you . . ."

Jeff stopped in confusion as his dark eyes swept hungrily over the curve of Sam's still partly exposed breasts. "Hey, look, I'm sorry. I should have realized. I didn't mean . . ."

Lord, her body was even more beautiful than he'd imagined, and lately he'd imagined plenty. With the sleepy baby in her arms, her breasts heavy and full, she made his head swim. Were nursing mothers supposed to inspire erotic thoughts?

Sam felt herself flush as she slowly finished buttoning her blouse, her gaze locked on Jeff.

Maybe it would be worth it. Maybe the sex would be enough.

Jeff sucked in his breath sharply. Soon, Samantha, his dark, smoldering eyes promised silently. Soon.

After tucking Amber back in her bed Sam went downstairs. She wasn't exactly sure what was happening to her, but she decided she liked it. Maybe Ellie was right. Maybe it was high time!

"Oh, Samantha, you missed it!" Daisy cried. "The subject of today's show was *Sex for One*. My goodness, I had no idea there were so many ways to . . ."

Sam nearly fell on the floor. "Aunt Daisy!" Sex for one! What next?

Jeff made a strange, choking sound as he tried not to laugh. "Yes, indeed, it was very informative. Is Amber all taken care of?"

Aunt Daisy stood up, chuckling mischievously. "With breasts like Sammy's there isn't much chance of her going hungry, now is there? She's a lucky little girl, all right!" Daisy shook her head.

Sam felt hot all over, and it wasn't the temperature of the house. She could well imagine what Jeff was thinking. "Well, is anyone interested in lunch?" Her voice came out all thick and strange, and the heat in her body intensified.

"We're starved," Jeff said. "Come on, Aunt Daisy, come out to the kitchen and keep me company while I whip up one of my super-duper salads. Why don't you go see if Tim is hungry, Sam?" Jeff suggested.

Sam's hands actually itched. She would have loved to wrap them around Jeff's neck and . . . oh, who was she fooling? If she got close enough to Jeff to put her hands around his neck, she wouldn't be thinking. It would be all feeling, warm, delicious feeling. And her hands wouldn't stay on Jeff's neck for long, either!

A few minutes later, she reached Jeff's front door. "Tim? It's me, Mom. Want to take a break and have some lunch with us? Jeff is fixing a chef's salad."

"Come on in, Mom, but I'm afraid I can't stop now."

Sam stepped inside the little cottage. It was the first time she'd been there since Jeff rented the place. She looked around, amazed. Although the furnishings belonged to Aunt Daisy, there was a new, distinctly male flavor to the house. Was it the books lining the walls? The pipe rack and the pungent odor of tobacco? Sam's forehead puckered. Funny, she'd never seen Jeff smoke a pipe. Not that she would object. She hated cigarette smoke, but a pipe was different somehow. Suddenly, Sam felt dizzy from the slightly sweet apple scent. It was the scent of Jeff; The essence of him was in the very air she breathed. Suddenly she was weak and wobbly, and she sank into the nearest chair.

Swallowing, she made an effort to get control of herself. This whole day had been bizarre. Aunt Daisy's antics, the way Jeff had looked at her . . . the way she'd responded. And Dr. Ruth! Sex for one! Was everyone in the whole universe going bonkers?

"Some computer, huh?" Tim asked. He swiveled around in his chair and pointed to the electronic equipment proudly, almost as though it belonged to him. "I can make this baby do just about anything!"

Sam let out her breath in a whoosh of relief. Tim seemed to have forgotten their earlier altercation. "Maybe you'd better just concentrate on getting it to do what Jeff wants," she said dryly. "I never realized how much you liked this kind of thing, Tim. You took computer courses in high school, didn't you?"

"Yeah, but it was just the tip of the iceberg.

I've read every book the library has on computers, but what I really want to do . . . oh, what's the use? We don't have money for a computer course. I need to get a steady job and try to save some money. It will take me awhile, but . . ."

Sam looked at her son in astonishment. How could she have not known? "Tim, that's a wonderful idea. I'll help you as much as I can. Why didn't you ever mention your interest in computers?"

Tim shrugged. "I tried, but you're always so busy. You have enough on your mind without me dumping on you. And now there's the baby. She needs you more than I do, Mom."

Sam was thoughtful as she walked back across the road. Apparently, she'd misjudged her son all along. Maybe Tim wasn't lazy and irresponsible after all; maybe he was just bored. Just as Daisy had been before Jeff had come along and dragged her out of the doldrums. Maybe all Tim had ever needed was a challenge. Sitting in front of Jeff's computer, he was a different young man. There was an eagerness about him, a light in his gray eyes that she'd never seen before. After lunch she was going to ask Jeff's advice. He seemed fond of Tim, and he obviously respected her son's abilities with the computer.

Then Sam walked into the kitchen and temporarily forgot all about Tim and his problems. Someone had set the big, round oak table with pretty blue place mats and Aunt Daisy's best china. There was a glass bowl of silk daisies in the center of the table. An attractive, appealing setting, and very different from the way Sam was accustomed to eating lunch. She couldn't help smiling.

"How lovely," she said, smiling at Jeff and Daisy.

"It was all Jeff's doing," Daisy said. "Let me tell you, Samantha, this man is a prize! When you find a man who can make a decent salad and set a table, not to mention change a diaper . . . well, if it were up to me . . ."

"It's not, dear," Sam said sweetly. She was determined not to let her aunt's annoying but well-meaning interference spoil her pleasure. But poor Jeff! He must think he was being hunted by a sex-starved, man-hungry, husband-hunting hussy. If he had any sense at all, he'd be out the door and running as fast as his feet could carry him. Why wasn't he?

With her head tilted to one side and her

eyes filled with unspoken questions, Samantha reminded Jeff of a little girl, a vulnerable, innocent little girl who wasn't sure which end was up. It made him want to draw her into his arms and tuck her head down on his shoulder, the way he'd done once before. She was just the right height for that, he decided. He gave the salad one final toss and shook his head to chase away his erotic imaginings. Get a grip, old man, he chided himself. This is a family luncheon, not a late-night, intimate tête-à-tête. He grinned. But one day soon there would be one of those; he was willing to bet on it.

"Well, are we all ready to eat?" Sam pulled out her chair before Jeff could do it for her. She couldn't chance having him touch her right now. "I need to work in the kennels this afternoon, and I think you should take a little nap, Aunt Daisy."

Jeff watched as Sam helped herself to a small serving of salad and sipped her iced tea. He wished he could help her, wished he could take some of the burdens off her shoulders. But would she let him?

"I'm not taking a nap today," Daisy announced firmly. "Jeremy is taking me to town to look for a new dress. The center is having a special dance next week and I don't have anything to wear."

"I'll take you later on, Aunt Daisy," Sam said. "I'm sure Jeff has other things to do today. If you'll just wait until I get the whelping boxes cleaned and the pups bathed . . ."

"No need, Sam," Jeff interrupted. "I don't mind taking Daisy to the store. I have some errands to run anyway, and besides, I'll enjoy watching a pretty lady shop for a new dress."

He winked at Daisy, and Sam could have sworn her elderly aunt actually blushed.

"What will you do with Amber while you work?" Jeff asked, after refilling Sam's tea glass.

"I'll take her with me in her carry seat," Sam said. "She'll be fine."

"I'm sure she will be," Jeff agreed. But what about you, Sam? he wondered. How long before you bend beneath the strain of trying to do everything and be everything to your family? How long until there's nothing left of you but a burned-out shell?

"Is there anything we can get you in town?" he asked. "How are you fixed for diapers?"

Sam couldn't help laughing. Diapers? Jeff

was worrying about how she was fixed for diapers?

"How did you learn so much about women and babies when you spent your whole life in the service, issuing orders to recruits?" she asked. She couldn't hide her smile. On the outside, Jeff was a tough, no-nonsense military commander, a man who was used to having things done his way, but inside . . . now that was a horse with a different saddle.

Jeff pushed his empty plate away and smiled. "I'm a smart man. Women need TLC and babies need diapers. That's just the way it is."

"Well, I'll give you an *A* for observation, Commander." Sam was bubbling over with strange, unwanted feelings. Jeff was sitting much too close. While Aunt Daisy was in the kitchen, loading dishes in the dishwasher, Sam was having all kinds of crazy feelings. She wished Jeff would go outside so she could get a grip on her emotions.

"Do you smoke a pipe?" Ridiculous, she knew, but she had to do or say something to break the spell. She felt like a girl again, felt the way she had eons ago, before Doug and Tim . . . before the weight of the world had come crashing down on her shoulders. What she wanted to do more than anything was chuck the dirty whelping boxes, reschedule the pups' baths, and . . . what? Jump into bed with Jeff and forget all about her family? She couldn't do that any more than she could put Amber up for adoption and ship Daisy off to a nursing home. And at any moment Daisy could come roaring into the room demanding to be taken to town for her dress. Amber would wake for another feeding, and Tim . . . "The pipes?" Sam murmured, dragging her thoughts back to the present. For some reason she really wanted to know about the pipes.

For a moment Jeff looked puzzled; then he shook his head and smiled. "Oh. You saw my dad's pipes. No, I've never smoked, but Dad sure loved his pipes. He had quite a collection, and somehow I just couldn't throw them out. I decided to keep them as mementos. I also kept a tin of his favorite tobacco. Every time I smell it, it brings back pleasant memories."

"It smelled like dried apples," Sam said. "I think it's nice that you kept the pipes. Your dad must have been very special to you."

Jeff folded the place mats he'd just taken off the table and handed them to Sam. "He was. For as long as I can remember it was just the two of us. I think we were probably closer than most fathers and sons. That's why I feel bad about not being able to spend time with him when he needed me the most." Jeff paused and finished the last of his tea. "Daisy reminds me of him in some ways. Dad wasn't quite as outrageous as she is sometimes, but he was pretty outspoken. He let me know when he wasn't pleased with something. I really miss him."

Sam was at a loss for words. The things Jeff had just revealed to her explained a lot: his willingness to spend time with Aunt Daisy, and the hours he donated to the senior center each week. Apparently, she wasn't the only one who felt she had a debt to pay. Silently, Sam put the centerpiece back on the oak table and slid the place mats into a drawer.

Every day she learned something new about Jeff, and she was learning about herself in the process. It was touching that Jeff had kept his father's pipes, and endearing that he was considerate enough to worry if she had enough diapers for Amber. A grin tugged at Sam's lips. As Aunt Daisy would be only too happy to point out, the man should be nominated for sainthood.

"Well, I'd better go check on Tim and see how he's doing with that computer," Jeff said.

He cleared his throat. "When Tim gets going it's like he's in another world."

"I noticed that," Sam said, lifting her hair up and away from her face, then letting the shining strands fall back in place.

An extremely erotic gesture, Jeff thought. He wondered if Sam had done it on purpose. It didn't seem likely, but stranger things had happened.

"Do you think we could talk sometime, about Tim and his fascination with computers?" Sam asked. "Maybe some evening when it's relatively quiet around here?"

"I'd like that," he said, hoping he didn't sound like an oversexed, awkward schoolboy. "I have some ideas."

"Wonderful," Sam said. "Then it's a date." The minute the words were out, she regretted them. "What I meant was . . ."

But Jeff didn't seem put off. If anything, he looked pleased, even a trifle smug. "Tomorrow night," he said. "I'll bring the wine. You won't change your mind, will you?"

His words made her tingle. Lord, how long had it been since she'd tingled? "No. I won't change my mind. I'm looking forward to it."

But not as much as I am, Jeff thought. It felt like his heart was beating in triple time.

A night alone with Sam; he was determined to make the most of it.

He whistled all the way across Sam's yard and the road that separated their houses, and he wasn't a whistling man. What was it about Sam that captivated him so? Was it her sweetly caring nature, or the way she mothered them all, from Daisy on down to her infant daughter? A fleeting thought sobered Jeff: Did he have some kind of mother fixation because he'd lost his own mother at such an early age? He thought about it for a moment and decided it was definitely not the case. Sure, he'd missed not having a mother, and maybe his life would have been different in some ways if he'd had that benefit, but he and his dad had made out all right, and the way he felt about Sam was definitely not the way a man feels about his mother!

He admired her mothering instincts and he respected her sense of responsibility to her family. A sudden grin split Jeff's face as he remembered Aunt Daisy's brazen reference to Sam's ample breasts. Daisy was a pip, all right!

But he could understand why Sam got a little exasperated sometimes. Since Amber's birth Sam's patience had been a little thin, her temper quick to flare. Out-of-whack hormones, he decided, remembering what Ellie's husband, Tom, had told him. Women couldn't be trusted when their hormones acted up, Tom had said, lamenting Ellie's mood swings since she started into the change. There'd been times when he'd been tempted to run for cover, Tom had confided. Once, Ellie had actually thrown a half-cooked flapjack at him. Jeff smiled as he remembered the way Ellie and Tom had looked at one another. They might fight like drunken heathens, but he'd be willing to bet they had a hell of a good time making up!

Jeff stepped up to his front door and looked around, seeing Sam come out of the kennels with one of the big dogs. He shook his head. For a man who had initially been determined not to get involved, it seemed like he was getting in deeper and deeper with every passing second. But what the hell! His life was more interesting than it had ever been before. He liked the idea of helping Daisy enjoy her golden years, and he actually looked forward to the hours he spent volunteering at the senior center. And now Sam had asked for his help with Tim. Helping guide the young man toward a successful future wouldn't be that different than what he'd done in the service, when he'd taken raw recruits and turned them into competent servicemen and women. And as for Amber—well, she was definitely a superior child. When she snuggled trustingly against Jeff's chest or laid her fuzzy little head on his shoulder he felt ten feet tall. It made a man stop and think.

Ten

Tim was still working when Jeff entered the house. For a minute Jeff stood, quietly observing.

Tim looked eager and excited, as fired up as he had been when Jeff had left him hours earlier. His hands moved confidently across the keyboard, and he muttered instructions to himself under his breath.

"Hey, buddy, how's it going?"

Tim's hands stilled and he looked at Jeff triumphantly. "Take a look at this, Jeff. I didn't think you'd mind if I tried out a few ideas while I tested this baby out. What do you think?"

Jeff leaned over and stared at the screen. His mind registered the neat columns of figures and he whistled in admiration.

"Tim, this is great. It's fantastic. Does your mother know anything about this?"

The light faded from Tim's eyes and he shook his head. "Mom doesn't think much of my ideas, but I'm sure this would work. It could be the answer to all her problems. She'd have to hire a full-time groomer, and have some additional runs built, but for a relatively small investment I think the kennel could be made into a paying proposition."

"I'm impressed," Jeff said, sitting down next to Tim. "I knew you were interested in computers, but I had no idea you had this kind of ability, Tim. You could be a definite asset to a lot of companies. You're going to have to get some training. It would be criminal to waste this kind of natural talent."

Tim could feel his chest puff out. To have someone like Jeff compliment him this way was great.

"I've never said much to Mom because I know there's no extra money for schooling," he admitted.

"There are ways, Tim," Jeff said. "Don't ever give up your dreams. Let me think about this for a couple of days and then we'll talk again."

Sam frantically rooted through her closet. It had been a long time since she'd worried about clothing. During her pregnancy she'd been content to wear old jeans and loose shirts, but now . . . oh, why had she ever asked Jeff to come over and talk about Tim, anyway? And why hadn't she said something when he'd mentioned bringing wine? She knew what he was expecting, when all she wanted was . . . Her thoughts ran in chaotic circles. She knew exactly what Jeff was hoping for, and if she was willing to be honest, it was what she wanted, too. A little devil inside her urged Sam to give in to her feminine instincts and let nature take its course, but was she ready for a romantic relationship? Could she handle that, with everything else that was going on? Ellie seemed to think she could, but compared to Sam's situation, Ellie's life was relatively calm and quiet. There was just her and Tom and the two boys, no temperamental, elderly aunts, no teething babies, and no dogs needing to be bathed and fed and trained. Sam stopped, suddenly realizing she wouldn't change places with Ellie if she could. She laughed softly. What in the world did Ellie do with herself all day?

The dress she'd been holding slid through her fingers and puddled on the floor at her feet. Suddenly, determination replaced Sam's confusion. She was tired. Tired of doing everything for others and nothing for herself. Tired of always putting her own needs second to everyone else's. Tired of always doing the sensible thing, of seeing everything in sharp black and white. Whatever happened to all the shades of gray in between? she wondered. It was true, she wouldn't change her life if she could, except for one little thing: She needed some time for herself, a little pure, unadulterated pleasure.

She needed this evening with Jeff, and not just for Tim's sake. She needed a pleasant interlude, a few minutes of selfish enjoyment. She needed it and, by damn, she was going to have it! For once she was going to go with the flow and worry about the consequences later.

Tim let himself into the house quietly that afternoon. He felt great. Jeff wasn't the kind of guy to make idle promises. If he said they'd talk, he meant it. Tim knew he'd been drifting aimlessly for a long time, but he'd gotten used to having his mom do his worrying for him. He felt ashamed now as he thought about it. He'd convinced himself that he was sticking around to help his mother, but the plain truth was that he was afraid of trying to make it on his own. The women in his life had always been there for him. One or the other was always ready and waiting to cushion life's blows for him. He'd been leaning on his mom and

FULL BLOOM

his great-aunt for too long. If he wanted self-respect, he had to make a break. He thought back to some of the stupid, thoughtless pranks he'd pulled in the past and knew he couldn't blame his mom for thinking he was irresponsible, but all that was going to change.

Just then, he heard Amber start to wail. He headed for the cradle in the living room.

His mom came clattering down the steps, holding something soft and silky, her cheeks flushed. "I'll get her," she said. "She fell asleep down here. Did you finish what you had to do with Jeff's computer?"

"Sure did," Tim answered, scooping his baby sister out of the cradle and handing her to his mother. One of these days he'd show her what he'd done with the computer and, boy, would she be surprised!

The next morning, Tim good-naturedly chased Muffy out of the way, then picked up a brush to finish grooming Sam's newest bitch, Samantha's Summer Storm. Stormy, as Tim had nicknamed her, stood patiently as Tim brushed her thick, silvery white coat, but it was obvious she'd rather be romping with the other dogs.

"Isn't she a beauty?" Tim asked Jeff, who stood watching. "There's a show coming up in New York soon. Mom wants to show Stormy and maybe one of the big males; she hasn't decided which one yet. Her friend, Hank, will probably be entering some of his dogs, too."

Jeff felt something twist inside him. It wasn't the first time he'd heard about this Hank guy, and he couldn't help wondering just how friendly he and Sam were.

"You know Hank?" he asked, hoping he sounded casual and properly disinterested.

"Hank? Sure. We don't see him too often because he lives just outside the city, but he's a nice guy. He just breeds his dogs as a hobby, though. He doesn't do it as a business like Mom's trying to do."

"Oh." Now what? How could he find out more without acting suspicious?

"Hank's had a rough time," Tim said, brushing the area above Stormy's tail. "His wife just walked out and left him, and I think Mom said there was some trouble with his daughters. Anyway, he's a nice old guy and last Mom heard, he'd met a real nice lady and was thinking about getting married again."

Jeff broke into a smile. "That's great," he said. "I always like a story with a happy ending."

"Anyway," Tim continued, "a couple of our dogs are just a few points away from a championship. With champions in the kennel, the pups will be worth a lot more money." He grinned. "Of course, we both know that the green stuff is not Mom's primary concern."

Jeff nodded. He knew very little about dogs and shows and championships, but from listening and observing these past few weeks he was starting to understand what Sam was trying to do. Naturally she hoped to make money from the kennels, but she wasn't content to raise pretty puppies and make a few dollars. She was dedicated to bettering the breed. She chose her dogs carefully and studied their lines. She bred only the dogs she was reasonably sure carried no genetic defects.

As he thought of Sam's business tactics, Jeff felt a surge of warmth. How could any man fail to admire and respect a woman with such high principles? Then again, was this just another example of Sam letting other things come before her own needs? As Tim had so brilliantly pointed out, selling the pups the way Sam did was hardly lucrative. No, the Snow Storm Kennels needed other ways of generating income, and it looked like Tim had figured out just how to do it.

"Say, Tim, tell me about your mom, will you? What does she like to do for fun? What's her favorite color? Does she prefer white wine or red?"

Tim looked up at Jeff, clearly puzzled. "I don't know," he admitted slowly. "I honestly don't know."

Jeff shook his head. There was only one other person who could help him, and somehow he had a feeling she would be 100 percent on his side.

Sam opened the door to Jeff's knock a few minutes later. Lord, but she was a good-looking woman! Even with her face scrubbed clean of makeup, with tiny laugh lines crisscrossed around her eyes, and with a sprinkling of silver lighting her red-brown hair, she was beautiful. But the frown that puckered her brow wiped the smile from Jeff's face.

"Something wrong?" he asked. "Is this a bad time? Do I have egg on my chin . . . dirty socks . . . a rip in my shirt?"

Sam didn't want to feel what she was feeling. She didn't welcome the ridiculous rush of gladness she'd experienced when she'd opened the door to Jeff. She didn't want to acknowledge the ache of longing that lay in the pit of her stomach like a giant stone. Jeff was obviously a full-grown, mature man, but when she looked at him she couldn't help seeing the boy she'd fallen in love with so many summers ago. How innocent and carefree they'd been then. At least, Jeff had been carefree. Even at fourteen

Sam had felt family responsibilities weighing her down. She couldn't do all the things other girls her age did, couldn't let herself be free the way they were. Sometimes when she looked at Jeff she was reminded of all the fun she'd missed out on.

"I'm pretty busy this morning," she said, knowing she sounded stiff. "Was there something in particular you wanted?" She kept her wayward feelings under control by pretending she didn't care, by acting like Jeff was of no more importance than the boy who delivered their paper every day.

Jeff knew he should probably be offended by Sam's tone of voice, but he had learned to read the look in her eyes, to hear the words she didn't say. He was pretty sure he knew what was going on inside that head of hers. She was running scared, afraid of her feelings. He smiled. There's something I want all right, he thought. I want you, Samantha. I want you in my life, in my arms . . . in my bed. He wanted to recapture the feelings they'd both felt that long-ago summer. He wanted to bring back old memories and make new ones, but this wasn't the right moment to express his thoughts.

"I'm going to the shopping center in Rio Grande and I thought maybe Daisy would want to ride along with me." His grin widened. "I know there's no use asking you."

Sam felt an unreasonable rush of disappointment. For a minute she wished she could chuck everything and go. "Oh, then you've come for Aunt Daisy. I'll get her. I'm sure she'd love to go with you."

Jeff followed her inside, silently praying Dr. Ruth wasn't on television again.

"How's the baby?" Jeff asked. "Is she napping?"

Sam lifted the hair off her neck in that unconscious way of hers and smiled proudly. "Every day she does something new. This morning she rolled over all by herself. And then she smiled at me."

"No kidding? I wish I'd seen that."

Jeff tried to pull his gaze away from the swell of Sam's breasts beneath her blue sweatshirt. He was like a randy teenager lately. But that was what Sam did to him. The first time he had seen her she had been a girl. Now she was a mature, lovely woman. All woman. His heart hammered against his rib cage as he wondered what Sam was thinking and feeling.

Then she laughed and his gut tightened. Even her laughter excited him. He jammed his hands down in the pockets of his jeans and decided he liked everything about Sam.

"My daughter is a bright little girl, Jeff," Sam said. "Who knows, maybe she'll grow up to be the country's first woman president."

Aunt Daisy joined them then. Her faded gaze swung from Sam to Jeff and back again, and she clucked her tongue and chuckled.

"Good morning, Jake. Are you here to take me away from all this?" She waved her arm to take in the cluttered living room, where Amber napped in her cradle and Muffy happily gnawed on a rawhide chew toy.

"You're getting to be quite the shopper these days, Aunt Daisy," Sam remarked. "Are you interested in another new dress?"

Daisy laughed and happily tucked her arm in Jeff's. "I was thinking about a pair of jeans. The center is having a square dance soon. Maybe I'll get a straw hat, too."

"Are you sure you won't come with us?" Jeff asked.

"When are you going to take time to smell the flowers, Sammy girl?" Aunt Daisy asked. "When you're my age you'll realize that life passes all too quickly. You've got to grab the brass ring while you have the chance."

"I'm sure you're right, Auntie, but I really do have a lot of work to do today." Sam grinned. "Besides, it's your company Jeff enjoys."

"Fiddle-faddle! I wasn't born yesterday, my

girl! The day a handsome young fellow like Jack prefers my company to yours will be a snowy one in Tahiti. Isn't that right, Jim?"

"Aunt Daisy, you wound me," Jeff said, feigning hurt feelings. "I'm a man of integrity. Don't you know you're my best girl?"

It was good to laugh and tease this way, a new experience for Jeff. He'd always considered himself a fairly good-natured person, but years of military discipline and the need to keep a certain distance between himself and the men he commanded had tempered his personality. Now, freed of those restrictions, he was thoroughly enjoying himself. He was even getting used to the constant chaos that was Sam's household. Sometimes he even liked it.

"Well, come on, Jeremy. When we're done shopping I'll treat you to a nice cup of tea in that new little shop."

Jeff settled Daisy in the Blazer and slid behind the wheel.

"All right now, Jake, what's going on?" Aunt Daisy demanded. "Just what are you up to?"

Jeff laughed. He started the motor and pulled out into the road. It was quiet this morning, and cool for May. The trees were still fleshing out, and the birds were singing. He took a deep breath of fresh country air and glanced at his passenger. "You sure don't believe in beating around the bush. So you think you've got my number, have you? Well, would it surprise you to learn that I want to find out a few things about Samantha?"

"Not anymore than it surprises me to see you hanging around my niece with your tongue hanging down to your shoes. Got it bad, haven't you, Jake?"

Daisy shifted position until her arthritic knees stopped throbbing. Getting old was a real pain, but she had to admit that her life was a lot more interesting since the handsome man beside her had showed up on their doorstep. And unless she was mistaken, things were about to get even more interesting. She imagined Sammy and Jake together, and then she thought of her dance partner at the senior center. A soft flush colored her cheeks.

"My name is Jeff," Jeff said automatically, knowing even as he spoke that it was useless. "Don't go getting a lot of ideas, Daisy. Sure I like Sam, and I think she likes me, too. I just think she needs to loosen up and have a little fun. It worries me to see her so weighed down with problems and responsibilities."

They passed the Cold Spring Cemetery, and Daisy nodded in the direction of the headstones, some of which were incredibly old. "I know," she said. "You and Sammy aren't in love, right? Well, let me tell you, sonny, before I land over there I want to see my girl happy and settled. She's had more than her share of grief, and it's high time she saw the other side of the coin. I like you, Jack, I surely do, but if you've got any intentions of trifling with my Sammy's affections, you'd better think twice!"

Jeff felt the urge to wipe sweat off his brow. Nothing like good, plain talk!

"I won't hurt Sam, Aunt Daisy, I promise you that. But I need your help. I need to know more about her. What kind of music does she like? What makes her laugh? What's her favorite food?"

Aunt Daisy chuckled, and Jeff could have sworn her eyes brightened. "Hmm, not in love, are you? I should have known. Okay, Jim, my boy, I'll tell you everything you always wanted to know about Samantha, but first you have to promise me something."

"Anything," Jeff replied recklessly.

"You mustn't hurt her, Jake," Daisy said solemnly. "Sammy isn't the kind of girl you love and leave, understand? When she loves she gives it her all. She doesn't know how to hold anything back. If you take her love and then walk away, she won't have anything left." Aunt Daisy paused and reached out to grasp Jeff's arm. "She's the kind of woman a man marries and cherishes all his life, Jeremy. You can see that, can't you?"

Jeff nodded, not surprised to feel a huge lump in his throat when he tried to swallow. What Daisy said was true, and it scared the hell out of him, but it was too late to back away now. Much too late.

The new shopping center rated a grunt of disapproval from Aunt Daisy. "All these fancy shops," she grumbled. "I liked the old department stores much better. A body could walk right in and find what they wanted. Now it's all changed."

Jeff nodded, matching his long-legged stride to Daisy's somewhat stiff gait. "Arthritis acting up?"

"Some," Daisy answered, "but there's no use whining about what can't be changed, is there? Anyway, those exercise classes at the center are supposed to help."

"I'm sure they will," Jeff said.

By the time Jeff dropped Daisy off that afternoon his head was spinning. After much serious debate Daisy had purchased a pair of Levi Wranglers, a beaded, fringed western shirt, and a spiffy straw hat. Jeff made a mental note to get plenty of film for his camera before the big dance.

In between trying on clothes, Daisy had

filled him in on Sam's likes and dislikes. She adored country music, Daisy said, had a passion for red shoes, and loved Chinese food, especially egg rolls and won ton soup. She'd always loved children and had once announced she was going to have a dozen, six of each sex. "Of course, that didn't work out, not with that irresponsible husband of hers. Knew he was wrong for her from the start, but Sam didn't see it, not until it was too late."

Shaking his head, Jeff put the wine he'd bought into the refrigerator to chill. He'd been tempted to buy Sam a pair of red shoes but had thought better of it. One step at a time, old man, he told himself. First wine and a little conversation and then . . . what? Aunt Daisy's warnings came back to haunt him, to thwart his normal, masculine desires and bring his conscience galloping to life. The thing was, he knew Daisy was right. Sam wasn't the kind of woman you love and leave, but oh, how he wanted to love her!

Jeff picked up the telephone and called one of his old naval buddies.

Brian Alhart and Jeff had worked closely together for most of their respective military careers. Brian was happily married and the father of three healthy sons. His wife, Amanda, was a pleasant, soft-spoken woman Jeff had always liked. Brian had retired shortly before Jeff, and he and his family had moved to Virginia to live what Brian called, "the good life."

"Hey, buddy," Jeff said when he heard Brian's familiar voice. "How's it going? I've been thinking about you. How's the family?"

Brian groaned. "Don't ask! Paul broke his right arm playing baseball and Ricky just had three thousand dollars' worth of braces put on his teeth. Amanda is having hot flashes and is convinced she's no longer a 'sexual being,' and I can't figure out what the hell I want to do with the rest of my life. Other than that, everything is great. How about you?"

Jeff laughed. It was good to hear Brian's voice, good to know he wasn't the only one who was undecided about what to do with himself.

"I'm doing okay," he said, "but I've got a bit of a dilemma. There's this woman and . . ."

"Ah ha! So that's why we haven't heard from you for so long. Did the love bug finally bite?"

"That's just it," Jeff said. "I'm not sure. She's . . . well, Sam is special. She's beautiful and she has a sweet, loving nature. She also has an infant daughter, a twenty-year-old son, and a feisty, somewhat eccentric elderly aunt. Oh, and she owns and operates a dog kennel."

"And her name is Sam?" Brian asked. "Wow!

She sounds intriguing. How does she feel about you?"

Jeff could picture the smirk on Brian's face. He had no doubt his old buddy was thoroughly enjoying this. He'd always insisted that when the right woman came along Jeff would be a goner.

"I don't know," Jeff answered honestly. "I think she's as attracted to me as I am to her, but . . . well, she's not the kind of woman . . . hell, I'm not sure I want to take on all those responsibilities. Maybe it's too late for me to do the daddy thing, and is there any valid reason why two mature, consenting adults can't enjoy each other's company without hearing wedding bells in the distance?"

A chuckle floated over the telephone lines. "Not if that's all you want, buddy, but from the sound of your voice I'd say you've got it bad. Hark! Are those bells I hear chiming in the background?"

"Thanks, pal," Jeff said. "I knew I could count on you."

The two men talked a while longer, and Jeff mentioned Tim's natural talent with computers. As he'd hoped, Brian sounded interested. He'd always been a computer wizard and had talked of starting his own programming company after he retired. Before they hung up

Brian promised he'd call back with some suggestions for Tim.

By eight that night Jeff stood on the front steps of Sam's house, his hand poised to knock. For a minute he hesitated. Was he making a mistake? It wasn't too late to back out. Maybe he should just turn tail and run, making tracks back to his own place. Maybe he should just forget he'd ever seen a gorgeous, green-eyed redhead and her rosy, butterball baby daughter. Maybe he should stop caring about what became of Aunt Daisy and Tim, stop worrying about how Sam's dogs would fare in the big dog show in New York . . .

Then the door opened, and Jeff felt himself drowning in Sam's luminous green eyes.

"Hi," she said huskily. "Come on in."

Jeff's throat was dry and his heart was pounding. He took a step into the room and was immediately assaulted by Muffy, the walking dust mop. "Hi, Muff," he said, bending to pet the little dog. Muffy quivered with ecstasy, but she didn't piddle. Jeff's carefully polished brown shoes remained dry.

Slowly, Jeff straightened and met Sam's smiling eyes. That was it, then. Ready or not, he'd just become an official member of the family.

Eleven

All the things he'd meant to discuss with Sam went right out of Jeff's head. She was wearing some kind of floaty blue-green thing. It was a soft, silvery shade, and it made her eyes even more intense. And she was wearing makeup. It wasn't heavy or obvious, and he only noticed it because he was so used to seeing her with a clean, scrubbed face.

Sam pressed a hand against her belly to quell the tremors. Jeff looked and smelled wonderful. She wished she was the kind of woman who could just throw herself in a man's arm and get right down to it. Instead, she took his hand and led him into the living room. Wincing, she saw Jeff look at the clutter of baby toys and magazines scattered around the room. "I didn't have time to do much cleaning today," she said apologetically. "Tim and I are getting the dogs ready for a show. Did he tell you?"

"He mentioned it," Jeff answered. He

couldn't take his eyes off Sam. And even the messy house didn't bother him as much as it once had. What did neatness matter, anyway? Who cared about scattered toys and magazines lying where they didn't belong?

"I've never been to a dog show," he said. "Do you think I could go along?"

Sam's brows rose and she smiled. "You'd be more than welcome, Jeff, but it gets pretty noisy, and dog shows aren't the sweetest-smelling places in the world. Are you sure you . . ."

"Right now I'm not sure of anything," Jeff admitted, "except that I want to drink wine with you and get to know you a little better. Can we do that?"

Sam's smile spread to her eyes. "Well, I don't hear Amber wailing, and Aunt Daisy has been asleep since eight o'clock. Tim is out with some of his friends, so it looks like we're all alone."

"Then shut up and sit down," Jeff said, his voice sounding strangely rough. "Let's take advantage of every second."

Sam sat down, accepted the wineglass Jeff held out to her, and took a tentative sip. "Mm, good," she murmured, running the tip of her tongue over her rose-tinted lips. Then, to Jeff's delight, she kicked off her shoes and tucked her feet beneath her floaty gown.

Jeff knew his blood pressure was definitely on the rise. He'd have to call on all his military discipline to keep himself from falling on Sam like a wild beast, he wanted her that much. But he was determined to act like a gentleman. The thing was, he hadn't realized it would take this much effort. When Sam's tongue flicked over her full, sensuous lips, a quiver started deep in his belly. Could there possibly be a woman anywhere in the world more appealing than Sam?

"What do you call that thing you're wearing?" he asked, fingering the flimsy material. It was smooth and silky, but then, everything was sensitized tonight, he realized: sight, scent, touch. What he longed to do was run his hands over the softly rounded mounds beneath the silky fabric. He wanted to crush Sam against his chest, inhale the female scent of her, and taste her sweetness.

Sam sipped her wine, her eyes locked with Jeff's. "This is a caftan," she said. She could feel the heat rising between them. A part of her, the safe, sensible Samantha she knew so well, wanted to run away, to put distance between herself and this man. But the new Sam, the Sam she was just getting to know, was tired of running, tired of turning away from pleasure, the delicious pleasures that Jeff's dark eyes promised. She shivered and took another sip of wine. Maybe Ellie was right. Maybe she had been sexually deprived all these years. She knew Doug had always thought of himself as a great lover, but now she had to wonder. He'd always been in such a hurry, such a rush to obtain his own release. There had been many nights when Sam had lain awake, long after Doug was snoring, feeling cheated.

How old was Amber now? Jeff wondered. Six weeks? Seven? Was Sam physically ready for love? Through the years Jeff had known his share of women. He had always tried to be a considerate, caring lover. With Sam, it was essential that things be perfect. He wanted to give her pleasure, and he was prepared to protect her.

"Uh, about Tim . . ."

"Tim. Sure, Tim." A dash of ice water couldn't have been more effective. Jeff put a lid on his passion and shrugged.

"Tim is very bright," he said. "I think he has a lot of potential. He has a natural ability with computers. I spoke to a friend of mine the other day, an old naval buddy. Brian is retired and living in Virginia. He worked with computers in the service, and he has his résumés in with several large electronics companies in his area. He promised to see what was available, and if there is any way Tim can work and go to school at the same time."

"In Virginia?" Sam asked. Suddenly she felt desolate. "I never thought about him leaving the area. You don't think there's anything around here?"

Jeff hesitated before he spoke. He didn't want to set Sam's teeth on edge, but he also felt he had to be honest. "There may be," he said, "but, in all honesty, I think it would be good for Tim to be completely on his own. He's not a little boy anymore, and he needs to learn to stand on his own two feet. It will be easier for him to do that if you're not right next door."

Sam drained her wineglass in one last gulp. For a minute she felt sort of wobbly. "I know you're right," she said, "but he's still my child. It's hard to let go."

She leaned toward Jeff a little.

He reached for her empty glass, and her hair brushed his cheek, sending all thoughts of Tim out of his mind.

"More wine?" His voice was a husky mur-

mur as Sam's uniquely earthy scent assaulted his nostrils.

Smiling, Sam held out her glass. "This is nice, isn't it?"

Jeff didn't trust himself to speak. Being with Sam this way . . . it was more than nice. It was incredible. It was the stuff dreams were made of, and it scared the hell out of him. Who would have thought that at this stage of his life he'd meet a woman who could make him feel like an overeager boy again? And Aunt Daisy was right: Sam wasn't the kind of woman you love and leave.

Sam's second glass of wine went down awfully fast. Once again she held out her empty glass, but this time Jeff shook his head.

"Better not, pretty lady, or I'll have to carry you upstairs and pour you into bed."

Sam giggled. "Don't be silly. I'm not drunk . . . am I? Do you think I'm drunk?"

If she was, then so was he. Drunk with the sight and sound and smell of her, drunk with the tantalizing thought of how it would feel to touch her, to hold and caress her. He took the empty glass from her and placed it on the table. Then he gently drew her into the circle of his arms. This had to be; there was no use denying the feelings bubbling between them.

Sam allowed herself to relax. It felt wonderful. She savored each sweet sensation, inhaling Jeff's strong scent. The night was warm and all the windows were open. The sounds of night surrounded them. The sharp chatter of a bird, the wind in the trees . . . the distant drone of an automobile. "The whole world is sleepy," she murmured. "We're all alone."

Jeff drew lazy circles on her back with his fingertips until he was sure he would explode. He wanted to kiss her, hold her, crush her hard against his body, but he was afraid of rushing her, afraid of scaring her off. "There's nothing to stop us from loving each other, Sam," he said gently, praying it was true.

Sam raised her head and her voice was shaky. "Are we making a mistake?" She was in his arms and she felt as though she was wrapped around his heart, as he was with her, but she was still afraid. She'd only known one lover, and the way she was feeling now was new and frightening. What if Jeff was disappointed?

"Is love wrong?" Jeff asked.

"No, but is this love? I know we want to make love, but maybe it's just lust or loneliness."

"Maybe it's all three, and what would be wrong with that?" Jeff murmured, his lips trailing across her jaw and down the delightful curve of her neck. She tasted as good as she smelled, he thought, like wild honey and fresh strawberries. Like fresh-mown grass and the baby talc she used on Amber.

She lifted her face then, her eyes begging for his kiss. She reminded herself that this was her night, her time, and what she was about to do with Jeff wouldn't hurt anyone. She was quivering with need. It had been so long, and she had been so lonely.

Their lips met in blinding hunger; then the hunger eased as a feeling of rightness enveloped them. It was a homecoming . . . a reunion. Sam shivered, then burrowed tighter and closer in the circle of Jeff's arms. She remembered the first kiss they had ever shared, and she knew that this was much, much better.

"Lord, how I've ached for this," Jeff said. He groaned as their lips reluctantly parted. "I knew it would be this way, Sam. You're the warmest, most appealing woman I've ever known, and this may sound crazy, but I feel like this was meant to be, as if both our lives have been building up to this moment."

She trailed her fingers along his jawbone. Such a firm, strong chin, such safe, protective arms. It was so different from the way she'd felt with Doug. With her husband, Sam had always felt she had to remain in control, had to hold onto some shred of strength and common sense. With Jeff she felt safe, as though she could finally let go and be the soft, sensuous woman she had always wanted to be. With Jeff it was safe to surrender control, safe to just be.

"If this is a dream, please don't wake me," she whispered. All her cares seemed to be floating away. The tensions she had learned to live with were being replaced with tensions of another kind, with warm, sweet wanting and a desire to be as close with this man as it was possible to be. "I think I'm melting," she said, her lips a soft sigh against his neck.

Jeff did his best to hold back his mounting passion. His body was clamoring insistently, but he didn't want to rush this, didn't want to rush Sam. He rubbed his chin against her hair. "I'm not sure how much longer I can sit here, stroking you and breathing in your sweet musk."

Sam's heart swelled, and she wriggled closer.

"Come to my place?" Jeff asked. He felt it hovering over them, the endless responsibilities, the restraints. Here in this house it would be hard for Sam to really let go, hard for her to forget the people depending on her and just think of herself.

Jeff's question broke the spell and snapped Sam out of her mindless lethargy. She twisted away, suddenly feeling cold and bereft. "I can't," she said. "I can't leave Amber."

"Bring her with you," Jeff urged. He was desperate to hold her, even as his heart felt her slipping away. "She'll go back to sleep, won't she?"

Sam hesitated, and slowly her head began to clear. She longed to say yes, longed to put her own needs first for a change, but she couldn't. If she slept with Jeff, if wouldn't be a casual encounter, a one-time thing. Her feelings for him would tie her up in knots and make it hard for her to see where her loyalties lay. She simply wasn't the kind of woman who could take love in stride.

"No," she said, her voice thick with regret. "I can't. I'm sorry. I hope you can understand, but I'm just not free to do as I please."

Jeff smothered a king-sized moan. It was over. The moment was lost, and the funny thing was, he did understand. He knew about responsibility and duty, and about making hard choices. He was disappointed, but he couldn't be angry.

"I'm not mad, sweetheart," he said quickly. He saw the fragile slump of Sam's shoulders as reality crashed in on her.

Sam closed her eyes. Gone: her chance for pleasure and happiness. She ached to reach out to Jeff, to draw him back and push away the heavy demands that curved her slender shoulders, but she couldn't.

Jeff stood up and pulled Sam up to stand in front of him. For an instant he remembered the feel of her in his arms, a warm-blooded, sensuous woman who wanted him as badly as he wanted her. Not tonight, Jeff, he told himself, but someday. One way or another he was going to find a way for them to be together the way a man and a woman were meant to be.

"I do understand," he said, taking her hand and raising it to his lips. With his mouth against her fingertips he adored her, tenderly, lightly, and oh so sensuously.

Sam felt Jeff's warm breath on her flesh, the feather-light touch of his lips against her fingers, and she was butter, melting on a hot summer day. She was liquid, hot and smooth.

"This isn't the end, Sam," Jeff said. "It's just a little detour. We'll work this out, you'll see. Remember that long-ago summer? The beach in the moonlight? The way we hid under the boardwalk and . . ."

Sam shuddered, with longing and a terrible feeling of loneliness. "That was a lifetime ago," she said softly. "We were just kids."

"Yes, but the feelings have endured," Jeff said. He smiled, then lightly traced her eyelids with his fingers. He smoothed his palms down the sides of her face, to her neck and then on to her shoulders. He felt the heat of her through the soft, silky material. His smile widened as he felt her shiver at his touch.

"Soon, Sam," he promised. "Soon."

When the telephone rang it shattered the gentle feelings and brought them back to reality with a crash.

"Who can it be at this time of night?" Sam worried, reaching for the receiver.

Jeff saw the last remnants of passion fade from Sam's eyes and watched as fear and bleak disappointment replaced it.

"Oh, no," she said. "Are you sure no one was hurt?"

Jeff slid his arm around her waist, supporting her as she sagged.

"Tim?" he asked.

She nodded, looking sick. "He's in jail. He ran a red light and hit another car, and he was . . . drinking."

Twelve

"You stay here with Daisy and the baby. I'll go get Tim and bring him home."

"But won't I have to post bail or something?" Sam asked. She knew she probably looked as sick as she felt. Tim had done some crazy things but never anything as potentially dangerous as this.

"Don't worry, Sam. I'll take care of it," Jeff said, his jaw tight with anger. "But there's no sense in waking Daisy and dragging the baby out this late at night." He stared at her for a minute. "Are you okay? You won't faint or anything, will you?"

Sam managed a shaky laugh. "Do I look like the fainting type to you?" Then she sobered. "Why does he do things like this, Jeff? Isn't he ever going to grow up?"

Jeff shook his head. "I'd better go get him," he said. "We'll talk later."

After Jeff left Sam alternately paced and wrung her hands waiting for Jeff's call. He'd promised to let her know as soon as he got things sorted out. When the phone finally did ring she nearly jumped out of her skin.

"Sam? It's me, Jeff. Look, this thing is taking a little longer than I anticipated. Why don't you just go on to bed? There's no sense in you waiting up all night. And don't worry about Tim. He's fine, except for a headache and a sick stomach. We'll talk in the morning, all right?"

Sam wanted to protest but she was drooping with exhaustion, and she knew she'd be up before daylight to feed Amber. She drew a deep breath into her lungs, then let it out slowly. "Thanks, Jeff," she said simply.

In her bedroom she stripped off the floaty caftan. It had been a mistake to wear it. Maybe the whole evening had been a mistake. She wanted Jeff with an almost desperate urgency, but even in the heat of passion she couldn't forget her responsibilities. How long would any man put up with that? And now this trouble with Tim. This, drinking and driving, was more serious than anything he'd ever done before. Sam pinched her eyes shut and moaned. Jeff had to be sorry he'd ever gotten involved with any of them!

She washed her face, brushed her teeth, and slipped on a cotton nightgown. Then she stood over Amber's crib, looking down at her baby daughter. Amber slept soundly, secure in the knowledge that Mommy was here for her. "Don't worry, I will be," Sam whispered, patting the sleeping baby. "I'll always be here."

For her daughter's sake, Sam knew she had to stay focused and strong. Her own mother had left her for a man. She'd never do that to her child.

Coffee cup in hand, wearing jeans and a gray sweatshirt and feeling as though someone had flung fistfuls of sand into his eyes, Jeff crossed the road and headed for the kennels the next morning. It had taken three cups of coffee to prop up his eyelids after the evening's escapade. But, thank the Lord, no one had been hurt, and Tim would probably get off fairly easy since it was a first offense. Still, he'd given the young man a good tongue-lashing on the way home. He'd driven the point home again and again that Tim's little indiscretion could have had tragic consequences.

Jeff told himself to forget about Tim for the moment and think about Sam instead. If the way to a man's heart was through his stomach, then the way to Sam's heart must be through her beloved dogs. All through the long sleepless night, after he'd brought Tim home, Jeff had thought of nothing but how he could convince Sam that they were destined to be lovers. There must be a way she could have something for herself without neglecting her responsibilities. He smiled as he neared the kennels. Sam was definitely a strong, determined lady, and he guessed he wouldn't want her any other way. "If you can't fight 'em, join 'em," he muttered. Maybe Sam was determined, but so was he, and they'd just see who held the winning hand.

"'Morning all," he called cheerfully. Sam and Tim were hard at work, cleaning the dog runs. Tim looked like the devil, but that was to be expected. "Need some help?"

"Shouldn't you be at home, writing?" Sam didn't even look up. Good grief, the man might as well move in! Sneaking up on them first thing in the morning . . . haunting her sleep all night . . . filling her dreams . . . but she owed him for what he'd done for Tim the night before. It was only that she was more convinced than ever that there was no room in her life for romance.

"Hi, Jeff," Tim said. He hung his head sheepishly. "I'm sorry about dragging you out last night. What I did was really stupid. I'm not going to do it again."

"You can bet on that," Jeff said. "Look, I can see you're both busy. We'll talk about last night later."

"Thanks," Sam said quietly. But she wouldn't look directly at him.

Jeff sighed. Instead of the step forward he'd hoped for, it looked like their relationship had just leaped into reverse.

"Polar Princess's pups are going to their new homes today," Tim said. "Mom and I are trying to get everything cleaned up before the people arrive. And, of course, the babies have to be all prettied up. Pink bows for the girls and blue for the boys, naturally!"

"Sounds great," Jeff said, nodding at Tim. Then he turned back to Sam. "I'm taking the day off from writing. I need some physical exercise; I don't want to get flabby. Is there anything I can do around here to help?" He didn't feel it necessary to add that he had yet to write a single word of his proposed book. What he had done, however, was carefully study Tim's ideas for turning the kennels into a full-service business, with boarding runs and a grooming salon. The more he thought about it, the more he liked Tim's ideas. But he wasn't ready to discuss it with Sam yet. First he needed to study the layout of the existing kennels to see how much renovation would be needed. But it could be done, he was sure of it, and it could very well be the answer to all Sam's financial problems.

Sam raised her head and leveled a look at Jeff. What on earth was wrong with the man? Didn't he understand English? Couldn't he see that hanging around here was hazardous to his health? Then an idea sparked, and she lowered her eyes quickly, before Jeff could see the gleam of mischief. "We can definitely use another pair of hands, Jeff," she said. "The whelping area needs a thorough cleaning. There's a bucket over there, and the disinfectant is in the supply closet."

Tim tried to protest. "Wait a minute, Mom. I don't think Jeff meant . . ."

Jeff grinned, picking up on all the things Sam hadn't said out loud. "Hey, it's okay, Tim. I'm willing to do whatever is necessary. Which way to the supply closet?"

"What are you doing, Mom?" Tim demanded angrily when Jeff was out of hearing. "Isn't it a little much to ask our tenant to do this dirty work? I'm sure Jeff wasn't planning on scrubbing a dirty kennel when he offered to help. Hasn't he done enough for us?"

"He said he wanted to help," Sam answered reasonably, "and the whelping area does need a good cleaning. Since neither you nor I have the time to do it . . . besides, an old navy man should have plenty of experience swabbing the decks!"

Jeff was still scrubbing when the customers started arriving to pick up their puppies. Tim stood in the doorway, shaking his head.

"I still can't believe Mom asked you to do this."

Jeff shrugged. "I volunteered." He looked at the pup Tim was holding. There was a huge blue bow tied around its neck. "Is this little fellow going to a new home?"

"Yep, any minute now. Mom's out front greeting the prospective parents right now. Want to wash up and watch the ceremonies?"

Jeff nodded. There was nothing he wanted more. Each new thing he learned about Sam added to his fascination.

When he had cleaned up he took the female pup Tim handed him and followed the young man outside.

"These two will be the first to go," Tim explained. "Would you believe Mom sold them both to the same family? She sold the male first, then those people raved so much to their cousins that they bought the female."

Jeff absently held the little dog next to his face. He'd always thought of dogs as smelly, flea-ridden creatures, but Sam's dogs were different. She took perfect care of them and they smelled great, clean and fresh, as though they'd just come from a perfumed bubble bath, and he'd yet to spot a flea on any of the dogs. He grinned ruefully as the pup licked his ear. If the disinfectant he was using was what Sam normally used, it was no wonder. No self-respecting flea would dare to venture anywhere near!

Now the pup was licking Jeff's ear in earnest, the rough little tongue scraping over Jeff's flesh as the tail wagged ecstatically.

"She likes you," Tim said approvingly. "Mom always says that you can tell a person's character by the way a dog reacts to him. If Mom's dogs like you, you've got it made!"

All of a sudden they were surrounded by a bevy of children in assorted sizes. Or at least that's how it seemed to Jeff.

"That one is ours," a tow-headed little boy shouted, pointing to the puppy Tim was holding. "See? He's wearing a blue bow 'cause he's a boy like me and Trevor!"

"Well, the girl is prettier," a female of about eight declared. "The boy is bigger, but our dog is prettier!"

Two couples, apparently the parents of the children, laughed indulgently. "Come over here and let Ms. Wells show us how to take care of the puppies," one of the women said.

"Yes, gather around," Sam invited. "Tim, Jeff, would you bring the pups over here, please? I want to show the children the right way to pick up a puppy."

Intrigued by this new, confident, and knowledgeable Sam, Jeff put the pup down beside her and stepped back to listen.

Carefully making sure her hands supported the pup's hindquarters, Sam lifted the female puppy and held it out to the impatient little girl. "Always support the puppy's back end; otherwise you could injure it," she explained. "And never, ever, pick up a puppy by the scruff of its neck. I have a bag of puppy meal here for each of you. It will get you started until you can buy more at the pet shop. It's the best food for the pups, at least until they're a year old. After that you can feed them any good dry dog food. They should have a daily vitamin. You'll be surprised at how fast a Samoyed pup will grow, and they need good nutrition."

"Can I teach my puppy tricks?" the little girl asked, gazing at her new friend adoringly. "Will she learn to roll over and sit up?"

Sam nodded. "She can, if you train her

properly. Samoyeds are very intelligent dogs, but they can be stubborn."

"What do you do then?" one of the little boys asked.

"Then you must be firm," Sam explained. She smiled, watching the children nuzzle the puppies. "These dogs grow up to be very big," she explained, "so it's important to teach them to be obedient when they're young. Tim, will you bring Frosty out?"

Tim disappeared and returned a few minutes later with the adult male. Frosty was magnificent, Jeff thought. His silvery coat had been brushed to perfection, and the animal pranced proudly, his head erect and his tail curved up and over his back like a feathery plume.

"Oh, look at the big dog!" All the children were dancing with excitement. "Will our dog look like that someday?" one of the little boys asked. "Can we pet him?"

"Sure," Sam said confidently. "Frosty loves everyone."

When all the children had met Frosty, Sam snapped her fingers and called the big dog to her side. Then she put him through his paces. She commanded him to sit, then to lie down and stay while she walked away from him. She demonstrated how he came when she called him; then she walked him around the perimeter of the yard without a leash, showing how he walked by her side and sat down whenever she stopped.

Jeff smiled as he watched the children's expressions. It was clear they were thrilled, and their parents seemed just as impressed. Sam definitely knew her dogs. The love she felt for her animals was obvious in the way she spoke to them and touched them.

"Will our dog get that big?" the little girl asked.

"Just about," Sam answered. "The female will be a little smaller than the male, and the ruff around her neck may not be quite as prominent, but she'll be every bit as beautiful as the male in her own way."

The female certainly is beautiful, Jeff thought. Doing what she loved best, Sam's eyes were shining, and there was joy in every line of her body. Jeff suddenly wished the customers would take their pups and go home so he could be alone with Sam.

Sam gently caressed each pup as it left, and her parting gift to each new owner was a ragged piece of blanket. "This has been with them ever since they were born," she explained. "It has the mama's scent on it. It will help comfort them until they get used to their new homes."

But when the customers left, Sam and Jeff still weren't alone, and Sam seemed determined to keep it that way. She was trying to pretend that nothing had happened between them, that she couldn't feel the tension radiating from Jeff's body to her own.

"Well, it's just about time for me to feed Amber," she said, "and then it's back to work. There are more people coming this afternoon."

"What about lunch?" Jeff asked boldly. "You feed your workers, don't you?"

For a minute Sam looked confused; then she shrugged and smiled. "Hot dogs and baked beans okay? I don't have time to whip up a gourmet meal."

"Hot dogs and beans are just what I had in mind," Jeff assured her. He glanced pointedly at his watch. "It's almost noon."

"Oh, all right, all right," Sam said, throwing up her hands. "You and Tim clean up and I'll get things started. Twenty minutes, okay?"

She checked on Amber and found the baby still sleeping, her little behind poked up in the air.

After Amber there was Aunt Daisy to check on. She looked up hopefully as Sam entered the den. "This television program is boring,

Sammy. Is there anything I can help you with?"

In the past Sam would have refused gently and played with the dial on the television until she found something that captured Daisy's interest, but now she happily snapped off the set and held her hand out to the elderly woman. "Come on," she said. "You can help me rustle up some lunch. Jeff has invited himself to lunch, and I told him I'd fix hot dogs and beans."

Aunt Daisy clapped her hands like an excited child. "Oh, good! Jake's having lunch with us. I do like that young man of yours, Sammy."

As she worked, Sam tried to concentrate on her aunt's chatter, but visions of a strong male face with bluntly chiseled features and warm brown eyes kept intruding. The man who had taken her to the hospital, the man who had held her as labor pains racked her body and who had held his finger against her daughter's face when the baby was only seconds old. The man who had taken Daisy under his wing and had given her a new grip on life. Sam chopped onions and shook her head. Jeff's gentleness never ceased to amaze her. And Tim looked up to Jeff as though he were some kind of god, especially after the way Jeff had bailed him out of trouble. Even Muffy accepted him as one of the family. The excitable little Shih Tzu didn't even piddle on his shoes anymore.

"There now, that should do it," Aunt Daisy said, emptying a bag of potato chips into a large plastic bowl. "A feast fit for a king!"

Sam laughed. "I don't know about that, but at least it will fill up our hungry men . . ." Her voice trailed off in confusion as she realized what she'd said. "What I meant . . ."

"I know what you meant, Sammy girl," Aunt Daisy said, her face sobering. "You want him to be yours, don't you?"

"Well, of course not," Sam snapped. "It was just a . . . figure of speech . . . a silly slip of the tongue. Jeff is a friend, nothing more."

"Humph! Call it what you will, Sammy, sooner or later you'll have to admit the truth. You're falling in love with that man, if you haven't already. It's as plain as the nose on my face!" Daisy stood with her hands on her hips, daring Sam to argue with her.

"Don't be . . ."

"Ladies," the deep male voice came from behind Sam, effectively shutting off her protests. "Is lunch ready?"

Sam slathered mustard on a roll at least three times, and when she bit into the hot dog it tasted like sawdust. Her mouth was dry and she didn't know where to look. Had Jeff heard Aunt Daisy's remarks? Of course it was all in the old lady's imagination. She wasn't in love with Jeff. Simply being physically attracted wasn't love, was it?

Every time she dared to look up from her plate she met Jeff's smug, amused look.

It was the longest meal of her life, yet it couldn't have lasted more than forty-five minutes. When Jeff and Tim went back out to the kennels Sam's knees were weak with relief.

"I'll be out later," she called after them. "After I take care of Amber."

"Thanks for lunch, Sam," Jeff called over his shoulder. "The hot dogs were even better than I expected."

Sam hurried up to the nursery to check on the baby. She decided she was definitely going crazy. Everything had piled up and finally nudged her over the edge of rational thought. Her sanity and common sense had flown right out the window when Jeff had walked into her life.

Out in the kennels, Jeff whistled as he worked. So, Aunt Daisy thought Sam had fallen in love. Was it true? He knew Sam was attracted to him, but love? Part of him wanted it to be true, and it would certainly make his seduction plans a lot easier. But was that all he wanted from Sam? Was a satisfying sexual encounter enough to satisfy all his needs? He was beginning to doubt that it would. And even if that was all he needed, what about Sam? He'd promised Aunt Daisy he wouldn't hurt her, and he meant to keep his promise, but where did that leave them? As he watched Sam go about her daily chores, as he listened to her soothe and placate Daisy and watched her care for Amber, he was painfully reminded that no one in the whole world depended on him. There was really no one who would care very much if he dropped off the face of the earth.

Sure, he'd made some friends through the years, but somehow he'd been so absorbed in his military career that he'd avoided deep, intimate relationships. Consequently, he knew it was more accurate to say that he had many acquaintances but few real friends. And, as an only child, he'd never known the joy or the problems of having a sibling. Jeff leaned on the broom handle. It was a sobering thought to realize that he was totally alone.

Thirteen

"You need to relax and have some fun, Sam. It would do you good to get away, even if it's just for a few hours. After all, you've just had a baby, and it's a scientifically proven fact that new mothers can fall into a depression if they don't take some time for themselves." Jeff was doing his best to persuade Sam to put her family responsibilities aside, just for a little while. He touched her shoulder lightly and grinned disarmingly. "Besides, I need a playmate."

"Maybe," Sam said uncertainly. She couldn't help feeling a surge of excitement. Being a playmate would be a new experience; she couldn't remember when she'd last done something just for the fun of it. But reality came crashing down on her like giant hailstones as she thought of all the reasons why she couldn't or shouldn't. "How can I?" she asked. "Even if I could leave Tim and Aunt Daisy with the kennels, what about Amber?" A sudden gleam lit her green eyes. "Unless . . ."

Jeff shook his head, and his jaw tightened. "Absolutely not! Look, you know how I feel about Amber. She's a doll baby, but if we take her with us it won't be a rest for you. You'll be feeding and changing her, and worrying if she's warm enough. No, Sam, you need a day just for yourself. Now, no more arguments. I've made all the arrangements. Susan Lynch is a retired pediatric nurse, and she raised children of her own. She's got a lot on the ball. Daisy and I met her at the center. Amber will be in good hands."

"But if you met her at the center . . ."

"It's not like that, Sam," Jeff explained patiently. "Susan is at least ten years younger than Daisy. She just recently retired and she's kept her mind and body active. Trust me. Do you honestly think I'd suggest your leaving Amber with someone who wasn't perfectly competent?"

"Well, no, but . . ."

Jeff gripped Sam by her shoulders and looked her straight in the eye. "Shelve the buts, pretty lady," he commanded, giving her a glimpse of the strength and firmness that had stood him in good stead throughout his military career. "We're going and that's final! Doctor's orders!"

"Oh? And since when did you acquire a medical degree, Commander?" Sam's eyes were sparkling. She didn't even try to stem the pleasure and delight that swept through her body. A whole day free! A day to allow herself to feel young and free and unfettered. A day with Jeff!

"Can the commander stuff, okay? I'm just Jeff these days, and I don't need a medical degree to see that you're working and worrying yourself into a frazzle. Sometimes a little fun is better than the strongest antibiotic. Now say 'yes' and put me out of my misery, Sam. I've been planning this for a long time."

Maybe it was crazy. Maybe it was irresponsible. Maybe it was even wrong, but just this once Sam didn't care. "Okay, you're on," she said, as a thrill of anticipation bubbled up inside her. Fun. It had been so long since she had done anything that was purely for fun— too long.

Jeff hugged her briefly, his dark eyes dancing. So far so good, he thought.

But saying and doing were two different things, Sam discovered on the morning of the "Great Escape." A million last-minute doubts assailed her; a thousand horrifying "what-ifs" buzzed in her brain. How could she blithely go off and leave her precious little daughter in the hands of a perfect stranger? How could she callously throw her responsibilities aside for a few hours of fun? Tim had been on his best behavior ever since his arrest. Sam was convinced he'd gotten a good scare, and she knew Jeff had given him what for; still . . .

Daisy watched the play of emotions on Sam's face. Worry warred with wanting and guilt struggled with the need to be selfish just once.

"Now don't you go getting cold feet, Sammy girl," she chided. "It's long past time you forgot about us for a few hours and had some fun. My, I wonder what Jake has planned for you? He's such a dear, thoughtful man. I'm sure you'll have a wonderful time whatever you do." Making sure no one was looking, Aunt Daisy gave Sam a big wink.

"Jeff, Aunt Daisy," Sam answered automatically. "His name is Jeff."

"Whatever," Daisy said dismissively, shaking her head as she helped Sam fold the last of the baby's laundry. "You've got to loosen up, Samantha. First thing you know, you'll be an old woman like me, and life will have passed you by. A woman could do a lot worse than hook up with a man like Jim, you know!"

Samantha rolled her eyes heavenward and gave up. Aunt Daisy didn't understand how she felt. No one did. Responsibility wasn't just a word to her; it was a way of life. She simply didn't know how to be any different. Maybe it was because of what her parents had done—both of them walking away without a backward look—but the reasons no longer mattered. She was what she was, and at her age she wasn't likely to do an about-face.

Despite her last-minute fidgets, Sam was dressed and ready when Jeff arrived with Susan Lynch just after lunch.

A trim woman of medium height, with salt-and-pepper hair and a firm handshake, Susan had an air of competency about her that immediately reassured Sam.

"I've heard a lot about you," she told Sam, smiling as the two women shook hands. "Both Jeff and your aunt have been singing your praises ever since we all met."

Sam felt herself flush. "Well, that's nice to know. I'm pleased to meet you, Susan." She scrutinized the older woman carefully. She looked intelligent, but how could they be sure?

"Are you sure you're prepared to cope with my family?" she asked. "We can be a little overwhelming at times."

"Don't worry, dear," Susan said. "Daisy and I are fast friends. We both watch Dr. Ruth." She winked at Daisy.

Jeff groaned. Wrong shot, Susan. Definitely not the way to impress Sam!

But to his amazement he saw that Sam was

smiling as she headed for Amber's bassinet. "Ah, yes," she said, shooting Jeff a mischievous look. "Sex for one. I remember it well."

"What an adorable little girl," Susan cooed, leaning down to get a closer look at Amber. The baby was nine weeks old now, and just starting to smile and gurgle. "Did Jeff tell you I have three daughters? When mine were this age I would lay them across my lap and rock them when they were fussy. It almost always settled them down."

"Why, that's just what I do with Amber!" Now Sam was beaming.

Jeff looked slightly smug as he took Sam's hand and started tugging her toward the door. "See? Didn't I tell you Susan would take good care of Amber?"

"You ladies enjoy yourselves," he said, nodding to Susan and Daisy. "Tim is working in the kennels, and there's plenty of food in the refrigerator for everyone. I'm not sure what time we'll be home."

"Don't either of you worry about a thing," Susan said. "Just relax and enjoy yourselves. I'm prepared to spend the night, if necessary."

Sam's eyes widened. "Oh, no! That won't be . . ." She turned bewildered eyes to Jeff. "Did you tell her . . . ?"

Jeff tugged harder. "Come on, Sam. The clock is ticking. 'Bye, everyone."

" 'Bye, Jake, 'bye, Sammy girl," Aunt Daisy called.

"Now just you wait a minute!" Sam insisted, pulling back as Jeff steered her toward the Blazer. "Did you tell that woman we were staying out all night?"

Jeff hugged Sam close to his side and answered innocently. "Of course not. I just said I wasn't sure how far we would roam. I asked her if she would mind spending the night if we got in very late."

Sam still looked doubtful, but Jeff's arm was around her waist now and it felt too good to ignore. "Well, all right, but we have the rest of the afternoon and the evening. I'm sure we'll be home in plenty of time for Susan to leave at a reasonable hour."

Not if I can help it, Jeff thought.

He helped Sam into the car, his hand lightly caressing her arm as he gave her a long, searching look.

Sam felt the heat clear down to her toes. She couldn't hold back a surprised, "Oh!"

Jeff nodded. "Good. I take that to mean you haven't quite forgotten that you're a woman and I'm a man. I guess we can take it from there. This is our day, Samantha. Yours and mine. No one else matters, and nothing is going to intrude."

Jeff slid behind the wheel then, and turned to grip Sam's shoulders.

Her veins started to throb. Jeff was wearing a white shirt and a light blue sports coat. He looked every inch a strong, secure male. And he was so near. She could smell his aftershave, that distinctive, slightly spicy scent that made her head spin. It was so wonderfully male and erotic. She lifted her hand and touched his cheek.

"Yes," she agreed softly. "This is our day. There's no one else." She felt young and fresh, like a girl on her first date, a virgin just beginning to discover the mysteries of men and women.

Jeff resisted the urge to reach out and touch the fabric of Sam's dress. It was a soft blue-green that brought out the color of her eyes. It clung in all the right places and gave him ideas he knew he'd better put on hold if he expected to be able to back the Blazer out of Sam's driveway.

He cleared his throat and grinned. "Doesn't this feel great? Being totally free, even just for a few hours?"

Sam laughed lightly, and the sound sent pleasurable spasms coursing through Jeff's body. "Maybe you'd better pinch me. I must be dreaming. Is this another life?"

"I'd rather kiss than pinch," Jeff said, his dark eyes smoldering with a hot, sweet longing that made Sam tingle all the way down to her toes. "But I think I'd better put the car in gear and get out of here before we end up spending our day of freedom right here in the yard."

"Maybe you're right," Sam answered, her voice husky. "If you don't move pretty quick, we're likely to end up necking like teenagers in a parked car."

Jeff grinned and put the Blazer in reverse.

They drove in a comfortable, compatible silence. Now and then Jeff glanced at Sam's lovely profile. Despite the years in between, he could still see the girl he'd met on the beach so many years before. Sam. Sweet Sam. He hoped she was enjoying the blessed quiet, the absence of demands. If ever a woman needed a man to help her shoulder her burdens, it was Sam. She'd been trudging through life under a heavy load for too long. It was past time for someone to lighten the load, and maybe he was the man to do it.

His insides twisted as he realized how much he ached to possess her, but he couldn't help remembering Aunt Daisy's warnings. Could

Sam handle a love affair without getting hurt? For that matter, could he? Sam was a warm, nurturing woman. She would probably prefer a husband over a lover, a strong man to lean on in times of crisis. She would want a daddy for her little girl. Confusion muddled Jeff's thoughts. He knew what Sam needed, but he wasn't sure he was the man for the job. He'd been a loner for years. Could a stray ox learn to pull in harness? Could he be all that Sam wanted and needed? Even after all these years, Marcie's rejection stung. He hadn't been able to fulfill her needs. How did he know it would be any different with Sam? And what if he couldn't be the kind of father little Amber needed?

"Will you at least tell me where we're going?" Sam asked, bringing Jeff back to the moment. "I love surprises, but it would be nice to have a little hint."

Jeff momentarily took his eyes off the road and pushed his doubts away. "Well, I suppose you'll find out soon enough," he said. "We, my lovely lady, are going to Bally's Grand Casino in Atlantic City. We will cast our lot with lady luck, dine in stylish splendor, and enjoy a show that will rival anything Las Vegas has to offer. How does that sound?"

"Like a fairy tale!" Sam's green eyes widened with excitement. "We're really going to a casino? I've seen pictures on television, but I've never been to one. I've wondered what it would be like, but . . ." Her expression sobered. "I can't afford to gamble, Jeff. I know I sound like a silly old maid, but that's just the way it is."

"No problem. We're not going in for the big stuff," he assured her. "Just a few quarters in the slot machines, and for that I have come prepared!" Grinning, Jeff pointed to a bag on the seat between them. He tapped it, and it clinked suspiciously. "Twenty dollars in quarters for each of us. When that's gone we're done, okay?"

Sam nodded. Somehow she had never imagined this. She'd expected Jeff to take her someplace nice for dinner. She'd thought that maybe they would see a movie . . . but this—a day at the casinos, with dinner and a show as well. It really was like a fairy tale.

"Have you been to the casinos before?" she asked. A new and disturbing thought had intruded on Sam's happiness. Gambling was something Doug had enjoyed all too much. She remembered his weekly poker sessions with his buddies, the lottery tickets he bought with what should have been their grocery money . . . the countless get-rich-quick schemes in which he wanted to invest. As hard as she tried, she couldn't quite banish the ugly memories.

"I've been to Atlantic City a few times," Jeff answered, breaking into her memories, "and when I was in the service I went to Vegas a couple of times, but I'm not a hard-core gambler, if that's what's worrying you, Sam."

"The idea of gambling does scare me a little," she admitted.

"Do you know what I've been thinking about?" Jeff asked. "I was thinking about next summer, about taking Amber to the beach and to the boardwalk for cotton candy. She'll be old enough then, won't she? Can you picture her eating cotton candy?"

Sam groaned. "All too vividly! Do you think we could get her a small frozen custard instead?"

"We'll negotiate," Jeff promised. He sent a look her way that promised negotiating on more than one level.

Sam fell silent, digesting this new side of Jeff's personality. When he had first come back into her life she'd thought him stiff and rigid, maybe even a bit of a snob, but now she knew different. For all his military manners and his ability to command, he was the warmest, most loving man she'd ever known. For weeks she'd watched him cheerfully chauffeur

Aunt Daisy back and forth to her senior citizens' center, she'd marveled at his easy interaction with Tim, and she'd been thrilled with the concern and affection he'd shown her baby daughter. And most incredible of all, she was beginning to think he actually liked her dogs! But what did it all mean? Was it possible Jeff might want to become a permanent part of her life?

Daisy and Susan ate their dinner in the family room so they could keep an eye on Amber, who was sleeping peacefully in her cradle.

"Your niece is a handsome woman, Daisy," Susan remarked, spearing a baby carrot. "She and Jeff make a real nice-looking couple."

"Hm, you're right about that," Daisy said, "but I wonder if Sammy can relax long enough to let herself fall in love. She's always so worried about doing for all of us." Daisy chuckled. "I haven't worked up the courage to tell her about Ralph yet."

Susan smiled. "He's a dear old gentleman, Daisy. I don't blame you a bit for snapping him up."

"You don't think loving is foolish at my age?" Daisy asked. No fool like an old fool, she often thought. Was that what she was being, just an old fool?

"I don't think love and caring is ever wrong," Susan said. "Ralph is lonely, and so are you, even with your family. After all, they've got their own busy lives to look after. Why shouldn't you and Ralph take whatever happiness you can find?"

Daisy nodded. "That's what I think, too, but it's nice to know you agree." She flushed and giggled like a young girl. "Ralph's very affectionate, you know. He watches Dr. Ruth, too."

"Then you've already got a common interest," Susan said. She winked. "If you want my advice, Daisy, I say go for it!"

Daisy nodded and sipped her after-dinner coffee thoughtfully. She was tempted to do what Susan said, to just go for the happiness that seemed right around the corner, but she couldn't help remembering the way Sammy had come running home years earlier when she'd had her stroke. They'd never spoken of it, but Daisy knew Sam and Doug had been of two minds about settling down in her old house. Now she was thinking of leaving Sammy, but it wasn't desertion, was it? And if Sam and Jake got together, they'd be a lot better off without an old woman hanging around.

* * *

That evening Frank Fenwick and several other members of the senior center came to talk with Susan and Daisy about raising money for the center.

"What about setting up a small craft shop?" Susan asked. "I have some beautiful embroidered pieces I'd be willing to sell, and Daisy makes her own homemade blackberry jelly."

"I make crocheted afghans," Lily Parker said eagerly. "I've given most of them away for gifts, but I think they would sell."

"I enjoy doing decoupage," Mary Hartley said. "And I'm a whiz with knitting needles, as well. I've made some lovely baby sets. Do you think we could really sell our crafts, Susan?"

"I don't see why not. Is there any reason why we couldn't partition off a corner of the main room and open it to the public a few hours each day? We could all take turns manning our 'store.' Most people, especially young folks with limited time, love the idea of giving homemade gifts."

"Susan, I think you've got something," Frank said. "I took some oil painting classes a few years back. Some of the things I did were pretty good, if I do say so myself, but after I ran out of friends to give my painting to I slacked off. I wonder if my paints are still good?"

"It will take some planning and organization," Lily said. "I'll be glad to volunteer my expertise. As you all know, I ran a law office for several years. I don't think I'd have any trouble organizing a craft shop."

"Then let's do it," Frank said eagerly. "Maybe we've found the answer to our financial dilemma!"

A valet parked Jeff's Blazer, and Sam found herself being propelled toward the casino entrance. She couldn't remember when she'd last felt so free and happy. And all because of Jeff.

When she stepped inside she caught her breath. Her eyes widened as she tried to take it all in. It was just as she'd pictured it in her imagination: gleaming limos everywhere, women in beautiful gowns and furs, doormen dressed like palace guards. And the glitter nearly blinded her. She stood very still and tried to catch her breath. For a forty-six-year-old woman, she knew she was very naive. She didn't know anything about this kind of living. "Oh, Jeff!"

There were crystal chandeliers, acres of marble, huge, gleaming mirrors. Sam was dazzled and dizzy. "I've never seen anything like this, except on television or in the movies, and to think I only live thirty-five miles away!"

Jeff grinned, enjoying Sam's childish pleasure. It took all his willpower to keep from gathering her into his arms and kissing her senseless. She was so sweet, so amazingly innocent and unspoiled. He'd done this before, but now, with Sam at his side, it was all fresh and new. She reminded him of a child on Christmas morning, of a hungry kid pressing her nose against the candy-store window. He wanted to hold and protect her. He wanted her to belong to him in every way. "Come on," he said. "Let's go find the slot machines!"

Sam stared around her in amazement. Nearly every machine was taken, and people were feeding quarters into the greedy monsters with astonishing regularity.

"I don't even know how to do this," she admitted. "Is there some sort of system?"

"I doubt it," Jeff said, shaking his head. "I think it's just dumb luck. Ready to try?"

Jeff decided he really did like Sam's blue dress. It was nipped in at the waist to emphasize her newly slender figure, and the color brought out the red-gold highlights in her hair.

Sam bit her lip in concentration as she carefully, almost reverently, inserted her quarters into the machine. And all the while she was conscious of Jeff's nearness.

Jeff shifted position, moving away from Sam just a little. He could smell her, could taste her luscious lips, could feel the softness of her breasts against him as he watched her. Get a grip, old man, he warned himself. You've got a long night ahead of you.

Sam took a deep, deep breath. This was probably the one and only time she'd have this kind of adventure, and she intended to enjoy it to the fullest. She ignored the tiny flicker of guilt that swept over her at the thought of wantonly throwing money away.

"I feel deliciously wicked and decadent," she whispered to Jeff as he showed her how to operate the machines. All around them glasses clinked as drinks were ordered and accepted. Waitresses in ridiculously skimpy outfits strolled around on high heels that would have sent Sam flying. Behind Sam a man cursed as his luck ran out, while on her left side a woman cheered as her machine spewed handfuls of coins. It was heady and exciting and totally foreign to Sam, and she was loving every minute.

After that she fed her quarters into the machine recklessly, dreading the moment when her pile of coins would be depleted.

Just as she accepted her second glass of champagne from a redheaded waitress, it happened: Her machine suddenly went berserk. Lights flashed and bells clanged. Sam's eyes widened and the champagne sloshed in her glass. "What happened? What did I do wrong?"

Then people were crowding around them, and Jeff was shielding her from the crush. He laughed and hugged her. "You did it, Sam!" he yelled. "You hit the jackpot! Look at all the money you've won!"

She stared, openmouthed, as the machine spewed coins on the floor at her feet. Her eyes bulged and her throat was dry. The jackpot? She had hit the jackpot? Of course it had to be a dream, or was it real? Was it possible that Samantha Wells, mother and kennel owner, had just won the jackpot at the slot machines in Atlantic City? Then there was something else for Sam to wonder about as Jeff hauled her into his arms for a congratulatory kiss. It began gently enough, then deepened as Sam instinctively wound her arms around his neck. Her body pressed against his hard, male contours and a wave of heat rose between them. Skyrockets of sensation went off in Sam's body. Then a loud burst of applause and laughter brought her back to the moment. "Good heavens!" she said.

Fourteen

Jeff guided Sam to the cashier's window to make arrangements to pick up her winnings at the end of the evening.

"I can't believe I won all this money," Sam said. It was enough to pay off the balance of her outstanding bills and buy the crib and car seat she needed for Amber. She was still throbbing with excitement when she realized Jeff was leading her toward an elevator.

"Where are we going?"

"To the suite I rented," Jeff said, his voice deepening as he admired the flush of pleasure coloring Sam's cheeks. She was more beautiful than ever, and he wanted her so badly his body ached.

"Our dinner will be served in the suite," Jeff explained, "And later we'll see the show I told you about, but I just couldn't stand the thought of spending all our time together surrounded by a crowd of strangers."

Every part of Sam's body tingled with awareness. The two of them alone in a hotel suite! She had no doubt what would take place once the doors closed behind them, shutting out the rest of the world and allowing them to be totally alone for the very first time.

"Are you . . . sure this is a good idea?" she asked weakly. Suddenly, she was leaning against Jeff for support, holding on to him as if her life depended on it. Her legs were melting beneath her, the blood was roaring through her veins, and her heart was thumping wildly. Good idea or not, she wanted it. She wanted Jeff. Wanted to feel his naked skin against her, wanted to know the magic of having him deep inside her. Suddenly, she knew she wanted to make love to this man more than she'd ever wanted anything in her life. The need was all-consuming, all-powerful. It buried all her doubts and fears.

"I think," Jeff answered, in a voice husky with desire, "that this is the best idea I've had in years. I can't wait any longer, Samantha. I haven't slept the night through in weeks. Every time I'm close to you I go a little crazy."

"Me . . . too," Samantha admitted softly. "I want you, too."

When the elevator stopped they were tightly clasped in each other's arms. A discreet cough from some people waiting to enter the elevator brought them back to earth, but only long enough for Jeff to fumble in his pocket for the room key.

Once inside, Sam looked around in delight. "Oh, Jeff, this is beautiful!" And it was. It was a spacious, elegantly appointed room, with a lovely little sitting area, a sparkling tiled bath, and a huge, mauve-draped king-sized bed. Sam's eyes flew to the bed, and her breath caught in her throat. "You . . . this must have cost a fortune," she managed.

"And worth every penny," Jeff assured her, his fingers tangling in her hair as he pulled her close. There it was again, that wonderful, erotic fragrance that was the essence of Samantha. "I want to love you, Samantha Wells, like you've never been loved before." Then his lips found hers.

His raging desire would not allow for gentleness, but Sam didn't seem to mind. She gave as good as she got, her hands smoothing urgently over Jeff's shoulders, down the muscular plane of his back. She tugged at his shirt, wanting nothing between them, nothing to stand in the way of their loving.

Warm and knowing, Jeff's fingers slid under the neckline of Sam's dress. In his eager haste he almost tore it. He groaned impatiently, then slid the silky fabric off her shoulders, and shuddered with longing at the first glimpse of her lace-covered bosom.

"Ah, Sam, you're so lovely, so perfect. I knew you'd look this way, all soft and waiting. Ah, so sweet!" Sam had the full-bodied figure of a mature woman, and Jeff thought she was the most beautiful thing he'd ever seen.

He lowered his head and kissed the rigid buds through the pastel lace. His lips had hungered for this for so long!

Sam writhed against Jeff's hardness, loving the warmth and power of his embrace. She had no desire to be treated like a fragile rosebud. She held Jeff to her strongly and surely, knowing deep inside that this was right and good for both of them. An ache began to build within her as Jeff lovingly walked her to the wide, inviting bed.

Then she was lying on crisp, clean sheets, watching as Jeff quickly undressed. His body was firm and strong, his stomach hard and flat. His legs were long and well-muscled, and he gave off an aura of male power that made Sam feel small and feminine. It excited her beyond all reason. She sat up to undo the clasp of her bra, but Jeff quickly covered her hands.

"No, sweetheart, let me. This is a pleasure I want to savor."

Quickly, he unclasped the bra, then felt his

eyes widen as the lace fell away, baring Sam's lusciously full breasts to his heated gaze. He pulled her down beside him then, delighting in Sam's bold inspection of his aroused body. His desire throbbed urgently, and a hot, aching sensation began to build in him.

Hesitantly, Sam reached out, and as her slender fingers made contact with Jeff's pulsing manhood, his thin thread of control snapped.

Crushing Sam against him, Jeff's hands explored her womanly curves. Then his lips captured her mouth to devour her sweetness.

Breathless, Sam responded with all the pent-up desire of months of loneliness. She parted her lips and raised herself to meet Jeff's urgent caresses.

"Oh, Jeff, I need you so! I'm so tired of being alone. . . ."

Sam's whispered words struck a blow to Jeff's heart. Poor baby! She'd carried a huge weight on her shoulders for so long. His embrace tightened and his kiss deepened as Sam writhed hungrily beneath him. She was all woman, he thought proudly, and she was responding to him, to his body and his loving caresses.

Sam couldn't make her body be still. She was a quivering, trembling mass of pure desire. She'd never known this kind of urgency with her husband. What made this so special, so different from the almost mechanical joining she'd shared with Doug? Then there was no time for introspection as Jeff's hands and lips and body transported her into a magic land of pure and perfect pleasure.

His hands were on her breasts now, and Sam felt her nipples harden and swell at the sweet intimacy of Jeff's touch. She moaned softly, twisting against him, thrusting her pelvis against his lower body, where his desire throbbed urgently. "Now!" she begged. "Oh, please, now! I don't want to wait any longer!"

With a glad, proud cry, Jeff moved to cover Sam with his body, lifting his head to enjoy the sight of her passion-glazed green eyes. "Ah, darling, this is perfect, just as I dreamed it would be. Oh yes, my sweet, now!"

More aroused than she had ever been before, Samantha instinctively arched against Jeff's rock-hard body. Her thighs parted eagerly, and she felt him move against her. Then, with an exquisite smoothness, he moved inside her so that she tightened and rippled around him in sweet, wild spasms of ecstasy.

Jeff was overjoyed by the way Sam welcomed him into her body. Their joining was even more beautiful than he could have imagined. He smiled against her lips. She was earth mother, with not only a nurturing heart but a giving, loving body as well. Oh, and she knew how to give so well! Now he wanted to teach her to take, he wanted to show her how to capture pleasure for herself. Starting slowly, he waited for her to match his rhythm.

The turbulence of their passion swirled around them as they moved together in sweet, sensuous harmony.

Sam felt herself climbing higher and higher, until she could no longer hold back the tiny cries of joy and pleasure.

"Oh, my darling Jeff," she crooned. "I lo . . ."

Jeff's mouth captured her impassioned endearment as tongues of flame seared their bodies. His heart soared as he realized that Sam had been about to declare her love.

Then all thought was suspended as together they reached and touched the stars. Their bodies exploded in a wild shower of sparks. Then, slowly and gently, with a beauty neither had ever experienced before, they descended, floating back to earth gently, securely, wrapped in the warmth of their love.

It was a while before either of them could speak, and it was Sam who broke the contented silence.

"This may sound trite, but I've never felt this way before."

Jeff raised himself on an elbow to grin down at her. "And this may sound repetitious, but neither have I."

Sam felt as if she was one big smile. "That military control of yours came in handy, Commander," she teased. She was still tingling, every nerve cell alive and alert. She reached out and traced a fingertip along Jeff's fur-covered chest. When he quivered her smile widened.

"What control?" Jeff growled, bending his head to nibble experimentally at the rosy tips peeking out from beneath the sheet. "Hussy," he whispered huskily as he felt his desire rise again, hot and strong. "See what you do to me?" He guided Sam's hand to his eager manhood and laughed at her girlish blush. "I don't think I'll ever get enough of you, pretty lady. It's a good thing I've got a strong heart!"

Proudly, loving the way Jeff responded to her femininity, Sam felt her own body come alive again. She couldn't believe her shameless, erotic needs.

"Sure you can handle this assignment, Commander?" she taunted, rubbing against him teasingly. "You're not so young anymore, you know."

"Shall we find out? Right now I feel like I'm just hitting my stride."

They rolled and tumbled then, like the eager, playful puppies Sam loved so much. Then, when the situation grew serious, they abandoned themselves to passion once more, and this time Sam knew she'd touched the stars.

"Hit the shower, lazybones," Jeff commanded later. "Our dinner will be arriving shortly. You don't want the waiter to think you're a wanton, shameless creature who can't leave my body alone, do you?"

"Ha! I'd say the wanton shamelessness was mutual, my friend," Sam retorted. But she did sit up, holding the sheet to her naked breasts. Then a worried look puckered her brow. She pointed to her clothing, scattered helter-skelter around the room. "Is that going to be suitable to wear to the show?"

"Probably not," Jeff said calmly. "Here, why don't you open these packages?"

He thrust a pile of beautifully wrapped boxes at her and grinned happily.

Sam's brows rose and her mouth formed a perfect circle. "For me?" she squeaked.

"A little something to mark the occasion," Jeff explained. "Go on, open them."

Sam sat up straighter and swiftly knotted the sheet so that it covered her. "I can't believe this," she said, her green eyes dancing as she tore at the wrapping paper and bows. "This is better than Christmas!"

Jeff watched silently, too full of emotion to speak. He couldn't remember when he'd been happier, more fulfilled, and it was all thanks to a slightly disorganized, auburn-haired, green-eyed woman who could make him feel ten feet tall with a single look.

With a flourish, Sam opened the first box and lifted out a beautiful cream-colored dress. It was silky and slinky, unlike anything she'd ever worn before, but perfect for the way she was feeling right now. She held it against her cheek. "It's lovely, Jeff. How can I ever thank you?"

"You already have, just by the look on your face," Jeff said. "Now go on, open the other one."

Sam obeyed willingly, blinking back tears of happiness. She lifted the lid off the box and gasped. "Red shoes! How did you know?"

Jeff cocked his head and grinned. "A little bird?" Sam's pleasure was contagious. He knew that no matter what came later, he'd remember this day for the rest of his life.

Sam nodded. "A little bird named Daisy, I'll bet. Can't a gal have any secrets?"

"Not from me," Jeff stated firmly. "Now hit

the shower before the waiter finds you draped in nothing but a sheet and calls the vice squad!"

Sam scurried to do his bidding, but not before she gave him a quick thank-you kiss.

In the sparkling bathroom, Sam pinched herself to make sure she wasn't dreaming; then she let the sheet fall to the floor and stepped into the shower. There was no way to describe how she felt. She was excited and happy, eager and alive. Her heart was full to overflowing. As she felt the stinging shower spray she wondered how she would cope when the magic ended. And it would, of course. Such happiness could not be sustained indefinitely, and this carefree freedom was merely a temporary oasis in her life. At home her responsibilities waited. This was just a brief taste of bliss. Like Cinderella, she'd soon have to trade in her ball gown for jeans and a flannel shirt, her lovely red slippers for tennis shoes. Her Prince Charming would cease to be her lover and become just a friend.

For just a moment she wondered if it really had to be that way . . . if there wasn't some way she could have it all: home, family, and a private, intimate life of her own. It was what she wanted, what she ached for, but was it possible? Only time would tell, but no matter what happened, she would have these precious memories. They would be like fine jewels, wrapped in gossamer, tucked away in a corner of her heart, to be plucked out and savored anew when the realities of life grew burdensome.

A bittersweet smile tugged at Sam's lips as she dried herself. No matter what, she was glad she'd come, and she wasn't going to waste a single moment worrying about what would come after.

Jeff was waiting for her when she came out of the bathroom, a look of boyish eagerness on his handsome face. His thick, dark brows rose and his lips curved into a smile as he admired Sam in her finery.

"Do I meet with your approval?" she asked, twirling slowly in front of him. She felt like a queen, like the most beautiful, desirable woman in the world, and it was all because of Jeff and the loving look in his eyes.

His breath caught in his throat for a moment. Sam's hair glowed like copper fire, her eyes shone with a thousand emerald lights, and the smile that kissed her lips was fit for an angel. As she turned in front of him, her hips moved sensuously beneath the silky fabric. Once again Jeff felt his hunger begin to build. Lord, but he was insatiable! He laughed. He was middle-aged, and so was Sam, yet he knew there wasn't a young woman anywhere who could hold a candle to Sam's mature beauty.

"Uh-uh," Sam said, shaking her head as she correctly interpreted the gleam in Jeff's brown velvet eyes. "I want my dinner; I'm starved. Our little bout of acrobatics worked up quite an appetite."

"Selfish broad," Jeff taunted with a mock frown. "You have no heart."

"Oh, I have a heart all right," Sam said softly, sidling up to Jeff teasingly. She twisted sensuously, then planted a light kiss on his cheek and patted his hand consolingly. "Dinner first," she said. "Then we'll discuss the situation at length."

As if on cue, a knock sounded at the door, and Jeff opened it with a flourish. "Your dinner, Madame," he said, as the waiter wheeled the cart into the room.

Sam watched with unconcealed delight as a small table was set with lovely china, wine and water glasses, and heavy silverware. Something smelled scrumptious, but she didn't even try to guess what it was. She was content to take one pleasure at a time.

Finally the waiter left and they were alone again. It was growing dark outside, and the lights in the room glowed softly. The waiter had lit a tall ivory candle and placed it in the center of the small table. Jeff smiled and pulled out the chair for Sam.

Sam sat down, feeling as if she were in the middle of a fairy tale. A bottle of chilled champagne rested in a bucket of ice next to the table, and as she watched, Jeff expertly popped the cork and poured them each a glass of amber-colored bubbly. The dark hairs dusting the backs of his hands suddenly seemed incredibly sensuous. Sam impulsively reached across the table to touch him.

They feasted on tiny, tender, steamed shrimp and baby scallops, a melt-in-your-mouth filet of beef, baked new potatoes, and, finally, a sinfully rich raspberry cream torte.

When they finished Jeff poured them each a cup of coffee.

"I've never eaten like this in my life," Sam said, sighing with pleasure. "You're spoiling me, Jeff. How can I ever return to reality?"

"There can be more nights like this, if you want, Sam," Jeff said softly, leaning back in his chair. He laughed lightly. "Of course, I know it can't always be like this, but we should be able to manage a getaway night now and then, don't you think?"

Sam considered the new thought. Could they? Could she? Jeff was opening up a whole new world . . . he was forcing her to see things in a different way. She had never shared evenings like this with her husband. She had been too busy trying to keep the rent and utility bills paid to even think of this kind of indulgence.

"It's not wrong to take pleasure for yourself occasionally, is it?"

Jeff laughed happily. "Oh, Sam, you're learning! You really are! This is what I hoped for: that you would understand that you're entitled to something for yourself. And if you do take something for yourself, the sky isn't going to fall in. Being just a tiny bit selfish doesn't make you a bad mother or a neglectful niece. If anything, you'll probably be better for this little time away."

Sam nodded. "I know you're right, but I'm so used to taking care of everyone . . . to putting their needs ahead of my own. I may have to practice a little to learn how to be selfish."

"Well, I'm going to hang around and help," Jeff said firmly.

The floor show was everything Jeff had said it would be. Sam drank in all the glitter and glamour. She wallowed in the music and lights, marveling at the exquisite costumes and the beautiful people who entertained them. When it was time to leave she was thoroughly saturated with pleasure. She was also helplessly, hopelessly in love.

But, as they drove home, the magic was abruptly shattered.

"You've got to learn to let go, Sam," Jeff said earnestly, his profile stern and commanding. "You can't be everything to everyone, and by trying you're doing Daisy and Tim a disservice. You're making Tim into a helpless wimp and turning Daisy into a vegetable. If you'll just . . ."

Sam felt as if Jeff had sliced her heart wide open. Was that really what he thought? Dear Lord, was it true? Had she hurt the ones she loved when she'd only meant to care for them?

"Is that really what you think?" she asked, her voice trembling. "You think I hurt my aunt and my son?"

"Well, of course I know you didn't do it deliberately," Jeff said, "but in the service I learned that delegating authority is a very important . . ."

"I'm not running an army camp, Jeff," Sam said furiously, the coldness around her heart seeping into her bloodstream. "And I'm not a commanding officer. I'm just a woman, a mother, and I tried to do the best I could."

"I know that, Sam. I just meant . . ."

"I think I know exactly what you meant, Jeff,

and I also think this evening was a big mistake."

"Don't do this, Sam," Jeff said.

"I want to go home now," Sam said wearily, leaning her head back against the seat and closing her eyes.

Sam alternated between feeling blissfully happy the next day and painfully bereft. The hours she had spent in Jeff's arms had been heavenly, and she knew she'd cherish the memories forever. But what came after . . . Jeff's criticisms of the way she cared for her family . . . that was something she didn't know how to deal with. She spoke to Tim, dealt with Aunt Daisy, and mothered Amber all with a sense of unreality. Life was never smooth and simple; but then, she'd learned that when she was just a girl. Why should it surprise her now? Had she really expected to ride off into the sunset with Jeff and live blissfully ever after with nary a problem?

Aunt Daisy and Tim exchanged covert glances, smiled, then frowned worriedly when Sam's eyes grew dark with sadness. It looked like Jeff's campaign to change the course of Sam's life was moving full steam ahead, but apparently the magical evening out hadn't been as perfect as they had hoped.

"Susan and I had a lovely time chatting last night," Aunt Daisy said as she helped Sam clear up the breakfast dishes. "She's a remarkable lady. Do you know, she almost became a doctor?"

"Really? What happened to stop her?" Sam asked curiously.

"The same thing that happens to most people," Aunt Daisy said philosophically. "Life happened. She got married, had three daughters, and before you know it, it was just too late to do what she wanted to do for herself. Of course, she claims she enjoyed nursing, but I'll just bet she would have made a heck of a surgeon!"

"Surgeon? Is that what she wanted to be?"

"Oh, yes. She wanted to be a heart surgeon. I always think it's a shame when folks don't at least try to realize their dreams. Don't you think it's a shame, Sammy girl?"

"Dreams are nice, Aunt Daisy, but they don't put food on the table or make the mortgage payments, do they?"

Sam finished wiping the kitchen counter thoughtfully. She had dreams, too, but she wasn't sure they'd ever come true. She dreamed of making the kennel a success. She dreamed of raising her daughter to be a strong, confident woman. She had even dared to dream of having a loving partner by her side while she did those things, and that seemed the most illusive dream of all. Despite the haze of happiness still lingering from the previous evening, Sam knew she had to be realistic. She couldn't be sure the lovemaking had meant as much to Jeff as it had to her. She couldn't give herself casually, her heart or her body. The loving she'd shared with Jeff had been wonderful and magical, but had it only been a pleasurable interlude for Jeff? And what about the way Jeff had criticized her?

"Snap out of it, Samantha," Aunt Daisy said, chuckling. "Don't you hear Amber crying? She's tired of waiting for her breakfast!"

Sam pulled her thoughts back to the present and grimaced. That was her answer right here. Dreams were dreams, but reality was a baby crying, a kennel waiting to be cleaned, hungry dogs to be fed and groomed. Reality was Aunt Daisy's arthritis and Tim's need to find his niche. Reality was being in charge and being responsible, doing what had to be done, and sometimes pushing the dreams aside.

Nursing Amber a few minutes later, Sam once again allowed her thoughts to wander. The cream silk dress was lying on a chair in her bedroom; and the red shoes sat neatly on the floor of her closet. Would she wear them again? Would there ever be another night as magical as the one she had shared with Jeff?

This time Jeff wasn't embarrassed to see Sam's partly exposed breasts as he stood outside her bedroom. Only hours earlier, he'd shared the ultimate intimacies with this woman, and now he watched as she nursed her daughter, a tender, loving smile playing across his lips.

As though she felt him, Sam looked up, and an answering smile warmed her face.

"Hi," she said, sounding almost shy.

"Hi, yourself. Daisy told me where you were, and that it was okay to come up. You know, I think this is one of the most beautiful sights I've ever seen. You don't mind me watching, do you?"

Sam laughed joyfully. "Not if Amber doesn't."

"Ah, Amber," Jeff murmured, sitting down across from Sam. "Do you have any idea what a lucky little girl you are to have such a beautiful, loving mama?"

Sam's eyes darkened. She couldn't forget the harsh words she and Jeff had exchanged on the way home from Atlantic City. "Unless I smother her the way I did Tim," she said.

Jeff shook his head. "You misunderstood me, Sam. I was only trying to make you see that . . ."

Sam nodded, absently patting Amber's bottom as the baby shifted slightly.

"They're my family, Jeff. I did what I thought was best. If I made mistakes . . . well, they were loving mistakes. I'm not going to beat myself up over them, and I won't allow anyone else to do that to me, either."

"Mom? Hey, Mom, there's something wrong with one of the pups. Can you come down?"

Instantly alert, Sam looked at the infant drowsing against her breast. Hurriedly, she closed her blouse and put the baby into Jeff's outstretched arms. Tim sounded worried.

"Go ahead," Jeff said. "Go see what's going on. I'll take care of Amber."

Sam looked at the dark-haired man and the tiny baby. She had no qualms about leaving her precious little girl with Jeff, and that told her more clearly than anything else that she'd fallen in love. But there were still a lot of hurdles to jump, a mountain of doubts to climb.

"Thanks," she said quickly. "I'll be back as soon as I can."

"What's wrong?" she questioned Tim as

they hurried out to the kennels. "What happened?"

"I don't know," Tim said. "One of the little females is kind of limp and lethargic. She was fine yesterday, but when I picked her up just now she felt really warm."

Sam's heart was pounding. It could be a number of things, maybe serious, maybe not, but one thing was for sure: She had to isolate the sick pup from the others immediately.

Sam removed the female from the whelping box and carried it a few feet away. She held the tiny animal in her hands and examined it. Tim was right; the pup did feel warm, so chances were it was running a temperature, which would indicate some kind of infection. But what? Hopefully not something contagious that would spread to all the others, and maybe even the bitch.

"Tim, can you stay here and hold down the fort while I run this little one to the vet?"

"Sure, Mom, that's no problem. Here, let me get you a box to put her in."

Moments later, Sam was backing out of the driveway, leaving Tim to tell Jeff and Daisy where she'd gone. More vet's bills, she thought worriedly. It almost seemed like every time she took one step forward, she took three backwards. Was she fighting a losing battle? Maybe her dream of having a successful breeding kennel was just that . . . a dream.

An hour and a half later, Sam was home, armed with a prescription for the sick pup and the vet's assurances that it was just a flu-type virus and not anything to be too concerned about. She felt a little better, but doubts still tugged at her. Was she being selfish to put so much time and energy into the kennels? She knew she'd neglected Daisy in order to keep up with everything. Was she prepared to do the same with Amber? She'd thought she could do everything, be everything to all of them, but she was starting to realize that the load was too heavy. She couldn't do it all alone. But who would help her? Tim was on the verge of finding his own way in life and Aunt Daisy was too fragile to be much help.

After settling the pup in a separate box, away from the others in its litter, Sam went up to the house feeling unsettled.

Jeff met her at the front door. "Everything okay?" he asked.

Sam nodded. "It's just a virus. The pup should be back to normal in two or three days. But it gave me a scare. I was afraid it might be something serious that would go through the whole kennel. Was Amber okay? I didn't mean to dump her on you that way."

FULL BLOOM

Jeff put his arm around Sam's waist casually. "Everything is fine. Amber and Aunt Daisy are both napping. Tim finished what he had to do in the kennel so I sent him to the store for a steak and salad fixings. How does that sound?"

Sam looked up at Jeff and grinned. "Are you cooking?"

Jeff shrugged. "Why not? I'm a liberated man. And I was thinking that after dinner we could . . ."

"Whoa, hold on there, Commander. Do you think maybe we're moving too fast?" Sharing dinner and afterwards with Jeff sounded wonderful, but Sam was still afraid of assuming too much. Maybe Jeff was just floating in a hazy, lovely afterglow. Maybe when things calmed down—when he had a chance to think things through—he'd want to fly to the other side of the country.

"I want to be with you, Sam," Jeff said solemnly. "Isn't that enough for now?"

Sam pushed her hair away from her face, letting the meaning of Jeff's words sink in. And she decided that maybe it was time to start living life one day at a time . . . maybe it was time to live in the present and stop worrying so much about the future. But she'd done that for so long, it would be a hard habit to break.

She nodded, then stood on tiptoe and let her lips touch Jeff's. "It's enough," she said, and she pushed the nagging little worries away. It had to be enough.

That evening, as soon as they'd eaten dinner, Tim decided to take Aunt Daisy out for ice cream. Since it was the first time he'd ever done anything like that, Sam was just a tiny bit suspicious.

"Did you put him up to that?" she demanded of Jeff when they were comfortably settled in the living room with coffee and fresh fruit.

Jeff put his mug on the table and gathered Sam into his arms. He buried his nose in her hair and sighed appreciatively.

"I swear I didn't have a thing to do with it," he said. "Maybe Tim is just discovering that Aunt Daisy isn't so bad after all. Or maybe," he whispered, nuzzling her happily, "he felt the sparks between us."

"Maybe," Sam said. "I caught them both staring at me several times today. Him and Aunt Daisy. Do you think they know that we . . ."

Sam couldn't finish her sentence. Aunt Daisy might be outspoken now, but she had brought Sam up with strict morals. It was hard for Sam to imagine her son and aunt knowing that she and Jeff had been intimate.

Jeff chuckled. "Just relax and enjoy it, honey," he said. "You deserve a little pleasure and freedom, and I doubt if Tim or Daisy are going to criticize us. All they want is your happiness."

He pushed her away a little and looked at her intently. "You need to be spoiled. You give too much of yourself away, Samantha. If you keep on this way, soon there'll be nothing left. You have to take time off, do something for yourself once in awhile."

A sinking feeling was sweeping over Sam. It was nice that Jeff cared about her, but it was all too plain that he strongly disapproved of her devotion to her family. He thought she did too much, assumed too many responsibilities, but what choice did she have? Her family needed her. And if Jeff couldn't accept that . . .

"Did you shirk your duty to your father, Jeff?" she asked quietly, praying that he would understand.

Jeff looked startled. What did his father have to do with Sam's overblown sense of responsibility? "Sam, I don't think we're talking about the same thing. My father became totally helpless, and since there wasn't anyone else I *had* to take over. Your situation is different." He hesitated a minute. He knew Sam was sensitive about her family situation, and at the first hint of criticism she became defensive. Last night they'd almost gotten into a major fight. But he had to make her see what she was doing. He spoke gently. "I know your intentions are the very best, Sam," he began, "but I can't help wondering if subconsciously you want to keep Tim and Aunt Daisy dependent on you so that you can feel needed. Tim is an intelligent adult, not a little boy, and Aunt Daisy isn't nearly as helpless as you make her out to be. She was taking far too much medication, and it nearly turned her into a vegetable. I know you meant well, but . . ."

Jeff stopped, wishing he could suck back in the words he'd just spoken. Sam looked stricken, and her green eyes glittered with tears. She looked a lot like the way she had the day he'd met her at the beach and told her his summer vacation was over. "Sam, I didn't mean . . ."

"I think I know what you meant," she said softly. "You don't understand how I feel about my family. You think I should back off and let them do their own thing, right? Just live my life and not give either of them a second thought, right?"

"No, I . . . that's not what I meant at all, Sam. I was just trying to make you see that you could probably ease off just a little and everybody would be fine."

Jeff looked at Sam and felt his insides twist into a knot of frustration. He saw the glint of tears in her lovely eyes, the sad droop of her mouth, the way her shoulders sagged. The last thing he wanted to do was cause her pain. If he hadn't known it before, he knew it now. He loved this woman. He didn't just want to make love to her, he wanted to be her love. And yes, he wanted some of her compassionate concern for himself.

"Please listen to me, Samantha," he said urgently. "I understand why you feel the way you do. It's because of your mother, the way she left you. You're determined to make up to Tim for being neglected by his father and you're hell-bent on paying Daisy back for all the sacrifices she made in your behalf, but what you're not seeing is that neither Tim nor Daisy want to sit in a corner and be taken care of. Daisy needs and wants to be involved with life. And Tim is a man now, not a little boy. He should be making his own decisions, his own choices, right or wrong. It's the only way he'll ever mature."

Sam had gone beyond hurt; now she was furious. Her body was rigid and her eyes glittered like emerald ice. Jeff was wrong. She wanted nothing more than to see Tim go out on his own and build a life for himself, and she would certainly never do anything to make Daisy feel useless, but good grief, at her aunt's age there were certain physical limitations. All she had ever wanted to do was protect her family and keep them safe. How could that be wrong? And if Jeff couldn't understand how she felt about her family, what kind of relationship could they hope to have? Maybe it had been doomed from the beginning, she decided. Maybe they were both too old and set in their ways to accommodate another lifestyle. Jeff would always want to take charge, and she was used to holding the reins. They would always clash. There would be no peace or tranquillity, no happily ever after.

"You'd better go home, Jeff," she said, refusing to meet his eyes and shrugging away when he reached out to touch her. What did he know about families, anyway? And what right did he have to barge into her life and turn everything upside down?

"Sam, wait! Don't do this! Don't shut me out. We need to talk this through."

"There isn't anything to talk about," Sam said dully. "You just don't understand."

Jeff wanted to argue. He wanted to do something, anything, to make Sam see things as they actually were, but he sensed that she wouldn't hear anything he had to say. Sighing heavily, Jeff left.

It was very late when Sam slipped into bed. Tears stung her eyelids as she thought of everything that had happened in the past two days: the wonderful, magical hours she'd spent with Jeff, the dreams she'd dared to dream, and now this—Jeff ripping her to shreds with ugly, hateful words.

She lay wide awake, her head aching, a kaleidoscope of thoughts spinning in her brain. Jeff couldn't be right, could he? Maybe she had been a little overprotective of her aunt, but she'd never made the elderly woman feel useless, had she? And why on earth would she want to stifle the process of Tim's maturation?

He'd made her sound like a neurotic middle-aged woman who was afraid to let go.

Fifteen

Tim dropped his bombshell the next morning. "Mom, I'm going to move out," he said. "My friend Rod shares a house with a guy, and they're looking for another roommate. I've got a job lined up at a hardware store, and as soon as I can save up some money, I want to go to computer school."

"You're moving out? When did you decide this? Are you sure you can pay rent and your share of the utilities on what you'll make?"

Suddenly, Jeff's words came back to haunt her. Was she doing it again? Holding Tim back? Making him dependent?

She was his mother, but she wasn't his keeper. Years ago, when her husband had shirked his parental responsibilities, Sam had felt compelled to be both father and mother to her son. And now she was still doing it, with Tim all grown up and a good three inches taller than she was. She wasn't treating him like an equal. She was smothering him!

She looked across the table, saw Tim's earnest, almost pleading look. Set me free, his eyes seemed to be saying. Cut the strings once and for all. Something twisted inside her. She wanted to do it, but she just couldn't. Tim had never been on his own. What if he couldn't make it? What if he got in with the wrong crowd? What if he couldn't keep his job?

"Tim, maybe you shouldn't do anything hasty," she cautioned. "Why not wait a few months . . . see how the job goes . . ."

Tim's face twisted and his eyes darkened with a bleak look of disappointment. His shoulders slumped and he pushed back his chair angrily. "I should have known you'd throw a dozen roadblocks in front of me! Why do I keep on thinking that one of these days things will be different? Well, this time it is going to be different, Mom. I don't know why you're so determined to act like I'm a helpless little baby, but I won't let you do it anymore! I don't need your permission, and I am moving out! It's past time I took care of my own life. Jeff is right; it's time I take charge of my future!"

"My goodness, what's all this shouting about?" Aunt Daisy shuffled into the kitchen, her old flannel wrapper held closed with a length of clothesline. Despite the new wardrobe she'd acquired for her visits to the senior citizens' center, Aunt Daisy still got herself up in some strange-looking outfits when she was lounging around the house. Any other time Sam would have had to smother a smile at her aunt's comic appearance, but not now. She was too upset.

"Tim, wait!" she cried.

"No! No more!" Tim cried. "I've waited too long already. I guess this is what Jeff meant when he said I had to stand up and be a man."

Jeff! So he was behind all this! Sam knew she shouldn't be surprised, but there was a funny, hollow feeling in her chest. How could Jeff do something like this? He knew how she felt about Tim, how much she loved her son and worried about him. How could deliberately alienate Tim this way? And what right did he have to interfere, anyway?

"I demand to know what is going on here," Aunt Daisy said sharply. "What are you and Timothy arguing about, dear?"

"We . . . we're not fighting, Aunt Daisy," Sam said quickly. The last thing she wanted was to upset her aunt.

"Now don't you fib to me, Sammy girl!" Aunt Daisy said tartly, her faded blue eyes unusually bright. "I know a spat when I see one, and I insist that you tell me what is going on here! Aren't I a member of this family?"

"Oh, Aunt Daisy, of course you are! I didn't mean to shut you out. I just didn't want to upset you."

Daisy sniffed, then relaxed. The frown on her wrinkled face eased into a sympathetic smile. "I know, honey. You're just trying to protect me, but I don't want to be protected anymore. I'm tougher than I look. And since I've been going to the senior center I feel like a girl again." She laughed. "Well, maybe not a girl, but I do feel better. My, I'm so glad Jim came along and talked me into going to the center and making some new friends."

Sam's head was spinning. Was she going crazy? Had everything she'd tried to do been wrong? Had she hurt her family when all she wanted to do was take care of them? She forced herself to look at her aunt objectively. She saw a frail elderly woman, but a woman whose eyes now sparkled with a lively intelligence, a woman who simply wasn't content to sit in a rocking chair and stagnate. Sure, she was a little eccentric, but so what? She was sweet and kind and giving, and she deserved better than to be pushed aside and left to rot.

"Aunt Daisy, I . . . don't know what to say."

Daisy patted Sam's hand and smiled. "Don't

say anything, girl. You're too upset right now to make any sense. You just get yourself together and take care of that baby of yours. She's the one who needs you now."

Leaving Aunt Daisy at the kitchen table, Sam hurried up to the nursery to take care of Amber. Her aunt was right; Amber did need her, but for how long? And when the time came to let go, would she be able to? She nursed the baby with tears streaming down her cheeks. She'd only meant to take care of her family, but had she done more harm than good?

"Where is she, Daisy?" Jeff demanded, bursting into the kitchen a few minutes later.

Daisy raised her eyebrows. "My, what's gotten into you, Jake? Had a few too many? You look like you've got a hangover."

For the first time Jeff failed to smile at Daisy's outrageous remarks. He had only one thing on his mind: Samantha. He had to see her, talk to her.

"Where is she?" he repeated, his mouth drawn into a tight, thin line.

"She's upstairs with the baby, but I'm not sure . . ."

Jeff didn't stick around to hear the rest of

what Daisy had to say. He took the stairs two at a time.

"Sam? Samantha, we have to talk. We can't leave things like this. I have to explain . . ."

Sam turned slowly, and Jeff instantly saw that she had been crying. Damn Tim for blurting out the things they'd discussed the other day! Now Sam was probably convinced that he was trying to control her, but it wasn't like that at all! Damn!

"Look, Sam, you've got to listen to me. I don't think you understand what . . ."

"Oh, I understand all right," Sam said quietly, her voice so deadly, it chilled Jeff to the bone. "You don't think much of me, do you?" She didn't add that she didn't think much of herself at the moment. Her mind was whirling with confusion and her head was splitting. Why had she ever dared to hope that there could be something special between her and Jeff? Maybe she was just a manipulative, domineering woman who would end up alone and lonely. Maybe everything Jeff had said was right, but how could she know?

"You'd better leave," she said. "I'll have Tim bring a check over to you later." *Go before I make a complete idiot of myself and beg you to stay, before I sob all over your sweater and . . .* despite the pain Sam was experiencing, she could still feel the thrill of the moment Jeff had claimed her for his own. But maybe it wasn't the same for him. How could she trust her feelings anymore? How could she know what was right when her whole life had been wrong? Forty-six years down the drain, and nothing could be changed. She closed her eyes, but she could still smell him, the clean, masculine scent that made her head spin. She could taste him on her lips, feel his tongue inside her mouth, his hands moving slowly over her body, his heart beating next to hers. . . .

"Your deposit on the house, remember? You wanted it back so you could look for another place to live." Her voice came out stronger than she felt. "Well, I can afford to give it to you now, Jeff," she said. "You're free to go."

"Sam, don't be ridiculous! That was a long time ago. Everything is different now. I don't want the damn deposit back and I don't want to go away!"

She almost weakened. He was so near, and she wanted him so much! She wanted him to stay by her side, to live with her and love her and be the father her little girl needed. But she'd been the one in charge for so long, and maybe she wouldn't be able to relinquish her position of authority, even to Jeff. And he'd never understand how she felt.

"No, it's best this way," she murmured. "We're too different, you and I. It just . . . wouldn't work."

Jeff was stunned. Then he got angry. Samantha was just about the stubbornest female he'd ever laid eyes on! He didn't blame her for being hurt and angry. He knew he'd bungled things pretty badly, but he was trying to set things right, and if Sam thought he was going to turn tail and skitter off like a spooked jackrabbit, she had another think coming. He'd never retreated in his life and he wasn't about to start now!

Squaring his shoulders and firming his jaw, Jeff moved across the room, bent down, and gripped Sam by the shoulders. She tried to twist away, but he held firm and forced her to look at him. "I don't think you really mean that, Sam," he said. His pulse started to pound as the heat of her lovely body seared him. Lord, but she affected him like no other woman ever had! But this was no time to indulge his body's physical desires. He had to make Sam listen to reason. "Look, I can understand why you're angry. I know it seems like I'm butting in where I don't belong, but I only wanted to help. Sometimes a person on the outside can see things the insiders can't. Tim wants to make it on his own, Sam, and he'll be okay. And Daisy doesn't want to be shielded from life."

Sam twisted away from Jeff. She stood up slowly and carefully laid Amber in her cradle. "Your interference with Tim is only part of this," she muttered. "You'll never understand how I feel about my family. It would always come between us."

Her breathing was ragged, and she knew it was only a matter of minutes before she started to cry. And that, she decided, with what was left of her dignity, was something she was definitely not going to do in front of the perfect and wonderful Commander Jeffrey Brooks! She had to get rid of him before the tears broke loose and drowned them both. "Go away," she said. "Just leave me alone. I don't need you or your interfering ways in my life!"

Jeff's arms fell to his sides. He stood for a moment, his shoulders slumped; then he turned away. But he wasn't leaving, no matter what Sam said!

Sixteen

Jeff paced around the cottage. His muscles were tense and taut, and his head felt as though someone had thrown a brick at him, but he wasn't prepared to pack up and leave, not with Sam feeling the way she felt right now. She was hurt, deep down to her core, hurt by his careless words, his holier-than-thou attitude, his high-handed manner of taking charge. Who did he think he was, anyway, telling her she was handling her family all wrong? So what if he meant well? That wouldn't erase the pain from her eyes.

A sudden, sharp knock on the front door stilled Jeff's nervous movements. Tim come to commiserate?

He opened the door and felt like someone had knocked the wind out of him. Sam. Stunningly lovely in her righteous anger. Sam. The woman he'd fallen head over heels in love with when he'd thought all that was behind him.

Sam. The loving mother of the precious little girl he wanted for his own.

"Sam?" His voice was a hoarse croak. "Did you change your mind?"

"No. I want you to leave, Jeff, as soon as possible. It'll be better that way."

"For who?" Jeff asked. His heart seemed to stop beating as he waited for her answer. The walls of the cottage closed in on him, and the spicy apple tobacco scent clogged his nostrils.

"For ever . . . all of us," Sam said quietly. She stood on the front steps, looking pale and unhappy but very determined.

"I have a lease," Jeff said. "It's for a year, and I've only been here for a few months."

Sam's gaze shifted. "I had hoped we could handle this situation like mature adults. What does a lease matter when we're making each other miserable?"

"Are you miserable, Sam?" Jeff asked. "You seemed pretty happy the other night." He saw the memories darken her eyes, saw the remembered magic sweep down over her, and when she shivered he rejoiced.

"I'm staying, Sam," he said quietly. "I don't intend to leave this way. The only way you'll get me out is with a court order."

"You . . . you'd really do that? Stay here when you know how I feel?"

Jeff allowed himself the pleasure of smiling. "That's just it, Sam," he said. "Right now you don't know how you feel. I plan to stick around until you do."

Sam winced. "And then? What then?"

"We'll see," Jeff said. "When the time comes we'll see."

Daisy was dressed and waiting the next morning when Jeff knocked on the door. "Come on in, Jake," she said. "Want some coffee?"

"Thanks, but I've had my quota," Jeff replied. "Look, maybe we'd better just get on our way. It's probably better right now if I don't run into Samantha."

Daisy picked up her purse and a lacy shawl one of her new friends at the center had crocheted. She nodded wisely. "Smart move, Jeremy," she said.

"What's on the agenda today?" Jeff asked when Daisy was comfortably settled beside him in the Blazer.

"Actually, I don't want to go directly to the center," Daisy said as a faint tinge of pink colored her cheeks. "I promised Ralph I'd try to come by his place so we can talk, you know, and make some plans. You don't mind dropping me off there, do you, Jim?"

Jeff grinned. "Gonna do a little sparking, Aunt Daisy?" he teased. "I'll bet Sam wouldn't approve."

"That's precisely why I didn't tell her where I was going," Daisy said, lifting her chin stubbornly. "That fool girl thinks I'm dead from the neck down. I'd sure like to be around to see what she's like at my age. Why, I'll bet . . ."

"I know there's plenty of life in you, Daisy," Jeff interrupted. He chuckled. "And that goes double for Ralph. I've seen how tight he holds you when you're dancing."

Daisy's wrinkled face sobered. "Do you think it's foolish, Jake? Am I too old to look for a second chance at happiness? Sometimes I think maybe Sammy's right. Maybe it's crazy for me to be thinking of getting married. My arthritis is a bitch sometimes, you know."

Jeff nearly strangled as he struggled not to laugh. "What about Ralph? He has arthritis, too, doesn't he? It's not slowing him down, is it?"

"Not so I can see it," Daisy said, giggling like a schoolgirl. "My, that man is sure a good kisser! Makes my toes curl right up, and that's a fact, Jeremy!"

Jeff laughed. "Then what more do you need, Daisy? I say go for it!"

After dropping Daisy off at Ralph's beachfront home, Jeff drove back to Wildwood to the center. He was scheduled to help Frank and the others build shelves for the crafts they would display and sell. He was truly amazed at the beautiful craftsmanship of some of the items he'd seen so far. The seniors were certainly a talented group.

"Daisy and Ralph making plans?" Frank asked, after handing Jeff a well-used carpenter's apron. "Those two make a nice couple."

Jeff nodded and stood back to appraise a solid oak shelf. "I think so," he agreed, "but Daisy's a little uncertain. She's worried about being too old for romance."

"Nonsense!" Frank said. "I expect to be looking at pretty women when I'm a hundred! We're as young as we feel, and right now I feel like a teenager!"

Jeff grinned and began nailing boards into place. Frank was the perfect example of an active senior. He felt a pang wishing his dad could have had this kind of companionship.

* * *

Ralph and Daisy sat on the back porch swing, slowly rocking to and fro. Now and then a bird flew to one of the many feeders Ralph had placed around the yard, and the scent of the first rambler roses drifted through the air.

"This is lovely," Daisy said softly. "I like your home, Ralph."

"Then stop putting me off, woman," Ralph scolded. "Marry me and put me out of my misery. It's lonely here all by myself."

"But what if we're too old and cantankerous to adjust?" Daisy asked. "I'm used to sprawling across the whole bed."

Ralph grunted. "We'll buy a new bed; a king-sized one. That should give two scrawny old birds like us plenty of room."

"Sammy says I snore," Daisy added worriedly.

"So do I," Ralph confessed. He smiled and lifted Daisy's chin so she had to look at him. "I'll put up with you if you'll put up with me. How about it?"

"I want to," Daisy admitted, "but I can't help feeling a little foolish. Brides are supposed to be young and slender and perky. I lost all of that a long time ago, Ralph."

"And I'm not the stud I was forty years ago, Daisy, but when I've got you cuddled in my arms like this I feel like anything is possible."

He gave her a wicked wink and a little squeeze. "Wouldn't it be fun to find out?"

"You really want to do it?" Daisy asked. She was trembling like a girl, and there was a warmth in the pit of her stomach she hadn't felt in years.

Ralph kissed his future bride gently, then reared back to look at her. "Daisy, my girl, you're the prettiest thing I've seen in a month of Sundays. Now say yes so we can get on with it!"

"Yes!" Daisy said, her eyes locked with Ralph's. "Yes!"

Tim and Sam worked around the kennels. It seemed abnormally quiet with both Jeff and Aunt Daisy out for the day.

"Daisy's really getting into the senior citizen thing, isn't she?" Tim asked as he slowly and carefully brushed Polar Princess. "She's looking good these days."

"Yes. I'm happy about that." Sam kept her face turned away from her son so he wouldn't see the sadness in her eyes. She knew it was there; it stabbed her every time she looked in the mirror. She and Jeff were keeping an armed truce. When he wasn't chauffeuring Daisy somewhere he stayed in his cottage, and Sam refrained from looking across the road when she was in the yard. At least most of the time she did, but sometimes, like now, and at night alone in her bed, she couldn't help thinking of him and wishing that things could be different. But she'd suffered the pain of an unhappy marriage for many years, and she wasn't up for that agony again. And how in the world could she and Jeff be happy together? They'd always pull in different directions the way she and Doug had, wouldn't they?

"Does Aunt Daisy really have a boyfriend?" Tim asked, putting down the brush and comb and giving Princess a pat. "Gosh, I can't picture that, can you?"

Sam shook her head. "I thought at her age she'd be content to be a spectator to life, but instead she seems to want to jump right in and sample everything that's out there."

Tim laughed. "When are we going to meet her beau? That's what they called boyfriends in her day, isn't it?"

Sam stood up and stretched her cramped muscles. "According to Jeff, Ralph is a paragon of virtue. Jeff swears we don't have anything to worry about in that department. It seems Ralph has a nice little house in Cape May right across from the beach, and is comfortably fixed financially."

Despite herself, Sam grinned. "Aunt Daisy thinks living across from the beach would be romantic. Waves crashing against the shore and all that, I suppose."

Tim laughed and shook his head. "Life is full of surprises, isn't it, Mom?"

He hadn't said anything about the girl he'd met recently; one shock at a time was enough for his mom to digest. As he put the grooming supplies back where they belonged, Tim let his thoughts drift to Marnie. She was special, all right, the nicest girl he'd ever met, and when she smiled at him . . . well, it was like Fourth of July and Christmas all rolled into one. He was pretty sure she was the one for him, but he was trying to take things slow and easy, as Jeff had advised. He trusted the commander's judgment, and Jeff didn't preach. He just stated his views and allowed you to make up your own mind. But Tim knew he was right. Choosing the girl you wanted to spend your life with was serious business. Even as a little kid he'd known there was something vitally important missing from his parents' marriage. He wanted more when he married, so he was going to be very careful and take things slow.

* * *

Sam finished cleaning the runs. Jeff was staying out of her way in a physical sense, but in other ways he was insinuating himself into her life, and there was nothing she could do to stop it. Aunt Daisy thought he should be nominated for sainthood, Tim thought he could do no wrong, and even little Amber was enamored of him. So how on earth could she put the man out of her mind? Sometimes she felt like her entire family was ganging up on her, forcing her to admit feelings she . . . but they weren't real. That's what she had to keep reminding herself. What she felt for Jeff was just a foolish infatuation. She'd been alone for months, and lonely for years before that. It was only natural that she would respond to a handsome, caring, considerate man. Only normal that her deprived hormones would go into overdrive when that same man was constantly underfoot. She really did have to figure out a way to make him leave, but how? He remained adamant about staying through his lease, a lease that still had almost nine months to run. Sam groaned. Nine months! She'd be in a straitjacket by then, if she didn't jump off the nearest cliff in the meantime.

* * *

"How'd it go?" Jeff asked as he pulled out of Ralph's driveway. "Did you two get everything settled?"

"Just about," Daisy admitted, a blush coloring her cheeks. "Ralph seems to think we can be happy together." She shrugged and grinned mischievously. "He even thinks I'm pretty. I knew he was a blind old coot, but what the heck? It's still nice to hear."

They rode the rest of the way home in comfortable silence.

Jeff was pleasantly tired from his morning's labors. The craft shop was coming along nicely. He believed, along with Frank, that the center would be able to raise enough money to help with their expenses through the shop. Once the local people saw what the seniors had to offer, he was convinced the shop would prosper.

If only he could work things out with Sam as easily as he was working with the seniors. But maybe Sam was right; maybe he was crazy to hang on here and hope that in time Sam would accept his presence in her life, maybe even crave it. Were they really too different? But that was crazy. Everyone knew that opposites attract. It was no wonder he was batty about Sam, and wouldn't their differences complement one another? Wouldn't Sam's somewhat overblown sense of responsibility counter Jeff's tendency to look the other way? Not that he'd done much of that since coming to Cape May. How could he look the other way when Daisy had been crying out for help? Or when Sam desperately needed a sympathetic labor coach, or when Tim was falling asleep on the sofa when he was supposed to be baby-sitting Amber? Or when he saw Sam driving herself into a mental and physical breakdown? How could anyone turn the other way?

"So what do you think, Jake?" Aunt Daisy asked, breaking into his thoughts. "Should I wear white for this wedding, or would that be pushing it?"

Seventeen

Jeff stood in his front yard, staring across the road to Sam's kennels. He was waiting for her to come out of the house and enter the kennels. And when she did, if she was alone, he was going to march right over and kiss some sense into her.

It had been two weeks since their big blowup, since Sam had told him in no uncertain terms to get out of her life. Well, he hadn't, and he wasn't going to, at least not until he'd exhausted every possible means of getting her to admit that she cared for him as much as he cared for her.

In his calmer, more rational moments, Jeff knew that a large part of Sam's reluctance was fear—fear that she'd be hurt again, as she had been in her first marriage, and an even deeper, more painful fear that she might be abandoned as she had been as a child. Well, he'd never do either. Unless he was forcibly kidnapped and dragged kicking and screaming, there was no way he would ever abandon Sam and Amber. Hell, right now he was aching to be part of their lives. His arms actually itched to hold that little baby, to raise her high in the air and watch her giggle. And holding Sam had been one stair step away from heaven. He wanted to show her that he wasn't the kind of man to turn tail and run when the going got rough. He wanted to prove to her that he could be counted on in good times and bad, and most of all he wanted her to look at him the way she had that night in Atlantic City, with her eyes filled with love and trust and pure, sweet pleasure.

Sighing, Jeff drained his coffee mug and turned toward the house for a refill. Then he saw Sam step outside Aunt Daisy's kitchen door.

She wore jeans and a soft T-shirt the color of buttercups. Her red-brown hair was pinned back from her face and, as usual, Amber was riding in a carrier on her back.

Jeff's heart turned over. Such motherly devotion; Amber was a very lucky baby. But he wanted some of that love for himself, wanted Sam to realize she was a woman as well as a mother.

He waited until she disappeared inside the

kennels, then strode across the road after her. Procrastination was a mortal sin; Aunt Daisy had told him so.

"Good morning, Sam," he called as soon as he entered the kennels. "Beautiful day, isn't it?"

She whirled, startled, her eyes wide and full of questions. "You! What are . . ."

"I'm just being neighborly," Jeff said. "After all, we are still neighbors. Let's see, I have eight months, three weeks, and two days left on my lease. That means we'll probably see each other at least . . ."

Sam put down the dishes she'd been holding and placed her hands on her hips.

Jeff could hear Amber babbling in the background.

"This is ridiculous and childish," Sam said. "I don't understand why you won't just take your check and leave."

Jeff shook his head. "I can't," he said. "I'm not a quitter. It's not in my genetic makeup. And in the service I was trained to stay and fight." He smiled and shook his head again. "I'm afraid I never learned how to retreat."

Sam sighed. "So where does that leave us?" Her initial anger had evaporated a long time ago, but she wasn't about to let Jeff know that. She decided a little humble pie would do him a world of good. "I'm too busy to stand around and spar with you," she said. "I have a family to look after and a kennel to run."

"Precisely," Jeff said, nodding solemnly. "And I'm here to help. Sooner or later you're bound to realize what a sterling character I am, and when that happens we can start fresh."

"You really want to help?" Sam asked, her green eyes narrowing suspiciously. A little voice warned her that she was treading on shifty sand, but ignored it and faced Jeff boldly. "You'll do whatever I ask you to do?"

Jeff looked a little wary as his dark eyes met Sam's intent, penetrating gaze. "Well . . ."

"All or nothing," Sam said, struggling not to laugh. "I don't do things halfway."

"All right. I'm in for one hundred percent. All the way."

"Good."

"There's just one thing," Jeff said, advancing on Sam in a very determined way.

"What?"

"I think a kiss is in order to seal our bargain."

"Oh, I don't think . . ."

"That's right," Jeff said huskily, as he quite effectively cut off Sam's protest. "Don't think. Just let yourself feel."

He drew her into his arms then, baby and all. He was careful not to jostle Amber, but he had the feeling that if the innocent baby had any idea what was going on, she would be all for it. Then he let his lips touch Sam's mouth, let his tongue ever so lightly skim across her teeth. She opened to him instantly, as if she'd been as hungry for his touch as he had been for hers.

Instinctively, Sam raised her arms and clasped her hands around Jeff's neck. Her whole body felt as if it was melting. She knew if she didn't hang on tight she'd slide right down Jeff's body and puddle on the kennel floor in a soggy heap. I'm putty in his hands, she thought weakly as the warm, delicious sensations swept over her. She forgot everything for the moment: the baby riding in the carrier on her back, Aunt Daisy having a boyfriend, Tim's new independence. It was all pushed aside by the heaven of Jeff's touch.

He ached to do more than kiss her. He would have taken her right there in the warm, doggy-smelling kennel if it had not been for the baby riding on her back and the possibility of Tim bursting in on them at any moment. So a kiss would have to do for now. Knowing that was all he was going to get, Jeff was determined to make it a good one.

It seemed to go on forever, the wild, wanton plundering of her lips, the brush of his warm, strong hands on her breasts, the white-hot heat that began to build down low in her belly. Sam knew she should push Jeff away; Tim would be coming out at any minute. But it felt so good to be held and caressed this way. Instead of struggling away, she found herself pushing closer to Jeff, desperately draining every drop of feeling from what she knew would be an all-too-brief embrace. It must be as Ellen said: Her hormones were completely out of control.

Jeff heard the cheerful whistle first. It registered in his brain, then sent signals to his inflamed body. Reluctantly, he lifted his lips from Sam's moist, softened mouth. Gently, he put her and the baby aside, and when Tim entered the kennels a few minutes later all he saw were two slightly flushed individuals.

" 'Morning. Hey, Jeff, great to see you. What are you doing here?"

Jeff grinned. He felt great, even if his body was protesting the deprivation of Sam's soft curves. "I just stopped by to offer my services as a kennel hand," he said. "I decided I need more physical exercise. Sitting in front of that computer is hard on the body."

Tim nodded. "I guess, but it sure stimulates the mind, doesn't it?"

"I suppose it depends on what you're doing with it," Jeff said. "Well, Sam, what do you want me to do first?"

"The runs need to be disinfected," she said evenly, looking more composed than she had a moment before. "You know where the cleaning supplies are, don't you?"

"Sure. Uh, all the runs?"

"All of them," Sam said firmly.

When she turned and walked away Sam tried to keep her shoulders from shaking with laughter, but it was hard. So Jeff thought he could kiss her into submission, did he? Well, two could play the same game. If Jeff needed physical exercise, she was just the woman to see that he got it!

Daisy hurriedly slipped the bridal magazine under the sofa pillow. If Sam caught her ogling ruffles and lace, she'd never hear the end of it. Still, there was nothing wrong with a lady looking a little festive at her own wedding, was there? And what did age matter anyway? She was still a size twelve, and that wasn't bad for an old lady. Not having had any babies, she'd never had to worry about losing her figure. A fleeting feeling of sadness washed over Daisy as she remembered the day when she and Harold had learned they could never be parents. It had been one of the saddest days of their lives, but their deep and abiding love for one another had carried them through the sadness and grief back into the sunshine. They'd had a good life, despite the disappointment of being childless. Then Harold had died, and her sister had left Sammy on her doorstep. Like a gift from heaven, Sammy was, Daisy remembered. The sweetest, bravest little girl on earth. And now the tables were turned and Sammy was taking care of her old aunt. Well, maybe it wouldn't be for much longer. Daisy decided she felt better, stronger and more alive than she had in years. It was because of Ralph and dear Jeremy and her new friends at the center. Oh, Sam was a sweetheart and would always be the core of her heart, but Daisy knew she needed more. She needed more than sitting in front of a television and listening to some old woman talk about sex. She needed to be out there doing! She wondered if Susan would help her pick out a wedding nightgown.

"Aunt Daisy? Where are you?"

Daisy chuckled. Just in the nick of time, she thought, patting the sofa cushion fondly.

Picking out her wedding dress would have to wait for another time. "In the living room, Sammy girl," she called. "I'm just finishing my dusting."

"Honestly, Mom, you're treating Jeff like a regular hired hand, and he's not even getting paid!" Tim speared a pickle and slid it between the bread of his tuna sandwich at lunch. "Do you think that's right, Aunt Daisy?"

"Well, I . . ."

"He volunteered," Sam said quickly. "It was all his idea."

"What I want to know is, why?" Tim insisted. "I mean, the guy is a former naval commander, for pete's sake, and he's writing a book. Why would he want to clean out smelly dog kennels?"

Sam smiled, shrugged, and bit into her tuna sandwich. "Who knows?"

I do, Daisy thought, smothering a wicked chuckle. Jake will do whatever he has to do to worm his way into Sammy's life and heart. She lowered her head so Sammy and Tim wouldn't see her joy. Way to go, Jack! she cheered silently.

"I'm planning to take Stormy, Frosty, and Son of Sam's Pride," Sam said, pointing to a seven-month-old Samoyed pup that Tim was grooming.

"He's a beauty," Jeff said, noting the dog's strong, solid build and the thick, beautiful coat. "And if he takes any prizes, it will go toward his eventual championship, right?"

"Right, if he proves to be show quality. See, it's more than just his looks that will win him points. A champion has to have a certain presence, a willingness to work in the ring, a desire to prance around in front of thousands of people. Some dogs just don't show well, even if they have the physical attributes the judges look for."

"So what you're saying is that this young fellow is untried. This upcoming show will be his maiden voyage, so to speak."

Jeff was surprised to find that he was intensely interested in this dog show business, and he wasn't quite sure why. Was it just because Sam loved it so? Or was he learning to like these dogs more than he'd ever thought possible? He wasn't sure what the reasons were; he just knew that he was looking forward to the upcoming show with almost as much eagerness as Sam and Tim.

"What are you going to do about Daisy?" he asked. "She's not going along, is she?"

Sam shook her head. "She's been invited to

spend the weekend with Susan. It works out perfectly. We'll drop her off early Friday morning before we leave and pick her up Sunday evening when we return."

"And Amber?"

"Amber goes with me," Sam said adamantly. "She's too young to be left with a sitter for a whole weekend. With you and Tim along to help with the dogs, we'll be fine."

"You actually think I'll be of some help?" Jeff asked, unable to hide his smile. He'd literally forced his way into this dog show thing, and he hadn't been sure exactly how Sam felt about it until now. Was she really starting to depend on him?

Sam smiled and snapped the leash on Frosty in preparation for putting the big male through his paces. He was only a few points from his championship, and it was vital that he make a good showing. "Time will tell, won't it, Commander?"

Jeff sat on the grass, leaning back against a huge old oak tree, and watched as Sam walked Frosty around the perimeter of her yard. First a normal walk, then a slightly faster trot, then an out-and-out run, and finally the sit, stay, and down commands before Tim, playing the part of a judge, moved in to examine Frosty. That was the tricky part, Sam had explained.

Some dogs simply would not stand still and allow the judges to run their hands over their bodies, check their teeth and jaws, and examine their genitals. Show dogs could never be spayed or neutered, Sam had said. A show dog must always be in its natural state.

Frosty stood still as a statue as Tim performed the examination in exactly the same way the judge would in just a few days' time. When Tim was finished and stepped backwards away from the dog Jeff realized he'd been holding his breath.

"That's amazing," he told Tim when the young man joined him.

"Not really," Tim said. "We've been training Frosty since he was a pup. He's used to it. He knows it's all part of the routine. He's been in shows before and he's always a favorite."

"I still think it's incredible. I guess it's because I'm such a novice where dogs are concerned. I always thought of them as furry creatures that barked and deposited piles on the lawn."

Tim laughed. "Don't let mom hear you say that. She'd never forgive you."

"Don't worry," Jeff said. "Where your mom and her dogs are concerned I've learned to tread lightly. I just hope I can be of some help at the show."

Tim flopped down on the grass beside Jeff. "I'm glad you and Mom patched up your little disagreement. For a while I was afraid . . ."

"Yeah, me, too," Jeff said. "I almost lost my happy home."

"Well, don't worry about the show," Tim said. "If I know Mom, she'll find plenty of chores to keep us both busy!"

Jeff echoed Tim's laugh. That, he decided, wouldn't surprise him a bit!

"We have to wait a little while, Ralph," Daisy said. "I want to be sure Sammy's got her life on track. You can understand that, can't you?" A vivid blush colored her wrinkled cheeks. "And we'll have this coming weekend."

"I can hardly wait," Ralph said, hugging Daisy. "You won't back out at the last minute, will you?"

Daisy shook her head. "I won't," she promised, "but you've got to promise not to tell anyone. I don't want wind of this to get back to Sammy. Not yet."

"I promise," Ralph said solemnly as he and Daisy moved around the dance floor. He knew his bride-to-be doted on her niece and he understood why, but he was getting impatient, and Daisy, that feisty woman who'd made him feel more like fifty than seventy-nine, had refused to do more than give him a good-night kiss so far. So who could blame him for getting impatient? But, ah, this weekend! It was going to be something special!

"Have any idea when you'll be able to tell her?" Ralph asked, giving Daisy another little squeeze and smiling as she blushed a soft shade of apricot.

Daisy chuckled. "You devil, you! Soon, Ralph," she said. "I'm sure it will be soon." To Daisy's amazement, her voice came out sounding slightly breathless. Who would have thought it, she wondered, pressing close to Ralph and giving her hips a slightly naughty twist. Who would have thought it?

Eighteen

Early Thursday morning, Tim, Jeff, and Sam were all busy making final preparations for the show. Daisy's overnight bag was packed and waiting, and some of Amber's gear was waiting to be loaded in Jeff's Blazer. Since they were taking three dogs as well as the baby, Sam needed all the space in her station wagon for the dog's traveling crates and grooming supplies. Jeff had offered to follow behind them in his Blazer with their suitcases and Amber's folding bed and other paraphernalia. Now, as he pictured it in his mind, he laughed. They'd make quite a caravan, and who would ever have imagined him right smack-dab in the middle of something like this? Jeff knew that if his friend Brian could see him now, he'd never hear the end of it! When he spoke with Brian the other day he said he'd located a computer software company that was hiring. They were looking for people they could train, and part of the benefits of the position would be continuing education in the field of electronics. It sounded ideal for Tim. At least it was a way to get him started in his chosen field. But Jeff hadn't said anything to Tim or Sam yet; he wasn't sure how Sam would take the thought of her son moving so far away.

He had to tell Tim soon; Brian didn't expect the position to be open for too long. How could he make Sam see that it was a golden opportunity in more ways than one? It was the chance of a lifetime for Tim to get a foothold in computers, plus the distance would help him become more sure of himself, more independent. It might not be easy, but Jeff honestly believed it was worthwhile. Tim couldn't stay tied to his mother forever. He needed to break away and make his own way in the world. And if Sam would just loosen up, she'd realize she no longer needed Tim. Jeff was ready and willing to step in and take up the slack in helping with the kennels. He'd discovered that after years of paperwork and stuffy, smoke-filled offices, he actually enjoyed working with the dogs. And most of all, he enjoyed being close to Sam and Amber.

Sam packed the clothing she would need for the weekend and picked up the telephone to confirm the hotel reservations she'd made. A room for herself and Amber, another for Jeff and Tim. As she wrote the confirmation number on a slip of paper, her thoughts flew backwards to the last time she'd been in a hotel.

There were still nights when she lay in bed, unable to sleep, remembering. Heaven. She had truly touched the stars that night, and now, weeks later, she hungered for more. Her anger at Jeff's remarks and interference had dimmed, and they had formed what was a comfortable friendship—unless, of course, they happened to brush too close to one another while working around the kennels. As long as Jeff kept his physical distance, she was hanging on to her equilibrium, but for how long? She decided it was definitely a good thing her son would be along on this trip; otherwise who knew what could happen?

Later that afternoon Jeff offered to buy pizza for supper so Sam wouldn't have to cook. "I figure there'll be plenty of last-minute things to do before we leave in the morning."

Sam groaned. "You've got that right. Before I go to bed tonight I want to double-check and make sure I have everything I'll need for Amber." Her forehead furrowed as she remembered something. "Tim, you did put that special dry shampoo in with the other grooming supplies, didn't you?"

"It's all set, Mom. Hey, relax. We've done this before, remember, and it always turns out okay."

"But that was BB, before baby," Sam explained. "Now, with Amber coming along, there's twice as much stuff to haul."

"It's probably not too late to get a sitter, if that's what you want to do," Jeff said. He loved Amber as much as Sam did, but he knew that the next couple of days would be hectic enough without an infant in tow. And what was wrong with leaving Amber at home as long as they had a competent sitter?

"I told you, she's too young to be left with a sitter for a whole weekend," Sam answered. She sounded irritated, and her eyes were narrowed angrily.

Jeff started to apologize, then felt his own anger rise. He'd be damned if he'd say he was sorry for simply voicing an opinion! And there was no way he was going to spend his life with Sam measuring every word and pussyfooting around!

"It was just a suggestion, Sam, not a command. I think this weekend will be as hard on Amber as it will on you, but it's your decision."

Sam was momentarily speechless. Jeff had

quite effectively put her in her place. She had been acting like a bitch, letting Jeff do all the dirty work and then jumping all over him when he voiced an opinion, and the thing was, she was beginning to think he was right. A smelly, noisy dog show really wasn't the best place to take a small baby, but to just go off and leave Amber with a sitter felt like desertion. It felt as if she was foisting her child off on someone else for her own convenience. But would it really harm Amber to stay with someone warm and motherly like Susan Lynch? And Daisy would be there, too, so there'd be someone from the family. Maybe it wasn't too late to call Susan.

"I think you may be right," she said quietly, looking at Jeff. "I wonder if Susan would consider keeping Amber at this late date?"

"Susan?" Jeff was sure his voice cracked. Susan Lynch was planning to cover for Daisy this weekend. Sam thought Daisy was staying with the retired nurse, when she was really planning to spend the weekend with Ralph.

"I don't know," he said. "How about if I call her and sound her out? I'm not sure what plans she and Daisy have made."

"That's right," Sam said. "They may have planned to take in a movie or something."

Or something, Jeff muttered under his breath.

"Let me run up and check with Daisy," he said, "and then I'll call Susan for you. You just go on with your packing, Sam."

"Okay, and thanks. I do appreciate all your help, Jeff."

He managed a weak smile. "I know," he said. "I'll be back after I talk to Daisy."

He tapped on the elderly woman's door, then turned the knob when she called for him to come in.

"Why, Jake, how sweet of you to come calling," she teased. "Are you all packed for the dog show?"

"That's what I have to talk to you about, Aunt Daisy," Jeff said, carefully closing the door behind him. "We've run into a snag. Sam is thinking about leaving Amber with Susan, and of course she doesn't know . . ."

"Oh dear, let me think a minute," Daisy said. She stood up and pushed something pink and silky under the pillow on her bed. "Well, maybe Susan can just come out here," she said thoughtfully. "Frank can pick me up here as easy as at Susan's apartment. Now, don't worry, Jeremy," she said, noting Jeff's worried look. "Frank and Susan are both sworn to secrecy. My, isn't all this intrigue exciting? Who would have thought that at my age I'd be planning an illicit weekend?"

"I'm sure your weekend will be fine, Aunt Daisy," Jeff said. "That's not what I'm worried about. If Sam finds out I had a hand in all this . . . well, she really will boot me out on my ear!"

"Oh, don't be such a worrywart, Jack! I'll call Susan and explain the change of plans. I'm sure she'll be delighted to look after Amber for a couple of days."

Jeff paced as Daisy dialed Susan's number. "Susan?" he heard her say. "There's been a change of plans. Would you be willing to come stay here at the house with Amber? Oh no, my plans haven't changed. I'll just have Frank pick me up here instead of at your apartment. You're sure you don't mind? Wonderful. I'll have Jake tell Sammy."

Daisy hung up the phone. "Well, that's all taken care of, Jim. That wasn't so hard, was it?" She was beaming, and Jeff just shook his head. Talking to Daisy was like having the whole earth spin around you at warp speed.

"You're sure we're going to get away with this?" he asked.

"It'll be a piece of cake, Jack," Aunt Daisy assured him. Then she calmly pulled a slinky pink nightgown out from under her pillow. "What do you think, Jeremy? I need a male viewpoint, and Tim's too young. Besides, he'd probably blab everything to Sam. Do you think Ralph will like this?"

With the lacy nightgown held up under her chin, there was something almost girlish about Aunt Daisy, and Jeff knew that no matter what happened, he couldn't deny the elderly woman this happiness.

"It's perfect, Daisy," he said. "Ralph will be bowled over."

Daisy nodded and stuffed the gown back under her pillow. "That's what I'm hoping," she said. "I learned a long time ago that a woman's got to keep her man guessing!"

"Everything is all set, Sam," Jeff said a few minutes later. "Susan said she would be delighted to stay here with Amber. Oh, as it turned out, she and Daisy didn't have anything special planned. It's my guess they'll probably just eat frozen yogurt and watch old movies on TV."

Sam nodded. "I feel comfortable about Susan. I trust her."

Jeff was conscious of a terrible sinking feeling in his gut. Would Sam still trust Susan after she found out how Daisy had spent the weekend? Then again, maybe she didn't have to find out. Wasn't there a saying about ignorance being bliss? But Jeff's pizza tasted like cardboard that night, and he was sorry he'd ever gotten involved in Daisy's little love scheme.

"All right, is that everything?" Tim finished loading the last of the grooming supplies into the wagon and stood back, lifting a hand to push a stray lock of hair out of his eyes. "Did you check your list, Mom?"

Sam looked eager and excited and just a little worried as her gaze swung from the loaded station wagon to the silver-haired woman holding Amber. "Are you sure you don't mind?" she asked Susan for the hundredth time.

"Don't worry about a thing. Amber and I will be fine," Susan said. "I love babies. This will be a pleasant change for me."

"Well, there's plenty of food in the refrigerator and freezer for you and Daisy. Help yourself to whatever you like."

Susan shot Daisy a quick look and smiled. "Don't give us another thought, Samantha. Daisy and I are going to have a delightful weekend. Now, go on; you'd better get out of here if you're going to show those beautiful dogs of yours. And remember, Amber and I will be rooting for you."

"All right then," Sam said. "I guess that's it. Are we all ready?"

"As we'll ever be," Tim said, nodding at Jeff.

Since they didn't have to drag Amber's baby furniture along, there was room for all three of them in the wagon. Tim slid behind the wheel to take the first stretch of the drive. Sam slid in beside him, and Jeff sat on the outside. Sam could feel the heat of Jeff's body where his thigh rested against hers.

Jeff hadn't been to New York in years, but it was just as he'd remembered it: noisy, busy, and filled with excitement. Beside him he felt Sam lean forward as they neared their hotel.

"How do we handle the dogs?" he asked.

"The hotel has a special kennel. We'll get the dogs settled first, then see about our rooms."

"Man, this is a great place to come for a visit," Tim said, "but I don't think I'd want to live here. Makes a guy feel hyper, you know?"

Sam laughed. "You're a homegrown country boy, son," she said, her voice exaggerated into a drawl. "Don't worry; we'll only be here for a couple of days."

It took a while to settle the dogs; they had been stirred up by the ride. When the three of them finally got to the front desk they were all looking forward to a shower, a nap, and a nice dinner.

Jeff's brows rose as he watched Sam retrieve two keys from the desk clerk.

"This is yours and Tim's," she said, handing one of the keys to Jeff. "I don't know about you, but I want to relax for a while."

"Good idea," Jeff agreed. "Shall we meet in the lobby for dinner around six?"

"Oh, Mom, there's something I meant to tell you. My friend Paul is here visiting his uncle. They kind of planned on showing me around tonight."

"Tonight? But we have to be at the show early tomorrow, Tim. Do you really think you should be out running around the city all night?"

"It won't be all night, Mom," Tim said, "but I do want to spend some time with Paul."

"But . . ." The struggle was apparent in Sam's eyes.

Jeff watched as she swallowed and forced a smile. "Well, of course," she finally managed. "If that's what you want. See you in the morning, then?"

"Sure, and don't worry. I'll be bright-eyed and bushy-tailed."

"You better be," Sam said.

"Nicely done," Jeff whispered against Sam's ear as she watched her son jog down the hotel corridor.

"It wasn't easy," Sam answered, uncomfortably aware of Jeff's proximity. Lord, but he smelled good! Like a strong, secure man, a man a woman could count on, the kind of man Sam had had little experience with. "I really do need a shower and a nap," she said, staring hard at the piece of plastic that served as a key.

"Me, too," Jeff said. "The lobby around six?"

Sam nodded, too stirred up to speak.

She had splurged and bought a new dress for the occasion, something she would not even have considered a year earlier. But she'd counted on having a nice dinner with Jeff at least once, and she wasn't about to embarrass him by looking like a frump.

Jeff had apparently had the same thoughts, because he wore a pair of light gray slacks with a deeper gray sports coat, a crisp white-on-white shirt, and a gray tie with cranberry accents.

"Wow!" Sam said, shaking her head. "Is this

really the same man who cleans my kennel runs?"

Jeff grinned, and despite the silver at his temples he looked young and boyish. "And is this the woman who clumps around the kennels in worn jeans and faded flannel shirts?"

"We clean up pretty good, don't we?" Sam teased.

Jeff felt desire swell deep in his belly. And if he didn't get a grip, something else would begin to swell. It was always this way when he was near Sam. He had to call on every ounce of the tight control he'd learned in the service. And it was much worse now, with Sam looking and smelling so sweet, with that soft look of bemused expectancy on her face.

"I thought you'd probably want to have dinner here in the hotel, but if you'd rather go out . . ."

"Right here is fine," Sam said, swinging her head toward the hall leading to the hotel dining room. "This looks elegant. I'm sure it will be perfect."

And it was, or if not perfect, as near to it as Jeff could reasonably hope to get. The atmosphere was quiet and refined, the music soft and melodic, and the woman across from him everything he'd ever dreamed of, all rolled up in a neat, five-foot-five, 135-pound package.

"I'm glad I came," he said, as a white-coated waiter appeared with the wine Jeff had ordered. "This is nice."

Sam nodded. She waited until the waiter had poured their wine and left. "I'm actually glad Tim went off with his friend," she admitted. "We haven't had a chance to talk about anything personal for a long time, have we?"

"No, but I didn't think you wanted to."

"At first I didn't, but now . . . Can you forgive me for acting like a silly twit?"

"If you'll forgive me for acting like a strong-armed, overbearing . . ."

Sam laughed and held up her hand. "Let's skip the apologies and drink a toast, shall we?"

When their dessert arrived, a towering confection of sinfully rich cream and chocolate curls, Sam thoughtfully toyed with her spoon.

"You've never said much about your marriage, Jeff. Does it still hurt to talk about it?"

"No, it doesn't hurt," Jeff said, shaking his head. "I got over all that a long time ago." He leaned back in his chair and his eyes darkened. "Marcie and I were together such a short time, it sometimes seems like a dream. I was twenty-three when we met. Marcie was cute, smart, and had a bubbly personality. She captivated me. We were married six months after we met." Jeff shifted and seemed to be looking backward.

"We hadn't even celebrated our first anniversary when she started complaining. She didn't like military life; she thought it was too rigid and restricting. She didn't seem to want to mix with the other wives on base, and when I was transferred to a new base shortly after our anniversary she was really unhappy. We struggled on a few months longer, constantly bickering and snapping at each other, and then one day she just left. She said she wasn't going to spend her life being ordered around by a military macho, whatever that meant. I asked her to give us a chance. I thought maybe counseling would help, but she wasn't interested."

"I'm sorry," Sam said.

"Yeah, so was I. But we weren't right for each other, and I guess it's just as well we found out before there were any children. And if I'm being completely honest, I have to admit that the feeling of failure bothered me more than the simple fact of losing my wife. My dad brought me up to excel in everything I did. Failure was hard to accept."

Sam nodded. "I think that's part of what kept me from leaving Doug. I was very young when we married. Doug was handsome, and he had a magnetic personality. He could sweep you along with him with no effort. He made it sound as if we were going to have an exciting, glamorous life. After the first glow began to fade, I realized Doug was living on pipe dreams. He had a head full of dreams, but no clear plan to make them come true. And when things didn't happen the way he expected them to . . . well, he wasn't really abusive—at least not physically—but he managed to let me feel his disappointment." Sam brushed a strand of hair away from her eyes. "I don't know," she went on, "I guess there was just something inside me that wouldn't allow me to admit that I'd made a mistake. I didn't have the guts to cash in my chips and call it a day. So I hung on, hoping against hope that things would change. Then I got pregnant with Tim right around the time Aunt Daisy had her mild stroke. I was tired of living out of suitcases and chasing empty dreams, and I was determined to have my baby and repay Aunt Daisy for some of the care she'd given me."

"So you came home and Doug followed?"

Sam nodded. "He didn't like the idea, but he had no place else to go."

"And things just went on as usual?"

Sam nodded. "Pretty much. God, this all makes me sound like a wimp, doesn't it? But at the time I didn't see it that way. I wanted

Tim to have a father, and I still considered my marriage vows sacred. I guess I never, not until the very end, gave up hope that things would change, that Doug would wake up one morning and realize that Tim and I were what was important, that working at a steady job and making a decent living was enough. He never did."

"It's over, Sam," he said softly. "And look what you got from those years—a handsome, intelligent son and a beautiful, healthy daughter."

Sam smiled. Her fingers trembled beneath Jeff's, and a sweet, aching desire sprang up between them.

"Ready to go upstairs?" Jeff asked.

"Let's go."

"My place or yours?" he asked when they stepped out of the elevator on the fourteenth floor.

"Definitely mine," Sam said. "Who knows what time Tim will wander in?"

Jeff's hand was still on the doorknob. "Would it bother you if Tim found us together?"

Sam flushed. "Jeff, he's my son, my little boy . . . it would be awkward for both of us, I think."

"Awkward, maybe, but not the end of the

world. I think Tim would like us to get together."

He opened the door and they stepped inside. Sam's room was identical to his, except that instead of two double beds there was one king-size bed with a peach-colored spread.

"Nice," Jeff said, locking the door behind them, "but definitely too much room for one single woman to rattle around in all alone."

"Definitely," Sam agreed, standing perfectly still as Jeff gripped her arms. He didn't try to pull her into his arms at first, just held her there, barely touching. But they were close enough for Sam to feel the warm bulge that just barely grazed her belly. She felt the heat begin to build inside her, swelling and growing until she thought she'd faint from it.

"Jeff, I want you," she murmured thickly, standing on tiptoe to whisper in his ear, then slowly sliding back on her heels so that her lower body moved down against Jeff's blatant arousal.

He backed her up until she felt the mattress against her knees. Then he slid his hands down her arms and briefly released her.

Sam thought she would die if he didn't let her feel him soon. "Don't make me wait, Jeff," she pleaded. "It's been forever."

That was all he needed to hear. He had wanted to be gentle with her, to prolong and savor each delicious sensation, but the hunger was too great, the need for affirmation and physical release too strong to be denied a moment longer.

With a harsh groan he clasped her hard against him, and they fell together on the bed. Their clothing was suddenly hot and restricting. Frantically, they tore at each other's buttons and zippers until finally they were totally nude. Silk and satin, Jeff thought, before all coherent thought ceased in a flood of hot, raw sensations.

Steel and warm mahogany, Sam thought, writhing hungrily against Jeff's full, hard arousal. She wanted him now, deep and tight inside her. She was too impatient to wait for soft words and gentle caresses. That could come later. Now there was only a primitive need driving her, and she knew, as Jeff impatiently spread her thighs and entered her, that it was the same for him.

She gasped as he plunged into her, filling all the empty places she'd lived with for so long. Then thought fled as sensation replaced it. There was no time for doubt, no time to worry if her well-rounded body would please him. Sam could only feel.

***

It was hard for Jeff to go back to his own room, but Sam insisted. As he lay in the double bed, after showering and slipping into pajama bottoms, Jeff relived the evening. Dinner had been perfect, the talk he and Sam had shared had cleared the air, and the loving . . . well, he had no words to describe that. With Sam he felt as though his lost youth had been restored. He was young, strong, and capable of anything. Now if he and Sam could just hold onto that closeness . . .

A sound interrupted his musings. He heard the knob turn on the door, and then the sounds of Tim creeping into the room.

"It's no use, Tim. I'm awake," he said.

The young man jumped, then laughed nervously. "Oh. Well, it's pretty late. I didn't want to disturb you."

"No problem. Did you enjoy yourself?"

"Yeah. It was great. Steve's uncle took us to an all-night club. It was wild. How about you? Did you have a nice night?"

"The best," Jeff said quietly, then he closed his eyes and drifted into a deep, contented sleep.

Nineteen

"Okay, Tim, this is how we'll work it: I'll show Frosty and the pup, and you do Stormy, all right?"

"Sure, whatever you say, Mom. I sure wasn't looking forward to tackling that pup. Not while he's a virgin."

Sam laughed. "He'll be okay, but I do think it's best if I show him. I've had a little more experience than you."

Frosty pranced importantly, as though he understood exactly what was going on. As though he knew the importance of this show.

"Think he'll make it?" he asked Sam, flicking a glance at the big male. There were many other Samoyeds in their area, but none that compared with Frosty as far as Jeff was concerned. He grinned as the pup, Son of Sam's Pride, tried to lick Sam's nose.

Sam laughed. She felt light and free this morning, certain that everything was going to turn out exactly the way she wanted it to. She had slept well the night before, better than she had in weeks. A soft flush colored her cheeks as she met Jeff's knowing look. "You slept well, too?" she asked.

"Never woke up once. I guess I was worn out." Jeff winked, laughing as Sam shot a quick warning glance in Tim's direction. *Behave*, she mouthed silently. But her eyes were filled with laughter and her smile was lit with contentment.

Before they knew it, it was time for Sam to take Frosty into the ring for the preliminary judging. When Jeff heard the announcer call Sam's name as owner and breeder his chest puffed with pride. Sam wasn't his—at least not yet—and he'd had little to do with these beautiful, immaculately groomed canines, yet he felt as though they all belonged to him, as if he was part of it. Did cleaning the kennels make him a viable partner? "Go for it, beautiful," he whispered as Sam snapped the lead on Frosty's collar. "Bring home the gold!"

Sam walked tall and proud as she and Frosty entered the ring, and Jeff was amazed to feel a lump in his throat as he watched Frosty prance proudly beside Sam, his perfectly brushed plume of a tail arched high over his back. The dog was magnificent, Jeff decided, cutting a glance toward Tim, who was watching avidly.

"Way to go, Mom!" Tim cheered softly. "Way to go!"

There was an appreciative burst of applause from the crowd as Frosty and Sam broke into a smooth run around the ring. "I see what you mean about Frosty being a favorite," Jeff said to Tim. "If that applause is any indication, his championship is in the bag."

"I hope so," Tim said, sounding tense. "It would mean a lot to Mom."

By the time they packed up and got ready to go home on Sunday morning Frosty was a champion, with the ribbons to prove it. Son of Sam's Pride had scored points in the puppy category, despite Tim's concern about how he would show, and Stormy, with her delicate female beauty, took more points toward her championship.

Sam was euphoric: all three of her Samoyeds taking points!

"I never believed they would all win!" she exulted, urging the excited pup into his traveling crate. "What a coup!"

"You were wonderful in that ring, Sam," Jeff said, managing a quick kiss on her neck while Tim's back was turned. "You're as much a champ as your dogs."

She allowed herself to lean into him for a moment, then carefully slid the bolts on the crates into place as Tim turned to grin at them.

"Man, what a weekend this was! Now I know why Paul likes to come up here and visit his uncle so much. This place is wild!"

"Too wild for my blood," Sam said, stepping back so Jeff could close the tailgate of the wagon. "I'll be glad to get home."

"Missing Amber?" Jeff asked as they climbed into the wagon and prepared to leave. "Because I am. I never realized how a tiny baby can get under your skin until now. I can't wait to see her smile and hear her happy gurgles."

"Me, too," Sam said; then lines of worry creased her forehead. "I've been so busy, I have to admit I've hardly thought of Daisy and Susan. I hope they didn't have any problems with Amber."

"I'm sure they're all fine," Jeff said. "Everything was okay when you called yesterday, wasn't it?"

"Yes, but . . . maybe I should call before we start home."

"Sam, we'll be pulling into the driveway in

less than four hours. Come on, relax. Don't spoil a great weekend by getting uptight now."

Once Sam would have taken instant offense at words like those, but now she simply smiled. She knew Jeff meant well, and that he was almost as crazy about her little daughter as she was. This weekend had done them all good: Tim was relaxed and cheerful, Jeff was one big, nonstop smile, while she . . . well, there weren't any words to describe how she felt. And it was much more than the sex, although that had been incredible. Oddly enough, in Jeff's arms she didn't worry about stretch marks on her tummy, or the fact that her breasts hung a little lower than they once had. With a woman's deepest instinct, she knew that in Jeff's eyes she was perfect, that her beauty was not measured solely by the circumference of her waist.

She dared to look at him and found him studying her intently. "What?" she asked.

"I was just thinking," Jeff said. "It's a good thing you stopped breast-feeding Amber a few weeks ago; otherwise you wouldn't have had a choice about bringing her along."

Sam felt wistful for a moment. Discontinuing Amber's breast feedings had been a purely practical decision. With the kennel and all the accompanying chores, she simply didn't have the time to sit and nurse Amber several times a day. Now that she was on a formula, Aunt Daisy or Tim or even Jeff could feed her if necessary. Sam had made the switch after receiving the pediatrician's blessing. And it made her life easier, even if she did miss the quiet times in the rocker with her baby. But she made up for it in other ways. She was determined that Amber wouldn't suffer from neglect in any form.

They were all tired by the time they got home late that afternoon. Jeff was inordinately relieved to see that Aunt Daisy was quietly watching television with Susan when they walked in.

"Well, how did it go?" Daisy asked, her eyes roving from one to the other and back again. "Did your doggies do you proud, Sammy girl?"

"They did splendidly, Aunt Daisy, but what about Amber? Was she all right? Did you and Susan have any problems with her?"

"Heavens no, Samantha," Susan said, gesturing toward the baby, sleeping in the cradle. "She was playing away until just a few minutes ago; then she just lay down and closed her eyes, as sweet as can be."

Sam tiptoed toward the sleeping infant, and Jeff followed close on her heels.

"Oh, look; I think she's grown," Sam cried. "Look at her little cheeks, Jeff!"

They stood there, bending over the sleeping baby, and three pairs of interested eyes met and exchanged wordless comments.

Yep, it had happened all right, Daisy thought happily, Damn if Jake and Sammy hadn't fallen smack-dab in love! She smothered a chuckle as she remembered the old rhyme, "First comes love, then comes marriage, then comes Sammy with a baby carriage." Well, things were just a little cockeyed here, but who cared? What did anything matter where there was love? She caught Susan's eye and winked.

"So, what did you two ladies do all weekend, when you weren't playing nursemaid to my little dumpling?" Sam asked as she gratefully accepted the cup of tea Susan offered. "I hope you got a chance for some good old-fashioned girl talk."

"Uh, we . . . well, to be truthful, Sammy . . ."

Jeff's heart skidded to a stop. He held his breath. His eyes, filled with mock panic, telegraphed a silent message to Daisy. Not now, his dark eyes screamed. Not yet!

"Yes? Go on, Aunt Daisy. What did you start to say?" Sam prompted.

"Well, I just . . . the last couple of days just flew by, didn't they, Susan?"

"Oh, yes, indeed," Susan said, nodding vigorously. "They certainly did."

"Well, it was the same for us. We hardly had a minute to breathe." Then Sam remembered the night Jeff had spent in her room. Well, maybe she had had a few minutes, but there was no reason for her aunt to know about that!

But Daisy looked different in some way. There was something about her that Sam couldn't quite figure out, a new softness in her eyes, a gentle glow to her skin. If she didn't know better . . . but that was the craziest thought she'd ever had in her life. Aunt Daisy was seventy-eight years old. She might have a boyfriend, but she would never . . .

Daisy felt Sammy's inquisitive gaze and prayed she wouldn't blush and give it all away. Then again, what could her niece do if she did find out? And now that she thought about it, hadn't Tim said something about going off on his own with some friends who were visiting in New York? That meant Sammy and Jeff had been all alone, just like her and Ralph. Sammy might be a little uptight, but she wasn't a fool! So who knew what had gone on in that fancy New York hotel? And, Aunt Daisy decided, what was good for the goose was also good for the gander!

Later, when everyone was settled down, Daisy napping and Tim off with some friends, Sam and Jeff sat side by side on the sofa as Sam gave Amber a bottle.

"What a weekend!" Jeff said, drawing a finger gently along Amber's plump cheek. "But you're right; it's great to be home."

Sam's heart swelled. It was true; Jeff was beginning to consider this old house his home. He'd blended into her family almost effortlessly. He'd filled a void she hadn't even realized existed.

"I'm glad you went with us," she said.

Jeff grinned. "Me, too."

Twenty

Life settled into a comfortable routine in the first few days after the dog show. The ribbons the dogs had won were proudly displayed on the kennel walls, and Sam placed a small ad in the local paper, announcing Frosty's championship and the fact that a litter of his pups would soon be available.

Daisy hummed contentedly to herself as she puttered around the house. She'd always liked her little home, but now, after spending such a delightful weekend with Ralph, she was getting the itch to leave it. She felt a lovely warmth in her body as she thought about the time she and Ralph had spent together.

Ralph was such a dear, such a gentleman, and yet sexy as the devil when he wanted to be, which had turned out to be pretty often for a man his age!

Now Daisy knew she was blushing up a storm, and she peeked to make sure Sammy wasn't in sight. She wasn't ready to make her declaration yet, but it would be soon. She'd promised Ralph. And somehow, some way, she had to make her sweet but sometimes misguided niece understand. Life was an hourglass filled with sand, and for Daisy the sand was almost gone. The thought didn't sadden her, nor did it frighten her. She had always believed that there was a season for everything. She'd had a good life, all things considered, and she didn't think she was being morbid to face the fact that time was running out. Nor did she think she and Ralph were wrong to want to cram every bit of living they could into their twilight years. Why not, for heaven's sake? Life was meant to be lived, wasn't it?

Jeff sat by his telephone, trying to figure out the best way to tell Sam about the job offer Brian had scared up for Tim. He knew she wasn't going to be thrilled about Tim moving all the way to Virginia, but Jeff had explained the situation to Brian briefly, and his old navy buddy had promised to keep an eye on Tim. That might reassure Sam a little, as well as the fact that Brian had volunteered to help Tim find a small apartment.

And, of course, the final decision had to be Tim's. If he wasn't interested in relocating, that would be that. But Jeff was pretty sure he would be. It was easy to see that Tim loved his mother deeply, but Jeff was convinced the young man knew that the only way he'd truly learn to be independent and stand on his own two feet was to get away for a while. It made perfect sense to Jeff, and Brian had agreed that it sounded like Tim needed a change of scenery. But would Sam see it that way?

And Aunt Daisy! How was Sam going to react when she found out Daisy was getting married?

Jeff reached for his mug and realized his coffee had gotten cold. Why was he sitting and staring into space anyway? When he first went into the service he'd learned that the best way to get things done was just to do them, so the sooner he faced the situation head on, the sooner he could relax. He threw the cold coffee in the sink and headed out the door.

Samantha felt great. The dog show had been successful beyond her wildest dreams. It was what she'd been hoping for, because now Frosty's offspring would command a higher price. Sam stopped sweeping for a minute and leaned on her broom. She needed another way to increase the income. She'd been kicking around some ideas for a while, but she wasn't quite ready to implement them. She was thinking of talking them over with Jeff, of asking his advice. Even though the kennel business was new to him, she respected his intelligence, and she needed a sounding board. For an instant she remembered all the "ideas" Tim was always getting. Of course he meant well, but Tim had a little of his father in him. He tended to dream bigger than life size. No, Tim's ideas, whatever they were, probably weren't very practical.

When Sam thought about talking with Jeff and asking his advice she felt perfectly comfortable. She might get a little annoyed with Jeff for his occasional bossiness, but she knew she could trust him.

She glanced up toward the house. She'd left Amber sleeping and Aunt Daisy baby-sitting. Sam shook her head and started sweeping again. Aunt Daisy's behavior was a puzzle these days. She continued to visit the senior center on a regular basis, and on more than one occasion, when Jeff escorted her to one of the dances, Sam had thought her aunt looked younger than she had in years. There was something different about her, but Sam couldn't quite figure out what. She grinned and swept harder. Whatever it was, something was agreeing with Aunt Daisy very nicely these days.

When she finished sweeping Sam decided to check on Amber. It wasn't that she didn't trust her elderly aunt, but whenever she was away from the baby for any length of time she felt an almost irrational need to see and hold her. It was almost as if she was afraid she'd wake up one morning and discover that Amber had been just a dream.

Sam went in the back door, the way she usually did, and heard the now familiar sound of Jeff's laughter mingling with Aunt Daisy's high-pitched cackle.

"Just what's going on here?" she demanded, hands on her hips. She shook her head. Jeff was on his knees, a pained expression on his face as he moved his arms and legs. Next to him on a blanket lay Amber, waving her chubby limbs and making gurgling noises.

"What in the world . . . !"

"Jake is trying to teach Amber how to crawl, Sammy. Isn't it sweet of him to give his time this way?" Aunt Daisy asked. "We saw a television show the other day, and the pediatrician said that babies who don't crawl sometimes have trouble later in life. It's a necessary part of their development, he said. So Jim and I thought . . ."

Sam started to laugh. "Please get up off the floor, Jeff. Do you have any idea how ridiculous you look?"

"I think she was starting to get the idea," he said, "and the concept makes sense if you think about it, Sam. Babies develop in a certain way and . . ."

"Jeff, she's still too young to crawl," Sam said, automatically giving Jeff her hand as he struggled to his feet. "She's only four months old. Maybe you'd better wait a couple of months before you try that again."

"Yeah, I guess you're right. I suppose right now she just likes lying on the floor and babbling, huh?"

"That's about it," Sam said, bending down and scooping the baby up in her arms. She kissed first one plump cheek and then the other. "What are they trying to do to you, pumpkin? Make you into some kind of child prodigy?"

"I wouldn't hurt her, Sam," Jeff said quietly. "You know that, don't you?"

"Yes," Sam said. "I do know that." And she did. She would trust Jeff with her life, and with her child's life as well. What more could she say?

* * *

That afternoon, when Jeff drove Daisy to the center, the normally chatty woman seemed abnormally quiet.

"Something wrong, Daisy?" Jeff asked. "You didn't have a spat with Ralph, did you?"

To Jeff's surprise, Daisy nodded, and her eyes filled with tears. "Damned old fool wants to get married right away and I keep telling him I'm not ready."

"Why not? I thought you liked him a lot."

"Well, of course I like the man, Jason! For heaven's sake! Do you think I'm the kind of woman who would spend the weekend with a man she didn't like?"

"No, what I . . ."

"It's Sammy, Jack. I can't leave Sammy just yet. Lately she's been letting me do a few little things around the house. Oh, I know it's not much, but it helps a little, and when I'm gone . . . well, I know Tim's getting ready to fly the coop, so where will that leave Sammy? All alone with Amber?" Daisy dabbed at her eyes and sniffed.

"What about me?" Jeff asked, "or don't I count?"

Aunt Daisy narrowed her eyes and peered at Jeff. "I don't know, Jake," she said. "Do you?"

"What the hell is that supposed to mean, Aunt Daisy? You know I don't like it when you talk in riddles. Why don't you just come right out and say what you're thinking?"

"Don't swear, Jake, especially not in the presence of a lady. All right; you want it straight, that's what you'll get! I told you before that my Sammy wasn't the kind of woman a man trifles with." Daisy paused, drew a deep breath, and then lifted her hand and shook her finger in Jeff's face. "Just what are your intentions toward my niece, Jeremy? Are you prepared to make an honest woman of her?"

Jeff groaned. "Oh, Aunt Daisy! What am I going to do with you? What do you think I am, some kind of love 'em and leave 'em lothario?"

"Well, of course not, Jack! If I'd thought that, I'd have run you off a long time ago! What I mean is, have you declared your intentions yet? In plain English, Jim, are you contemplating matrimony with Sam?"

"I . . . oh hell, Daisy! Now you've ruined everything! I wanted to propose to Sam when the time was right, and I sure didn't plan on it being secondhand."

Daisy's wrinkled face was wreathed in smiles. "Why, what do you know! I was right about you all along, Jake. You are a decent man!"

"I just don't want to rush Sam into anything, Daisy," Jeff explained. "In some ways she's still skittish. I think she wants to trust me, but she's still hauling a lot of garbage from her first marriage."

"Humph! Not to mention the way my sister dumped her," Daisy said. "I still can't figure out how anyone could just walk out on their own flesh-and-blood. Can you figure that, Jeremy?"

Jeff shook his head. He'd been going crazy trying to figure out how to tell Sam about Brian's job offer to Tim. If he couldn't pull that off, everything else he and Daisy had talked about would be academic. "I found a job for Tim, Aunt Daisy," he said, "but I haven't told Sam yet. The thing is . . . the job is in Virginia."

Aunt Daisy's eyes widened, and Jeff was sure he could hear the wheels turning inside her head.

"Oh, dear," she said, her hand fluttering up to her throat. "Oh, dear, you do have a problem, don't you, Jake?"

Twenty-one

"Sam, we need to talk."

Sam turned away from the pregnant Samoyed she had been examining. "Sure. What's up, Jeff?"

"No," he said. "Not here. Later tonight, when everything settles down."

"Tonight? All right; why not? Tim has a date again, and Daisy said something about staying overnight at Susan's. Those two are really getting close, aren't they? Anyway, that means all I have to do is get Amber settled down, and then we'll have our talk." Her smile faded as she noted Jeff's solemn face. "Is something wrong?"

"No. At least, I hope you won't think so. Shall I come by around eight?"

"Sure. Eight will be fine."

She watched Jeff walk back toward his cottage, and a funny, sick feeling settled deep in Sam's stomach. Something was wrong. She could feel it.

The day was spent the way she spent most of her days, caring for Amber, cleaning the kennel, and looking after her dogs, and in the afternoon, while Amber napped, Sam wrote out some checks and looked over the books for the kennel. Thanks goodness the expenses for the dog show were all deductible. It was going to be close again this month, but if she could just hold on until the next litter of Frosty's pups arrived . . .

Suddenly, Sam was tired. Tired of struggling to make ends meet, of letting one bill ride so she could pay another, of pinching pennies until her wallet squeaked. It had been that way for as long as she could remember. Was the struggle really worth it, or was she just kidding herself, thinking she could make a living raising her beloved dogs? Maybe it just wasn't feasible, especially now that she had a daughter to raise. As time went on Amber's expenses would grow, just as the baby grew. And how long could she go on this way, driving herself until she was so tired her muscles screamed? Until her head throbbed and her belly was twisted with nausea?

Suddenly, Sam had a horrifying thought. She hadn't felt well at all the past few days. She'd attributed it to fatigue, but now a sickening suspicion was nagging at her. She'd stopped nursing Amber, and although Jeff had used precautions both times they had been together, she knew that condoms weren't foolproof. God, it wasn't possible that she was pregnant again, was it?

Jeff thought Sam looked pale that evening when he arrived with a bottle of white wine.

"You look a little tired," he said, following her into the living room. "Amber all settled down?"

"Finally," Sam said. "I think she's teething. She was fussy all day, and her gums look a little swollen."

"I guess I don't know much about that," Jeff said, "but it must be painful for the baby."

Sam managed a weak laugh. "Even more so for the mother, I think. Tim was a terror. I can still remember walking the floor with him all night."

Jeff poured wine into the glasses Sam had set out and handed one to her. "You look like you could use a little bubbly."

Sam started to reach for the glass, and then she remembered. "Thanks, but I think I'll pass," she said. "I've got a headache and I'm afraid wine will make it worse."

"I can cure your headache in nothing flat," Jeff promised, setting his own glass down and patting the seat next to him. "Sit down, Sam. I'll give you one of my special massages."

She wanted to say no, wanted to stay on the opposite side of the room where it was safe, but her head did ache, and she needed relief from the fear swirling around in her belly. She was being silly. She was just a little under the weather. It was crazy to think she was pregnant again. But if she was, what? She'd been too old with Amber, and it had been only dumb luck that had allowed her to deliver a normal, healthy baby. She couldn't go through all that fear and stress again, not to mention the fact that she had her hands full now. There was just no way she could take on anything else.

"Sam, are you worried about something?" Jeff asked, his fingers kneading the tight skin on her neck and shoulders. "You're really tense."

"Just the usual," Sam lied. "All I need is a good night's sleep."

He debated about telling her. She seemed strung out, and he sure didn't want to do anything to add to her distress. Still, Brian was pressing for an answer, so it seemed he really didn't have a choice.

"Sam, we need to talk about Tim. An old navy buddy of mine is living in Virginia now that he's retired. Brian has always been a computer nut, so he knows what's going on in the field. It seems there's a job opening near where he lives. He thinks it would be a great opportunity for Tim. He can work and study computers at the same time. The pay is decent for someone just starting out, and Brian said he'd be glad to help Tim find a little apartment."

"Virginia? The job is in Virginia?" Sam sounded stricken.

"It's really not that far, Sam, and it would give Tim the chance to see some different scenery. After all, he's young and single, and now is the time for him to explore a little."

"But he's never been away from home! What if he gets in trouble?"

"There's no reason to think that will happen, Sam," Jeff argued. "Tim is a decent, intelligent young man. In fact, he's come up with some great ideas for expanding the kennels and increasing your gross income. I was waiting for the right time to tell you, but . . ."

Sam's headache was getting worse. Tim moving all the way to Virginia? And what was this about ideas for the kennel? Why was she the last to know? Suddenly, it was all just too much . . . Jeff finding Tim a job in another state . . . the two of them discussing her kennels behind her back . . . the insistent throbbing at her temples. She shrugged away from Jeff's stroking fingers.

"I guess it's up to Tim," she said slowly. "Have you mentioned it to him?"

"Not yet," Jeff said. "I wanted to tell you first."

"Thank you for that," Sam said. She knew she sounded dull and flat, but she couldn't help it. Her voice was echoing the way she felt.

"Jeff, I really don't feel well. Could we continue this some other time? I think I'd better just go to bed."

"I hope you're not angry, Sam. I really am just trying to help."

"I know," Sam said. "I know you mean well."

Alone in her bedroom, Sam tossed restlessly. Why did the thought of Tim's leaving frighten her so? She couldn't keep him forever, and it was past time he flew from the nest, but somehow when she let herself think about losing him everything inside her tightened up. Feeling unbearably warm, Sam flung the blankets aside and took a deep, calming breath. She felt herself breaking out in a sweat. She was really losing it, reacting this way at the thought of her grown son leaving home. What did she expect—that Tim would hang on to her apron strings until middle age, until all his youth and opportunities had passed him by? God, Sam didn't want that. She wanted him to mature and prosper, and if going to Virginia was the path he needed to follow, so be it. She had to let go.

A moment later, when her overheated body had cooled down, Sam quickly pulled the blankets up and snuggled into the now welcome warmth. Something was wrong, terribly wrong. She was either pregnant or suffering from some horrible, incurable disease! Just before she fell into a restless sleep, Sam decided she would see her doctor first thing in the morning.

At breakfast she asked Tim and Daisy if they would mind looking after Amber while she went into town.

"Oh good, a morning with our precious little girl," Aunt Daisy said. "There's nothing I'd like better, Sammy girl."

"I'll keep an eye on things, Mom," Tim said quietly. "I don't have to work this morning."

"Good. I'd appreciate your sticking around until I get back," Sam said. "And when you get a chance, you'd better speak to Jeff. He has a lead on a job for you with some kind of computer firm."

"Computers? No kidding! Did he give you any of the details?"

Sam shook her head. "You'd better talk to Jeff. He can explain everything."

"Sure. Thanks. Boy, if I could work with computers that would be great!"

Sam drove straight to her obstetrician's office. She'd called ahead and the nurse had promised to work her in, even though appointments were usually made weeks in advance.

I have to know, Sam thought. I can't stand not knowing. But when she knew, what then? If she was pregnant, it was Jeff's child. His *only* child. But dear God, she didn't want another baby! She wasn't sure she could handle it. Twisting her hands in her lap as she waited for the nurse to call her name, Sam prayed it wasn't true.

"Well, Sam, what brings you here? Carol said something about headaches and nausea?"

Sam nodded. "And last night I felt so hot I threw all the blankets off. Then a few minutes later I felt cold. Maybe I'm coming down with something."

"Mm, could be. Sam, have you been sexually active since Amber's birth?"

"I . . . well, I'm not sure how active you'd call it, but yes, I have had . . . sex."

"Did you take precautions?"

"My partner did, and the first time I was still nursing Amber so I thought . . ."

"That's an old wives tale, Sam. Surely you didn't believe nursing your baby would prevent you from getting pregnant?"

Sam shook her head. She felt miserable, and stupid to boot. "I don't want to be pregnant," she said.

"Well, you probably aren't, but it's a possibility we need to check out. I'll send the nurse in to help you into a gown and then we'll see."

He thought she was pregnant! Sam was shaking with fear as she stripped off her clothes and slid her arms into the thin paper gown.

The doctor's examination seemed to take forever, but finally Dr. Bergstrom straightened up.

"You can get dressed now, Sam, and I'll see you in my office in a few minutes."

"But . . ."

"He'll explain everything to you in his office, Samantha," the nurse said, patting Sam's hand, "and don't worry. It's all perfectly natural."

Of course it was, Sam thought as she quickly pulled on her slacks and blouse. Pregnancy and childbirth were as natural as breathing . . . for young women, but not for someone her age. Not for a woman who could conceivably become a grandmother at any time.

The doctor was smiling when she sat down across from him, so Sam felt safe in assuming that she hadn't contracted a fatal disease. She took a deep breath and told herself to relax and stay calm. Whatever it was, she could deal with it. After all, what choice did she have?

"Well, am I pregnant?"

Dr. Bergstrom chuckled. "So, you did think that was a possibility?"

"Well, it crossed my mind, but . . ."

"You're not pregnant, Samantha," Dr. Bergstrom said, "but I must caution you: If you're going to continue to be sexually active, you'd better be extremely careful. It would be very easy for you to get pregnant right now."

Relief flowed through Sam and she felt herself sag. "Thank God!" she murmured.

Dr. Bergstrom nodded. "I did a pap test while I was examining you, Sam, and we'll know better when the results come back, but it looks to me as though you're starting menopause. What you experienced last night—the hot, flushed feeling, and then the chill? That's what's commonly called a hot flash. You were probably starting when you got pregnant with

Amber. I know you've heard of change-of-life babies."

"Sure, but menopause? I just turned forty-six!"

"It is early, but the onset of menopause varies with each woman. Some start in their forties, others not until their mid- to late-fifties. I really believe that's what's causing your symptoms—that and stress. I know things haven't been easy for you since your husband's death."

Sam shook her head. "Things have been pretty hectic, and now it looks like Amber is starting to teethe." She laughed. "That's why I was so panicked at the thought of another baby. I love Amber with every breath in my body, but . . . well, I just don't think I'm up for any more morning sickness and amniocentesis. I think I'll concentrate on raising puppies from now on."

Dr. Bergstrom laughed. "Wise move, Sam," he said. "Now, let's discuss birth control."

Sam left the doctor's office feeling like she could break into song at any moment. The thought of menopause and its accompanying discomforts didn't exactly thrill her, but the doctor had explained that for most women menopause was no more than a minor inconvenience, and in some ways it brought freedom. But she wasn't pregnant!

She thought about Jeff, and wondered what he would have thought if he'd known she was worried about being pregnant with his child. Would he have wanted a child? Would he feel cheated when he learned that she would soon be physically unable to bear children?

Jeff was seated at the kitchen table with Tim and Aunt Daisy when Sam got home. Three pairs of curious eyes focused on her.

"Everything all right?" Jeff asked.

He looked concerned, and Sam hastened to reassure him. "I'm fine," she said. Then she turned to Aunt Daisy. "Where's Amber?"

"Sleeping like a lamb," Daisy answered. "But I think she's cutting teeth, Sam. Her little gums are swollen. I rubbed some of that teething lotion on them."

Sam nodded and sat down next to Jeff.

"Did you tell Tim about the job?" she asked. Somewhere, between last night and her ride home from the doctor's office, Sam knew she had come to terms with Tim's need to try his wings and be independent.

"I want to go, Mom," Tim said seriously. "This may be the best opportunity I'll ever get. I'll miss all of you, but I think this is something I have to do. Do I have your blessing?"

Sam nodded. Tears were stinging her eyelids, but she held them back. "I want you to go, son," she said, and from the corner of her eye she caught Jeff's surprised look.

"Really?"

"Really," Sam said, "but before you go, could you enlighten me as to some of the ideas you dreamed up for the kennel? Jeff said you and he had some plans."

"Sure. Yeah! You really want to know?"

"Absolutely," Sam said, "but first let me check on Amber."

Amber was sleeping peacefully, just as Daisy had said. Sam stood looking down at the baby for a long time. Amber was a miracle, a precious gift, but she meant what she'd told the doctor. She didn't want any more children. While her family would always come first, the kennel was a lifelong dream, and there was only so much one person could do. If things had been different when she was younger, she would have loved more children, but now it was simply too late. She would have to tell Jeff what was happening to her, and make him understand how important it was to be careful.

Twenty-two

"So, if you add a grooming salon and boarding kennels, this place could become a paying proposition, Mom. Of course, you'd have to hire a groomer, and you'd need some capital to build new runs, but in the end the investment would be well worth it, don't you think?"

Sam was quiet, digesting all she'd heard. Some of the ideas weren't new to her. She'd considered them herself, but she'd always rejected them as too risky. Now both Jeff and Tim seemed convinced they would be feasible.

"I have to think about this," she said finally. "It sounds good, but . . . I guess I'm conservative to a fault. What if it doesn't work out? I'll be stuck with a loan I can't pay back."

"Nothing ventured, nothing gained," Aunt Daisy said flippantly. "Sometimes we have to take risks, Sammy girl; otherwise we just sit and stagnate. And since we're on the subject of stagnation, there's something I have to tell . . ."

"Hey, Daisy, shouldn't you start getting ready for the meeting at the center this afternoon? Frank wanted us to be sure to get there on time. It's got something to do with the craft shop, right?" Jeff looked at Daisy meaningfully.

Daisy's eyes snapped open as she nodded and hurried off to her room. "Be ready in a jiffy, Jake," she called over her shoulder.

That, Jeff thought, had been a close one. Unless he was mistaken, Aunt Daisy had been about to tell Sam about her wedding plans, and as far as Jeff was concerned, that would have been a big mistake. Sam had had a lot dumped on her, what with Tim's job and the ideas he and Tim had dreamed up for the kennel. He wasn't sure she could absorb much more right now.

But Daisy was getting impatient, and so was her beau. They wanted to be married and get on with their lives, and Jeff could sure understand that. He was starting to get impatient himself. He wanted to make his place in Sam's life permanent, but one thing at a time.

"Just a little longer, Daisy," Jeff pleaded as he drove her into town. "I'm a little worried about Sam. She seems so stressed lately. Actually, I'm amazed at how well she took the news about Tim's job, but if you dump on her, too . . ."

"All right, all right, Jake, I see your point," Daisy said, "but I can't wait too much longer. Ralph is getting anxious."

It wasn't going to be easy for Sam to let go of her family all in one fell swoop, even if Jeff was there to fill in the gaps.

"So, are we all in agreement about opening the shop on September first?" Frank asked. "How about a show of hands?"

Jeff sneaked a look at Ralph and Daisy. They sat off in a corner, away from the others, holding hands like starry-eyed teenagers. Reluctantly, they let go of each other and raised their hands.

"The place looks great, Frank," Jeff said after the meeting was officially closed. The seniors stood around, chatting and enjoying cookies and lemonade. "I really think the craft shop is going to be successful."

"I hope so," Frank answered. "Contributions are down lately, what with the slump in the economy. I guess most folks figure charity begins at home. Lord, I can't count how many times my folks said that when I was a kid."

Jeff nodded. Things were tough everywhere, and that was one of the reasons he thought Tim should jump on the job offer in Virginia.

He might not get another opportunity like it in a hurry.

"What's the deal with Ralph and Daisy these days?" Frank asked. "I figured those two were fixing to tie the knot."

Jeff nodded. "That's the plan, but Daisy's waiting for the right moment to break the news to her niece. You see, Samantha is . . ."

Frank held up his hand. "Say no more. I get the picture. This Samantha thinks her aunt is too old and frail for romance and such, eh?"

"Something like that," Jeff said, "but Sam means well. She has Daisy's best interests at heart."

"Sure she does, but doesn't she realize that time is running out for those two? Hell, they're not kids! Either one of them could keel over at any time. There's no time to waste, if you ask me."

"You're absolutely right, Frank," Jeff said, nodding.

Sam tucked Amber into her crib and sighed wearily. The baby was definitely teething; she'd been cranky all afternoon and Sam was exhausted, but she still had to feed the dogs and fix something for supper. Actually, she didn't feel much like eating, and Tim had said something about going out. She wondered if Daisy would be content with a sandwich when she got home from the center. Just then, Sam heard the sound of Jeff's car. She looked out the window and saw Jeff helping Aunt Daisy from the car, and . . . good heavens, Daisy's ankle was heavily bandaged and she was using a crutch!

"What happened? Aunt Daisy, are you all right?"

"Now just simmer down, Sammy girl," Aunt Daisy answered quickly. "I just sprained my ankle. It's no big thing."

"No big thing? A sprained ankle at your age? Why, you could have broken a bone! How did it happen?"

"Sam, it was just a stupid accident. Daisy tripped on a loose piece of carpet and . . ."

"Oh, my God! Don't you realize how badly she could have been hurt? What if she'd broken her hip?"

"She didn't break anything," Jeff said. He was trying to be patient, but Sam was building this whole thing out of proportion. What Daisy needed right now was a nice cup of tea and a nap.

"I think Daisy should lie down, Sam. The doctor who checked her ankle said it will be fine in a few days as long as she takes it easy and keeps her weight off it. And I think a cup of tea would be in order."

"Oh . . . oh, of course. Aunt Daisy, are you in pain? What can I do for you?"

"Just get me that tea and leave me be, girl," Daisy snapped. "Good heavens, you're making a big fuss about nothing!"

"But . . ."

"The tea, Sam," Jeff reminded her. "I'll help Daisy to her room and see that she gets her ankle propped up."

While she waited for the kettle to boil, Sam seethed along with the water. She'd been afraid of something like this. No matter how much Aunt Daisy enjoyed going to the center and dancing and carrying on, she was going to have to put a stop to it before something terrible happened. All that bouncing around was too strenuous for an elderly woman.

Sam fixed her aunt a tray with tea and some homemade almond cookies. By the time she carried the tray to Daisy's room, her heartbeat had resumed its normal rhythm. As she approached the room she heard the sound of urgent whispering.

"You've got to help me, Jake," Aunt Daisy was saying softly. "If Sammy has her way, I'll be locked in this room until I go to meet my maker! You saw how she was. Why, a body would think I was at death's door!"

"Am I that terrible, Aunt Daisy?" Sam demanded, advancing into the room, her shoulders stiff and her face flaming with angry color. "Is it wrong of me to be concerned for your safety?"

"Well, of course it isn't, Sammy. It's just that I know how you are, and you'll use this as an excuse to keep me away from the center and . . . well, it won't work. As soon as I'm back on my two feet I'll be at the center. I've made friends, and the center gives me something to do besides watch that silly television set. I've had more fun these past months than I have in years."

"It's not that I don't want you to enjoy yourself, Aunt Daisy. I do, but sometimes I think you forget your age."

Aunt Daisy started to shake her head, but then she nodded. "You're right, you know. Sometimes I do forget my age. I forget all my aches and pains, and the fact that I probably don't have too many more years left on this earth. Is that wrong, Sammy girl?"

Sam had no answer. She watched silently as Jeff fixed Aunt Daisy's tea for her. When she was finished he plumped her pillows and settled the prop more firmly under her ankle.

FULL BLOOM

"You rest now, Daisy," he said, "and if there's anything you need, just yell."

"Thank you, Jack," Aunt Daisy said. Then she closed her eyes.

Sam stood for a moment, not sure what to do or say. She couldn't help worrying, yet Jeff and Daisy were both acting as if it was no big deal.

"Come on, Sam, let's let her rest," Jeff coaxed. He put his arm around her waist and gently nudged her out of the room.

Sam groaned. "What next? Jeff, are you sure it's just a sprain? A fall can be deadly for an elderly person like Daisy, and . . ."

"She didn't actually fall, Sam. She just tripped on the loose carpet. Ralph kept her from falling. And the doctor really did say she would be fine in a few days." Jeff looked at Sam intently. "I wouldn't lie to you, Sam."

"I know," she said, but the words came out sounding like a sob. "Why can't I stop worrying, Jeff? Even Aunt Daisy is getting tired of having me hover over her. The first thing you know, everyone will leave and I'll be all alone, and it will be my own fault for being too clingy." She laughed then, and looked up at him. "Is that a word? Clingy?"

"If it wasn't before, it is now. Sam, your family knows how much you love them. Tim and

Aunt Daisy both know how much you care, but I think that what you need to realize now is that they're both struggling to be independent. Tim is ready to try his wings and fly away on his own and Daisy . . . well, she's desperate to maintain a little dignity in her twilight years. You can understand that, can't you, darling?"

He drew her into his arms and held her close, calming her with his love.

"Come into the living room and sit down. Have you eaten yet?"

Sam shook her head. "It was a hellish afternoon. Amber was as cranky as a bear who's lost his jar of honey. I was just trying to decide what to do about dinner when you pulled up with Aunt Daisy."

"Well, Daisy is probably set for the night. Despite her bravado, she was pretty shaken up. The doctor gave her something to settle her down. Tim's out with friends?"

"Right."

"Then I guess it's just us. How about one of my famous gourmet omelets?"

"Sounds wonderful," Sam said. She followed Jeff to the kitchen, feeling her tensions draining away.

By the time they finished their third cup of tea Sam felt mellow and relaxed, better than

FULL BLOOM

she had all day. She sighed. "Now, if Amber will just sleep through the night . . ."

Jeff smiled. "Not a very likely prospect, hm?"

Sam shook her head, then impulsively scooted closer to Jeff and leaned against him. "Not while she's teething," she answered.

They both fell silent, enjoying the quiet, restful atmosphere. Jeff's arm was around her shoulders, and Sam could feel the warmth of his body through her clothing. Suddenly, she wanted to make love to him so badly, it was like a physical pain. She shifted position and pressed her lips against Jeff's neck.

She heard him catch his breath and felt his arm tighten.

"Sam, are you . . ."

"I want you, Jeff," she said, her lips parted and waiting under his.

It was all he needed to hear.

They went to Sam's bedroom quietly, taking care not to disturb Amber as they passed the nursery. Please stay asleep just a little longer, baby, Sam pleaded silently.

Then they were standing beside her bed. There was a sudden look of dismay on Jeff's face as he looked at it. Without a word, Sam understood.

"Don't worry," she said softly. "I bought a

new bed after Doug died. Somehow it just seemed like the right thing to do."

Jeff nodded, and then he began to undress her; slowly at first, and then his fingers moved faster as Sam rubbed against him, heightening his own fiery desire. How was it possible, he wondered, for a man of fifty to feel such raw, eager passion? Such unbridled lust? It was as if he'd been starved for a woman, and maybe he had. Maybe his whole life had been spent hungering for a woman like Sam.

"Hurry, Jeff," she urged. "I can't wait much longer."

She was fumbling with his belt buckle now, then his zipper, and then her hand slipped inside his trousers. She felt his warmth and strength.

"Oh, Jeff," she moaned. "Please, please hurry!"

In minutes they were on the bed, writhing hungrily against one another. Sam felt alive and eager, and she knew she'd never get enough of this wonderful man, this man who could take her to the stars and back again. This man who could soothe her fears and calm her nerves, who could be tender and tough in turn. This man who had turned her world upside down. Because she would never, ever be the same. She'd been married and had borne two children, but she'd never really known what it was to be wholly female until Jeff walked into her world.

She was hungry for him, impatient to be filled with him, to feel his weight crushing her into the mattress. Then, suddenly, she remembered.

"Jeff, we have to be . . . careful. I could get pregnant very easily right now."

For an instant he was still, and his dark eyes seemed to glow as he stared down at her. Then he reached down for his pants, and she knew he would protect her.

If this is what happens in menopause, I love it, Sam thought, as she opened herself to Jeff. She was like a flower, its petals open wide to the sun, like a tender, leafy shoot reaching out to a raindrop.

Then Jeff's lips covered hers, and his strong, hard maleness filled her. She gasped against his mouth, then felt herself tighten around him. She began to move, slowly at first, then faster and faster as the need for completion drove her on. She reached the peak seconds before him; as he caught and followed her, she held him, her nails biting into the flesh of his buttocks.

"Wow!" Jeff said later, when he carefully lifted his weight from her. It was starting to get dark, but he could still make out the soft contentment on Sam's face. He could almost feel the relaxation that had taken over her body. "You must have missed me."

"Always," Sam admitted. "I wish you never had to leave."

"Maybe one day I won't," Jeff answered. He wanted to say more, wanted to declare his "intentions" as Daisy would have put it, but the time still wasn't right. He believed that Sam was learning to trust him, and he was convinced that someday soon the last of her doubts and fears would dissolve, but until then it was best if he tread lightly.

Twenty-three

Sam lay close against Jeff, her hand pressed against his chest. She could feel his heart beating under her palm, and she was almost content. She loved this man; maybe a part of her always had, ever since she was a shy, lonely, fourteen-year-old. She wanted nothing more than to share the remaining years of her life with him, to have him by her side through good times and bad. To laugh and argue with him, to have him help her guide Amber through a happy childhood. And Jeff loved her. She felt it in his touch, in the things he said, the look in his eyes when he smiled at her as she held Amber. But love wasn't always enough, and she and Jeff were so very different. Maybe he wasn't interested in spending his retirement changing diapers and listening to a teething baby cry. She remembered the day he'd arrived at her aunt's cottage, when he'd insisted that he wanted peace and quiet so he could write his book. Well, there was precious little peace around this house, and there probably wouldn't be for a long time to come. So maybe this was simply the wrong place for Jeff, despite the way his masterful lovemaking made her feel. Maybe the passion they shared wouldn't be enough to make up for what Jeff would be giving up if he joined his life with hers.

"Penny for your thoughts," he said, his hand lightly caressing her throat and sending fresh spasms of desire from one end of her body to the other. "Why so solemn?"

Sam's lips parted and she almost blurted out her thoughts, the doubts that nagged and taunted her. But then she smiled and shook her head. "Just thinking of Tim, and wondering how he'll manage on his own."

"He'll do fine," Jeff said. "I have a feeling that one of these days that young man will do you proud. He's got a lot to offer, Sam."

"I know. I think I'm just beginning to realize that. For so long I thought of him as my baby, and then my little boy. It's hard to think of him as a grown man."

"I'm sure it's that way for most mothers," Jeff said. "But I think that in the months to come you'll find that Tim is much more capable than you ever imagined."

"And speaking of my beloved son, he'll

probably be home at any time, so we'd better make ourselves decent."

Jeff pulled her back against him to kiss her, and Sam felt her body respond instantly. "Jeff, we can't," she managed, breaking away. "I don't want Tim to find us this way."

"Okay. I guess you're right. Tim and I have a pretty good relationship right now; I wouldn't want him to think he had to beat me up to defend your honor."

Sam laughed. An image of Tim and Jeff slugging it out crossed her mind. But for the fact that she didn't want either one of her men to get hurt, it might have been fun to have two handsome males fighting over her honor.

When she came out of the bathroom a few minutes later she discovered that Jeff had already gone downstairs. For a moment she stood, staring at the rumpled bed, letting the warm, musky scent of lovemaking swirl around her. She hated to think of how she would feel if this was taken away from her, if Jeff decided it was time to pull anchor and drift away. For years she'd thought of herself as a woman with a low sex drive. During her marriage she'd rarely initiated lovemaking, but now everything was different. She actually hungered for Jeff, and she was no longer afraid to enjoy her sensuality. Better late than never, Sam, she told herself as she headed downstairs to find Jeff.

"Daisy is still sleeping peacefully," Jeff said. "I just looked in on her. As I said earlier, I think she's out for the night."

"Amber is still asleep, too," Sam said, "but I know she's not out for the night."

"Come sit with me for a few minutes," Jeff said, leading Sam to the sofa. "Then I'll go home and let you get some rest. Do you know there are circles under your eyes?"

Sam started to laugh, but it turned into a sob. "I'm not a young girl anymore, Jeff. When Tim was a baby I cared for him with one hand tied behind my back, but now . . . I hate to admit it, but caring for Amber takes a lot out of me."

"For an old broad you look pretty good to me," Jeff said, arching his brows comically as he tried to leer at her.

"Thanks," Sam said, "but today I found out I really am getting old."

"Oh? Did you find a gray hair?" He held her loosely, letting his warmth and strength flow into her. "You're a beautiful woman, Sam. If you live to be a hundred years old, you'll still be beautiful."

"I . . . I'm going through the change of life, Jeff. I thought . . . I was afraid I was pregnant again, but Dr. Bergstrom said it's early menopause. He warned me to be especially careful with birth control from now on."

Jeff was silent for a moment, and a fleeting pang of regret stabbed at him. Through the years he'd pushed thoughts of fatherhood and family life away, believing it just wasn't in the cards for him. Then along came Sam and Amber, and he'd begun to realize what he'd missed. And he had actually wondered if Sam would consider having his child.

"But you're all right, aren't you?"

Sam hesitated, then knew she had to ask. "Would you have wanted a child, Jeff?"

He continued to stroke her gently, his fingertips sending a message of love. "It would have been wonderful," he said honestly, "but as long as I can share Amber with you, I'm content."

"Really?"

"Really. Now I'd better go home, and you'd better go to bed and get some sleep."

"I'll dream of you," Sam promised.

Jeff kissed her one last time, then stepped back. "Ditto," he said.

Jeff lay in bed, his hands linked behind his head. He was having trouble sorting out his feelings. Being honest with himself, he had to admit that the idea of having a child with Sam had crossed his mind. It wasn't a prerequisite, but it would have been wonderful, and now he knew that it was never going to happen.

Well, it was probably for the best, he decided. As it was, if he and Sam did get together, he'd be a doddering old man by the time Amber was Tim's age. He grinned, picturing himself and Sam attending PTA meetings, leaning on their canes and peering through their bifocals. Well, bifocals or not, he intended to be a damn good father to Amber, if Sam would let him.

Twenty-four

The day Tim left for Virginia, Sam steeled herself to be brave and cheerful. After all, she didn't want Tim to remember her holding a tissue to her swollen eyes. She wanted him to carry a picture of a smiling, waving mother, and she wanted him to leave home with confidence and a hopeful heart.

"What are you going to do with my room now, Mom?" Tim asked. "Maybe you can fix up that sewing room you always wanted."

Sam laughed and jiggled the baby in her arms. "With this little creature to look after, I doubt I'll have time to sew, Tim, but I'll keep your idea in mind—or maybe," she said, winking at Daisy, "we'll take in a handsome male boarder."

"Hey, wait a minute. I'm not sure I like that idea," Jeff said, boldly putting his arm around Sam's waist, not caring who saw him.

"So, that's the way it is, eh?" Tim grinned and lifted the last of his bags into Jeff's Blazer.

"I hope so," Jeff answered before Sam could speak. "I sure hope so."

"Good luck and Godspeed, Timothy," Aunt Daisy said, planting a kiss on the young man's cheek and patting his shoulder.

Tim grinned down at the frail but feisty lady. "Aunt Daisy, there were times when I never thought I'd say this, but I really am going to miss you."

"Go on now. You're turning into a regular charmer!"

Daisy blushed as Tim leaned down, hugged her, and whispered something in her ear. She started to shake her head, then changed her mind and nodded instead. "Maybe I will," she said. "Maybe I'll just do that."

"Maybe you'll do what?" Sam asked. She was sure her eyes were narrowed suspiciously, and she was equally sure she wasn't imagining the slightly guilty looks on the three faces surrounding her. "What's going on here?" she demanded.

"Nothing," three voices said in nearly perfect unison.

"I'll bet," Sam said. "Well, go ahead, keep your secrets." She smiled. "And maybe I'll have a few of my own."

Aunt Daisy clapped her hands. "Oh, good, secrets! I love secrets!"

By the time Jeff and Tim drove away Sam's tears had dried. Tim was off on an exciting journey, doing what she'd urged him to do: building a life of his own.

"Well, that's that," Aunt Daisy said. "I know you'll miss him, Sammy girl, but it's for the best. A young man has to make his own way in the world."

Sam hugged her aunt. "He'll be fine, Aunt Daisy," she said. And for the first time she believed it.

Late that afternoon Jeff returned from driving Tim to the airport. "Well, he's on his way," he said. "He promised to call as soon as he got to Brian's house." Jeff studied Sam's face, looking for traces of tears or anxiety. "Are you okay?"

"I'm wonderful," Sam said, and she meant it. Amber had finally cut her first tooth, and her disposition had improved dramatically. Daisy's ankle seemed to be as good as new, and everything was going along just fine.

Jeff's face relaxed into a smile. "I believe you mean that."

"I do. I'm happy for Tim. He's going to be doing what he wants to do, and the job sounds like the opportunity of a lifetime. What kind of mother would I be to try to hold him back?"

Jeff's smile widened. "Come on," he said.

"Wash the kennel dust out of your hair and put on your best jeans. This has been a special day. Let's take a ride over to the boardwalk and gorge on hot dogs with the works. And if you're very good, I might even buy you an ice cream sandwich for dessert."

"But Amber . . ."

"We'll take her along, and Aunt Daisy, too. We'll make it a regular family affair. Come on, Sam. What do you say? We all deserve a treat."

Sam closed her eyes and let the memories wash over her. Hot dogs smothered with mustard and sauerkraut, a slice of ice cream sandwiched between waffles and dusted with powdered sugar, and Jeff by her side. It was heaven, or else she was dreaming. But when she opened her eyes Jeff was still there and, suddenly, she wasn't a middle-aged mother. She was young again, energetic and vibrant and ready to face life head-on.

"Why not?" she asked, shrugging. "If you'll tell Aunt Daisy, I'll get Amber. And I'm holding you to that ice cream sandwich!"

It was a weeknight, and the boardwalk wasn't as crowded as it could have been. Propped in her stroller, wearing a white lace-trimmed bonnet, Amber took in the sights and sounds with wide-eyed interest. Aunt Daisy, delighted to have a chance to test her ankle, walked beside them with her eyes snapping.

"Goodness, it's been a long time since I've done this," she said. "Aren't we lucky to have Jeremy bring us, Sammy?"

"Indeed we are. This was a wonderful idea, Jeff," she said, giving his arm a little squeeze. "I'd forgotten how exhilarating this place can be."

Jeff grinned, and for just an instant he was once again the shy young man Sam had fallen head over heels in love with so long ago.

"I love the smell of the ocean," he said. "I even like the noisy, honky-tonk atmosphere."

"Me, too," Sam admitted, smiling.

It was a night of smiles, a night to rejoice for Tim's good fortune and to look forward to the future. And for Sam it was also a night to remember the past, to call up the feelings she'd felt during that long-ago summer. She didn't even have to close her eyes to feel the shivers of fear that had danced along her skin, the thrill of anticipation she had known while she waited for Jeff to kiss her, both dreading and craving the unknown.

A sound from the baby brought Sam back to the present. I'm not that shy, awkward little girl anymore, she thought. I'm a widow and a mother, a woman entering midlife. And Jeff was no longer the slender young man who had captured her teenage heart. They were both mature and sensible, too smart to make rash decisions that could end in disaster. So, for the time being, Sam decided she would be content to take things slowly, one day at a time. She'd see if the physical passion she felt for Jeff could be sustained despite the pressures of daily life, if they had enough common interests to keep them together once the first blaze of desire burned down. Because she'd married for lust and what she thought was love once, and it had ended unhappily. She wasn't going to make the same mistake twice.

"Oh, Jeff, look! There's the Ferris wheel! Do you remember how many times we rode on it that summer you were here with your father?"

Jeff laughed. "I don't have the exact count, but we kept that wheel turning, that's for sure. Want to give it a spin, for old time's sake?"

"Could we?" She felt like a kid, pleading for one more candy. "Please?"

Jeff turned to Daisy. "Will you watch Amber while Sam and I ride the Ferris wheel?"

Daisy nodded happily. "I was hoping for a chance to sit down and rest a minute. Amber and I will wait right here on this bench while you ride."

Behind Sam's back, Jeff gave Daisy the okay sign, and the elderly woman nodded.

High above the earth, Sam and Jeff looked out over the beach. The moon made a path over the water and the soft, splashing sounds of waves on the beach were music to their ears.

"God, I feel like a kid," Jeff murmured, pulling Sam hard against him and letting his lips lightly touch her ear. "This place is magic, Sam. Can you feel it?"

She could. She did, and she wished it never had to end. She wished she and Jeff could go round and round, in slow, languorous circles, with the lights of the boardwalk twinkling and the sound of crashing waves surrounding them. She lifted her face until her lips were nearly touching Jeff's. "Kiss me, my prince, before I turn back into a middle-aged mama."

"Hm, did I ever tell you I like middle-aged mamas? Especially when their breasts are so soft and full, when their . . ."

"Stop!" Sam cried, "We're almost at the bottom, and the people down below can see that lecherous look in your eyes."

"Who cares?" Jeff asked, and then he kissed her, and Sam felt as though the Ferris wheel was spinning in double time. And she realized she didn't give a fig who saw them!

* * *

"Aunt Daisy was worn out," Sam said when she returned from settling Amber into her crib, "and Amber, too. It must have been that salt air."

"It is magic, isn't it?" Jeff asked. "I really did feel like a kid again tonight."

Sam sat down next to him and handed him a glass of wine. "But we aren't kids, Jeff, and our lives are a lot more complicated now than they were then."

"Oh, I don't know about that. Some things never change. Like the way we feel about each other. It must have been lying dormant all those years."

Jeff carefully put his wineglass on the table, and then he placed Sam's beside it. Then slowly, so slowly Sam thought she'd die of anticipation, he drew her into his arms. "I love you, Samantha," he said, the words so soft and solemn they seeped right into her heart. "I think I've always loved you, and I want to spend the rest of my life right here beside you."

"Oh, Jeff! I want that, too, but I . . . I'm still afraid. It isn't just you and me. There's Amber and Daisy . . . and even Tim. I mean, what if he doesn't make out with his job? He could end up right back here. And the kennels . . ."

"I love Amber and Daisy," Jeff said, "and Tim and I understand each other. The kennels aren't a problem, Sam. I'm actually starting to like your dogs."

As if on cue, Muffy raced into the room, trailing one of Tim's old tennis shoes behind her.

Jeff laughed and shook his head. "Now that one is another story!"

"She's part of the package," Sam said.

"And a delightful package it is," Jeff responded. "You can't scare me off, Sam. I like it here."

Sam looked into his eyes. They were filled with love and concern. "I like it here, too," she said, snuggling close and lifting her face for his kiss. "I like it just fine."

Twenty-five

The little house seemed awfully quiet with Tim gone. Funny how one member of a family could make such a difference. It wasn't that Tim had been especially noisy, or even that he'd been around all that much, because during his last few weeks at home Tim had spent all of his free time with his girlfriend. As Sam bathed Amber and dressed her in a cool pink cotton sunsuit, she thought about her son, hoping with all her heart that all his fondest dreams would come true.

"He really was a good boy, you know," she told Amber. "It was just that he didn't know where he wanted to go or how to get there."

"Ga," Amber replied, giving Sam a wide smile that revealed her two new teeth.

"But you won't have that problem, sweetheart, because I won't make the same mistake twice. I'm going to make very sure you have every opportunity to figure out what you want to be when you grow up."

"If she's half as smart and sweet as her mother, she'll be doing great," Jeff said. Once again he'd entered the house without Sam realizing it. But she didn't mind. She'd gotten used to looking up and finding Jeff watching her, his face full of love.

"Hi," she said, lifting her face for the kiss that had now become a delightful habit. "Did you come to see me or Daisy?"

"Both," Jeff said. "And this little sweetheart, too. How's she doing this morning? Any more new teeth?"

"She's working on them," Sam said. She finished snapping the crotch of Amber's playsuit and handed the baby to Jeff, surprised at how comfortable she felt doing it. It was almost as if Jeff was the baby's natural father.

"Well, look what we have here," Jeff said, holding the clean, sweet-smelling baby high in the air. Amber gurgled happily, and Jeff carefully lowered her so he could sniff her neck and inhale the baby scent of her.

"Nothing smells as good as a baby, does it?"

"Nope." Jeff cradled the little girl in his arms and smiled at Sam. "How am I doing for a crusty old bachelor?"

"Crusty?" Sam asked, her eyebrows arched. "Old?"

"Not that old!" Jeff said. "What's on your agenda today?"

"Amber is due for a checkup and a booster shot," Sam said, putting the baby's bath things away, "and I thought maybe I could drop Daisy off at the senior center while I'm in town."

"I was planning to do that," Jeff said. "Today's my day to help Frank finish the shelves for the craft shop."

"The shop is going to be great, isn't it? Aunt Daisy is certainly excited about it."

"Everyone is," Jeff said. "I'll tell you, Sam, this is what the elderly need, something to occupy their minds and their hands, a reason to get up in the morning."

Sam nodded. Jeff was right, of course. The change in Daisy since she had started attending the center was nothing short of a miracle. It even seemed as though the older woman's arthritis was less troublesome lately. "You're not still beating yourself up over your dad, are you, Jeff?"

"No. I've made peace with that. I did the best I could at the time. No one can do more than that. I'm sure Dad understood."

"So there you are, Jake!" Aunt Daisy came hurrying into the room, all smiles. "Are you ready to leave for the center? There's a lot to do today, you know. If we're going to open the craft shop next week, we'd better hop to it!"

"Ready when you are, Daisy," Jeff said. "Is your jam all ready to go?"

"It surely is," Aunt Daisy answered.

There was a proud gleam in her eyes, and Sam smiled as her elderly relative pecked her cheek.

"Later, Sammy girl," Aunt Daisy called over her shoulder, herding Jeff toward the kitchen to pack up her jelly.

Sam shook her head as she watched them go. Aunt Daisy's renewed zest for life was wonderful, and she knew most of the credit had to go to Jeff. "Have a good day, you two," she yelled as she carried Amber to her playpen.

"So, how's your love life, young fellow?" Frank asked as he and Jeff arranged shelves to hold the handmade crafts that would soon be on sale. "I heard tell you're romancing that pretty niece of Daisy's."

Jeff had to laugh. "News travels fast," he said.

Frank stopped what he was doing and regarded Jeff soberly. "It's not just nosiness, Jeff. All of us here . . ." he stopped and waved his arms toward the elderly women and men diligently working, arranging and pricing their crafts. "Well, we consider you part of our family. We care about you, young fellow."

"I know you do, Frank, and thanks. I appreciate your concern. As for my love life . . . well, let's just say I'm working on it, okay?"

Frank grinned and slapped Jeff on the back. "That's the spirit, boy! Hang in there!"

As Jeff worked, the muted sounds of the other workers hovered at the edge of his consciousness, and Frank's words rattled around inside his head. He really did feel like part of a family here, both at the center and with Sam. And he liked it. He realized that deep down inside he'd missed this warm comradeship for most of his life. The friendships he'd made in the military had been different. He would always value them, but this . . . this easy, homelike feeling was something he couldn't put a price on. When he walked into the center he felt needed and wanted. All the seniors greeted him by name and seemed genuinely glad to see him. Hammering a nail into a smoothly sanded board, Jeff grinned. It was like having a big, extended family of aunts and uncles. And when he watched the seniors bustling around, busy and happy, he felt warm all over. This was what he would have liked for his father.

"Say, Jeff, how are things going with Daisy and Ralph? I get the feeling that old Ralph is getting anxious to tie the knot. Why do you suppose Daisy's dragging her feet?"

It was Pete Howard who'd come up behind Jeff when he stopped for a well-deserved break. Jeff turned to greet the older man.

"Hi, Pete. How are you?" He took a swallow of the lemonade one of the ladies had brought him. "I think Daisy and Ralph will work things out. Daisy's just waiting for the right time to break the news to her niece."

Pete glanced across the room, where Daisy was huddled with a group of the women, and groaned. "Don't I know how that is," he said. "My daughter's worse than a mother hen since her mother passed on. She acts like all my brain cells have atrophied!" He shook his head. "Don't know what gets into young folks sometimes."

"She's just concerned for you," Jeff said. "I guess it's easy to be overprotective when you love someone."

"I suppose," Pete said, "but it's sure hard to take. I've tried telling her I'm still able to tend my own affairs, but I don't think she hears me."

"Well, at least you know she loves you," Jeff

said. "You'd feel a lot worse if no one cared about you."

Pete looked surprised for a minute; then he grinned. "I never thought of it that way," he admitted. "I guess love has a price, doesn't it?"

It sure does, Jeff thought as he finished his lemonade and went back to work. But then, everything in life had a price. You gained one thing and gave up another. Like him and Sam. If they were successful in getting together, Sam would have to surrender a little of her stiff independence, and he, in turn, would have to learn to curb his bossy, managing nature. They would have to meet on middle ground and learn to compromise. And they could; he was sure of it. He and Sam were both intelligent people. There was no reason they couldn't meet on common ground, if they wanted to badly enough.

He sure did. He wanted it more than he'd ever wanted anything in his life. When he thought of going back to his old life, of holding people at arm's length and never really being intimate, he felt cold and dead inside. Sam and her little family had led him in from the cold and given him warmth and light. They'd given him a new reason to get up in the morning, a new set of goals to strive toward. They'd given him a whole new life.

Sam hummed contentedly as she made the final preparations for dinner. It was nothing fancy, just Daisy's recipe for a cold pasta salad and some fresh steamed shrimp. She'd discovered that Jeff loved shrimp, and she wanted to surprise him. There was also a fresh peach pie cooling on the counter, and it looked like she was just about done. If she hurried, she would have time to bathe and change before Jeff and Aunt Daisy got home. Maybe Jeff would enjoy seeing her in something other than torn, faded jeans for a change.

Stripping off her soiled clothing so she could shower and dress before the baby woke from her nap, Sam stepped into the shower and turned on the water. She sighed as the warm water pelted her flesh, and as she slid the lightly scented soap over her body she felt her cares wash away down the drain. Things were finally starting to work out. She and Amber had a momentary break from the trials of teething, Tim was happily established in his new job, and Aunt Daisy was happier than Sam had seen her in years. So everyone was happy except her and Jeff. As she rinsed off,

Sam revised her last thought. It wasn't that she and Jeff were unhappy, it was more that they felt unfinished . . . at least that was how she felt, and unless she was sadly mistaken, Jeff was having some of the same feelings. They were lovers, but it wasn't enough. Both of them wanted more. She felt that they were inching toward a total commitment, but a part of each of them held back, scared to take that last, final step.

Sam wrapped herself in a thick, fluffy terry towel and shook water from her hair like one of her dogs after a swim. She kept telling herself she had nothing to fear from Jeff, that it wasn't in his nature to hurt anyone. How could a woman be afraid of a man who held a baby so tenderly and had such endless patience with a cantankerous old woman? Why was she so afraid of giving up her independence? Part of it was due to the insecurities she'd suffered in her first marriage, but there was more, and try as she might, she couldn't figure out what it was.

When Jeff and Aunt Daisy came in, Sam was feeding Amber her dinner. The baby sat in her high chair, and she banged a spoon happily when she spotted Jeff.

"I think she's glad to see me," Jeff said, bending to kiss the top of the baby's head.

"We both are," Sam said, smiling up at him. Then she turned to Daisy. "Did you have a good day at the center?"

Daisy nodded. "Good and busy. My poor old muscles are worn out." She glanced toward the table, set with three places. "Will you be too disappointed if I don't join you, Sammy? I'm afraid I ate a few too many of Martha Beck's oatmeal cookies. All I need right now is a nap."

Sam's antennae went up instantly. "Aunt Daisy, did you overdo today? You're not sick, are you, dear?"

"Now just you turn it off, Sammy girl. I'm fine. I'm just a little tired, and that's perfectly normal, isn't it, Jeremy?"

"Aunt Daisy, for the last time, his name is Jeff," Sam said.

Daisy grinned. "Isn't that what I just said?"

"Sometimes I think she just calls you all those different names to get a rise out of us," Sam said, after Daisy had gone to her room. Then a worried look covered her face. "You don't think she overdid it, do you?"

"Not a bit. She had a great time, but she did eat a few of Martha's cookies. Actually, so did I."

"Go get a shower," Sam said, shooing him away. She'd seen the gleam in his eyes and knew he was about to kiss her, and if he did . . . well, poor Amber might not get to finish her applesauce. "By the time you get back I'll be finished with Amber and we can eat." She smiled innocently. "Unless you're too full of cookies to want any of the steamed shrimp and pasta salad I fixed."

"Steamed shrimp? Pasta salad? I'll be right back."

Amber finished her applesauce and took her bottle like a lamb. It was almost as if she sensed that her mama needed some free time.

Sam was taking the salad out of the refrigerator when Jeff came in.

"Is Amber all tucked in?" he asked, coming up behind her and slipping his arms around her waist.

"Sleeping like an angel," Sam reported, leaning back against Jeff gratefully. She'd missed him all day. She was definitely getting used to having him around.

"Can that salad wait?" Jeff whispered against her ear.

Sam thought of several cute answers, but the words all stuck in her throat. She straightened and put the salad back into the refrigerator. Wordlessly, she led Jeff to her bedroom.

It wasn't fully dark yet, and at first Sam felt self-conscious. Being with Jeff like this was still relatively new, and it was still a little scary. She wasn't a young girl anymore and she couldn't help wondering if Jeff saw the flaws and marks of time on her body.

"Don't be shy with me, Sam," he said, as if he sensed her misgivings. "We belong together like this. It was meant to be this way."

Sam allowed him to finish unbuttoning her blouse. She shivered as cool air touched her naked flesh. "Jeff . . ."

"No talk now," Jeff insisted, capturing the hands that would have stilled his progress. "Just feel, Sam." He took one of her hands and pressed it lightly against his arousal. "This is what you do to me. All I have to do is think about you . . . remember that night in Atlantic City or the time we spent together in New York, and I'm ready."

"It's the same with me. I'm working with the dogs and all of a sudden I have to stop and catch my breath."

Jeff's movements became frenzied as Sam continued to stroke the front of his trousers. "Oh, Sam!" he said, groaning. "Stop! Just for a minute."

She obeyed him, and they finished undressing frantically as the hot, steamy desire enveloped them.

"God, I can't believe this!" Jeff whispered against her neck when they were finally naked together on the bed. "I've been on this earth for half a century! I never expected to feel like this again."

"Me neither," Sam admitted. She pushed closer to Jeff's hard warmth. "I have a confession to make. I . . . didn't enjoy sex very much when I was married to Doug. I thought I wasn't . . . very highly sexed."

"Big mistake," Jeff murmured as his hands cupped her full, heavy breasts. He chuckled softly. "Who would have thought it? That a skinny, flat-chested little fourteen-year-old could turn into such a hot-blooded, sensual wench."

Sam began to laugh, but it was quickly smothered by Jeff's lips as his hot, insistent mouth moved over hers. His tongue slipped between her teeth and began a love dance with her tongue.

Then, when Sam thought she would die from lack of oxygen, Jeff lifted his head and let his lips trail downward until they circled the tip of her breast. Sam felt herself swell against his mouth, felt a warm, tugging sensation deep in the pit of her stomach. She began to move beneath him, rubbing herself against his hardness, so that the feelings intensified.

"Jeff!"

"Slow, baby," he coaxed. "Patience."

"I . . . don't have any," Sam said, panting with a desire so strong, it consumed her entire body. A tornado could have blown the roof off her house at that moment and she wouldn't have cared, as long as Jeff continued to kiss and caress her.

But he made her wait, and the sensations that flooded Sam's body were unlike any she had ever known. A warm, pulsating need was driving her to completion, urging her to writhe passionately against Jeff. Only his hands on her hips stilled her movements when they would have sent him over the edge prematurely, and finally, when neither of them could bear a moment more of the exquisite torture, Jeff moved inside her.

A sigh whispered against Sam's lips as she welcomed him into her woman's warmth. Then she began to move, the age-old dance of love, slowly at first, then faster and faster as the heat rose around them like steam. Then she felt herself tighten and begin to pulse. They came together in a glorious burst of sensations, then slowly, gently, drifted back to earth, and the reality of a baby's fretful cries.

"Amber," Sam said. "I thought she'd sleep awhile."

Jeff laughed and gave her one last kiss before rolling away. "I'll bet she senses we're having fun without her. Want me to get her?"

"Would you?"

"How could I refuse you anything, Sam?"

Twenty-six

After changing Amber and propping her up in the high chair, Sam bustled around the kitchen, setting out their cold supper.

"Now I do have an appetite," Jeff teased, holding Sam's chair and then sitting down across from her.

Sam smiled. She was filled with Jeff's love, saturated with his warmth and caring, and she wanted nothing more than to spend the rest of her days sharing moments like this with him. At times like this she could believe that they were right for one another, that she and Jeff could live together in love and harmony. But the niggling little doubts still plagued her. They ate at her when Jeff wasn't around, when she thought of all he would be taking on if he married her.

"A moment ago you were smiling, and now you look as though someone just dumped a ton of troubles on your shoulders, Sam. What's wrong?"

Jeff had heaped his plate with steamed shrimp and pasta salad, but now he put down his fork and regarded her soberly. "What's bothering you? Is it Tim? Are you missing him?"

Sam shook her head. "Oh, I miss Tim, all right," she admitted, "but that's not the problem." She pushed her plate away, feeling tears sting her eyelids. "Oh God! I'm not even sure there is a problem, and if there is . . . well, it's of my own making. I just . . . I guess I can't let go of the past, Jeff, and I'm afraid of the future."

"I want to share the future with you, Samantha," Jeff said. He was out of his chair now, and his hands were on her shoulders. He wanted to infuse her with his strength, with his certainty that together they could make it work. That they could have it all, marriage, a family, and a love that wouldn't die. But there was a part of Sam that he couldn't seem to reach, no matter the physical intimacies they shared.

"Jeff, I . . . sometimes I don't know what's wrong with me. I love you, and I believe you love me, too, but what if love isn't enough? I don't think I can handle another failure. I'm not up for another mistake." She looked over at the baby, happily gumming a teething biscuit. "And I don't want to give Amber a daddy and then have him disappear from her life."

"Is that what you think I'd do, Sam? Cut and run? Don't you know better than that by now?"

Sam sensed a change in Jeff. She felt his fingers stiffen on her shoulders. Suddenly, she was icy cold, despite the early fall warmth. She looked up at him and saw the way his jaw was tensed. "Jeff, I . . ."

"I think I'd better get out of here for a while," Jeff said, his hands dropping from her shoulders. "I need to do some thinking."

With tears sparkling on her lashes, Sam nodded wordlessly. She kept her head down so she wouldn't have to watch him go.

After Amber had been put back to bed Sam cleared the table, putting the uneaten food back in the refrigerator. The beautiful evening she'd anticipated had been ruined, destroyed by doubts. What is wrong with me, she asked herself? Why am I doing this? It's as if I'm hell-bent on ruining everything, as though I'm determined to chase Jeff away, when my heart aches for him to stay.

With a heavy sigh, Sam locked the front door and put out the lights. She was tired, but she knew she'd have a hard time getting to sleep. In fact, she knew she'd be damned lucky if she closed her eyes at all.

Jeff paced the perimeter of his small living room. What he really wanted to do was throw something, or smash something, or crush a beer can in his bare hands, the way he'd once seen one of his recruits do. His entire body was hot with rage. He couldn't remember ever being so angry. He peered out the window toward Sam's place and snorted. So! Sam was snug and safe in her bed, having sweet dreams while he stormed and stewed! It just figured! Women! No wonder his dad had never remarried!

But he knew he was just letting off steam. His dad hadn't remarried because he hadn't been lucky enough to find a second love. For him there'd been no Sam, no sweet, seductive, maddening female to turn him inside out.

But hell, he'd been patient, hadn't he? And he'd done everything he could to make Sam see that he was willing to share fifty-fifty, rearing Amber, helping Daisy and Tim . . . even running the kennel. Why wasn't it enough? Why did she always get that scared, panicky look on her face every time they got close to making a commitment? Did she really trust him and his love so little? Finally, deciding that he wasn't likely to come up with any brilliant answers, Jeff took a shower and lay down on his bed. For a long while he stared into the darkness, wondering what he could do to convince Sam that what they had was worth taking a chance on. As Daisy was always saying, time was slipping away like grains of sand in an hourglass. It was time to grab the brass ring and hang on. There was no time to waste, and all he had to do was convince Sam.

Samantha tossed restlessly, and when she heard Amber's faint whimpers, she crawled out of her bed almost eagerly. She'd sat by her bedroom window, staring out into the darkness until she'd seen Jeff's light go out. She shrugged. She was glad someone was getting some sleep! But even after she curled up in a ball in bed and told herself how tired she was ten times in a row, she couldn't fall asleep, so it was actually a relief to hear Amber start to whine.

"What's wrong, sweetie?" she asked the baby a moment later. "Is something hurting you?"

A wet diaper was part of the problem. After changing the baby and washing her hands Sam ran her finger over Amber's gums. Sam had a feeling the brief reprieve from teething pains was over. She warmed a bottle and sat down in a rocker to feed Amber.

With just one lamp lit the nursery was dim and peaceful. Sam rocked gently while Amber drank. She wouldn't blame Jeff if he got fed up and took off. He'd already shown an unusual amount of patience, but how long would it last? How long before he got tired of being on the defensive all the time? How long before he gave up on her?

When he couldn't stand lying sleepless any longer Jeff rolled over and sat up. From his bedroom window he could see Sam's place. He looked, blinked, and squinted into the darkness and realized there was a light on in the nursery.

What did it mean? Was something wrong with the baby? Was Amber sick? Should he call and see if everything was all right, or would Sam resent the intrusion? Just as he reached out for the telephone the light went out. With a heavy sigh, Jeff fell back on the bed. It was going to be a hell of a long night.

* * *

Wearily, Sam crawled back into her bed. It felt cold and lonely, even though the weather was exceptionally warm for late August. She wanted Jeff beside her, but not just for tonight; she wanted him for all the nights to come. But she wasn't at all sure that what she wanted would ever come true.

"What's the problem, Sam?" Ellie demanded the next day, her hands on her ample hips. "You just admitted that you love the guy, so what's keeping you from doing everything you can to hang on to him? From everything you've told me, the man is a treasure beyond price. Take it from me, pal, those kind of men don't grow on trees!"

"It's hard to explain, Ellie," Sam said slowly. She sipped her coffee and stared off into space. How could she expect Ellie to understand when she didn't understand herself? She just knew that there was a hard core of fear inside her, and no matter what Jeff said or did it wouldn't go away.

Ellie's tone softened. "Look, Sam, I know some of what you went through with Doug, but Jeff . . . well, he's a different type. Even

I can see that. He's dependable, and he seems honest, and what he's done for Daisy . . . well, you have to admit it's little short of a miracle. Before Jeff arrived you were about ready to be carted off to the funny farm. Now . . . well, look around you, Sam. Daisy is as happy as a clam, Tim is gainfully employed, Amber is thriving, and it must be great to have a pair of broad shoulders to lug in those heavy sacks of dog food."

Sam had to laugh. "You make Jeff sound like a pack mule. I don't think he'd appreciate that."

"You're running scared, Sam. I can see it in your eyes. Remember, this is me you're trying to con, and it won't work. There's not a thing in the world wrong with Jeff. You're putting up roadblocks because you're scared stiff. Sure, I know your marriage to Doug wasn't sweetness and roses, but it's more than that, Sam, and nobody knows that better than you. You're afraid of being abandoned again. You're scared that Jeff will take off just like your pitiful excuse for a mother did all those years ago! That's what this is all about, isn't it, Sam?"

Twenty-seven

Samantha winced, but she knew that what Ellie was saying was true. Intellectually, she knew it, but sorting out her emotions and keeping them separate from what she knew in her head was an almost impossible proposition.

"Maybe he's in love with me now, Ellie," she said slowly, "but what will happen when the reality of daily living sets in? When Amber gets sick and upchucks on his best pants? When the kennel operates in the red and he has to watch me struggle to pay the bills? Or what if Daisy relapses and starts acting crazy again? What if he can't handle it and wants out? What will I do then? I'm not as strong as you are, Ellie. I don't think I could just shrug and get on with it. I'd probably fold up into a soppy heap of tears and wail myself into a breakdown or something."

"Oh, Sam! You are something else! I'll let you know when I figure out what. A soggy heap of tears indeed! You forget who you're talking to, my friend. I was here when you discovered you were pregnant, remember? And I was here when Doug acted like a royal shit and stormed out of here and smashed himself against . . . look, I'm sorry. Sometimes my mouth really does run away with me. But you know it's true, Sam." Ellie caught Sam's pained expression and subsided. "Okay, okay, I'll say no more, but you're not a useless piece of fluff and you never have been. You're one of the bravest, strongest women I know. I guess I'll just have to trust you to make the right decision, won't I?"

Sam smiled weakly. For a moment it had seemed as if the past was crashing down on her, and that was the last thing she needed now. "That would be nice," she said.

"Was that Ellie I heard in here?" Aunt Daisy asked. She shuffled into the kitchen, wearing one of the oddest-looking outfits Sam had ever seen.

"Aunt Daisy, are you . . . uh, you're not planning to go out today, are you?"

Daisy grinned, and a naughty twinkle sparked in her eyes. "Why? Don't you approve of my new look? Split skirts are all the rage, you know."

"Yes, but . . ." Sam caught herself in time. She'd been about to say that Daisy was much too old to worry about fashion.

"Well, it will take some getting used to, I suppose," Daisy murmured, fingering her silk shirt and crocheted vest thoughtfully. "But Jim said I looked spiffy. At least that's the word I think he used. Oh dear, sometimes my memory fails me."

Sam rolled her eyes heavenward. Fringed crocheted vests and split skirts. What next?

"Did Ellie leave any of those jelly doughnuts she usually brings?" Daisy asked.

"I think there's one left, but you know sweets aren't good for you, Aunt Daisy."

"Oh, pshaw! What is good for me at my age, Sammy girl? What harm can a little sugar do at this stage of the game?"

Sam nodded absently; her aunt had a point. The woman was in her late seventies and, all things considered, she'd had a good life. Why deny her a little sugar?

"Help yourself," she said, sliding the plate toward her aunt. "Want some caffeine to go with it?"

"No, thank you, I'll pass on that. I think I'll have milk instead. The calcium is good for my bones."

Sam shook her head helplessly. "Whatever," she said.

Sam folded laundry as Daisy nibbled her doughnut. For a while she listened to her aunt's chatter with half an ear, then suddenly her ears pricked up. She whirled to face Daisy. "You're what?"

Sam knew her eyes were probably as wide and round as the marbles Tim had once played with. Of course she'd misunderstood. She was so preoccupied these days . . .

"I said," Aunt Daisy repeated, enunciating each word carefully, "that I'm thinking of getting married. I've been waiting for the right time to tell you, but Ralph is getting impatient, so I guess this is it." Aunt Daisy smiled calmly, as though the words she'd just uttered held no more significance than the nightly weather report.

Sam felt as though her bones had turned into rigid steel rods. "I must be going insane," she muttered. Amber woke and began to wimper, and Sam bent and picked up the baby, jiggling her to quiet her fussing. "I knew I shouldn't have had that glass of wine last night. I could have sworn you said you were thinking of getting married, Aunt Daisy. Isn't that a riot?"

"Ummm."

"What?"

"I said, that's right. I am."

Sam knew she must look confused. "What's right?"

"What I said about getting married." Aunt Daisy licked the last of the jelly off her fingers and nodded. "I've been thinking about it for a long time. Marriage is an important step, you know? I didn't want to jump into anything impulsively. I've never been that kind of person. I always weigh all the pros and cons before I act. Then again, as Ralph says, at our age there's not much time to waste, is there?"

Sam plopped down in the nearest chair and hoisted Amber to her shoulder. As if she had sensed the tension in the air, the baby had stopped fussing and was watching the adults in wide-eyed fascination. Sam's head was swimming. "Now I know I'm sick! I must be hallucinating! Aunt Daisy, you're seventy-seven—no, almost seventy-eight years old! You have arthritis, colitis, memory lapses . . . not to mention that you snore! How can you even consider getting married? And who is this bum who's been putting such crazy ideas in your head? Who is he, some silly gigolo who thinks you have money?"

Now Sam was quivering from head to toe.

She had to put Amber back in the playpen. She'd never heard anything so silly in all her life. Aunt Daisy getting married! It was ridiculous!

But as Sam stared at her elderly relative, Daisy drew herself up to her full height of five feet, two inches, a couple of inches less than what it had been when she was in her prime. With her lips pursed and her faded eyes flashing angrily, Aunt Daisy was still a formidable opponent. Boldly, she faced Sam down. "Don't you dare call my Ralph a bum! He's a wonderful man! Am I so terrible that no one would want me just for myself? It may be hard for you to understand, Sammy girl, but I love Ralph, and he loves me. We've both been lonely for a long time. We think we'd like to spend what time we have left together. Is that so wrong? What law would we be breaking? Who would we be hurting?"

Sam opened her mouth, then closed it without uttering a sound. She was hot, flushed with shame and remorse. Oh Lord, she'd done it again! She'd alienated one of the people she loved most in all the world! Just because her aunt was getting on in years didn't mean she didn't have feelings and needs like everyone else. How could she have been so blind, so self-centered . . . so hurtful? And wasn't this just part of what Jeff had tried to tell her? Still, the idea of Aunt Daisy getting married was going to take some getting used to.

"I'm sorry, Aunt Daisy. I didn't mean . . . it's just that I worry about you, and I never thought you would want to remarry. And especially now, at this time of your life."

Daisy nodded, and her eyes softened. "I know you didn't mean to hurt my feelings, Sammy. You've always been a good girl, but you young folks tend to forget that us oldsters need more than bed and board. I've never stopped missing your uncle, Sammy. I always liked having a man around the house, and in my bed. Now, with Tim gone and you trying to run Jake off . . . well, I'm seriously considering Ralph's proposal."

Actually, it had gone a lot farther than that, but Daisy wasn't sure Sam could absorb much more at the moment. Ease her into it, Daisy, old gal, she reminded herself. Heck, even if she hadn't been wildly in love with the old boy, she would have pretended. Anything to bring Sammy to her senses before it was too late! They thought she didn't notice, but she'd seen the way things were going: Sammy and Jeremy drawing closer, then one or the other of them pulling back, and most of the time it was Sammy. That girl just couldn't seem to make a commitment! Well, maybe if she thought she was about to be left all alone except for the baby, she'd get her act together. It was sure worth a try!

Sam couldn't seem to clear away her confusion. "Where would you live, Aunt Daisy?" Much as she loved her aunt and wanted her to be happy, Sam couldn't see herself living with another senior citizen.

"Don't worry about that. Ralph has a lovely little house in Cape May, right across from the beach. Isn't that romantic, Samantha? I'm sure you remember me telling you about it. We'll be able to lie in bed at night and listen to the waves crash on the shore, and oh, I do love that salt-air smell!" Then she laughed. "And if it's any consolation to you, girl, Ralph has arthritis, too. We take the same medication. And he snores almost as bad as you say I do."

Sam's eyes narrowed. "Oh? And how would you know about that?"

Daisy chuckled and winked. "Don't even ask, Sammy girl. I'm a woman, and a woman's entitled to a secret or two, isn't she?" She sobered as she took in Samantha's worried frown. "Come on, honey, perk up. You don't need a forgetful old woman around here anymore. Why, with all you've got to do, my leaving should be a blessing. And if you'd hook up with that Jake fellow . . ."

"His name is Jeff, Aunt Daisy. Jeffrey Brooks." Sam sniffed, trying to blink back tears. "I hope you know I've never thought of you as a burden, Aunt Daisy," she said. "After all you did for me, I was glad to take care of you, but I do want you to be happy, and if this Ralph person . . . just promise me you'll think this through carefully."

Aunt Daisy grinned mischievously. "I will, but caution is for you young folks, honey. At my age there's not much time to shilly-shally! And I know what your young man's name is. I just like to tease."

Somehow, Sam made it through the day, but later she stopped in the middle of cleaning one of the runs as a horrible feeling of desolation swept over her. Tim was gone, and soon Daisy would be leaving, too. It would be just her and Amber, unless she could make a commitment to Jeff. She wanted to; deep down she wanted it so badly she ached, but she was afraid. Jeff was like a dream, too good to be true.

Sam looked at Frosty, her champion stud. He was in one run alone, and in the next was Polar Princess. All of Princess's pups were gone now, and the bitch had a sad, lonely look in her dark eyes. On impulse, Sam took Princess and put her in the same run with Frosty. There would be no mating for a while, but at least the dogs could keep each other company.

"So, what do you think, Princess?" Sam asked the pretty female. "Frosty is some hunk, isn't he? 'Course, you'll have to watch out that he doesn't just move in and take over. Some males do that, you know. They just run in like bulldozers. They take over your life and nothing is ever the same. . . ."

The tears came then, and Sam swiped at them viciously. Dr. Bergstrom had warned her that she might feel a little down and weepy now and again. Maybe this was just one of those times.

When she finally returned to the house late that afternoon all Sam wanted was a shower and a chance to sit down quietly with Amber, but when she entered the house there was Jeff, comfortably ensconced at the kitchen table with Daisy. The two of them seemed to be having a high old time.

"Sam, join us," Jeff invited, as though it was his house and she was a guest. "Want something cold to drink? Daisy made some great iced tea."

"No, thanks, I just need a shower. Aunt Daisy, will you keep an eye on Amber if I leave her in the playpen for a few minutes?"

"Here, give her to me," Jeff said, holding out his arms.

"No. She . . . likes to be in the playpen with her toys."

For some reason she couldn't explain Sam was afraid to hand Amber over to Jeff. It was almost as if she expected him to snatch her and run off somewhere. Sam shuddered. Then she would really be alone.

"Sure. Okay. I'll just help Daisy keep an eye on her, and maybe you'll have some tea when you come down."

Sam didn't answer. She trudged upstairs, feeling like the bottom had dropped out of her world. Jeff. Why hadn't she realized before? This was all because of Jeff. He'd taken Aunt Daisy to that senior center and put silly notions into her head. He'd told her she could dance and party like a much younger woman, and now look what was going on! She wanted to get married and move into her elderly lothario's home! And he'd taken Tim away as well. Without Jeff, Tim would eventually have found a job nearby; instead, he was hundreds and hundreds of miles away. Someday he'd marry and have children, and

Sam would hardly ever get to see them, and it was all Jeff's fault! Why hadn't he kept his nose out of her business? And more to the point, why had she ever allowed him access to her life? Loneliness, and the need for a strong shoulder and a kind word. Well, look what it had gotten her! Her family was disintegrating before her eyes, and when Jeff decided he'd had enough and left it would be just her and Amber.

She stayed upstairs as long as she could, and it was only when she heard Amber fussing that she made herself go down to the kitchen.

"I have to take Amber upstairs for her bath," she said. She avoided looking at Jeff and Daisy, but she could feel them watching her.

"What's wrong, Sam?" he asked. "Daisy told me she told you about her and Ralph getting married. Is that what's bothering you?"

"How long have you known?" she asked, finally turning to face him.

"Well, I . . ."

"Now don't go getting mad at Jake over any of this, Sammy," Daisy said.

The elderly woman twisted her hands nervously, and Sam's heart ached. The last thing she wanted to do was hurt her aunt, but she was starting to believe there was a lot more to this little romance than met the eye.

"How long, Jeff?" she insisted.

"From the beginning," Jeff said. He sighed heavily. "Look, Sam, no one deliberately kept you in the dark, but . . ."

"Funny, but that's exactly how it feels. I suppose Tim knows all about this, too?"

"Oh, Tim just loves Ralph," Daisy blurted out innocently. "They met at the center, and Tim said he wished he had a grandfather like Ralph."

"I see," Sam said quietly. She felt like a bomb about to explode. She was holding herself under tight control, but she wasn't at all sure how long the bands would hold before they snapped.

"I do know what I'm doing, Sammy girl," Daisy insisted. "You see, I spent the weekend with Ralph when you went to the dog show in New York. We had a lot of time to talk and . . . get to know one another. It was wonderful. I want my life to be that way all the time from now on. Can you understand that?"

"Sam, I don't think you do understand," Jeff began. "No one wanted to keep anything from you, but we all knew how you would react so . . ."

"Oh, I understand all right," Sam said. "I understand perfectly!"

Twenty-eight

Jeff followed her upstairs. "I know you're upset, Sam, but going off in a huff isn't going to solve anything. You don't want to hurt Daisy, do you?"

Sam felt like a snarling tiger. "Oh, sure! That's how I get my kicks, you jackass! I smack old women in the teeth! Of course I want to hurt her! How else am I going to have any fun?"

"Oh, Sam . . ." He'd never seen her like this. She was out of control, the hurt inside her so hot and hard she couldn't see past it to the people who loved her. "Look, I guess I'd better leave you alone to think. I'll be back later."

"No."

"What?"

"Don't come back. I won't feel any different later."

"Sam . . ."

"Go away, Jeff," Sam said as she undressed

the baby with shaking hands. "This . . . our getting together was a big mistake. I knew it, but I . . ."

"We are not a mistake, Sam," Jeff argued. He stood close behind her, but he held his hands rigid at his sides, afraid to touch her. "You are the most wonderful thing that's ever happened to me, and I hoped you felt the same about me. I thought we could start to plan a future together."

"And it was really convenient for you to get rid of my family, wasn't it? First Tim and now Daisy. You encouraged and made it possible for both of them to leave, didn't you?"

"Tim is a grown man, Sam. He couldn't stay tied to his mother's apron strings forever, and as for Daisy, why, even your neighbors can see the difference in her. What's wrong with you, Samantha? Don't you want your family to be happy without you? *Do* you have some kind of sick need to keep them under your control?"

Now he'd really done it! Jeff saw the anger flash in Sam's eyes as she whirled to confront him, the naked baby in her arms.

"So that's what you think? It's what you've always thought, isn't it? Get out, Jeff. I don't want you here. I'll write a check for your security deposit and you can find another place to live."

Sam listened to him clatter down the stairs. Then she heard the front door slam, loud and hard and final.

Only then did she allow herself the luxury of tears. Dear God, why did it hurt so much? From the beginning she'd known that she and Jeff weren't right for each other. She'd seen how bossy he could be, and she'd known he disapproved of how she handled her life. He'd hinted on more than one occasion that she was smothering both Tim and Daisy. So why was she so surprised to discover that he'd been plotting behind her back all this time? She paced the room, Amber bouncing in her arms. She didn't doubt that Jeff meant well; he was a decent man. But he'd never be able to understand what her little family meant to her. He would pull in one direction, while she would tug in another. How could they be happy? She should never have allowed him to make love to her; now she would have to erase that memory from her heart. If she had kept her distance, she wouldn't be so aware of what she was missing, so achingly aware of what might have been.

Amber began to cry; she needed her bath

and her bottle. Sam patted the baby's bottom gently. "It's all right, sweetie," she said. "Don't worry. Mama will never leave you." She wouldn't. And Jeff would never understand.

Jeff threw clothing into his valise haphazardly. He'd tried and tried to talk to Samantha, but she was like a rock. She wouldn't let herself hear a word he said. So it was over. His dreams were never going to come true. "The sooner I'm out of this mess, the better it will be," he muttered angrily. "I must have been crazy to stay here in the first place. Right from the start I should have been warned. Everything they say about redheads is true! Especially redheads with green eyes!"

"Hey, Jeff, may I come in?"
Jeff flung the door wide. "Sure. Why not? It won't be my place much longer. I'll be on my way as soon as I finish packing." He suspected Daisy had sent Tim an SOS, and he had come home for the weekend. "I can't get over the way you've changed in just a few weeks," Jeff said, shaking his head. "You must really like your new job."

Tim nodded. "It's fantastic. The people I work with are great, and you wouldn't believe how much I'm learning. But I didn't come here to talk about my job, Jeff. I wanted to tell you how sorry I am about the way things worked out with you and my mom. Isn't there any chance you two could patch things up?"

Jeff swallowed, but the lump in his throat wouldn't go away. If circumstances had been different, the young man in front of him might have been his son. He turned away long enough to snap the locks on his suitcase, then he sat down on the bed and motioned for Tim to join him.

"Don't feel too bad, Tim. None of this is your fault. Sam and I . . . well, I guess we're both used to being in control. Your mom has done a real good job of caring for her family so far, and I guess she just doesn't want any outsiders messing things up. I guess I can't really blame her."

"But you didn't mess anything up. You helped all of us, me and Aunt Daisy. And Amber loves you."

"Amber is a cutie, all right," Jeff answered slowly, "but maybe I'm just not cut out for this family stuff. I've been a loner for a long time. I'll find another place to live, and maybe without all the distractions I'll finally be able to get my book written."

"Is that what you really want?" Tim asked. "I thought . . . well, it seemed as though you and Mom were getting pretty tight. I was kind of hoping you two would get married." Tim laughed, looking self-conscious. "I guess it's crazy, but I was getting to like the idea of having you for a stepdad."

Jeff swallowed convulsively and clamped his hand on Tim's shoulder. "It would have been my privilege," he said.

It was crazy and there was no use saying anything to Tim, but he'd liked that idea, too. The thought of being there for Tim, of helping to guide him toward a successful, secure future, had excited him. And as far as his book went, in his heart Jeff knew he'd probably never write it. He'd never been able to get past the first chapter. And he knew there were other ways to honor his father's memory. Donating his time to the senior center was one of them, and helping people like Daisy and Ralph find each other was another.

Jeff stood up and began pulling clothes out of his closet. Recently, he'd started to think about what it would be like to be Amber's daddy. Jeff thought that would have been a fine way to honor his father's memory—by being the best darn daddy a kid could have. But now he wasn't going to get that chance.

Tim wandered around the room, picking up a book and putting it back down. "You know, it's funny," he said slowly, "but for someone who likes her life exactly the way it is, Mom's looking pretty gloomy these days. I heard her crying last night, and this afternoon I surprised her in the kennels, sobbing all over Frosty. The poor dog didn't know what to do."

"People cry for lots of reasons," Jeff snapped, forcing down the quick surge of hope he'd felt at Tim's revelation. "Uh, did she get the crib she wanted for Amber?"

"Yeah, we all went to town yesterday. We dropped Aunt Daisy off at the center and Mom and I did some shopping." Tim sneaked a look at Jeff's stern profile. "I tried to talk Mom into buying herself some new clothes, but she said what for?"

Jeff coughed. "Well, I'm glad she got the crib. Amber is growing like a weed."

"Yeah," Tim said. "Too bad you won't be around to watch her. You know, I never thought much about babies until she came along, but lately I've been thinking I'd like one or two of my own someday." Tim laughed self-consciously. "But first I have to learn to be independent, right?"

"Right," Jeff said. "Look, I've got to finish packing. I plan to clear out tomorrow, but I'll keep in touch, okay? And Brian will keep me posted on how you're doing."

The two men shook hands, and then Tim hurried away. "Thanks for everything," he called over his shoulder.

Jeff stood by the window. There were no signs of life in Sam's yard this afternoon. No dogs, no Sam, not even a glimpse of Amber's playpen. It was almost as if the house was in mourning. He snorted. Fat chance! Sam was counting the minutes until he left, and she probably already had an ad in the paper for a new tenant.

In just a few short months Jeff had started to think of Sam's family as his own. As if they all belonged to him, and he was equally responsible for their well-being. He'd never really acknowledged his own needs, so he'd come up with every possible rationalization. Sam was a woman alone in need of protection. Right! Sam needed protection like Amber needed a prom gown. Aunt Daisy was lonely. Well, maybe once, but certainly not now. She had Ralph and her other friends at the center. Then he'd told himself that Tim needed a man's guidance and little Amber needed a daddy. Hell, maybe some of those things were valid, after all. Whether she would admit it or not, Sam did need someone. She needed someone to share her life, someone to lean on in times of trouble. But Sam had quite effectively cut him out of her family. She'd made it abundantly clear that she didn't want him around anymore.

Jeff sat on the edge of his bed. Wasn't there any way to make her change her mind? Was there any use in trying? He felt a sharp, stabbing pain in his chest and realized he was learning what people meant when they spoke of a heart breaking. He felt as if his was cracking and chipping into a million tiny fragments.

Tim walked back across the street to the kennels. Too bad things weren't working out for his mom and Jeff. Jeff was a decent guy, and despite what his mom said, Tim knew she'd been more than a little fond of the man. Heck, they'd all taken to him right from the start, even Aunt Daisy. He didn't understand why they couldn't work out their differences. Wasn't that what adults were supposed to do—talk things through until they solved their problems?

Tim entered the kennels and started feeding the dogs. He shook his head. He and Jeff had worked out a great plan to make the kennels a viable, self-supporting business, but now it looked like all their plans would have to be scrapped.

"Samantha, are you listening to me?"

Sam snapped out of her fog and turned to stare at her aunt. The elderly woman was modeling yet another new dress, and the smile on her wrinkled face was more suitable for a twenty year old than a seventyish woman.

"The dress is lovely, dear," Sam said absently. "That shade of rose is very becoming on you."

"Yes, that's what I thought," Daisy said. "It gives me a little color, and the saleslady said the pleats make my hips look a little fuller."

"Um, yes, they do," Sam replied, sneaking a look out the window at Jeff's house. Of course, soon it wouldn't be Jeff's place anymore. "I'll have to put an ad in the paper," she said. "Maybe I should specify a woman tenant this time."

"Humph! You had a perfectly good tenant, if you ask me!" Aunt Daisy scolded, her hands on her hips. "Sometimes I just don't understand what gets into you. If I were in your shoes, I'd never let him get away!"

"Aunt Daisy, you just don't understand." Sam backed away from the window and turned to her aunt. "Jeff and I . . . well, we're just not right for each other."

"Well, Jake is a hunk, or is that word outdated now? I can't keep up with the language young people use these days. All I know is that he's a good-looking, kind-hearted man, and you're a fool to let him get away."

"Aunt Daisy, didn't you think . . . well, wasn't Jeff kind of bossy?" Sam kept her eyes on the tiny nightgowns she was folding and avoided her aunt's eyes.

"Bossy? Oh, good heavens, Samantha! Is that what all this fuss is about? Is that why you were doing all that hollering the other day? Why, most men are a little bossy, at least the ones with any gumption. It's the nature of the beast, honey. You wouldn't want Jim to be one of those mealymouthed fancy pants, would you? My, I remember how your uncle used to love to give orders, God rest his soul. I never paid a bit of attention, but he didn't know that." Daisy chuckled. "He was perfectly happy all those years, thinking he ruled the roost."

Sam was shocked. "But . . . that's dishonest!"

Daisy rolled her eyes. "Maybe, but it made your uncle happy, and what was the harm?"

Daisy rattled on then, but Sam had stopped listening. Her thoughts drifted back to the afternoon in Atlantic City. Why couldn't she forget it? Why couldn't she wipe the memories out of her mind? It hurt so to remember, and now she knew that memories were all she would ever have. There would be no more lying in Jeff's arms, satiated with his love. Fighting tears, Sam left Aunt Daisy with her new dresses and went up to her room. For the first time in years she lay down on her bed in the middle of the day, and who knew how long she would have stayed there if Amber hadn't wakened and demanded to be fed?

Two days later, Jeff drove away. Sam hid in the kennels like the silly little coward she was while he went up to the house to say goodbye to Daisy and Amber. She tried to keep busy cleaning the dog runs, because it was a sure thing he wouldn't want to say goodbye to her.

Both Daisy and Tim thought she was crazy to let Jeff walk out of her life. Time and again they had hinted that a word from her would keep Jeff from leaving, but neither of them understood. It wasn't just that he'd interfered with her relationships with her son and her aunt, or even the way he frequently tended to take over. She and Jeff were just wrong for each other, and there was simply no way they could go the long haul. "And I'm just not interested in a short-term frolic," she muttered.

Samantha ticked off the reasons why she and Jeff were wrong for each other as she furiously scrubbed down the kennel runs. At best Jeff tolerated her business. He had tried, she had to give him that, but she was convinced he was hiding his true feelings. He'd probably be a lot happier if she was a nurse or a schoolteacher. She was certain he'd love it if she had a job where she could get all dressed up like a lady and stay clean and sweet-smelling all day long. And she knew the messiness of her house bothered him. How could it not when he was the kind of man who had closet organizers and the neatest dresser drawers she'd ever seen? But most of all, in her heart she knew it simply wasn't fair to expect a man like Jeff to take on a ready-made family, to expect him to change his whole lifestyle in one fell swoop.

Sam wrinkled her nose. She clumped around the kennels all day wearing faded jeans and old shirts. She never seemed to have time to have her hair styled, and manicures were an unknown. What man in his right mind would want a woman like that?

And if all of that wasn't enough, she came equipped with a rather bizarre family. Elderly, eccentric aunt, adult son, squalling baby . . . no, Jeff was better off without her, and if he didn't know it now, he would soon.

As far as she was concerned, she knew she would never find another man who would be so caring and concerned for her family. She swiped the kennel walls viciously. Why did life have to be so complicated, anyway? Why couldn't people just fall in love and live happily ever after without messy disagreements?

For just a minute Sam allowed herself to dream. If Jeff stayed, they would continue to be lovers—and she knew the loving would be heavenly—but what if that was all he wanted? What if taking her to bed occasionally was enough for him? She needed more than that for herself and her baby daughter. She needed permanence and commitment. If she let a man into her life, it had to be more than a temporary who could disappear at any time. Shaking her head, Sam scrubbed harder. It was best that he left now, before things got any messier. Best for everyone.

Jeff looked down at the sleeping infant. It was very possibly the last time he'd see the baby, and he was trying to memorize her delicate features. How could he have known how much it would hurt to say goodbye? At first he had thought to stay and fight, to badger Sam until she realized they were right for each other, despite their individual quirks and flaws. He'd planned to make her see that she needed him as much as he needed her and her family. But after telling him to get out of her life she'd determinedly avoided him, and her coldness had finally convinced him he would be fighting a losing battle. He still believed Sam had feelings for him, but old hang-ups were getting in the way. It was too late. Maybe it had always been too late.

This infant girl had crept right into his heart and captured a corner for herself. Jeff reached out and gently touched the plump, rosy cheek, marveling once again at the sweet softness of a baby's skin. Amber was so helpless and vulnerable, so much in need of caring, loving parents to help her grow strong and healthy. Damn it, why couldn't Sam see what she was doing? He was ready and willing to be a father to this child. Somehow, some way, they should have been able to work things out.

Sure, there were problems. Sure, he and Sam were different. But what did that matter if there was love? What was a little disorganization compared to the way he felt about her?

Jeff grunted and tore his gaze away from the sleeping baby. He touched her one last time; then he shook his head and straightened up.

"Are you sure you won't change your mind, Jeremy?"

Aunt Daisy watched him, her faded blue eyes filled with regret. She reached out and gently touched his arm. "We're going to miss you, Jake."

"I'll miss you, too, Daisy, but this is the way Sam wants it." Jeff hugged the elderly woman and sniffed her familiar lavender scent. He realized he was going to miss the feisty senior even more than he'd thought. She'd made him laugh so many times, and he genuinely cared about what happened to her.

He was going to miss them all, and his life would never be the same. Before, during his service career, he'd been reasonably content, but here . . . in this messy little house he'd had his first real taste of family life. Until Sam he hadn't known how much he'd missed a woman's softening touch. His father had done his best to provide a secure home for his young son, but something vital had always been missing, and now Jeff knew what it was. Sam had started to soften some of his rough edges, and maybe if they'd had a little more time . . . if he'd handled things differently. . . .

"I think you could change her mind if you tried, Jim," Aunt Daisy persisted, her eyes pleading now.

Jeff hesitated, and then he forced himself to remember the sting of Sam's rejection, the harsh, flat look in her green eyes. "No," he said, shaking his head. "She's made up her mind. She wants me out of her life and her house. I have no choice but to honor her wishes."

"But . . ."

"No more, Daisy," Jeff said. "Please. And don't worry, you'll be fine without me. After all, you've got Ralph now. You're going ahead with your wedding plans, aren't you?"

A healthy blush colored Daisy's cheeks and she lowered her eyes almost shyly. "Ralph is a good man, Jack. Just like you."

To his horror, Jeff felt his eyes start to sting. He never cried. Early on, his father had told him that men don't cry, and he never had, until now. He blinked hard and forced a smile.

"You're a very special lady, Daisy," he said. "I won't forget you."

She walked him to his car, her eyes widening

as she spotted the pet carrier in the back of the Blazer. "You're taking Cat?"

Jeff laughed ruefully. "What else can I do? I have to admit, I've grown fond of him. Crazy, isn't it?"

"No, not crazy, just human. You're a decent man, Jack. I wish things could have been different."

"Yeah, me, too. Well, best of luck, Daisy. Take care of Ralph."

Jeff slid behind the wheel of his car. He'd prolonged the moment as long as he could, but now he had no choice but to put the Blazer into gear and drive away. He cast one last, lingering look at the kennels. If Sam gave just one sign . . . but she didn't, so Jeff turned the key in the ignition and lifted his hand to Daisy in a final wave.

Sam stood by the window, weeping into a soggy Kleenex. She'd cried more in the last few days than she had in her entire life. And she wasn't a weeper . . . She'd get over this. Once Jeff was out of sight she'd be able to push him out of her heart and get on with her life. Things would go back to normal. She sniffed. But what was normal? Being lonely, even when she was surrounded by family members? Crying into her pillow at night when she thought no one would hear? She turned away, not wanting to watch Jeff back out of the driveway.

She had done the right thing, sending him away. There was no way they could have a future together, so why set herself up for even greater heartbreak? She would take care of her little family the way she always had, and it would be enough. And who knew, maybe someday she'd meet someone to whom she was better suited. But somehow she couldn't picture it; her future seemed dim and hazy.

Trudging back up to the house later that afternoon, Sam fought back tears. Things were better now than they had been when Jeff had come into their lives. Aunt Daisy was happy, and Tim was working toward his own bright future. Amber had arrived safe and sound, and Sam was getting caught up with her bills. Everything would be okay. It had to be.

But thinking of her baby made Sam remember the night Amber had come into the world. She ached with the memory of Jeff's sweet concern for her comfort and welfare, the way he had pitched in and acted as her labor coach. She remembered the stunned, awed look on his face as he gently touched Amber for the first time. The memories were precious, and Sam knew she would never forget them.

Twenty-nine

Sam had just finished straightening up the kitchen when the phone rang. She folded the dish towel she was holding and picked up the receiver.

"Hank?" she said a moment later. "How are you? Gosh, it's good to hear from you. I was thinking about you just the other day. I missed you at the show."

"Good thoughts, I hope," Hank Richards responded. "How's that baby of yours doing?"

"Amber is perfect—healthy and pretty as a picture—but what about you? How's that new lady friend of yours?"

It sounded like Hank tried to laugh. "Pat is probably almost as perfect as your daughter, Sam, but I'm afraid things aren't going too well for us. I may have to sell the kennels, and if so, I'd like to give you first dibs on my breeding stock."

"Oh, Hank! Why do you want to sell the kennels? Are you ill?"

"Not physically," Hank answered. "But my wife decided to pop back into my life without any warning. She wanted to get back together, but when I told her that was impossible she got nasty. So I may have to sell the house and the kennels to settle the divorce."

"Hank, I'm so sorry. Isn't there any other way?"

"I'm looking into that now, Samantha, but I just wanted you to know what was going on, so you could be thinking about whether or not you'd like to buy some of the dogs, if it comes to it."

"I'd love to," Sam said. "I mean, if . . ."

Hank laughed. "I know what you mean, Sam, and thanks. At least I'll know that some of my dogs will get a good home."

Sam hung up the phone feeling thoroughly confused. Was life never simple and straightforward? Hank Richards had some wonderful animals. He had a couple of bitches that would make a great addition to her kennel, but she felt terrible to think that Hank might be forced to give up his beloved Samoyeds.

Sam opened the refrigerator and took out a diet cola. Then again, life was growth and changes, wasn't it? She smiled as she sipped the soft drink. Slowly but surely, the message was getting through. Life simply didn't stay the same. Hank's life was changing, and so was hers.

Sam woke with a start. For a moment she'd thought . . . but no, Jeff was gone. He was out of her life for good, and now she had no choice but to get on with things on her own. She sighed. For Amber's sake she would.

As she prepared breakfast a few minutes later, Sam began making plans. If Aunt Daisy was truly determined to get married, so be it. She wouldn't try to stop her, wouldn't say one word to try and talk her aunt out of matrimony. After all, who was she to decide anyone's fate? But she was determined to meet this Ralph, and the sooner the better. She needed to see for herself just what kind of person he was. She could do that much without meddling. After all, if the wedding did take place, she and Ralph would be related. Like it or not, he'd be part of her family.

"So, I'd like you to invite Ralph to have dinner with us, dear," she told Daisy over cereal and fresh fruit. "Any night this week that is convenient with him is fine with me. After all, if we're going to be related, we should have a chance to get acquainted, shouldn't we?"

Daisy studied her niece suspiciously, her forehead furrowed, her eyes narrowed.

"So, you've had a change of heart, have you, Sammy girl?"

"I only want you to be happy, Aunt Daisy. And I should certainly meet Ralph before the big day, shouldn't I?"

"I suppose, but don't get any ideas about talking us out of getting married, you hear? We're determined, Sammy." Aunt Daisy suddenly smiled. "Say, while you're issuing dinner invitations, why not invite Tim's little girlfriend, Marnie? She's such a cute little thing. Hard to imagine she's old enough to be thinking about marriage, too."

"Marriage? With . . . Tim? Aunt Daisy, what's going on? I didn't even know Tim had a special girlfriend. Are you making this up to take some of the heat off Ralph?"

"Call your son and ask him if you don't believe me. He was going to tell you, but with everything else that's happened lately . . . well, I suppose he thought he'd better wait. But I'll tell you, my girl, if Tim's job works out, I don't think it will be long."

"Oh, my God!" Sam said. She put her head in her hands and groaned. "Tim's too young to get married, Aunt Daisy. He's not ready for that kind of responsibility."

"That's what you say, but his hormones are telling him otherwise. Lighten up, Sammy. Tim's not a teenager, you know, and if he really wants to marry Marnie, there's not much you can do to stop him."

"I suppose everyone's met her but me?"

"Well, Tim brought her by the center one afternoon before he went to Virginia. I'm sure he would have brought her here, too, but . . . well, I imagine he was worried about how you'd react."

"What am I? Ogre of the month?"

"Why don't you call Marnie and invite her to dinner, Sammy? I think you'll feel a lot better after you meet her. She's really a sweetheart, and she dotes on Timothy."

Sam threw up her hands. Why not? Why not meet all her potential in-laws at one time? As Daisy said, there wasn't anything she could do to stop things, so she might as well join in.

The dinner was arranged for Friday night, and as the week wore on, Sam found herself missing Jeff more than she could ever have imagined. She was positive the dinner would go a lot smoother if Jeff was by her side.

On Friday Sam spent very little time in the kennels. Instead, she worked in the kitchen, while Aunt Daisy dusted and polished the living room. Several times she stopped what she was doing and chastised herself. Why was she working this way? She was fussing more than she had in ages. After all, she wasn't the one who had to make a good impression, was she?

But she was as nervous as a cat when Tim's girlfriend arrived.

Lord, she was so young! So shy and sweet and anxious to please. Sam felt her heart melt.

"Please come in, Marnie. I'm sorry Tim can't be here with us, but it's just too far for him to come home every weekend."

Marnie nodded. "I know, and he's trying to save some money."

For a wedding, no doubt, Sam thought, a funny sinking feeling in her stomach. It wasn't that she didn't like the girl Tim had chosen. It was just that they were so young, and marriage was such a serious proposition, and she couldn't, no matter how hard she tried, picture her little boy as a married man.

Shortly after Marnie, Ralph arrived. Daisy explained that his nephew had driven him over and would pick him up later.

Sam sighed with relief. At least the elderly gentleman wasn't driving; she really didn't think that would have been a good idea. Sam wasn't sure what she'd been expecting, but it wasn't the slender, almost dapper man who held out his hand to her.

"Well," she said brightly, "Daisy has told me about your plans, Ralph, so it seems we should get to know each other. I . . . understand you like to dance?"

"I do, when this little lady here is my partner," Ralph said, putting an arm around Daisy's waist and pulling her close to his side. "She cuts quite a rug, you know."

Sam hadn't known, and she was rapidly learning that there was a lot she didn't know. Like the fact that Tim had given Marnie his high-school class ring.

Marnie tried to explain when she caught Sam staring at her hands.

"It's just until he saves up the money for a real ring," she said. Then the young girl blushed furiously. "I mean, well, we . . ."

"It's all right, Marnie. Aunt Daisy told me you and Tim are serious. Do your parents know?"

"They've met Tim and they like him very much. They have no objections as long as Tim has a steady job and we wait until we save up some money."

"That sounds sensible," Sam said, nodding. Then, looking at the young girl's earnest face, she softened. "It must be hard on both of you, being separated this way."

"Yes, it is," Marnie said, "but it's the best

thing for Tim's . . . for our future. Tim really loves working with computers."

"Yes. I recently discovered that."

"I'll have to snare that young man the next time he's home," Ralph said. "My computer has been acting up again, and I'm afraid I'm not a very good Mr. Fix-it."

"You use a computer?" Sam asked, not exactly sure why she was so surprised. After all she'd learned in the past few weeks, she should be shock-proof. But the man was nearly eighty years old, for heaven's sake!

Then Ralph laughed, and Sam could tell by the twinkle in his eyes that he knew exactly what she was thinking. "My son bought it for me for my seventy-fifth birthday. Told me I was never too old to learn something new. Well, I couldn't let him down, so I took some classes, and now I really enjoy keeping track of all my investments and such. Would you believe it even prints out my checks for me?"

"Why I . . . that's wonderful," Sam said, and oddly enough she meant it. If Ralph was spry enough and brave enough to tackle electronic technology at age seventy-five, then what was there to worry about? Handling a wife couldn't be much harder, could it?

"You know, you should have a computer here, to help you manage those kennels,

Samantha. You'd be amazed at what a help it would be. And if you decide to get one, I'd be glad to help you get started with the proper software."

"Thank you, Ralph. I'll keep that in mind. Tim has been after me to get a computer for years, but it seemed like such an unnecessary expense."

"Once you see what a computer can do you won't feel that way," Ralph insisted. "You'll wonder how you ever got along without it."

Daisy was beaming. Things were going much better than she'd dared to imagine. And Ralph was at his best when talking about his computer. My, he did love that silly machine! She'd have to make sure he understood that when they were married she wasn't about to play second fiddle to that little blinking cursor he liked so much!

And Sam was being kind to Marnie as well. Daisy chuckled silently. If she didn't know better, she'd think her sweet niece was beginning to see the light.

"Well, what do you think, Sammy girl?" Daisy asked, when she and Sam had gone to the kitchen to dish up dessert. "How do you like my man?"

"I do like him," Sam said, sounding surprised. "I didn't think I would, but . . . why didn't you tell me he was so . . . so lively and intelligent?"

Daisy chuckled, but this time it was out loud. "Oh, Sammy, you've still got a lot to learn. Did you think he was going to hobble in here leaning on his cane and be mute or something? Why, Ralph is one of the most interesting men I've ever known. He's done a lot of traveling, and he keeps up with all the latest news . . ."

Sam smiled and cut off the rest of her aunt's words by wrapping her arms around the older woman and hugging her as hard as she could. "For what it's worth, you have my blessing, Aunt Daisy. I think Ralph is just perfect for you."

Daisy was beaming. "I hoped you'd feel that way once you met him. Now what do you think of Tim's little lady?"

"She's as cute as a button," Sam admitted, "and very sweet, but I still think they're awfully young to be contemplating marriage."

"Maybe, maybe not," Daisy said calmly as she sliced pie and added a dollop of whipped cream to each serving. "You thought I was too old, and now you're beginning to see you might be wrong, so maybe . . ."

"Okay, okay," Sam said, lifting the tray of

coffee things. "I'll reserve judgment. How's that?"

"Couldn't ask for more," Aunt Daisy said.

Ellie stopped in just as Sam was rinsing out the coffeepot the next morning.

"Uh-oh, I'm too late, and look what I brought." She held out a paper bag.

Sam's mouth started to water. She never could resist Palmer's Bakery's fresh-baked cinnamon rolls. "Sit down," she commanded her friend. "I'll make a fresh pot. What the hell!"

"My, you're cheery this morning," Ellie said, plopping down in the nearest chair. "Bad night?"

Sam shook her head. "Actually, it went very well; much better than I thought it would. Aunt Daisy's beau is a sweetheart. Can you believe he learned to use a computer at age seventy-five?"

"Amazing," Ellie said, shaking her head. "I just hope I can still walk by that age!"

"And I met Tim's girlfriend," Sam said.

Ellie's brows rose. "And?"

"She's a doll, pretty and sweet, very polite. But God, Ellie, she's so young! I almost wanted to spoon-feed her!"

Ellie laughed. "That's just the mother instinct in you, Sam. When they handed out nurturing skills, you got more than your fair share."

"Maybe, but I just can't imagine my little Timmy married. Good Lord, do you realize he could make me a grandmother?"

"He could," Ellie said, grinning as she stirred cream into her coffee. "Would that be so terrible?"

"Well, no, of course not, but . . . well, good grief, I've got a young baby of my own."

"Speaking of, where is the little princess this morning?"

"Aunt Daisy took her for a walk in the stroller. She's decided she wants to exercise regularly so she'll be fit for her wedding."

"Good for her," Ellie said. "I always did think there was more to that lady than met the eye. Now if I could just get her to realize the same thing about me."

Sam laughed. "Aunt Daisy likes you, Ellie. It was just that for a while she was doing a lot of complaining. That all stopped after . . ."

"Jeff moved in," Ellie finished. "You might as well say it, Sam, because we both know it's true. Aren't you about ready to throw in the towel and admit that you made a mistake chasing Jeff off into the sunset? I know you miss him. I can see it in your eyes."

Sam opened her mouth, then closed it without uttering a word. She lowered her eyes, stubbornly refusing to confirm or refute Ellie's statement.

"Okay, I can tell you don't want to talk about it, so I'll be on my way, but remember one thing, Sam. It's not a crime to change your mind, or admit you were wrong. No one is going to lock you up and throw away the key if you decide to go after Jeff. I, for one, would stand up and cheer."

After Ellie left Sam hurriedly straightened up the kitchen and got ready to start her workday. One of her bitches had just delivered and she was anxious to check on the new arrivals. But as she walked across the yard to the kennels, Sam heard Ellie's parting words: It wasn't a crime to admit you were wrong.

Thirty

The next afternoon, while Aunt Daisy sat in front of her favorite soap opera, Sam rocked Amber to sleep and gave in to the nagging suspicion that had bothered her throughout the day.

"Aunt Daisy? Aunt Daisy, wake up! There's something I have to ask you."

"Mm? What? Oh, dear, I must have dozed off. Did Philip ask what's-her-name to marry him yet?"

"I don't know," Sam said. "When was the last time you saw Jeff, Aunt Daisy? Do you know where he is now?"

Aunt Daisy cocked her head, her blue eyes as innocent as a newborn baby's. "Well, now, I don't know, Sammy. When did he leave? Last week? Didn't he tell you where he was going, dear?"

Sam laid Amber in her playpen and pulled a light blanket over the baby. "Don't fence with me, Aunt Daisy. You know perfectly well Jeff didn't tell me where he was going."

"Well, what if I do?" Aunt Daisy challenged, her eyes sparkling with mischief.

"Where is he? Where is he hiding out?" There was a niggling little dollop of hope blossoming in Sam's heart and a longing so deep and strong, she couldn't put it into words. She just knew that suddenly she wanted to see Jeff so bad it hurt.

Aunt Daisy couldn't hold back her grin. Sam always did have expressive eyes. Despite the words that tumbled out of her mouth, all you had to do was look at the girl's eyes and you'd know exactly what she was thinking.

"Instead of giving Jim a piece of your mind, why don't you hand him a piece of your heart, Sammy girl? That's what you really want to do, isn't it? I believe he rented a room at the Holiday Inn in Wildwood, or maybe it was Howard Johnson's." Daisy grimaced. "Oh, dear, you know how I am with names."

"He's living in a motel?" Sam cried. "He won't like that, and what has he done with Cat? I'm sure I saw him carrying a pet carrier when he left."

"Hmm, so you were watching, were you? It's just as I thought. Why don't you stop fighting your feelings and admit it, girl? You're soppy about that young man, and you're sorry you acted like such a fool and chased him away, aren't you?"

Aunt Daisy reached out to pat Sam's arm. "Give up the past, Sammy. Let go of the hurt and pain you felt when your mama left you. You're not responsible for the things she did, and there was nothing you did or didn't do that could have changed things. Your mama had problems. Leave it at that." Daisy shook her head. "Poor Jake. I don't think he knew where he was going or what he intended to do when he left here. If you could have seen his face when he came to say goodbye, the way he looked at Amber . . . I tell you, Sammy, that man needs a home and a family as much as you need to make one. If you ask me, the two of you will make one super whole!"

"You think Jeff and I are right for each other?"

"Good heavens, girl! A blind man could see the way you and Jack fit together, like the last two pieces of a puzzle. But I'll tell you, if you don't do something soon, he'll be gone for good."

"Wha . . . what do you mean?" Sam's heart was hammering now, and a cold wedge of fear was lodged in her chest.

"Well, good heavens, now that you've pushed

him out of the family he's got no ties here. He's free as a bird. He'll probably travel to exotic places. My, doesn't that sound exciting? A handsome bachelor all on his own? I saw a television show the other day," Aunt Daisy added. "It was a travel show. My, those Caribbean islands are pretty, and all those tanned young bodies . . ."

Indeed! Sam's blood pressure took a sharp upward swing. She could just picture it: Jeff sitting in a hotel room, poring over travel brochures with pictures of warm, tropical islands and beautiful women in bikinis . . . Good grief, if he took off like that, she'd never see him again! She saw him lying on a beach, his body beautifully bronzed by the sun, while a beautiful, dark-haired island girl leaned over him, feeding him sweet, juicy grapes. Sam moaned, and she wasn't sure if she'd done it out loud. What's more, she didn't care. Oh, she could see it, all right. Jeff would probably meet some glamorous, sophisticated woman without a lot of messy family obligations, a woman who could come to him unencumbered, who wouldn't resent his take-charge attitude. Maybe he'd find someone who would appreciate his tenderness with babies, his patience with old ladies, and his understanding of a young man who was trying to find himself. Maybe he'd find a woman who liked to play the slot machines in Atlantic City and make love with the sound of ocean waves crashing outside the window, a woman who liked red shoes and pretty dresses . . .

Oh, Lord, Jeff already had found that woman! All right, so maybe it was stretching it just a little to call herself glamorous or sophisticated, and maybe she did have a few too many family obligations, but darned if they weren't rapidly dwindling, and when it came to the glamour business, Sam was willing to bet her prize pup that if she gave it a good try, she could give the best of them some competition. She'd make Jeff's eyes light up with that special, appreciative glow.

What a fool she'd been!

"Aunt Daisy, I've got to go out for a while. Will you be all right by yourself?"

"Well, of course I will. Go on with you, Sammy girl. Don't let Jeremy get away!"

Sam hesitated for a minute. Even though her aunt protested that she was perfectly capable of taking care of herself, she didn't like leaving her all alone. Sam decided she'd call Susan Lynch and ask her to stay with Daisy. Then her jaw dropped in astonishment as Aunt Daisy pulled a magazine out from under the sofa cushion. It was the latest issue of *Bride* magazine! Sam groaned and hurried out of the room.

Jeff walked slowly, letting the atmosphere sink in, trying to recapture the old feelings. But he couldn't do it. He wasn't nineteen anymore. And the boardwalk was different, too. The people working the concession stands were different, younger. Or was it just that he was older?

He grinned ruefully. Wildwood was still a great place. The beaches were beautiful, and the boardwalk, with its bright lights and rowdy music, could still help him remember what it had been like to be young and carefree. But the Ferris wheel was bigger than the one he and Sam had ridden when they were kids, and now there were three merry-go-rounds along the boardwalk, instead of just one.

Jeff bought a hot dog and loaded it with mustard and sauerkraut. Sixty-nine cents now, instead of three for a dollar, and soon it would be closed up for the winter. The boardwalk would be barren and empty, just like his heart.

Everything had changed. The boardwalk, the town itself, even him and Sam. They weren't nineteen and fourteen anymore. They'd both known love and disappointment, and they had both learned how to shoulder responsibilities. He thought of Sam, remembering the way she'd looked when she told him to go away. Despite everything, he'd bet his last dollar she hadn't really meant it. She was just scared and confused, afraid of sharing her responsibilities with anyone else, afraid to trust and be disappointed again. Jeff finished his hot dog and tossed the paper wrapping into a trash container. Then he squared his broad shoulders and headed back to his hotel room.

Soon he was pacing the perimeter of the small, impersonal room. He frowned. If there was one thing he'd learned since meeting up with Sam again, it was how to pace. From his container beside the bed, Cat howled piteously.

"Hush," Jeff cautioned, bending down to scratch Cat behind the ears. He feared the wrath of the motel manager if he discovered Jeff had smuggled a cat into the room.

Jeff resumed his agitated pacing. There had to be some way he could make Sam understand that they were right for each other.

He closed his eyes, remembering the way Sam had looked that night in Atlantic City, with the red shoes and the creamy silk dress. There had been a glow around her, the kind of glow that can only come from being loved. "And oh, how I loved her! I do love her!"

Cat meowed sympathetically.

Jeff paced some more. It didn't matter how many dependents Sam had, or how many people she felt responsible for. Hell, he didn't even mind the dogs. And Sam . . . well, he probably wouldn't love her the way he did if she wasn't so sweetly unselfish.

"Maybe if I go to her and tell her how I feel . . . do you think that would work, Cat? Maybe she'd realize I'm not such a bad guy after all!"

Cat blinked and continued cleaning himself. He was apparently still mad at Jeff for locking him in the cage, and had washed his paws of the whole affair.

Sighing, Jeff flopped down on the bed. It was hard as a rock. His gaze wandered around the room. Neat, clean and impersonal. Suddenly Jeff was tired. Tired of pacing, tired of thinking, tired of not having a real home anymore.

He rolled onto his side. What he wanted was warmth, warmth and light and noise. He wanted the warmth of Sam's body next to his, the sound of her laughter filling his senses. He wanted to hear Amber's baby gibberish, and he'd even enjoy the sharp, piercing bark of the dogs. But did he have the nerve to show up on Sam's doorstep after everything that had happened? What if she really didn't want him?

Maybe it wasn't so much that he'd interfered as how he'd gone about it. Maybe if he'd discussed things with her first, if he'd respected her place in the family . . . He sat bolt upright, suddenly able to see things clearly. No doubt about it, he'd come on too strong, even though his motives had been pure. All he'd wanted to do was help Sam see that she couldn't be responsible for the whole darned world. He wanted to teach her that life should be fun. That there was room for pleasure as well as responsibilities. He'd tried to show her all those things, and in the process he'd learned a few things himself. Caring meant work and sacrifice, sure, but it brought with it the purest joy Jeff had ever known.

He grinned and swung his legs over the side of the bed. Neatness and order were nice, but a warm body next to his would be even better. And peace and tranquillity were to be treasured, for sure, but so was the happy, chaotic noise of a healthy, loving family. A baby's cry, a dog's bark, a woman's tears . . .

Jeff hopped out of bed, suddenly seeing everything in sharp black and white. He'd been a fool to leave Sam the way he had. Maybe his retreat had been just one more way of avoiding a full, complete commitment, of protecting himself against another loss. Instead of staying and fighting like a man, he'd slunk away like a dog with its tail between its legs. He should have held his ground and slugged it out verbally with Sam. He should have battered her with words of love and soft kisses until she admitted she loved and needed him, too. "Maybe it's not too late, Cat," he said. "Maybe even an old dog like me can learn new tricks!"

Thirty-one

Sam fumed as she drove. She was excited and hopeful as well as damned good and mad! Jeff had one heck of a nerve! Ripping her life apart the way he had and then calmly walking away! Hit and run, that's what it was! Wasn't there anyone in the whole damned world who was willing to stay and fight for what they believed in? Anyone who would stick around right to the finish line?

"Well, my own mother didn't, that's for sure," Sam told Amber as the baby drowsed beside her in the car seat. "But you know what? That was her problem, not mine, and I made out just fine. And I . . ." Sam stopped. Was it so wrong to admit that she needed someone, that caring for her family, as much as she loved them all, just wasn't enough? A man around the house, Aunt Daisy had said. Well, that wasn't a bad idea, but it couldn't be just any man. Jeff was the man she wanted around her house. She wanted him beside her in the mornings and next to her at night. And she wanted some pleasure for herself. And suddenly, she felt no shame in admitting that she was tired of struggling through life alone. She'd weathered a bad marriage, raised her son alone, and looked after her aunt. Some of her concern might have been misplaced, but she'd meant well, and that's what counted. So, sure, she could make it on her own if she had to, but maybe she didn't have to. Maybe it wasn't too late to see if Jeff was willing to share the joys and problems of family life.

Sam's grin widened and she touched Amber's cheek with the tip of her finger. "He'd better look out," she said, "because we're not backing down this time, are we, baby?"

Jeff heard the knock just as he finished putting on his shoes. It was probably the old gent he'd met on the boardwalk a few days earlier. He'd taken to stopping by with hamburgers or pizza. It was nice of him, but right now Jeff wasn't in the mood for fast food and small talk. He flung the door open. "Look, Bill, could we . . ."

His voice trailed off and his Adam's apple bobbed. "Sam?" he asked, the name sounding like a croak. Before him was a vision: Samantha, with a plump, rosy baby in her arms, wearing red shoes and a creamy silk dress. Samantha, with her beautiful face, her loving hands and caring heart. Samantha, holding his heart in her care for now . . . for always.

"You . . ." He tried to speak and failed. The words he longed to say were lodged in his throat.

For a long moment Sam stared, drinking in the sight of him. His hair was rumpled, and he looked thinner. She longed to put Amber down on the bed and throw herself into his arms. She wanted his hands and lips and body to make her forget the misery of the past few days. She wanted to weld herself to him so he could never get away, so he'd never want to. She shivered, then squared her shoulders and stiffened her back. First things first.

Pushing past him, she deposited Amber's carrier on the floor beside the bed. "You've got some nerve, Jeffrey Brooks," she said. "You push your way into my home and my heart, you emotionally seduce my aunt, dazzle my son, and wrap my baby girl right around your little finger. . . . You turn my life upside-down and then you walk away! Why, you even mesmerized poor Muffy! What kind of man are you, anyway? Why didn't you stay and fight? Why didn't you try to make me see how foolish I was?"

She stopped to catch her breath, then darted a look at her sleeping baby. "Or are you just scared? Is she the problem?" Sam pointed a shaking finger at Amber. "Are you one of those men who can't imagine themselves raising another man's child?" She stood right in front of Jeff now, her breasts heaving, demanding an answer.

Jeff felt something inside him stiffen. "Another man's child? That baby is as much mine as if I'd sired her myself. I felt her kick when she was still in the womb, or have you forgotten? I was the first person to lay eyes on her besides the doctor and nurse. I saw her take her first breath." Jeff paused for a minute, letting Sam digest his words. Everything he'd just said was true; Amber belonged to him. She was the daughter of his heart, the child he'd never hoped to have. He stared at Sam. She was so beautiful, so womanly . . . so everything he'd ever need or want. He felt his indignation soften as he watched the confusion on Sam's face. And then he laughed. Even fighting with Sam was fun!

"You really feel that way? Like she's yours?

You don't think of her as a burden?" Sam was trying to organize her thoughts, to remember all the things she'd wanted to say to Jeff. Of course she'd known Jeff was fond of Amber, but she hadn't realized he thought of her as his own child.

Sam felt as though everything about her was soft now. Her lips, the look in her eyes, even the way she held her body, as if she was offering herself and all that came with her to Jeff for now and always. She was no longer a confused, middle-aged lady. She was young and in love and filled with the wonder of it. "That night in Atlantic City we became lovers in the truest sense. It went far beyond just physical pleasure for me. But I've been so afraid, not knowing if it meant as much to you as it did to me."

Jeff nodded, wanting to haul Sam into his arms and love her right then and there. But there were things that needed to be said first, words they both needed to hear. "It was that way for me, too."

Now Sam allowed herself to smile. A tiny kernel of hope was blossoming, promising to bloom into a rose more magnificent than any she had ever seen.

"It meant so much to me," she whispered. "It was a blending of our bodies and our hearts. I gave all of myself that night, Jeff. In my heart I made a solid, unbreakable commitment. I know that's probably old-fashioned, but it's the way I am. If you don't feel the same . . ." She paused, catching her breath, then bit the bullet and said what was in her heart. "If you're not willing to stand beside me and work to build a life, then I guess I'll just have to go on without you." Her feisty spirit broke through and she stiffened her shoulders. "It'll be hard, but I can do it," she said firmly. Then she smiled, and the softness was back. "But I decided I wasn't going to give up a dream without a damned good fight! For a long time I've put my own needs and wants on a back burner, but I don't want to do that anymore. I'm acting for myself now, for the life I want to live, for the man I want to share everything with."

Jeff couldn't hold back his grin any longer; it nearly split his face in two. Here they were, two mature adults, spinning their wheels, running in circles, all hot and steamed, when underneath they both wanted exactly the same thing. What a pair they were going to make!

"Why don't you finish all this by telling me what I mean to you, Samantha?" he taunted, his voice deep and husky.

They were standing very close now. Sam could smell him; the clean, slightly lemony scent stung her nostrils and made her feel dizzy. She saw the tiny scar on his chin, the way his lips curved upwards even as he tried to hide his triumphant smile. She watched the hot passion begin to build in his eyes and felt her own lightning response as the electricity sprang to life between them. She sighed. She had no choice. Her knees were so weak, she simply had to slide her arms around his neck and hold on. It was time now, time for honesty and openness. Take the risk, Sam, she told herself. Go for it!

"I'm in love with you, Jeffrey Brooks," she admitted, "and I do not love lightly. If you don't feel the same way, you'd better tell me now. I'll try to understand, but you'd better know now that if you love me, too, there is no way I'll allow you to walk out of my life without one hell of a fight."

Jeff's smile was blinding, and he saw that Sam's eyes were bright with love and hope. "Ah, Sam, I love you, too, more than I ever thought possible." He spoke softly; then his arms slid around her waist. He bent his head and their lips touched, hesitantly at first, like children testing the waters. It was almost as if neither of them was really sure the other was there, as if they still believed it might be a mirage. But the moment his mouth tasted Sam's something broke loose inside Jeff, and he held her with something close to desperation. Hungrily, his lips devoured hers. His heart thumped, his mind sang, and his body rejoiced. "Ah, Sam, never leave me again."

With a wrenching groan he crushed her to him, loving the feel of her womanly softness. His lips moved across her cheek and down to the sweet hollow of her throat. Then his mouth moved back to claim hers once again.

When she broke the contact Sam was gasping. "I'm drowning . . . I'm going down for the last time, but it's wonderful. We were meant for each other, Jeff. This was meant to be."

They melted together, fused by the heat of mutual desire. Their passion flared brightly, searing them, stunning them with its power and strength. Sam held Jeff tightly and her lips parted willingly to taste the sweetness of his probing tongue. With each new feeling and sensation that swept over her, she was reminded of how much she loved this man, how much she trusted and admired him. After days and nights of deprivation, Sam was suddenly full of life and love. Her blood sang in her veins as she felt Jeff's throbbing desire press against her. She had waited for this man all her life, this man who could make the sun shine and the clouds disappear. And he was strong and hard against her.

The past faded into oblivion as Jeff impatiently tore at the clothing separating them. It was the first time for both of them; the first time they had truly loved and been loved in return.

"Oh, Jeff, I'm glad you're not perfect," Sam cried. "I love everything about you, your strengths and your weaknesses, your good qualities and even the ones that aren't so good."

"Do I make your heart flutter?" Jeff murmured thickly as his hands expertly unhooked her lacy bra. "Does your flesh tingle? Am I the reason for that sparkle in your eyes?" He looked down at her and his hands never stopped, smoothing, caressing, fanning a tiny spark into a smoldering inferno.

"Yes, oh, yes," Sam cried. "Make love to me, my darling," she pleaded urgently, opening herself to him as a rose reaches its petals to the sun.

Jeff laughed, a strong, triumphant laugh that thrilled Samantha. "With the greatest of pleasure, my beautiful Samantha." He swept her up in his arms and carried her to the bed.

Just moments before it had seemed huge, a cold and lonely place. Now, with Sam lying on it, waiting for him, it seemed warm and cozy. Quickly, Jeff stripped away the last of his clothing and then he was beside her.

Jeff's voice was soft, almost reverent, his touch magical as he tenderly slid Sam's lacy panties down.

She forgot everything then, everything but Jeff and the exquisite joy of having him next to her.

Slowly and gently, as though they had all the time in the world, Jeff began to love her. He laughed softly as his fingertips lightly caressed the tips of Sam's breasts, and she quivered against him. "Lovely," he murmured. "So lovely. You are deliciously wild and wicked," he whispered against her cheek, his hands trailing lower now, causing Sam to arch off the bed. "You're a teasing, taunting temptress, and I love it."

Sam responded with her own words of love, urging Jeff on when he would have hesitated. Knowing Sam wanted him as badly as he wanted her made Jeff's breath quicken and his manhood stiffen. Sam was so beautiful, so perfect. She had a ripe fullness, a mature beauty that excited him beyond all reason. Abandoning himself to temptation, Jeff let his lips caress first one sweetly rigid bud and then the other.

Sam moaned, writhing deliriously against him. Even though she'd been married and had borne two children, she felt fresh and new and gloriously young. She was soft and dewy with love, warm and damp with desire. When Jeff slid his hand between her legs and lightly kneaded the bud of her desire she cried out, "Oh Jeff!"

Again he laughed triumphantly. He was more than ready but determined to take things slow, to prolong the pleasure for as long as possible. "Slow, baby," he crooned. "Nice and slow."

Sam was beside herself with sensation. She allowed her fingers to roam and lightly tickled the inside of Jeff's thighs before her hand closed around his rigid shaft.

Jeff let out a deep, throaty growl. Then he raised himself to stare at her lovingly. "You are so beautiful, so wonderful. You are my everything."

The ache of longing was building deep inside Sam now. She wanted, needed, to become one with this man, to be held closer than close, to feel him throb with passion inside her.

"Please, Jeff," she begged. "Love me now!"

Jeff moved over her then, tentatively, almost

as though he feared her delicacy. Then Sam clutched him to her and he plunged with a swift sureness that left them both gasping. They met and exploded in blinding ecstasy as waves of wild and wonderful sensations rolled over them, drowning them in sweetness.

Sam arched against Jeff, lifting to meet his strong, deep thrusts. She couldn't get enough of him, knew she would never have enough of him. Their movements were perfectly choreographed as Sam met Jeff's thrusts with warm, pulsing spasms. They started slowly and built to an almost agonizing peak before Sam exploded around Jeff, drawing him along with her as she burst into flames, then slowly and gently cooled.

"Am I dreaming?" Jeff asked moments later, his body slick as he tenderly drew circles on Sam's breasts with his fingertips. "Maybe you should pinch me."

"If you don't stop tantalizing me, maybe I will," Sam threatened. "Let me rest a minute, will you?"

"Can't," Jeff mumbled against her earlobe, while his fingers did crazy things to her equilibrium. "Got to make up for lost time. But we can't, you know," he said, sounding sad as he raised himself up to look at her. "Once something is lost it can't be brought back."

"Then we won't look back," Sam said. "We'll just march forward."

"Together?"

"Can you pull in harness?" Sam asked, sobering,

Jeff also grew sober. "I've never really tried," he admitted, "but I've been told I'm a quick study, and I'm willing."

"Then it's a done deal," Sam stated firmly, grinning. "Uh, did I just propose to you?"

"I think it was more of a royal command," Jeff teased, moving against Sam in a very suggestive way. Then, before Sam could form a suitable reply, he slid out of bed and knelt on the floor.

Sam stifled a giggle. Jeff was naked and ridiculous and very, very sweet.

"Since this is the only time I'm ever going to do this, I might as well go all the way. Samantha Wells, will you marry me? Will you put up with my quirks and flaws and allow me to help you shoulder the burdens of life?"

"Burdens?" Sam asked, her eyes automatically flying to her sleeping infant. She would never consider her child a burden, but if Jeff did. . . . "A child is a big responsibility, Jeff. I can't blame you if . . ."

"Oh, Sam, stop! When I said burdens it was just a figure of speech. I could never consider Amber a burden. She's a miraculous gift, a treasure. She's my daughter, my own child. I never hoped to have a child; I thought it was too late. I fell in love with Amber the instant I saw her. Remember how she closed her tiny hand around my thumb? If you'll allow me to help you raise Amber, you'll be giving me the most precious gift in life, Sam. Now, please, will you say yes? My knees are killing me!"

"So much for romance," Sam griped, unceremoniously dragging Jeff back into bed. "I suppose I'd better say yes, just to keep you from injuring yourself."

"Whoopee!" Jeff bounced up and down on the bed like a rowdy little boy. Then he sobered. In light of Samantha's scandalous, wanton behavior, he decided no further words were necessary. He figured it would behoove him to make an honest woman of Sam as soon as possible.

Later, when the first fiery needs had been temporarily satisfied, Sam felt the all-too-familiar stirrings of duty. "I have to go home," she said regretfully. "I left Susan with Aunt Daisy."

Jeff picked up the telephone and dialed Sam's number. "Let's check and see if Susan is willing to spend the night. If so, we won't have to worry."

Before Sam could utter a protest, she saw Jeff nod. "Susan? Hi, this is Jeff. Is everything okay? Good. Look, uh, Sam is with me and we've been having a little talk. There are still a few things we need to iron out so . . . great! That's what I was hoping you would say. We'll see you in the morning. And thanks again."

Sam was sitting up in bed, the sheet held modestly to her chin. Strange that she could still feel a little shy. "What's going on?" she demanded.

Jeff grinned and put the receiver back in its cradle. "All's quiet on the homefront. Daisy is sleeping like a baby, with visions of orange blossoms swirling around in her head. Susan assured me she'd be glad to spend the night."

"Oh, no, I can't . . . well, on second thought, maybe it would be okay, just this once." She sighed as Jeff pulled her back against him; then she remembered.

Orange blossoms, no less! She might love

this man, but he was getting away with murder. Folding her arms across her chest, she glared at him. "And that's another thing. What is all this nonsense about Aunt Daisy getting married anyway? I know I can't stop her, but I can't help worrying. And I know you put her up to it, Jeffrey Brooks!"

Jeff laughed. "Is it nonsense, Sam? Think about it for a minute. Ralph is a nice guy, and he's been lonely, just like Daisy. Your aunt has never been happier. They dance pretty good together, and they take the same medication for their arthritis. How much more compatible can you get at their age? Come on, Sam, you don't want to deny Daisy a little happiness, do you?"

"Of course not," Sam flared. "but I'll worry myself into a fit if Daisy isn't where I can keep an eye on her. You know how she is. Why, she can't even remember your name!"

Jeff shook his head. "Sometimes I wonder about that. Even so, being a little forgetful shouldn't keep a person from enjoying a warm and satisfying relationship with a caring partner, should it? Look at it this way, Sam," Jeff continued earnestly. "With Tim out on his own and Daisy happily married, you and I will be on a permanent honeymoon."

"Ha! With a hungry baby and a bunch of dogs?"

"Well, okay, maybe not every minute of every day, but we'll have our nights, won't we?"

A delicious shiver marched up Sam's spine. "Oh, yes," she said. "We'll have the nights. But I still can't picture Daisy being married. I met Ralph and he seems like a nice old man, but what do we really know about him?"

Jeff laughed. "As far as I know he's not an ax murderer, and Daisy thinks he's kind of cute." Jeff coughed and looked away. "And eighty's not really that old."

But old habits died hard. Jeff knew that all too well. Sam would often find herself worrying about her family, whether they lived with her or not; it was in her glands. Her heart would always lean toward those in need. She might take some clever managing and a lot of diplomacy, but Jeff knew he wouldn't want her any other way. She was Sam. His Sam.

He pulled her back against him and tickled her until she started to giggle like a young girl. "Trust me, Sam," he said. "Ralph is okay. He's just a lonely old man who's found something special and beautiful in your aunt. As I said, look at the bright side of this. Once you get used to the idea, you can stop worrying about Daisy and concentrate on me."

"But I specialize in the needy, not the greedy, Jeff," she teased. Sam moaned. "An eighty-year-old bridegroom!" Then she had to smile. She rolled over on her stomach and buried her face in the pillow. "Good Lord, now I'll have two of them to worry about!"

Jeff began to stroke the delightful curve of Sam's buttocks and grinned. Sam wouldn't change overnight, that was for sure. Maybe she'd never change at all. Maybe she'd never be able to stop worrying about her family, but who cared? For the moment, at least, Jeff had her right where he wanted her. He bent down and nuzzled her shoulder as he ran his hand up and down her spine.

"This . . . isn't the answer to everything, you know," Sam whispered. "There are still some things we need to discuss, problems we'll have to solve." Lord, but the man was sexy! There should be a law against a man Jeff's age being so . . . potent! He could melt her with a single look or touch.

"Sure, I know that," Jeff said agreeably. "But right now things look pretty rosy to me. I've got you and Amber. Tim's future looks bright. Daisy is happy. . . . Say, do you suppose she'll want me to give her away?"

"Jeff, I'm serious! What about the kennel? The dogs? How will you write your book with all the noise and confusion with a kennel full of dogs and a baby underfoot?"

Jeff sat up. "There isn't going to be a book, Sam, at least not from me. I gave the project up. Writing really isn't my forte."

"Really? Are you sure? When did you decide that?"

"About a week after I started," Jeff said sheepishly. "You see, I wanted to write the book as a sort of penance for not being able to spend more time with my dad during his last years. I wanted to make things better for Daisy and all the others like her, but there are a lot of other people out there who can do a better job of writing a book like that. I'll honor my father's memory in some other way. Maybe I can do it by being a super daddy to Amber. As for the kennels, well, I'd really like to put some of the ideas Tim and I came up with into practice, if that's okay with you. What would you think about adding a boarding kennel and maybe a grooming salon as well? I could take a course in dog grooming and we could work the kennels together."

"Really? You really, truly mean it?"

"Honest injun," Jeff said, putting his hand

over his heart. Then he kissed Sam in a very determined manner, effectively silencing any further chatter.

Thirty-two

They went home together and tiptoed into the still sleeping house as quietly as possible, amid giggles and stolen kisses. Amazing what love could do, Samantha thought happily. It could turn the stodgiest man into a youthful Casanova, the dullest woman into a femme fatale. Suddenly, like an alarm going off in her brain, something about the silence in the house started to bother her.

"Something's not right, Jeff. It's too quiet. Aunt Daisy is usually awake by now."

Jeff pulled her back into his arms for one last kiss. "I'll check on her. You see about Susan."

Sam mounted the stairs with an odd feeling of foreboding. She wasn't exactly frightened; just puzzled. Aunt Daisy had always been an early riser. Please don't let anything bad happen now, Lord, she prayed silently. Not when Jeff and I have finally gotten together.

Then Susan stepped out into the hall from the guest room.

Wrapped in a bright, floral-printed robe, the retired nurse blinked sleepily, then smiled as she took in Sam's rumpled appearance. "What time is it?" she asked, holding her hand over her mouth to stifle a yawn.

"It's still early," Sam said, "but I expected you and Daisy to be up, rattling around in the kitchen. What did you do, stay up late last night gossiping?"

Susan flushed. "Well, actually . . ."

"Sam, maybe you'd better read this," Jeff said, coming from Daisy's room with a folded piece of paper in his hand. "I think this will explain everything."

Sam took the paper with shaking fingers.

"Dear Sam," she read. "I've thought about this long and hard, and decided that at my age procrastination is one of the seven deadly sins. Also, I couldn't find a thing in *Bride* magazine that suited me. Anyway, Ralph and I decided that eloping sounded romantic, and he thought my new rose dress was perfect. Susan will drive me to Ralph's house, and then Ralph's nephew will take us the rest of the way. Ralph lost his license for speeding a few months ago, so he can't drive right now. We'll call when the deed is done. Please be happy for us, Sammy girl. I hope you patch things up with Jake, or is it Jack? Well, you know how I am with names. Anyway, he's a good man, and those kind are hard to find! Love and hugs, Aunt Daisy."

The lavender-scented notepaper fell from Sam's hand and fluttered to the floor. Sam looked at Susan accusingly. "You drove her?"

Susan nodded. "I couldn't stop her, Samantha, and, truthfully, I didn't think I had a right to try. Daisy is an adult of sound mind. She knows what she's doing. She loves Ralph."

Sam turned on Jeff. "Now see what you've done? She's eloped! My sweet, forgetful seventy-eight-year-old aunt has eloped!"

Jeff started to laugh. "All right!" he said, raising his hand in a victory salute. Even he hadn't expected anything like this. Then again, he knew he shouldn't have been too surprised. Daisy was a remarkable lady, and hadn't he urged her to grab for the brass ring? Thank God she was feisty enough to do it!

"Oh, Samantha, this is great! Don't you see what this means? Now you can stop worrying about Daisy; Ralph can do it. Now come here and give old Jake a kiss!"

"Nooo!" Sam wailed. "Now I have two elderly relatives to worry about. A man as old as Ralph . . . losing his driver's license for speeding . . . good heavens!"

Jeff laughed until his sides hurt, and Susan joined in.

"Ah, my precious, loving Sam. I never doubted you would add Ralph to your list of people to worry about, but what does it matter? What does anything matter when we have each other? Now, shut up and kiss me, woman," he commanded firmly, calling on his full military bearing. "We might as well start this relationship off right. From now on I wear the pants in this family. I really do like you in dresses, Sam," he added huskily. "Silky cream dresses and floaty green things . . ."

At some point Susan discreetly disappeared back into the guest room.

Sam felt herself start to melt. There was nothing else to do but kiss Jeff, Jack, Jim, Jake, Jeremy . . . whoever.

Later that morning, just when Sam thought she was regaining her equilibrium, the telephone rang. It was Tim.

"Mom? Guess what? I'm engaged . . . well,

not officially, but as soon as I save up the money for a ring I will be. Marnie told me she thinks you're great."

"Engaged? You and Marnie? Good Lord, it's contagious!"

"What? Oh, wow! Did Aunt Daisy get hitched to that Ralph dude? Hey, Mom, that's great, isn't it?"

Sam felt dazed, but also incredibly happy and hopeful. It was out of her hands now. Daisy had taken control of her own life, and Tim had as well. All she could do now was stand back and be supportive.

"Whatever makes you happy, son," she said. She started to feel a little weepy, and when Jeff came up behind her and slid his arms around her waist she leaned into him gratefully. Then they heard it: Amber's strong, urgent cries of hunger.

Jeff felt a tug on his pants leg and looked down to see Muffy growling fiercely as she diligently worked his shoelaces. He grinned. He decided that, for Sam's sake, he'd better stop grinning like a demented fool and lend a hand. Yeah. They were home. They were definitely home.

Epilogue

Sam leaned her head back and sighed, relishing the rare moment of peace and quiet. Amber was bedded down for the night, and Sam finally had a free moment to think back on all that had happened in the past few months. She smiled at the diamond and matching gold band on the third finger of her left hand, sparkling in the lamplight.

She hadn't waited long to follow in Aunt Daisy's footsteps and marry the man she loved, but she and Jeff had opted for a simple little home wedding. Romantic or not, she hadn't felt up to an elopement!

Anyway, Aunt Daisy was doing great. She was comfortably settled in her new husband's lovely little house, and dancing up a storm at the senior center every Wednesday night. Once in a while she and Ralph came to have dinner with Sam and Jeff, but usually they were too busy with center activities to be pinned down.

Sam's lips curved into a gentle smile as she

thought of what a cute couple Daisy and Ralph made. Ralph was much taller than Daisy, yet he allowed his new bride to boss him around shamelessly. He even seemed to like it.

Tim's job was going well, and he was saving to buy Marnie an engagement ring, and the young couple had asked if they could be married at home when the time came. Sam brushed a stray tear from her eye. It was still hard to realize that her son was all grown up, but she was trying, and it was getting easier every day.

Jeff entered the living room, a tray with coffee cups and a plate of cookies in his hand.

"This is the best time of the day," he said, setting the tray down on the coffee table. "Don't look now, Muffy," he cautioned, wagging his finger in the Shih Tzu's face, "but you're going to have to vacate that lap. For the moment, at least, the lady is all mine."

He poured them each a cup of coffee and sighed contentedly. "It's good to sit down."

"Mm," Sam agreed. With the kennel expansion, she and Jeff were kept hopping from morning until night, but she was thrilled with what they were doing. It looked as if the business venture was going to be a success.

Pushing aside all thoughts of business, Sam glanced around the living room. It looked the same as it always did these days. A discarded teddy bear lay on the floor beside the sofa, along with a scattering of magazines. Amber's playpen sat in royal splendor beneath the front window. And the new blue carpet was covered with dog hair. Sam sighed. Tomorrow she would definitely have to run the vacuum. She knew their home was certainly not a model of housekeeping efficiency, and every now and then she wondered if Jeff was annoyed with the mess. She winced, thinking of his immaculate closets and organized drawers.

"I'll never be a great housekeeper," she said into the comfortable silence. "I guess I might as well admit it: I'm a tad messy."

Jeff grinned. "Yep, and I'm a wee bit bossy."

"But you're getting a little bit better," Sam conceded, leaning over to kiss his cheek. There it was again, that crisp, slightly lemony scent that made her head spin.

"I'll never be totally cured," Jeff admitted. "I kind of like giving orders, especially to Amber. For the moment at least, she doesn't talk back!"

Sam laughed, then sobered as her eyes met Jeff's dark, smoldering gaze. "Tell the truth; don't you ever wish for order and peace and quiet? Those are pretty rare commodities around here."

Jeff grinned. "Sure, just about every day, especially when the telephone rings just as Amber wakes up demanding to be changed and fed, and when Muffy does one of his famous wastebasket-dumping tricks. But when that happens all I have to do is remember those days I spent in that cold, lonely motel room. I had plenty of peace and quiet then, but I didn't have this." Jeff waved his arm around the comfortably cluttered room. "I didn't have you either," he added. "All in all, I think I made a pretty good trade. There's just one thing that worries me: You've got to promise me you won't start taking in strays. I like this family just the way it is."

Sam knew he meant it. She sighed happily and leaned her head on his shoulder. It still tickled her to see him, her big, strong, ex-naval commander, meticulously blow-drying and brushing a toy poodle or a tiny terrier. But Jeff seemed to be enjoying his new career as a dog groomer; except, of course, for the time a high-strung Afghan hound nipped him in the buns. She smothered a not too sympathetic chuckle and moved closer to her husband.

All in all, everything was working out well. Jeff had insisted on buying Daisy's house from her. It was, he said, his contribution to their new life together, and they were slowly remodeling and making things more comfortable.

Aunt Daisy, her blue eyes twinkling mischievously, had promptly informed them that she was thinking of using some of the money to have a hot tub installed in Ralph's yard, and she might even buy some champagne so she and Ralph could sample the "good life."

Sam snuggled just a little closer to Jeff. Hot tubs were nice, but she didn't need one to live the "good life." Right now her life was just about as good as it got!

FULL MOON

Aunt Babby 'resolved to say nothing to her, so she had (wisely) concealed from her she was thinking of giving some of the money to Jane Forster 'usually in Ralph's vault, and she made it over to Jane. Champagne to the maid when could 'sample one' 'good sir.'

Sam answered her a little cheekily till the time 'we're alike' but she didn't mind could the "good sir." Slight mystery. He was just 'eog as a good as it was.'

Coming next month
from
To Love Again

Now's the Time by Kate Hanford
Never Too Late by Martha Schroeder

WATCH AS THESE WOMEN LEARN
TO LOVE AGAIN

HELLO LOVE (4094, $4.50/$5.50)
by Joan Shapiro
Family tragedy leaves Barbara Sinclair alone with her success. The fight to gain custody of her young granddaughter brings a confrontation with the determined rancher Sam Douglass. Also widowed, Sam has been caring for Emily alone, guided by his own ideas of childrearing. Barbara challenges his ideas. And that's not all she challenges . . . Long-buried desires surface, then gentle affection. Sam and Barbara cannot ignore the chance to love again.

THE BEST MEDICINE (4220, $4.50/$5.50)
by Janet Lane Walters
Her late husband's expenses push Maggie Carr back to nursing, the career she left almost thirty years ago. The night shift is difficult, but it's harder still to ignore the way handsome Dr. Jason Knight soothes his patients. When she lends a hand to help his daughter, Jason and Maggie grow closer than simply doctor and nurse. Obstacles to romance seem insurmountable, but Maggie knows that love is always the best medicine.

AND BE MY LOVE (4291, $4.50/$5.50)
by Joyce C. Ware
Selflessly catering first to husband, then children, grandchildren, and her aging, though imperious mother, leaves Beth Volmar little time for her own adventures or passions. Then, the handsome archaeologist Karim Donovan arrives and campaigns to widen the boundaries of her narrow life. Beth finds new freedom when Karim insists that she accompany him to Turkey on an archaeological dig . . . and a journey towards loving again.

OVER THE RAINBOW (4032, $4.50/$5.50)
by Marjorie Eatock
Fifty-something, divorced for years, courted by more than one attractive man, and thoroughly enjoying her job with a large insurance company, Marian's sudden restlessness confuses her. She welcomes the chance to travel on business to a small Mississippi town. Full of good humor and words of love, Don Worth makes her feel needed, and not just to assess property damage. Marian takes the risk.

A KISS AT SUNRISE (4260, $4.50/$5.50)
by Charlotte Sherman
Beginning widowhood and retirement, Ruth Nichols has her first taste of freedom. Against the advice of her mother and daughter, Ruth heads for an adventure in the motor home that has sat unused since her husband's death. Long days and lonely campgrounds start to dampen the excitement of traveling alone. That is, until a dapper widower named Jack parks next door and invites her for dinner. On the road, Ruth and Jack find the chance to love again.

Available wherever paperbacks are sold, or order direct from the Publisher. Send cover price plus 50¢ per copy for mailing and handling to Penguin USA, P.O. Box 999, c/o Dept. 17109, Bergenfield, NJ 07621. Residents of New York and Tennessee must include sales tax. DO NOT SEND CASH.

IT'S NEVER TOO LATE
TO FALL IN LOVE!

MAYBE LATER, LOVE (3903, $4.50/$5.50)
by Claire Bocardo
Dorrie Greene was astonished! After thirty-five years of being "George Greene's lovely wife" she was now a whole new person. She could take things at her own pace, and she could choose the man she wanted. Life and love were better than ever!

MRS. PERFECT (3789, $4.50/$5.50)
by Peggy Roberts
Devastated by the loss of her husband and son, Ginny Logan worked longer and longer hours at her job in an ad agency. Just when she had decided she could live without love, a warm, wonderful man noticed her and brought love back into her life.

OUT OF THE BLUE (3798, $4.50/$5.50)
by Garda Parker
Recently widowed, besieged by debt, and stuck in a dead-end job, Majesty Wilde was taking life one day at a time. Then fate stepped in, and the opportunity to restore a small hotel seemed like a dream come true . . . especially when a rugged pilot offered to help!

THE TIME OF HER LIFE (3739, $4.50/$5.50)
by Marjorie Eatock
Evelyn Cass's old friends whispered about her behind her back. They felt sorry for poor Evelyn—alone at fifty-five, having to sell her house, and go to work! Funny how she was looking ten years younger and for the first time in years, Evelyn was having the time of her life!

TOMORROW'S PROMISE (3894, $4.50/$5.50)
by Clara Wimberly
It takes a lot of courage for a woman to leave a thirty-three year marriage. But when Margaret Avery's aged father died and left her a small house in Florida, she knew that the moment had come. The change was far more difficult than she had anticipated. Then things started looking up. Happiness had been there all the time, just waiting for her.

Available wherever paperbacks are sold, or order direct from the Publisher. Send cover price plus 50¢ per copy for mailing and handling to Penguin USA, P.O. Box 999, c/o Dept. 17109, Bergenfield, NJ 07621. Residents of New York and Tennessee must include sales tax. DO NOT SEND CASH.

YOU WON'T WANT TO READ
JUST ONE – KATHERINE STONE

ROOMMATES (3355-9, $4.95)
No one could have prepared Carrie for the monumental changes she would face when she met her new circle of friends at Stanford University. Once their lives intertwined and became woven into the tapestry of the times, they would never be the same.

TWINS (3492-X, $4.95)
Brook and Melanie Chandler were so different, it was hard to believe they were sisters. One was a dark, serious, ambitious New York attorney; the other, a golden, glamourous, sophisticated supermodel. But they were more than sisters – they were twins and more alike than even they knew . . .

THE CARLTON CLUB (3614-0, $4.95)
It was the place to see and be seen, the only place to be. And for those who frequented the playground of the very rich, it was a way of life. Mark, Kathleen, Leslie and Janet – they worked together, played together, and loved together, all behind exclusive gates of the *Carlton Club*.

Available wherever paperbacks are sold, or order direct from the Publisher. Send cover price plus 50¢ per copy for mailing and handling to Penguin USA, P.O. Box 999, c/o Dept. 17109, Bergenfield, NJ 07621. Residents of New York and Tennessee must include sales tax. DO NOT SEND CASH.